A NOVEL

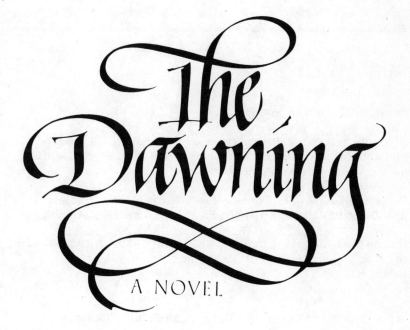

The Dawning

A NOVEL

A
JANET
THOMA
BOOK

THOMAS NELSON PUBLISHERS
Nashville

Published in Nashville, Tennessee, by Thomas Nelson, Inc., and distributed in Canada by Lawson Falle, Ltd., Cambridge, Ontario.

Scripture quotations are from the NEW KING JAMES VERSION of the Bible. Copyright © 1979, 1980, 1982, Thomas Nelson, Inc., Publishers.

Library of Congress Cataloging-in-Publication Data

Wise, Robert L.
    The dawning / Robert L. Wise.
      p.   cm.
    "A Janet Thoma book."
    ISBN 0-8407-3167-1 (pb)
    1. Jesus Christ—Fiction. 2. Bible. N.T.—History of Biblical events—Fiction. 3. Church history—Primitive and early church, ca. 30–600—Fiction. I. Title.
PS3573.I797D38   1991
813'.54—dc20   91–26250
                                                     CIP

Printed in the United States of America

1 2 3 4 5 6 7 — 96 95 94 93 92 91

*To
the Mother of all the Motherless
who still comforts those
who lose their way*

CONTENTS

ACKNOWLEDGMENTS

Many people have given me encouragement and assistance in my research on life in the first century. I could not have completed this project without them. Bernice McShane and Jane Carter Cole White gave invaluable advice as the story was being developed. I will always appreceiate Dr. Cliff Warren's guidance. Great time and effort were lent by my secretaries Jeanie Rogers and Kristin Jacobs in bringing the manuscript into its final form. A good editor who can find? Her worth is more than her weight in gold! I am grateful to Janet Thoma for her faith in me and her diligent work in editing. The services of these friends will always be greatly appreciated.

Robert L. Wise
Lent 1991

PART ONE

"The Sun Shall Be Turned into Darkness"

A.D. 32

ONE

Winter had fallen over Yerushalayim. The sky was an empty gray as the winds blew unmercifully. Darkness came earlier in the day, and the nights lengthened as the month of Tebeth* dragged on. Situated against the great city wall, the small building of the brothers Ben Aaron was often covered by shadows. The residue of the last infrequent snowfall still lingered around their jewelry shop.

A thick woven blanket hung on the inside of the door in an attempt to stop the constant encroachment of winter. The lamps throughout the building flickered as a sudden gust of coldness blew through the thickly woven canvas covers over the small windows, sending a chill through the small shop and quickly purging the large room of the smell of stale smoke and oil. Outside merchants and potential customers could be heard scurrying down the cobblestone street. Like the times, the mountain gales that swept down from the north were vicious and bitter.

*corresponds to December—January

Jarius Ben Aaron pulled his brown woolen robe more tightly around his wrinkled neck as he bent forward over his workbench. He pushed the little clay olive lamp closer to his work, but the cold continued to sting his fingertips. The warmth from the small fireplace in the back corner never quite reached more than a few feet. Huddling over his candle, he tried to keep his rough and stained fingers as nimble as possible.

"Ah," Zeda Ben Aaron chuckled from out of the shadows behind Jarius, "the winter's getting to you. Your blood's not as thick as it once was."

Jarius pulled at his graying beard for a moment before picking up his small hammer. His unusually strong arms and long tapering graceful hands always seemed contradictory. Gently he began working the small flat piece of gold, refusing to acknowledge what he clearly heard.

"Here I am, smaller and older than either of you," Zeda pushed further, "and I am still the toughest. Forty-five! Gray hair! And I can still take these Yerushalayim winters better than you both. Five years makes a difference, Jarius," he chided, holding up his fingers, which were gnarled and twisted.

"We recognize your authority, Zeda," Simeon Ben Aaron answered sarcastically. He pushed from the scroll he was studying, glancing across the room. "How can I study when there's constant banter?" He leaned back against the wall and crossed his arms. Long ago Simeon had discovered that he could use the back corner of their building as a command post. Simeon could watch his brothers without being seen by them. The strategic location was only one of the many ploys he used to compensate for being the youngest. "We both agree that you are the oldest and eldest in all respects."

Zeda roared. "My, my, I am surrounded by thin skin.

Age does have its advantages!" Zeda chuckled at his own joke as he rubbed his hands together vigorously over his clay lamp.

The brother's shop was spacious by Yerushalayim standards. Because the land had been in the family for years, they had been able to expand their stucco building while other merchants remained limited to small tent overhangs. In the winter the smell of burning oil and candles eventually permeated everything. The ceiling was black from thousands of hours of candle and lamp smoke and the brown walls were covered with gray and dark stains. Long ago the clay floor had become rock hard. And yet the artistic bent of the brothers Ben Aaron permeated the dullness of the room. Here and there bright swatches of cloth dangled down from the ceiling brightening the sides of the walls. The three brothers worked in different corners of the room on wooden benches. The massive display table was covered by a long bright red cloth, making an ideal backdrop for the gold pieces placed on display. Beautiful long necklaces were stylishly draped over bracelets and large solid gold rings. Magnificent headpieces were symmetrically arranged around trays of rings set in blue-green amalekite stones. Even the dullness of winter could not diminish the elegance of the soft glow of the luxurious display of gold.

Each brother's table was covered with the tools of their trade. Zeda had trays of stones, while Jarius worked the larger pieces of gold and silver. Always covered with at least one scroll, Simeon's table was littered with small strands of gold that he masterfully wove into chains.

Light exploded, filling the room as two Roman soldiers threw back the blanket and burst through the doorway. Each brother blinked momentarily, unable to comprehend what was happening. The soldiers quickly glanced back and forth, looking hard at the brothers. Suddenly they leaped at Jarius, grabbing him by his robe. The larger soldier pushed him against the wall while the other yanked his hair back and glowered into his face. "Is this him?" The burly soldier spit at the ground. "I can't tell."

"Mm—mm—m," the second man held the little clay lamp against Jarius's contorted face. The smell of singed hair filled the air. "No, I don't think so. The dog we want had a scar under his eye. He was younger."

"Maybe we're in the wrong place," the soldier growled and slung Jarius backward to the ground. "Keep out of trouble," the soldier warned the other brothers, "or you'll find out what we had in mind."

Without apology, the soldiers left as quickly as they had entered the store.

Jarius ran his hand across his cheek and through his thick black hair, feeling the pain of the burn on the side of his face. "Damn them! They had no right—no reason—"

Simeon leaped forward, extending his hand to help Jarius get up. Although he was thirty-five, Simeon seemed much more mature. He was the youngest; he was also the tallest. His natural handsomeness attracted women, who never caught him. The angular line of his profile and his square jaw gave him a firm, determined look, which accurately reflected his steel-trap mind. A razor sharp memory had made him a natural candidate to become a rabbi. His slim, muscular body moved quickly and with certainty. While he would never directly challenge Zeda's place in the family, Simeon often tried to take charge. Both his opinions and his grip were strong and unyielding.

"I hope those pigs rot in Sheol!" Jarius offered his

hand to let Simeon pull him up. He spit on the floor. "Damn those Romans!"

Streaks of gray ran through Jarius's long black hair. Even though he was only five years older than Simeon, he looked even older than Zeda at times. His eyes were set deeply in his face and circled by dark rings. His face was prematurely wrinkled and worn, showing the drain of too much sadness and loss. Perhaps the most handsome of the three brothers, Jarius seemed to carry disappointment with him like a lingering illness. Brushing off his robe, he asked, "How long will the Holy One tolerate our abuse?"

"A drink will help." Simeon reached for a wineskin that hung on the wall. "You are too good a man, my dear brother, to leave even your dust in the face of these swine."

Zeda quickly brought a cup from his table.

"Why?" Jarius pushed the goatskin pouch aside. "Why must we live with such insults to our dignity? Why doesn't the Messiah come to free us from these oppressors?"

"The day is coming when He will act. We will be liberated." Simeon assured him. "Remember Daniel, the Maccabees? When the Law, the traditions, were kept, they prevailed."

"I don't need history lessons. I need justice!" Jarius slammed his fist down, shaking the huge workbench. "Day after day the Romans coerce our people. Steal from us. Tax us to death. I want retaliation!"

"But all must come in His time." Simeon's gestures always looked condescending. "And in His way."

"The more I listen to you," Jarius's face reddened, "the more I think that just maybe the Zealots are right. At least they are willing to fight."

"You don't mean that." Simeon shook his finger in a

fatherly, superior manner. "Your frustration is speaking."

"Listen." Jarius leaned within inches of Simeon's face. "I am tired of your lectures from the Torah. I have just been attacked by two wild maniacs for nothing more than sitting peacefully at my own worktable. I want vindication." Jarius's voice suddenly rose to a shrill pitch. "Do you understand?"

"But," Simeon shrugged, "only through suffering can the world be redeemed."

"Suffering!" Jarius exploded.

"Stop! Stop!" Zeda threw his hands up in the air. "I can't stand this argument again for the one hundredth time. Jarius will keep demanding justice while Simeon counters with the Law and traditions. Please, not again."

Simeon sat down and Jarius turned away. Saying nothing more, Jarius drank from the wineskin. Finally Zeda, the eldest, sat down at the workbench between his brothers. For a long time no one spoke.

"Were you hurt?" Zeda finally asked.

"Only my pride."

"You always seem to be the one who is hurt," Zeda said compassionately. "Michele's death when your son was stillborn was unbearable. Then Mariam's illness. Heaven knows, you are a good man. If you were not so strong—"

"Remember, you are the Nisi, the president of the synagogue, Jarius," Simeon added. "You received the honored position at a very young age because few have borne suffering as nobly as you."

Jarius's head drooped even further until it rested in his hand. After a long silence, he said very slowly, "The Romans I can bear——— but ——— I don't think I could stand the loss of another child."

Zeda hugged him gently. "She was worse this morning?" He gripped Jarius's shoulder.

Jarius reached up to squeeze Zeda's hand and felt the twisted and bent fingers. He froze. Jarius always tried to not look at Zeda's deformity lest he make him feel uncomfortable. Seldom had he touched Zeda's left hand. Quickly Jarius let go.

"Each sunrise becomes more frightening than the last. Mariam is unable to leave the house. About all she can do is read the scrolls."

"Ah!" Simeon beamed. "And what family has a girl that can read both Hebrew and Greek? Her body may be weak, but Mariam has a magnificent mind."

"But without a body, a strong body—" Jarius's words faded. "We must hope," Simeon's resoluteness seemed strangely out of place.

"Oh, my little brothers," Zeda sighed deeply, "we must not be morose nor succumb to cynicism. You are both so serious. Along the way we must enjoy life a little!"

Jarius's eyes seemed even darker and more deeply sunken. "That is possible?" Jarius reached for a metal working tool without looking at Zeda. "I don't know."

"Of course, of course." Zeda went back to the tray of precious stones he had been sorting. "But we must remember to laugh some. I will not let either the Romans or the times rob me of a little pleasure. After all, we are among the most prosperous jewelry merchants in Yerushalayim. Jarius is esteemed at the synagogue, and our little brother Simeon is the most promising young Pharisee in the Great Sanhedrin and the best rabbi in the whole stable of Hillel's pupils. My wife treats me well. We eat well. I am a man who should be happy."

Zeda rubbed his bent fingers together. Because of his

deformity, Zeda couldn't do the detailed craft work. In turn he had become the buyer for the business, working the trade routes to Elilat, where the best buys in amalekite were. He looked around their spacious shop. Gold bracelets and even emeralds set in magnificent necklaces were everywhere. There couldn't be a better location than the heart of the lower business district of the city. Jarius was one of the finest craftsmen in the whole nation. The Romans bought his work to send back to Rome itself. And Simeon's fine gold chains were excellent workmanship. The brothers' accomplishments were considerable. "Yes," Zeda said aloud, "I can smile today."

"Try being a widower for a while," Jarius grumbled and pushed his graying hair back.

"Jarius—" Zeda pleaded.

"He thinks of Mariam," Simeon interceded. "Her health weighs heavy on his mind."

"I know, I know," Zeda's voice dropped, "but the two of you are always so sober. The world hangs around your necks like a millstone. I swear you will not drag me down with you."

Two men abruptly stepped through the canvas door while a third held the blanket back.

"See!" Zeda nudged Jarius. "The Holy One compensates us with customers. Friends, we offer you the finest wares in the city." Zeda quickly stepped behind the counter.

"Perhaps we should offer you a knife." The man leaned across the display.

"What?" Zeda choked.

"Do you think we didn't see the soldiers. You think we don't know that you do business with the Romans."

"Zealots!" Jarius sprang to his feet.

Suddenly the second man pulled a long thin dagger

from beneath his robe. "We know collaborators when we see them." His voice was low and menacing. "We keep a record."

The third man dropped the canvas door and stood in front of it.

"You're threatening us?" Zeda eyes narrowed.

"Warning," the first man hissed.

"I sit on the Sanhedrin." Simeon stepped beside his brother. "Are you calling us traitors?"

"Listen." The man with the knife grabbed Simeon by the robe, bending him over the display. "Conspirators are everywhere." He swung the knife back and forth in front of Simeon's face. "We have taken a vow to cut the throat of every publican we catch. We are not adverse to carving up anyone who deals with Rome."

"Stop it!" Zeda grabbed the man's wrist pushing the knife back. "You're crazy."

"Not as crazy as those who consort with the Romans." He tried to jerk the knife back but couldn't budge Zeda's grip.

"Please!" Jarius waved his hand in the air. "The soldiers attacked me. Look at my face. They made a mistake."

"Who were they seeking?" The man jerked his hand again, but Zeda's hold only tightened.

"None of your damn business," Zeda began bending the knife-wielding hand to the table. "How dare you fanatics break into the store of God-fearing patriotic Jews and threaten us. If I ever see the likes of either of you again, I'll turn the Romans on to you."

"How dare you . . ." the man was cut short as Zeda smashed his hand into the table, causing the knife to fall to the floor.

"Don't trifle with an old man," Zeda chided him. "Might prove dangerous."

"We're watching you all the time." The first man began backing away. "Zealots make for bad enemies."

"You will see us again." The second man bent down to retrieve the knife while the third opened the blanket door.

"The House of Ben Aaron is above reproach!" Zeda yelled at the top of his lungs. "We will not be intimidated by petty thugs from the streets. If we see you again the wrath of heaven will break on your heads," Zeda screamed as if all of Yerushalayim might hear.

The Zealots made a hasty retreat, moving even more quickly as Zeda became louder.

"To hell with you!" Simeon yelled after them.

"God help us." Jarius heaved, slumping back on his workbench. "Two attacks in one day."

"I don't know which is worse." Simeon shook his fist. "Our enemies from Rome or our supposed friends from our own backyard."

"We shouldn't have offended them," Jarius lowered his head into his hands. "They are dangerous."

"Yes," Zeda shrugged, "a treacherous lot indeed, but one cannot live with fear."

"Never!" Simeon stomped his foot.

Jarius covered his eyes. The whole weight of his body sagged against his table.

Zeda watched Jarius as Simeon went back to his scrolls. Silence settled over the shop as each man faced what had just happened. Zeda continued to lean against the display counter, stroking his beard and looking at his middle brother from the corner of his eye.

"Fear is a terrible burden to bear," Zeda looked at the ceiling as he spoke.

"I am not afraid for myself alone," Jarius finally answered. "I fear for all of us. Perhaps, there is no justice, no truth left in the world. Maybe we are at the mercy of whoever throws the last spear." Jarius turned toward

Simeon as if expecting a retort. When Simeon said nothing, Jarius waited as if he hoped to be rebutted. "I fear for Mariam," he concluded.

Zeda pursed his lips and carefully measured Simeon's face for a moment. The rabbi seemed to have escaped once more into the Torah. Zeda turned to Jarius. "I have heard of a young rabbi in Galilee," Zeda picked up a ring from the counter, "who effects marvelous cures."

"Oh, please," Simeon suddenly protested. "Let's not chase those rumors."

"We have a cousin's house near Gennesaret," Zeda ignored Simeon. He held a stone up to the light. "Perhaps you could take Mariam near to where he is teaching and—"

"You are speaking of Yeshu Ben Yosef*," Simeon interrupted. "The man is most controversial and even speaks against some of our leaders. Moreover, he is only thirty-two, and we don't need additional trouble from associating with a probable heretic. Aren't the Zealots enough?"

"We take hope wherever we can find it," Zeda answered sternly. "I don't care what he teaches if he can make Mariam well."

"Really!" Simeon answered indignantly. "You know better."

"Absolutely, but I still don't care. Anyone who helps us carry our fear is to be considered." Zeda's eyes narrowed and he looked threatening. "Think about it, Jarius. I know you have heard the stories of the amazing things this rabbi does."

Jarius nodded his head as if the idea had already been considered many times.

Simeon looked back and forth between his two broth-

*Jesus, Son of Joseph

ers for a moment as he rolled the scroll. "You've discussed this before," he said slowly. "Perhaps, often—"

Neither man answered.

"You knew I wouldn't like this idea," he turned the scroll. "Go home," Zeda said to Jarius. "After all, it is the ninth hour, go make sure she is all right. You will work better when you return."

Slowly Jarius stood and began placing some of his large pieces in the bag that he used for carrying the expensive items home each evening for the sake of security.

"We must not let fear make us succumb to superstition and gossip," Simeon warned. "The times and the turmoil can make people irrational. Unless we cling to the Law and the prophets, we betray ourselves. We can't go off chasing after magicians!"

Ignoring Simeon, Jarius stood up and shook his robes. Without another word, he picked up his black bag and left the shop.

"Jarius—" Simeon started to follow him, but Zeda caught his arm.

Jarius slowly walked up the street, passing the section where the silk and wool vendors' goods were displayed. The expensive silks had come even farther across oceans to reach the Yerushalayim market. Who knows how many times those caravans might have been beset by robbers and thieves along the way.

"Alms." A dirty, blind beggar held his hand out.

Jarius looked at the withered dirty palm, the sores on the man's shriveled arms, and the tattered soiled tunic. The wretch couldn't live much longer. Thinking of Mariam, he dropped two shekels in the beggar's hand and breathed a prayer.

Immediately he clutched the black bag at his side more tightly. No one could make a yerushalayim dedaheba as he could, and it was his responsibility to hide his own special creations. Jarius's gold head ornaments were worn only by ladies of the highest rank. His "golden yerushalayim" was the crowning piece to complete the elegance of the nobility of the city. As his fingers traced the outline of the metal, Jarius smiled. He carried a most valuable commodity in the black leather bag.

Jarius walked faster past the rest of the hanuyots— the craftsmen's shops—that lined the Lower City where he had worked for so many years. The Tyropoeon Valley divided Yerushalayim into an Upper City and a Lower City, and through each of these areas ran the main avenues where the bazaars would be found. Jarius's eyes peered into each of the side streets that finally ran into the Tyropoeon Valley itself. Should a figure be lurking in the shadows, he would scream for a hated Roman soldier. Not far ahead was the street that led from Herod's palace to the Temple across the Krystus Bridge. But even in the shadows of the sacred place, a man might be mugged. Life had become cheap. One's whole existence could be exacted over a little gold. Jarius felt for the outline of the small knife beneath his robe.

Jarius turned aside at the food market. Straight ahead the goats and lambs hung quartered and in slabs. The smell of old stale carcasses filled his nose and turned his stomach. A goat's head lay on the counter. Skinned, the eyes stared from their bloody sockets. An unexpected swirl of wind whipped at his robe, cutting through to nip at his skin. Yet, the sensation assured him that he was alive in a world that was filled with so much deadness.

Jarius quickly crossed to the grain vendor's side. "A full measure," he pointed to the wheat in the merchant's bin.

Without a word, the bent old man scooped up the grain. An ugly scar ran down his forehead, under the black patch that covered his left eye, and down his cheek. The skin had drawn and wrinkled around the disfigurement. He never looked up, as if all normal human dignity had long since departed.

When Jarius paid for the wheat, the vendor made no response. "Shalom." Jarius placed the coins in his hand.

"Humph," the old man grunted.

Everywhere he looked, Jarius saw emptiness in the eyes of the people. Save for the hope of a Messiah, there was little to encourage his fellow Jews to continue on the perilous journey called life. A widespread failure of nerve had settled over most of the nation. With the exception of the mindless fanatical outbursts of the Zealots, the populace understood well the Roman legions' capacity to smash all resistance quickly, effectively, and permanently. Fear had taken possession of every last one of them.

A sudden shriek from overhead took his breath away. A professional mourner had just stepped out on the balcony. From within the house more cries pierced the evening. Tearing at his clothes, the man doubled over the railing, screaming at all who passed by. The wailing and crying rose and fell in ever-increasing crescendos. Jarius knew all too well the ancient custom. Inside the house a family lay prostrate around the bed where a beloved one no longer breathed. Perhaps, a father held the limp hand of his only child. Even though death was an ominous fact of everyday life, the thought remained unbearable. Jarius began to walk much faster.

Jarius thought about how death had also become an expected intruder in his own house. When his wife died in labor, numbness had crept into his mind, stealing from him any capacity to feel. Two years passed before he would allow himself the luxury of facing even the pain. If it had not been for Mariam's sudden illness, he might have closed the world out forever. Yet, her malady had forced him to come out of his emotional hibernation. For the first time, Jarius realized that the pain which had first left him in shambles had also strangely rehabilitated him. Now, as he rubbed his numb fingers together, the bite of the cold was a sign that at least he was alive.

Turning off the major thoroughfare, Jarius headed for his home. Regardless of the danger, he resolved that he would not be ruled by fear. Seeking help for Mariam would be better than sitting and waiting for another intrusion from his final ultimate Enemy. Death would not be entertained again without a fight.

During the next three days, the weather became warmer. More customers came in to look, and the week's receipts were unusually good. As the sun set and the Sabbath was about to begin, each of the brothers quickly and efficiently completed his part of closing the shop. Expensive pieces of gold were slipped into bags to be taken to each of their homes for security. The profits were hurriedly divided among them, lest the shadows overtake them and the sacred covenant of keeping Sabbath be violated.

"I will not be here when you open on the first day of the week," Jarius said factually. Zeda did not even acknowledge his comment but kept clearing the gems from his workbench.

"Oh?" Simeon looked suspiciously at the two of them. "Why?"

"I will be going to the Gennesaret." Jarius wiped the top of his working surface with a cloth.

Zeda turned his back as if he were completely absorbed in his work.

"You've both planned this for some time." Simeon walked to the center of the shop.

"She is worse," was Jarius's only reply.

"As a rabbi," Simeon drew himself up to his full height, "and as one who sits on the Sanhedrin, I must counsel against such action."

Neither brother spoke.

"Well, say something," Simeon snapped.

"I think, '' Zeda said respectfully, "that maybe life is more important than being correct."

"That is a dangerous idea!" Simeon's face hardened.

"You mean well," Jarius patted his brother on the shoulder, "and I respect you. But Mariam is all I have left."

"I sense that this is a very important journey for all of us," Zeda embraced his brother. "Whatever happens, we will pray for her and for you until you return. Time means nothing. Stay as long as is necessary." Zeda pressed a leather pouch into Jarius' hands. "A little extra help should you need something additional."

Simeon did not move, neither did the intensity of his displeasure diminish.

Jarius smiled at his younger brother, but said nothing. When he reached the entry to their shop, Jarius turned one last time. "Shabbot shalom," he waved.

TWO

Zeda and Simeon walked briskly along the same path that Jarius had taken home from the marketplace two weeks earlier. Lost in their animated conversation, they were oblivious to the merchants and people they passed along the way. The stone walls and stucco houses blended together into a passing blur. Even the cold winds of a Tebeth spring didn't distract them.

"Are you sure you understood the servant?" Simeon questioned Zeda. "I don't think you heard correctly. Such transformation cannot occur in the span of only two Sabbaths."

"I may be older, but I'm not deaf!" Zeda snapped. "Why can't you just rejoice in good news?" His quick gait set the pace, challenging Simeon to keep up with him.

"We must not be deceived by illusions. They are everywhere these days." Simeon shook his head. "False messiahs appear from out of the dust."

"We are close." Zeda pointed up the street, ignoring

his brother's cynicism. "That crowd in front of their house is not an illusion."

Jarius's faded brown stucco house was certainly adequate enough to hold a large number of people. The second story was so high it left the appearance of being the neighborhood fortress. Many people were milling around near the door. Unlike the wealthy merchants who filled ugly warehouses with goods from afar, the successful family Ben Aaron owned their own premises and produced their own goods. They could afford such a fine house.

"You don't want to believe the report." Zeda sounded disgusted. "Just be glad."

"I have my responsibilities," the young rabbi protested. "We must be open-minded."

Jarius's house was on the side of the hill, allowing him to see over much of the city. The extra rooms made it possible for him to add other servants who lived with him after his wife's death. Plain by ornate Roman standards, the rambling stucco-covered home compared well to those of the priests who served in the Temple.

"The word has spread quickly," Zeda pointed out. "Jarius has found the hope that our people crave."

"People will believe anything if they're frightened." Simeon pulled his robe more tightly around him.

The noise of conversations reached their ears while they were still fifty feet away. People were chattering, gesturing, coming and going as if Jarius's home had itself become a bazaar. Simeon automatically touched the slender mazusseh attached to the door jam invoking the blessing of the Holy One of Israel. He paused, remembering the time years ago when he and Jarius had put their own carefully chosen piece of scripture inside the little oblong box and fastened it to the entryway as a constant prayer for the Ben Jarius household. Inside the little metal box, the small piece of parchment still proclaimed the message of Psalm 133: "How good and pleasant it is when brothers dwell in unity."

"Please," Zeda pushed past the crowded doorway. "We are the family." He squeezed past observers who were clearly displeased at having their view disturbed. "Excuse us." Zeda led on down the hallway to the living room.

In the center of the large, central room, Jarius sat with his daughter. In contrast to the stark colorless stucco walls, Mariam's face was filled with color and vitality. Having not seen Mariam out of bed in a long time, they almost didn't recognize her. She was seated on a small stool against the far wall where she could be seen easily. Her father sat next to her.

"My brothers!" Jarius leaped to his feet. "Come and see. Look at my child!"

Mariam's dark black eyes were fixed on the floor in the demure way of every proper and modest Jewish girl. Her raven black hair hung over her shoulders and down her back. The brothers stared incredulously at their niece.

Small and slight, Mariam's face seemed molded by the hands of a sculptor whose touch created perfection. Her petite nose and perfect mouth completed a countenance that had been lovely even in illness. But now the dark circles under her eyes were gone. The gray pallor in her skin was a healthy olive tone. The arms and legs that had hung limp and drawn were now firm and steady. Gone was the wheezing and rattling sound in her breathing that had become the ominous predictor of the future. Her black eyes danced with life; yet there was a new depth in her gaze.

Standing at the threshold of adolescence, Mariam's face was now filled with a wisdom that exceeded her years. She was a transformed person.

Jarius gestured to his brothers to come close. "No one could diagnose her illness," he continued addressing the people who filled the room. "None of the doctors who examined her had any answers. Day by day she became weaker until she could barely move her body. Ask my brothers who are now here."

Both Zeda and Simeon only stared at the child who now seemed unknown to them.

"I had just found the young rabbi," Jarius became more animated with large sweeping motions, "when my servant came with the word that Mariam had finally succumbed." He choked as his eyes became moist.

A murmur of amazement spread among the crowd.

"But the rabbi was unshaken!" Jarius's eyes widened. "Instead, he took my hand, looked into my eyes with the greatest compassion I have ever seen, and told me that she was not dead. I cannot express the bewilderment I felt in having my servant weeping at my side while this amazing holy man told me with his eyes that I was not to mourn."

"But—" Simeon broke in—"did you know she was dead?" He walked toward Mariam. "Perhaps the servant was mistaken."

"I ran like a mad man to our cousin's house. As the servant had said, there was no life in her. Her skin had already turned blue." Jarius shook his head. "When I picked her up from the bed, she hung limp and lifeless. Oh, I would have died in her place, but I knew she had already gone." He paused, wringing his hands. "Yes, Simeon, death had claimed her."

"Dead?" Simeon's voice drifted away into a whisper.

"Then—" Jarius paused until every eye was on him

and the room was completely silent—"then the rabbi said, 'The child is not dead but sleeping.' He took her hand from me and said simply, 'Talitha cumi.' That is all he said. 'Arise, little girl.'"

Jarius waited a long time before continuing. "And then my little Mariam opened her eyes, and the color came back to her face."

Silence fell over the room. The sea of faces was perfectly motionless as each person gave rapt attention. Servants stood in unusual informality as they stared at the young mistress of the house. Even the smallest of the children sensed the impropriety of interruption and hovered close to their parents. Every eye was fashioned on the marvel who sat before them in complete composure.

Simeon sat down on the floor in front of Mariam.

Zeda finally reached out and hugged his niece. Gently he ran his hand through her long hair as he pressed her head against his shoulder. "Blessed be the God of Avraham, Yitzchak, and Yaakov." Mariam reached up and took his hand.

"Could this rabbi be the Messiah?" someone whispered.

"My child." Simeon leaned toward Mariam so that he could look directly into her dark eyes. "Your father says that you were dead. Were you?"

Mariam studied her uncle's face carefully. She searched his troubled eyes. "Yes," she said quietly. "A gray cloud rolled over my body until I was wrapped in darkness itself. I was swallowed by the gloom. Yes, surely death had come."

"You are sure?" Simeon persisted.

"When mother died—" Mariam looked away. "I learned how terrible death is. I heard her cries over and over again until exhaustion left her no breath. I couldn't

stand to hear her suffering." She turned back to Simeon, "And I held the little baby and cried that I would
never have a little brother. He felt so limp and heavy in
my arms. Everything human seemed to be gone except
the face. How could I ever forget what death is like?"

"But," Simeon pushed, "what happened to you? Did
your mind stop? Did your thoughts cease?"

"No." Mariam smiled. "I was aware of a terrible emptiness that pulled me further and further away from all
that had been my life. I felt as if I were going down a
tunnel into a land of perpetual doom."

"Surely she went to Sheol," Jarius responded. "As the
Psalms proclaim, she truly went down to the depths."

"I knew I could not come back again," Mariam added,
"and each of you would quickly become only a memory.
I wondered if Mother would be there, but I saw only
emptiness."

"Then—" Simeon became more intense—"then how
did you return?"

"In that dark place a wonderful light began to appear,
far away in the distance. At first I thought I was seeing a
sunrise. But it became as if the sun had left its orbit and
was descending to me like a great sunburst."

No one dared to interrupt. Her elders seemed to become naive children and she the seasoned scholar. Mariam smiled at their astonishment.

"The light began to take shape like a face. And the
face spoke words that echoed through my mind. Again
and again, I heard, 'Talitha cumi, talitha cumi, talitha
cumi.' Each syllable imparted life. Energy surged forth
until I knew I could not stay in that place any longer. I
felt myself being propelled back to this world."

"Great is the name of the Almighty!" a man in the
front of the crowd said as he raised his hands.

"Bless Adonai!" Someone else clapped his hands.

Sounds of awe and delight rippled across the room. Then everyone applauded.

"And you opened your eyes?" Simeon ignored the people. "Do you remember how it felt to be back in your body?"

"Oh, yes."

The room again became silent.

"I felt as if I were putting on a covering left behind like an old dress. Yet there was nothing unpleasant in recciving my life again. I was simply back."

"Back?" Simeon seized the word. "Back! How could this be?"

"When I opened my eyes," Mariam no longer spoke to her uncle but to the entire room, "I saw a man hovering over me. I knew him! I had seen him in the cloud of light that had led me out of the land of death. The man, the rabbi Yeshua was holding my hand."

An older man exclaimed, "Isaiah wrote in the scrolls, 'The people who sit in darkness will see a great light.' The Messiah has come!"

Immediately the crowd pressed forward. People stepped over Simeon. Each person wanted to look more closely.

"Is the hour of redemption at hand?" an old woman touched Mariam's arm. "The sick are revived and the lame walk!"

"Only God could do such wonders."

"The day of redemption draws nigh."

"He visits His people Israel once more!"

Simeon was brushed aside by the amazed and the curious. As the people pressed forward, he was squeezed to the back. "Please," he heard Jarius say over the uproar, "do not crowd. Give us room."

"Where can we find this Rabbi Yeshu?" An old woman pulled at Simeon's robe. "I have a sick grandchild. I must leave immediately to find this great wonder worker."

"I don't know." Simeon turned away. "I know nothing about the man." He deliberately inched his way back out to the hallway.

Once outside, Simeon shook his robes. He watched the people pouring in to look at his restored niece. He could only shake his head.

Jarius watched Mariam answering the questions of the people. He smiled as she effortlessly and casually picked up a baby that had crawled over to her. Kissing the baby on the forehead, she bounced him on her knee without interrupting the flow of her story. His sickly hesitant child had been replaced by a vibrant, confident young lady. Even her face was mature and womanly.

As she talked, Jarius's eyes rested on the necklace around her neck. The unusually large pearl in the middle stood out against the colored beads which surrounded it. While the gold work wasn't Jarius's best, few pieces had ever been made with as much affection. He was very young then and had wanted to create a supreme expression of his devotion. Even though Zeda had struck an unusual deal for the pearl, months of labor were needed to fully cover the cost. But then, no gift had been too expensive to please Mariam's mother.

As was the custom, their marriage was arranged before Michele was of age and they had even met. Jarius had only seen her twice before they were betrothed. Their second meeting sent him in search of a pearl of great price. Although he knew nothing of romance, the thoughts that filled his mind during those interim years created wondrous expectations. In the days that followed their marriage, Jarius had at times even worried that he might have fallen into the unforgivable error of worshiping Michele.

With a wife, Jarius had worked all the harder to become a craftsman who provided in the best of style. Although the business had been in his family for endless generations, Jarius's workmanship soon exceeded any of his predecessors. His long nimble fingers worked designs that were far more complicated than any of his competitors. Unfortunately, his talent had cost him the pursuit that he had always admired the most. The family insisted he stay an artisan. Jarius had hoped to become a rabbi. As skilled as he was with his hands, his mind was by far his greatest asset. Even at an early age, he had been admired at the synagogue. His questions could be haunting and pressing, but the family had recognized the financial promise in his creations. His father had decided that Simeon would make the better candidate for the rabbinate because of an extraordinary memory. Afterward, the competition between the brothers had been sharp and frequent.

Although it was never mentioned or discussed, his parents had always sided with Simeon in these disputes. In turn, Simeon had used their partiality as a lever to subtly but persistently elevate himself. Jarius always felt his brother to be somewhat arrogant and presumptive, but Zeda made sure they stayed a family. Keeping himself squarely and constructively in the middle, Zeda was the peacemaker. So as their parents departed for Sheol, Zeda became the fatherly source of concord.

How could Jarius not admire Zeda? His goodness and sense of humor had covered over many conflicts. Standing between his brothers, Zeda was ointment when Jarius and Simeon were sandpaper to each other. Zeda could laugh at himself and had always demanded little. He had taken his terribly deformed hand in stride, never expecting exceptions for himself. Jarius loved him dearly. Actually, except for his unsavory and un-avoidable contacts with the Romans and Zealots, there were few people for whom Jarius did not care.

Jarius smiled again as he watched his friends talk to Mariam. Something wonderful was happening to every-one who heard Mariam's story. Years had passed since his home was filled with joy. People were coming to re-joice, not to mourn. Saying little, he stood, watching with deepest satisfaction as the afternoon floated. Fi-nally enough was enough.

Jarius had to call twice for his servants to clear the house before the people would leave. No one had any idea of how many people had come and gone during that afternoon. Although Mariam was tired, she was still cheerful.

"Where's Simeon?" Jarius asked. "He's gone?"

"He left much earlier," Zeda sighed. "I don't think he approved of your miracle."

"Perhaps he was concerned for the business," Jarius shrugged.

"You don't really think so."

"Daughter," Jarius turned away without answering, "I know the day has exhausted you. Maybe you should lie down for awhile."

"Father, you have spent too many years worrying about my dying. You can set that habit aside now. I am going to live."

"You are different, my child." Zeda looked very care-fully at her face, studying her eyes as if some secret had not yet been revealed. "You are more than alive. A new dimension has been added."

"Her sensitivity," Jarius marveled, "reaches inside the heart. Mariam, you seem to know things that the rest of us cannot understand."

"I have spent so many years alone," Mariam was pensive, "and loneliness has been a teacher for me. Now it seems what has been building in the silence has come forth in me. I think that I have learned to see with more than my eyes. I do not understand how, but I know other people's pain and worry before it is even spoken. I sense what is in their hearts."

"See?" Jarius beamed. "My little girl came back a woman of mystery."

"I don't know." Mariam looked down as she pondered her own words. "I seem to sense what God is going to do when I feel the pain of others. I want to pray for them, and I know that if I do, they will be helped. In giving me life, He also gave me a strange new ability to be His instrument."

"Surely you have been given a special mission." Zeda moved closer. "What are you supposed to do?"

"I don't know," Mariam answered slowly, "but when the time comes, I will be shown."

"Mariam," Zeda took her shoulders and looked deeply into her eyes. "I have never heard of anyone going to the land of the dead and returning, much less that a rabbi could say the words that could make it so. Yes, our rabbis prayed for your health, and often the Holy One, blessed be His name, does visit us with His touch. But what has happened to you is beyond our comprehension. Yet this much I know. Whoever this rabbi is, only HaElyon can give life."

"He is a most holy man," she answered. "We will hear much more about him."

"I saw that at once," Jarius agreed. "When he begins to speak, there is authority and certainty. His words are simple but almost beyond comprehension."

"What I remember most was what I saw in his eyes."

Mariam smiled. "When we looked at each other, he invited me to know him. He was gentle but with great strength."

"Maybe he could heal my hand," Zeda looked at his twisted fingers.

"Some day he will come down from the north and the response of all Yerushalayim will be great," Jarius assured him.

"His coming will be filled with many surprises." Mariam looked out of the window across the Yerushalayim horizon line. "Some will be filled with joy, but others will be sad. The little people will be happy and the mighty confounded."

"What do you mean?" Zeda's eyes widened.

"I don't know except there is a purity in him that will judge everything that is less. Many will not be able to face the test."

"Can a thirteen-year-old child say such things?"

"She does," Jarius answered Zeda. "In restoring her life, Rabbi Yeshua gave her years of wisdom."

Mariam kissed her father and uncle as she left the room. "I love you both," she said. Then she stopped in the doorway for a moment. "Simeon may be among the offended," she said without looking back.

Mariam closed the door to her room. Once again she found the little chest that was so carefully kept hidden behind her robes. Mariam took the golden chain strung with beads from her neck and laid it out on her bedroll. Lovingly she ran her fingers across the brightly colored little pieces of glass that hung on each side of the pendant with the large pearl in the center.

"Oh, Mother, I miss you. If I could just tell you, talk to you. I need you more than I ever have. I don't know how to understand—"

Tears filled her eyes; she sighed deeply. "I wanted to

find you in the place of death. Any place would be tolerable if you were there. I would have gladly stayed and you could have come back. But here I am. Now what shall I do?"

Mariam picked up the necklace and tied it around her neck again. Holding the candle next to her face, she peered into the small hand mirror. Even though the mirror was smoky and distorted, it reflected the bright colors that now sparkled around her neck. Mariam rubbed each of the little beads, peering into the glass as if she might see another face there.

"There are so many secrets that I don't even know, and now I have been given this strange power. My mind is filled with pictures, ideas, dreams that overpower me. And there is no one to talk to. I am really so alone."

Once more Mariam took the necklace from around her neck and put it back in the little box. She closed the lid and slipped it into the hiding place once more.

She blew out the candle and quickly slipped out of her outer garments. The cold floor stung her feet, sending her immediately scurrying beneath the heavy woven blankets.

"Adonai," she prayed aloud, "blessed be Your name. Consider Your servant. Forgive me that I am so small and Your works are so great." Mariam drifted off to sleep, not knowing what else to say.

The canvas flaps on the front door of the shop gently swung in the early afternoon breeze. Halfway into the sixth hour of the day, the men worked busily at their workbenches. The night chill still hung in the air.

"We have become the talk of Yerushalayim." Simeon looked back and forth between his brothers. "After the demonstration at your house yesterday, the report that

a miracle had occurred even spread to the Sanhedrin."

"Oh—" Jarius turned the piece of gold over to work on
the back side. He let the afternoon sunlight bounce off
the bracelet. "Maybe all the commotion will be good for
business today." He laughed to relieve the tension.

"Some attention is not so desirable." Simeon's voice
was sour.

"Well, our little Mariam has been returned to us,"
Zeda answered from his table across the shop, "and
nothing else matters. Who cares if people are happy or
sad. We are among the blessed!"

"There are issues here," Simeon spoke slowly, dis-
counting his older brother, "and we must be cautious."

"Please," Zeda's voice had taken on an edge, "can't
you just receive the gift that has befallen us and stop
there?"

"Fortunately or unfortunately, I am a rabbi. I sit on
the Great Sanhedrin. I must ask questions."

Zeda threw up his hands and turned his back as if he
had other business to attend.

"Who did this rabbi say that he is?"

"Simeon," Jarius sounded annoyed, "he claimed
nothing, nothing whatsoever. He was teaching the people and healing the sick."

"But did he ever call himself the Messiah—or hint of
such a calling?"

"No," Jarius was firm, "in fact he commanded us to
tell no one who he was or what he had done."

"Hm—mm—m, that's very interesting."

"Why?" Zeda was exasperated. "What difference
does it make anyway?"

"You know the people's hunger for a Messiah," Simeon began to talk rapidly. "The least little provocation
will stir them to a feverish pitch. And we have certainly

had enough self-proclaimed rabbis. We don't need any more trouble from some strange teacher who sweeps in upon us from out of the desert."

"But this man," Jarius shook his finger at his brother, "makes the lame to walk and the blind to see. He made our little Mariam live."

"Such a man could be the most dangerous of all!"

"Stop it!" Zeda waved his hand at Simeon. "If you can't rejoice with us, then hold your tongue."

"Listen to me, my brothers." Simeon rose to his feet. "You must not forget what the law has taught us. If a prophet or a dreamer of dreams comes with a sign or a wonder, we must carefully test what he teaches. He may use his powers to lead us off after other gods. The law demands that such a deceiver must be put to death!"

"I want to hear no more of this nonsense," Jarius retorted in disgust. "I think you are envious of a younger rabbi who has helped our family more than you could."

Simeon clenched both fists tightly and flexed his jaw. "Even now the Galilean drives a wedge between us. I warn you that many in Yerushalayim know about his work and question his authority. You do well to listen to what I am telling you for the good of us all."

Zeda stomped to the entry and threw the canvas flaps aside to open the shop. Quickly he tied the other flap back so that their merchandise was visible to anyone going down the street. "Visit the shop of the family Ben Aaron!" he called to a passerby. "Receive a blessing. We are the people who have had a great miracle. Come and hear how the rabbi brought life to my niece after she had died."

"Really?" Two men stopped and turned toward the stall. "You are not serious? Can such be?"

"He asked us not to speak of the deed," Jarius hesitated.

"My brother, a respected ruler of the synagogue, will tell you," Zeda continued unabated.

"We are from Damascus and new to the city. What strange stories do you tell?"

"Jarius was there. Or perhaps, we will have some additional commentary from our younger brother, the rabbi." Zeda pointed toward Simeon.

"Stop it," Simeon ground his teeth. "You would do well to heed what I say. I told you in the beginning that we are playing with fire. You will get all our fingers burned."

Simeon pushed impolitely past the two men who had entered the shop. Once in the thoroughfare, he walked briskly into the crowd.

"Humph!" the smaller of the two customers brushed off his robe where Simeon had jostled him. "Tell us more."

"Come in, come in," Zeda bid them enter.

THREE

"**B**aruch atah Adonai Elohaynu," Jarius prayed the Seder prayer as he closed his eyes. The words slowly rolled from his lips, "Blessed are you, O Lord, our God. *Melech ha—olam boray p'ree ha'adonai*," he continued his adoration.

Flickering candles cast long shadows across the stucco walls and across Mariam's covered head. Zeda and his wife Rachael sat huddled together around one end of the table while Simeon, the rabbi, sat in the middle. Each of the men had their heads covered with their talliths as the hovering darkness and the dancing light continually reshaped each of their silhouettes.

"Blessed art Thou, O King of the Universe," a servant murmured as she placed a basket of figs on the table.

"*Baruch atah Adonai Elohaynu, melech ha—olam,*" Simeon continued the steady lilting flow of words. "*Boray p'ree magofen.*"

"A year has passed since you returned Mariam to us. We are filled with gratitude. For centuries and in countless places, we have prayed and awaited the coming of

—35—

the Messiah," Jarius spoke almost unconsciously, "and now—" He stopped as if suddenly aware of his own words.

Simeon jerked his head.

"Hamotsu alechim min ha—a—rets," Zeda quickly added as if uninterrupted.

Jarius closed his eyes again and tilted his head upward once more. Simeon slowly looked down again. The prayers glided on as the brothers alternately prayed until finally Zeda uttered a definitive "amen." From around the room a chorus of "amens" followed.

"Once more the cycle of the seasons is complete as we gather in the home of our eldest." Jarius toasted Zeda. "The month of Nisan* has come with this great festival. Another year has brought us to this Passover of thanking the Almighty for His protection and deliverance. We have survived when so many have perished."

"Well," Zeda smiled warily, "we could have done without last week's attack from the Zealots."

"But the Romans returned most of what was taken," his wife added quietly, "after they caught the men."

"True, true." Zeda patted his wife's hand. "I suppose one of the values of trading so heavily with our captors is they give us some attention that is denied others." He shook his head sadly. "But the fanatics will never learn."

Servants began moving among the family, adding dishes and platters of food. Little clay bowls of salt water were placed between each person. Next to the commemoratives of the tears of slavery, bowls of maror or bitter herbs were set for dipping in the salt water. The charoseth, symbolic of the mortar for bricks made without straw, was nearby. Moach, the chief steward,

*corresponds to March—April

brought in the large platter piled high with the roasted lamb. Here and there were little dishes filled with hard-boiled eggs. The savory aroma filled the room with wonderful warmth.

"Surely the Zealots must be angry with us?" Mariam asked as she reached for a piece of the flat, hard, unleavened matzos. "What will become of these men? Can they harm us again?"

The glow of the many candelabra around the room made the dark ceiling appear to be far overhead, as if the ceiling had become a black hole extending an ominous canopy of space over the Ben Aaron family.

"They will all be put to death," her father answered. "Tragic. I do not wish the death of any of them, even if they were trying to hurt us, but there will be no reprieve."

"They have been seeking the ringleader for a long time," Simeon noted, "a fierce man named Barnabba*. They will execute him quickly."

"How?" Mariam placed some figs on her plate.

"Crucifixion, I'm sure." Simeon tossed his head indifferently. "Makes the best example for the people to see."

"Surely there is no greater cruelty," Mariam shuddered.

"The Romans are masters when it comes to pain," Zeda added, dipping the unleavened bread in the heavy sauce. "They rule by intimidation."

"But won't his death only make matters more difficult for us?" Mariam raised her eyebrows.

No one answered.

"Well?" she asked again.

Zeda looked down. "Of course. You are right. Yes, we become the victims once more. Some people will blame

*Barnabus

us simply because the incident happened in our store. Such publicity we don't need!"

"The times are hard," Simeon sighed. "The city is filled with chaos and turmoil. We must expect continuing attacks. I see little hope."

"You know our feelings," Jarius spoke softly. "I think—"

"Plea—s—e," Simeon cut him off, "not on this night of all nights. We have already heard enough of this Galilean who only adds to the confusion. I don't want to hear any more."

"Now, now," Zeda began waving his hands as if to separate the brothers. "We must recognize that Jarius and his family owe a great deal to the rabbi. Here," he reached for a plate of grapes, "let us eat and be thankful."

"So I have heard for the whole past year," Simeon snorted, waving the plate away. "I know that Mariam has sought him out to listen to his teaching. Bringing up his name tonight is like adding leaven to the matzos."

"But," Jarius begged, "surely you and your friends can recognize what is so clear to the common people. Did you not see the demonstration when he entered the city just four days ago?" Jarius took a handful of grapes and settled back.

"I saw a crude attempt to emulate the predictions of the prophets. I saw his followers with palm branches trying to make it appear that the Promised One had come, but I expect better from my own family. I thank the Holy One, not this man, for Mariam's restoration to health."

"Anyone with such powers can dispel the Romans," Jarius shook his finger as if preaching an often repeated theme. "We must listen to him!"

"The Romans will hang him out to rot and us with him," Simeon shot back. "I tell you, this Nazarene will be the death of all of us."

"Yeshu brings peace. You will see!"

Zeda's wife stirred uncomfortably, pushing herself back from the feast.

"Brothers, brothers!" Zeda rapped on the table. "Please. We hear this all day in the shop." Once more he sent a plate around the table. "Let's not continue our arguments here. Please try one of these delicious olives."

"But justice will prevail!" The color began rising in Jarius's face. "The Messiah will restore David's throne. We have prayed for this time to come."

"The man tries to destroy our traditions!" Simeon hissed and spit an olive pit on his plate. "Listen to me. I sit with the rulers and I tell you that we can end up with more than the Romans and the Zealots down on us. Would you like to stand against the Great Sanhedrin as well? Big trouble is coming because of this man!"

"What are you saying?" Mariam's voice was low and intense. "Uncle, you know more than you are saying."

Simeon started to speak, but stopped. For a moment he studied his niece's black eyes with their penetrating darkness that seemed unfathomably mysterious and knowing. Simeon found it to be impossible to be angry or answer harshly to one so delicate.

"If your father will not listen, heed me, child." Simeon pushed his plate aside and reached out for his niece. "Trouble is brewing, and this family needs no more difficulties. Yes, the rabbi helped you, but that time is past. Leave the man be."

"You would deny us the opportunity to hear his teaching?" Jarius's voice turned caustic and mocking. "As we celebrate this festival of freedom would you deny us the right of inquiry and investigation?" Jarius chuckled. "Strange that a rabbi would fear the truth."

Zeda searched frantically for something else to pass. All he could find was a bowl of pomegranates. "Marvelous crop this year," he said as he offered the bowl.

His wife said nothing but took the bowl. Yet Rachael nearly dropped the bowl as it came by. Mariam leaned back into the shadows so that Simeon could no longer see her eyes. The roasted lamb was left untouched.

"The meat is excellent," Rachael suddenly blurted.

"There is going to be violence before this matter is over," Simeon directed his response to Mariam. "Who knows what can happen? The city is ready to explode. I am warning you to stay away from volcanoes that are about to erupt."

"Do the Romans also confer with you, Simeon, before they make their raids?" Jarius chided. "Are we so honored that we have a brother who knows what is hidden from the rest of us?"

"No more!" Simeon rose from his place. "Let everyone remember," he spoke loudly as if to make sure the servants heard, "I separate myself from any and all connection with this man who troubles Yerushalayim. I stand with the teachers and priests of Israel. So be it." Abruptly Simeon turned and stomped out of the room.

"Please, please," Zeda hurried after him, "we must not celebrate the Pesach in such a manner."

No one spoke. Nothing more was said when Zeda returned by himself. After several minutes Rachael noted how unusually cold the weather had been. The superficial conversation continued with pleasantry drifting from one nonoffensive subject to the other.

"I apologize," Jarius finally said softly. "I should have held my tongue."

"We understand," Rachael answered. "We must go on and keep our festival." She offered wine to Jarius.

"Simeon will see nothing but the controversy," he lamented. "I know the matter is complex, but he refuses to even be open to what we have heard and seen."

"Our brother bears a heavy weight," Zeda smiled feebly. "Who would have dreamed that he would find favor with the Sanhedrin at such a young age? I know he worries over the authority that has come to him."

"The respect he has found with men has closed the windows in his heart," Mariam said gently. "Our rabbi did not come seeking position, but peace. Neither of you has understood," Mariam said humbly to her father.

Jarius looked dumbfounded at his daughter. "I don't understand."

"What?" Zeda strained to hear. "What are you saying?"

"The battles that our Rabboni fights are of another realm." Mariam seemed to arise out of the shadows as she bent over the table. "That is why it is futile to argue over his teachings. In time all will become clear."

No one spoke as they all stared at Mariam. After a few moments she leaned back, looked down, and settled into her own quiet space.

"My child," Jarius pulled closer to her. "When you talk like this, it is hard for us to understand. Say more. Don't retreat from us."

Mariam blushed. "I don't know what to say," she spoke slowly. "But it is wrong to fight over what Rabbi Yeshu says because he brings a way of love." She added, "And many will be surprised at the true meaning of his destiny."

"How do you know such things?" Zeda's wife frowned.

"I don't know. But when he speaks, I seem to hear more than his words. Perhaps, I am wrong, but these are the thoughts he has left with me."

"I accept what you say," Jarius smiled at his daughter, "and I know that God is surely with you. I am only sorry I can't seem to find the same grace that lives within you. The pain and injustice I see all around me makes me want to argue, to protest, to fight. I suppose that I want this rabbi to rise up with a great sword and cut them all down."

"He travels without a weapon, my father. We must learn his lesson."

"No sword? No shield?"

"Then where is our help and protection?" Zeda pressed.

"Where was it those many centuries ago on this very night in Egypt?" Mariam smiled, "Perhaps the Holy One wants us to allow Him to be our sole defense."

"I only want justice," Jarius answered.

"Isn't there a virtue," Mariam turned to her father, "that goes beyond justice?"

"What?" Jarius only shook his head in consternation.

"But Simeon was right," Rachael added. "Matters are coming to a head. How can we avoid swords? The city is filled with rumors and fear. Intrigue lurks on every corner. Even the children can feel the tension in the air. Never forget that the Romans are unpredictable. Simeon knows they could turn on us."

The brothers looked knowingly at each other.

"We must ask for the Deliverer to come again quickly," Zeda ended the discussion abruptly. "Let us say our final prayers. The hour is late." At once he began the chant, *"Yisa Adonai Panai Aylecha V'ya saym Echa Shalom."*

As the last words faded away, the family embraced each other and prepared to leave.

Jarius and Mariam left quickly, with their servant following behind them as a security guard. The trio avoided the more narrow pitch-black alleys. Once they turned onto the broad thoroughfare, they knew they were not far from their home.

"Abba," Mariam said quietly once they had entered their house and bolted their door, "there *is* a virtue that exceeds justice."

"There is? What could that be?"

"Mercy." Mariam squeezed his hand. "Mercy will triumph over justice."

Mariam reached up, kissed her father on the cheek, and hurried off to bed.

As Jarius walked to work the next day he thought on other Seders when his father, mother, and wife had been alive. He pictured their faces gathered around the table, and melancholy filled his thoughts. He reflected on the momentary, intangible nature of things, hesitating only before the thought of who might not be present at the table in the coming year.

At the end of the row of merchants and vendors, Jarius could see his shop ahead. Several men were standing outside the door. Situated against the great wall, the building was at the end of the string of jewelry merchants. Traders and pilgrims knew that the family Ben Aaron was always the last stop after the lesser goods had been inspected. The dull stucco shop's exterior was punctuated here and there with large rocks where the cement coating had chipped away. The bright colored canvas door coverings were already peeled back, signaling that the shop was open. Because everyone knew that the jewelry merchants had exclusive control of the street, signs weren't needed.

Jarius exchanged greetings with his competitors as he walked up the street. While each dealer pushed for the best deal, the jewelry merchants shared a common calling that created its own fraternity. Jarius was obviously admired and respected. When he looked again he was surprised to see that a crowd of men had gathered in front of his store.

"It's their fault!" rang through the air. Shouts and accusations punctuated the morning air.

Walking faster, Jarius quickly realized that the men were not customers. A heated and animated discussion had spilled over into the street. Somewhere in the center of the controversy, Simeon must be debating again.

"What's going on?" Jarius worked his way inside. No one seemed to notice his question.

"Something has happened?" he confronted one of the young men who was talking loudly to another man.

"The Sadducees," he replied bluntly. "They're at fault," he turned back to his conversation.

"The Sadducees?" Jarius looked around for Simeon. "What have the Sadducees done?"

Once more he slipped between two other men as he worked his way closer to Simeon. His brother's face was flushed and his eyes flashed with anger. Leather straps around his forehead and arms held the little boxes with fragments of scripture in place. The phylacteries and plain austere robes marked the men Pharisees.

"They have only created more trouble for all of us." Simeon pointed his finger in the direction of the great Temple. "Arresting anyone during the night obviously creates wrong impressions."

Jarius listened for a moment as another man argued that the darkness probably prevented a riot. When Jarius looked over his shoulder, he recognized one of the rabbis who was standing behind him.

"David!" he reached for the man. "What in heaven's name is going on?"

"You don't know?" The white-bearded man opened his eyes wide in astonishment.

"This is the morning after Pesach. Nothing happens today!"

"Last night," the old man pulled at his beard, "the Sanhedrin arrested him—Yeshua—the young rabbi."

"Arrested Yeshua of Natzeret?" Jarius stared. "You're not serious."

"And there was a trial of sorts last night— before the high priest."

"What?" Jarius shook his head.

"They even took the man to the Antonio Fortress to the Romans. Pilate condemned him."

"What are you saying?" The surprise in Jarius's face twisted into anger.

"It's true." The rabbi gestured frantically with both hands. "But the Sadducees were behind it all."

Jarius whirled around, pushing the men between Simeon and himself aside. "What do you know of this?"

"Very little." Simeon looked annoyed at the intrusion. "I was home. But I told you these matters were getting serious."

"They can't condemn a religious teacher," Jarius gasped.

"They already have," one of the men answered. "The sentence has been fulfilled."

"Yes, the Galilean has already been taken to the hill."

"Happened early this morning."

"No!" Jarius shrieked. "Such cannot be!"

"I'm sorry, Jarius," Simeon lowered his voice. "None of us would have chosen this path."

"They moved so quickly." An older man shook his

head sadly. "The soldiers took him from the house of Kaifa* very early."

"No!" Jarius screamed in their faces. "He was a thoroughly good man. Arrest is completely unjust!"

For a moment the group of men became subdued, but the debate quickly continued again.

"Golgatha," an old man said apologetically. "They've already hung him on the tree."

"N—o—o—o—" anger rolled out of Jarius's mouth. Pushing people aside with his powerful arms, he bolted for the street.

"Jarius," Simeon called after him. "We didn't have anything to do with the arrest."

Jarius did not look back as he broke into a run.

"Jarius!" Simeon yelled again. "Don't . . . Be careful!"

Jarius didn't stop until he found the cross street that would eventually lead him out to the city gate. Barely slowing down, he turned the corner and set his face into the wind. Storm clouds were gathering and the sky had begun to darken. He stumbled several times on the broken cobblestone pavement, but didn't fall. Eventually he had to rest against a long rock wall, heaving and gasping to catch his breath. Blustering winds whipped dust up into his face.

For a moment he watched some children still trying to play their make-believe game in the street. A woman came out of a doorway to call the children inside. A shabbily dressed man leading a donkey down the street pulled his outer robe over his eyes. Suddenly the thunder rumbled overhead as the clouds rolled in and Jarius pushed on. A big storm was brewing.

Jarius tried to run harder when the immense Ephraim gateway came into view. Even though he had

*Caiaphas

to move carefully when he began cutting across a small market full of food vendors that lined the street, he didn't slow down.

"Stop! You're in trouble—" A Roman soldier suddenly stepped in front of him.

Jarius had to spin sideways to avoid a direct collision.

"People who run are trying to hide something," the soldier grabbed his arm.

"No, no," Jarius could barely speak as he sucked in large gasps of air. "I am just— in a— hur—ry."

"Who are you?" the soldier asked indignantly.

"A busi—ne—ss man," he could barely breathe.

"Then act like one," the soldier pushed him back. "This is no place to look like you're trying to start trouble or escape from someone."

Jarius bowed his head in compliance, nodded respectfully, and quickly walked on. When he saw that the soldier had turned away, he once more began trotting toward the final gate that led out of the city. As he stopped under the large archway, the wind lashed at his face. Jarius knew well that once he crossed the huge threshold, he would be outside the city, and the hill of execution would be directly in front of him.

Because the staggering cruelty that the Romans meted out was more than Jarius could bear to witness, he seldom came this way. The monstrousness of the whole matter grabbed at his throat. To die outside the city was to be completely cut off from the people, from all that was holy. Clenching his fists, Jarius slowly walked on toward the stone outcropping the Greeks called Calvary.

FOUR

The flow of travelers was light for the third hour. The few wayfarers coming toward the city moved quickly, apparently knowing that loitering could result in conscription by the Romans for some grizzly service. Stumps of used crosses pointed starkly toward the sky. On several timbers the cross members still dangled, swaying back and forth. Increasing winds banged the planks against the center poles and whipped the robes and cloaks of the sojourners like tattered flags.

Jarius shielded his eyes against the blowing sand that stung his face. Turning away, he could not avoid looking straight into the strange countenance that time had worn into the soft limestone and gypsum rock outcropping. Two small, jagged caves added eye sockets to what looked strikingly like a skull. Black and purple clouds boiled behind the huge hill, making the chalky, bony shape even more menacing. For a moment he froze in place. The landscape of death looming before Jarius seemed poised to swallow him. Like a small child who feared that a specter might leap from the umbrage of the darkest night, Jarius blinked twice to force the shape of terror to become a mound of rock again.

Jarius hesitantly picked his way along the treacherous rocky path upward to the top. Another distant crash of thunder unnerved him again, and he lost his footing. Stumbling, he tried to walk faster. The remainders of old crosses and the endless line of sinkholes trailing down to the highway were unavoidable reminders of the rank injustice of his oppressors. The higher Jarius trudged, the more clearly he saw the places of execution, stretching far out down the winding road. Countless Jews had been put to death there as examples to the populace. Perhaps Jarius could still smell the lingering residue of their rotting bodies, which had often been left in the sun for days.

Near the top Jarius used his other hand to keep from seeing what was in front of him. The burning dirt was far less offensive than the sight of the bodies dangling from the poles scattered around the hilltop. A first glance told him that no more than three or four men were being executed.

"Stand back!" a soldier yelled at some people milling around one of the dying prisoners.

Noisy and rumbling voices of people standing in groups floated through the air and then were momentarily lost in the sudden roar of thunder. Dogs with protruding ribs cowered on the edge as if opportunity were at hand. Their whining and barking added to the distraction as the clamor of confusion merged into a blend of bewildering and detracting sounds.

As Simeon had claimed, most of the Jews looked like they were Sadducees. More elegantly dressed than the rest, with their gold-banded robes and distinctive dark flowing head scarfs, the Sadducees aloofly hovered together as if moving beyond their tight circle would bring instant contamination.

Another swirl of dust exploded in Jarius's face, forcing him to pull his robe more tightly around his head. The blackening clouds seemed to be descending on the starkly bone-white rocks. When he looked up again, Jarius could see that only three men hung from crude wooden crosses, which had been set in the ground. Instantly he turned his eyes to the rock-covered earth. Usually a prisoner was beaten or tortured before he was spread out on the makeshift beam that was affixed to the top of a barren tree trunk. The entire rig was set upright and dropped into a hole in the ground after the victim was nailed or tied to the crossbeams; the crucified was left to hang from the cross without support. Often his feet were tucked up and nailed to the shaft to keep the crucified from finding any relief as he dangled haplessly waiting for life to be drained out like a sheep slowly bleeding to death from a slit throat. Eventually the diaphragm collapsed and the prisoner suffocated in his own fluids. Crucifixion literally drained the life out of its victim. Jarius covered his mouth, fearing the wave of nausea could not be restrained.

Breathing deeply and quickly, Jarius tried to cover his ears. He had heard the victims when they became delirious. Their eyes bulged and their thickened tongues hung out like dying cows. Hours might pass before the agony snuffed out the gurgling rattle, finally devouring its victims. Jarius pulled his robe tightly around his neck.

Slowly Jarius forced himself to look up at the three men, stretched out like animals ready to be skinned. At first he did not recognize any of them. Stripped naked with hair hanging over each face, their chins were buried into their necks. One was particularly bloody and beaten. A crude makeshift sign had been tacked to the top of his cross. Metal spikes had been driven into his wrists and feet. Blood had run down his arms and dried into crusty dark brown stains on his body. Recognition of that downturned face made Jarius feel dizzy, and he quickly looked away.

"Jarius! Jarius!" someone called to him.

Ahead he recognized a group of men that he knew. "Yosef! Yosef of Ramatayim*!" Jarius lowered his voice immediately, remembering the seriousness of public identification. Quickly but silently he walked to the group.

"How can this be?" Jarius clenched his fist.

The old man was weeping and could only shake his head.

"Is there nothing to be done?"

Yosef's elegant silk robe was strangely out of place in the barren crude hill. He lifted his hands helplessly.

"He gave my daughter life!" Jarius pleaded. "Surely God was with him."

"No one can understand," another man answered.

"I thought he might be Ha Mashiach*," Jarius pleaded, "but even if I were wrong, I would never have believed he could come to this."

"We are all undone," Yosef heaved. A gold chain swung heavily around his neck. "Apparently he was sold out, betrayed, by one of the inner circle. His people scattered. Many are hiding. We don't have the full story." His words trailed away, "I don't know—I—just—don't—know."

"The crowds were with him. The people cheered him. Where are they?"

*Joseph of Arimethea
*the Messiah

"Very few people even know that he was arrested." Yosef covered his eyes. "By the time the city discovers the truth, Yeshua will be dead. Their treachery was well planned."

"My God," Jarius cried out. "When does it stop?" He struck his palm with his fist as hard as he could.

Immediately Yosef restrained him. Any form of reaction or demonstration could summon a Roman soldier. And yet, the well-intentioned caution made Jarius even more angry. Even simple, normal emotion wasn't allowed!

Jarius wanted to rush at the nearest guard and at the same time to flee. He set his jaw and ground his teeth as hard as he could to swallow the primal scream that was about to erupt from the depths of his soul. "My God!" he finally choked. "Where does it stop?"

No one answered. Each man avoided looking at the other lest they convey their own cowardice and impotence.

"Aren't any of the Twelve here?" Jarius looked over his shoulder.

"Some of the women are over there," Yosef pointed toward one of the crosses. "His mother is there with Yochanan*."

"His mother? Here?" Jarius stared incredulously. "How unspeakable. Maybe I can say something of comfort."

Walking toward the women and the man, Jarius avoided looking up. The little group was huddled around one woman as they stood close to the base of the cross with the sign on top.

"Please," Jarius slowly entered their circle, "I knew him. He gave life to my daughter."

*John

"I remember you," the apostle extended his hand. "I am Yochanan. You listened to his teaching. Often your daughter was with you. Please meet his mother, Miryam*."

"Yeshu's mother?" Jarius started to extend his hand and then stopped. A plain, thickly woven veil covered most of Miryam's face making it impossible to see her eyes. She was petite, but seemed even smaller as her whole body sagged against the apostle. Reaching up and pushing the covering aside, she offered her hand.

"I would have gladly taken his place," Jarius was surprised by his own words.

Miryam smiled feebly, but said nothing. Her tear-stained face was drawn and etched in weariness. She did not look much older than Jarius. "Try to trust," she mumbled. Once more she lowered her head and leaned against Yochanan.

"Trust?" Jarius winced. "I don't know what to say." He glanced around at the group of women, but none looked up. "I have seen terrible injustices," he appeared to speak only to himself, "but his death is the most monstrous."

No one answered or even seemed aware he had spoken. When the thunder cracked again, the women huddled more closely around Miryam to protect her from the impending storm. Darkness continued to roll in; thickening black clouds filled the sky. Although the sixth hour was approaching, night had come in midday.

A Roman centurion stepped closer. Leaning on his spear, he alone looked up at the figure hanging just above Jarius. The long low moan that settled down on the whole group made Jarius feel weak in his knees. Once more his nausea churned.

*Mary

—53—

Although surrounded by people, Jarius felt completely alone on the barren, god-forsaken hunk of rock. Everything was empty and hard, void and without life. When he closed his eyes, another day drifted into his mind. In solitary grief, he watched his wife, Michele, being sealed in a rock room. Once more the grinding crunch filled his ears as the huge stone door was rolled in place, forever banishing her to the family burial cave. An unrelenting conclusion had been etched in his mind in that moment: *Life would never be the same again.* When he opened his eyes, the same thought buried him once more. Directly in front of Jarius was the centurion, leisurely looking up at the rabbi suspended between life and death. In that moment Jarius thought that he might never again believe in anything.

The words floated down.

"Father, for—give them." Each syllable was more labored than the other. "For they kn—ow not wh—at they do."

Jarius couldn't move. At first, he thought he misunderstood. But the words couldn't be denied. He had heard them correctly. The very idea was totally inconceivable. Whatever Yeshu had meant, Jarius knew he couldn't stand what he was hearing.

"No, no," he shook his head. "No!"

And then Yeshu said it again, "Father, for—give th—em."

Jarius looked into the faces of the women and Yochanan, straining forward, hoping to hear another word. Forgive?

"Forgive them?" Jarius whispered under his breath, "Forgive them?"

The Roman soldier looked at him, equally dumbfounded. Jarius's face twisted, and he thought he might scream. Instead, his hot anger made it hard to speak. "Forgive them!" he finally sputtered.

Jarius bolted past Yochanan and the women, and ran toward the back side of the hill. Without any sense of direction or reason, he ran straight out toward the winding road that led from the city. All he could do with the pain that was exploding in his head was to run as fast and hard as he could. The scenery blurred as his sandals pounded the hardened surface. When a muscle cramp began to knot, he realized he must have run seven or eight furlongs.

Doubled over in pain and close to exhaustion, Jarius felt his heart pounding in his chest like a nearly spent drum. At that moment he saw one of the multitude of small caves that dotted the hills beyond Yerushalayim. Turning off the road, he limped toward the wind-worn opening. He stumbled near the entrance and fell head-long onto the floor. The fall knocked out what was left of his breath, and for a few moments he could only groan and roll up in a ball. Finally, Jarius pulled himself up next to a rock and sat very still. He dropped his head into his hands until his heavy breathing subsided for a few minutes. Sweat ran down his forehead and neck, stinging his eyes.

Only then did the tears begin. When Jarius wiped his eyes, long brown streaks covered his hand. Jarius had no idea why he was crying. Certainly he wept for the death of a totally good teacher and the death of another of his dreams. His tears told him that he could no longer live with the cruelty that threatened to swallow his entire life at every turn. Possibly he cried for the future. But when he stopped weeping, Jarius shook with rage. He pounded his fist into the palm of his hand.

Yet the words would not leave him. They kept pushing through every chain of thought. No matter where he turned, the slow agonizing syllables kept intruding.

"Father, forgive them, for they know not what they do."

The notion was maddening. Such ideas were not rational or possible. Although racked with pain, Yeshua had seemed without fear. No one hanging in total agony pushed to the final limits of all endurance could possibly turn his attention from himself to ask for absolution for his persecutors. The more Jarius thought of it, the more he raged.

And then Jarius knew the deepest point of his pain. This incredible teacher of truth and goodness had insulted and confounded the very core of everything Jarius valued. Yeshua should have cried out for his own vindication and revenge. Why didn't he call fire down from heaven to consume those treacherous dogs? Why didn't he pray for lightning to strike the centurion, incinerating him to ashes?

The very idea offended every value, every intention, every justification by which Jarius lived. He was confused and befuddled. Most of all, the notion released the anger that had lurked for years beneath his other thoughts. God's wrath should have been invoked!

And then, the words came again.

"Father, for—give them, for—give them, f—or they kn—ow no—t wh—at they do."

No one could live by Yeshu's creed lest they, too, end up dangling helplessly before the cruelty of the human race. His death was evidence enough of the absurdity of his own impulse to pardon.

But the words came again—

"Father, for—give them—"

Only then could Jarius scream. The incongruity, the incomprehensibleness, the inconsistency rushed forth in a bloodcurdling cry of anger. When there was no more emotion or voice left in him, he stopped.

For a long time Jarius stared at the ground. Then from deep within, other strange words came again. Mariam's voice from the night before filled his ears.

"Mercy," she had said. "Mercy will triumph over justice. A virtue exists that exceeds justice."

"No!" he tried to scream one last time, but the words wouldn't come.

Broken and bewildered, Jarius began the long journey home. He walked very slowly, stumbling aimlessly along the highway, oblivious to the thunder that roared overhead and the rain that soaked through to the skin.

Jarius was completely drenched by the time he reached his house. The terrible thunderstorm had sent lightning crashing into the mountaintops around Yerushalayim, but the rain had fallen on him almost unnoticed. He did find it impossible to ignore the unusual darkness that had made the afternoon seem like twilight. The black tempest had felt strangely comforting as he walked indifferently in the downpour.

Only after he entered his house did Jarius realize that Mariam probably knew nothing of what had transpired. The misery of her sorrow turned his attention from his own preoccupation. How could he tell her what had happened, much less what he had seen?

"Mariam," he called twice before the small voice answered far away in the center of the house. Jarius knew Mariam must be outside.

The Ben Aaron house was built around a large open area with rooms opening into the patio. Protected, the garden was also a natural place for reflection. When he found her, she was sitting under an overhang, looking out over the rain-drenched inner courtyard.

"Abba," Mariam called gently, "is that you?"

"Yes."

"My poor papa," Mariam touched his wet face, "you are filled with hurt."

Jarius reached for the towel she handed him.

"Simeon came much earlier looking for you. He was concerned."

"You know?"

"He thought I already knew. Yes, Simeon told me."

Jarius sat down on a wooden bench next to her and looked out over the garden. A small almond tree had just begun to blossom. The grapevine that ran up the wall had sprouted again, and the leaves were pushing out. There was a fresh moist smell in the air.

"You are so wet. I was afraid you would be caught in the storm."

"I am all right."

"No, you are not all right."

Jarius finally turned to look at her. To his surprise, her eyes were astonishingly reassuring and composed.

"I was there," Jarius said before she could stop him. "I saw—I saw—" his voice faded away.

"And what did you see?"

"I don't know," Jarius shook his head. "I just don't know. I don't think I will ever know."

"Why?"

"As Yeshua was dying, in complete agony, he asked the Holy One of Israel to forgive those who were putting him to death. He said that they didn't know what they were doing."

"Oh, my," Mariam's eyes opened wide in wonder. "He lived his teaching to the very end."

"But what good are such words? They killed him!"

"Father, I don't understand." Mariam touched his face with another dry towel, "But I remember often Rabboni taught that forgiveness would overcome the hate in the world. Yeshua conquered fear long ago. Surely through his death he has gained a triumph that Rome can never defeat."

"But he is dead," Jarius slumped. "You must understand. Dead."

"Death is one thing that I, perhaps, do understand

better than you, Father, even if I am only your little daughter. When I crossed that final Jordan, the rabbi met me there. Even in the last weeks, he taught the multitudes that that which was torn down will be rebuilt. I think we need not fear for him."

Jarius turned away, sinking further into silent despair.

FIVE

No one doubted that the ancient religious court could keep life on an even keel as it had always done. Every synagogue had its Sanhedrin where the daily and persistent conflicts of congregational life were sorted out. The wisdom of the Torah and the disciplines of the Traditions were meted out as properly as grain was weighted in the marketplace. Yet only the sagest and most learned were selected to sit on the Great Sanhedrin in Yerushalayim. Though antagonists, the Pharisees and Sadducees even sat side by side on the high tribunal, pondering the weightier matters that concerned the Holy City itself. After all, the Great Sanhedrin was the guarantor of the integrity of the faith.

Today acrimony and bitterness hung in the air like stale incense. Even the usually more amicable members of the Sanhedrin sat hunched over with scowls on their faces. Ten days after Pesach the venerable chamber of leaders was in complete disarray.

Although the Pharisees predictably squared off against the Sadducees, both sides generally tried to maintain a stoic attitude of superiority in the presence of the other. Irritation could always be interpreted as a sign of weakness. Sadducees saw their opponents as narrow-minded legalists, while Pharisees viewed their counterparts as compromising opportunists. Each sat on opposite sides of the room. Because the cohanim* were Sadducees, the balance of power almost always swung their way.

Simeon quickly slid by the guards at the door. Ducking his head, he avoided the group of men who were arguing by the back door. He stopped a moment to survey the scene. He saw many of the leaders intentionally turn their backs on the officers in the front. The intensity of the shouting meant that the meeting had been going on for some time. Even though it was morning, the room still seemed dark and foreboding. Simeon wanted to slip inconspicuously into his seat.

The assembly hall was large with an unusually high ceiling. The dark wood paneling made the room feel elegant. Lined in rows, the wooden tables and benches had been rubbed into a smooth glowing finish. Members sat facing a raised diadem that dominated the front of the room. The high priest of the year always sat on a heavy wooden thronelike chair, moderating the assembly.

"We cannot fight with a ghost!" A Pharisee leaped up beside the speaker. "More stories surface every day. He is first seen here and then there. In death you have made him to be more than he ever was in life!"

Simeon watched Yehosaf Ben Kaifa* squirm in the high priest's chair. He knew how much Ben Kaifa enjoyed parading in the attire of his office. Because the room was void of all images and pictures, the high

*Levitical Priests
*Caiaphas

priest took on an aura of an icon in his sparkling breast plate and white domed hat. His dark blue robe was covered by an elaborately embroidered chasuble. Hanging around his neck was a large silver plate set with different colored stones for each of the twelve tribes. The gold band on his high rounded headdress made him look much taller than he was.

Yehosaf wore pomposity and arrogance as easily as he donned the extravagantly expensive robes of his position. But today was different. Even though Ben Kaifa leaned forward with his hand resting on his forehead, Simeon could still see his eyes snap. Anger and malice were etched in the lines of his face.

"With every reported citing of Yeshua, his followers multiply." The first speaker shook his fist again. "They have found the perfect story to vindicate themselves and make us look like fools."

"Belief in resurrection," a Sadducee from the opposite side of the room jeered, "is the foolishness that begets such nonsense."

"No!" The speaker pounded the table. "Your arrogant blindness makes all of us vulnerable."

While the Pharisees believed in the doctrine of the resurrection from the dead, the Sadducees did not. Expecting nothing more than the present life, they attempted to manipulate and maneuver every possibility. No one was more calculating than Ben Kaifa. His perfectly emotionless face was betrayed only by his rapidly shifting eyes.

Behind the high priest another large chair was set against the wall to his left. The former high priest, Annias, sat with his arms across his chest. The old fox's obese form spilled over his chair. Annias's head sunk into his chest deceptively as if he were totally disinterested or asleep.

Ben Kaifa straightened up and looked away.

"Time will take care of the rumors," a Sadducee from the front row interrupted. "Hysteria will die out and be forgotten. We must not panic over a little madness." His voice echoed off the wooden walls, giving it a hollow foreboding sound.

"Why were there secret meetings?" the question rang from the dim in the back of the room. The three large windows were high upon the walls and never illuminated the room well. A shaft of light fell on the center stage where the high priest's chair was set to capitalize on the appearance of divine illumination. However, the tables in the back always appeared to fade into the gloom. No one noticed that Simeon spoke from his chair. "A clandestine trial? If you had not acted at night under the cloak of secrecy, we would have credibility. As it is, no one believes or trusts any of us."

"We cannot escape the weight of leadership," an old Sadducee shot back. "We must do what is best for the people, whether they understand us or not. Even if the rabble doesn't like the fact that a crucifixion occurred, at least the Romans aren't sending any of us to prison."

"Let us not forget," another richly dressed Sadducee interjected smugly, "it is expedient to sacrifice one life for the good of the nation."

"No!" Simeon rose to his feet. "I do not want to hear that argument ever again! Romans think like that, but not Jews. Since when has any Jewish life become expendable? Who is to know from which family the Messiah will come?"

"Here! Here!" echoed around the room. Several of the Pharisees applauded, but Ben Kaifa folded his arms and glared.

"Roman soldiers are telling the people," Simeon continued, "that our leaders paid them to say his followers stole the body while they slept. Is that so?"

Annias, the father-in-law of Yehosaf Ben Kaifa, immediately straightened up and lifted his hand to command silence. "Of course," he answered condescendingly, "his followers were the only ones who could have taken the body." He quickly and dramatically swirled his high priestly robes with great authority. "The drunken soldiers probably fell asleep while they were supposed to be standing guard."

"Everyone knows Romans don't fall asleep while on duty," Simeon was defiant. "They pay for such mistakes with their lives. What did happen?"

Annias looked blank as if he were momentarily speechless.

"What are you suggesting?" Ben Kaifa spoke for the first time. His voice was low and menacing.

"If the guards did fall asleep, they were in jeopardy," Simeon's eyes narrowed, "but if they were offered money to tell a story, they had an excuse, not only for whatever happened, but for themselves. Their superiors would only laugh at their extorting money from us. So now they are going around the city saying that you gave them money to spread rumors, and we are made to appear doubly foolish."

"Of course, you Pharisees are easily persuaded by resurrection theories," Ben Kaifa sneered. "We never believed in the idea. Apparently, Simeon, the Ben Aaron family has affinity for stories about the raising of the dead."

Simeon's face flushed as the blood surged up his neck. "I am saying," he said slowly and carefully, "that bribing guards is not worthy of this high institution."

"Yes! Yes!" rang across the room and echoed off of the high ceiling.

"We have only acted," Annias stammered, "to try to quiet the unfortunate situation."

"Then I would suggest," Simeon began to sit down, "that we let truth present its own defense."

"But what are we going to do now?" The old man in the front faced the assembly once more. "People are going to believe their stories."

"Arrest his followers!" someone shouted. "Find the members of the sect and put them in jail!"

"You can't arrest rumors," Simeon shouted back. Unsure of the extent of Jarius and Mariam's involvement with Yeshua and his followers, Simeon twisted uncomfortably in his seat. Obviously, Yehosaf Ben Kaifa knew a great deal about Mariam's healing. Maybe Simeon could himself become suspect. His arguments with Jarius were only family quarrels; he had never even considered that there was the vaguest possibility he and his brother could end up real enemies.

"We can arrest their leaders," a Sadducee said, pounding on his chair.

"Stop it!" Simeon leaped up again. "The more you speak of arrests, the more you spread the controversy. You can't stop rumors any more than you can control the wind."

"Then let it die here." Ben Kaifa stood abruptly. "Silence your accusations and let them die within these chambers." He turned and walked out, leaving the gathering in stunned silence. Annias quickly followed his son-in-law.

"Brilliant." The Pharisee next to Simeon patted him on the back. "Worthy of a man twice your age!"

"You made them look like fools," a colleague joined in. "Well done! But remember—it is dangerous to embarrass the high priest's family."

"Thank you," Simeon acknowledged, moving toward the door, "but I think they have too many problems today to worry with one young Pharisee." Pausing at the door, he looked back over the room, listening to the arguments, which continued to fly like arrows. He mused aloud, "What *were* the soldiers doing that night?"

The next morning Simeon spent an unusual amount of time stopping to talk with friends and associates on his way to work. Like a sponge, he absorbed the rumors that were rife on the streets. Everywhere he turned, people were engaged in heated and animated discussions.

Arriving at their store, Simeon pushed the canvas flaps aside and found Jarius hard at work bargaining with an Ethiopian. The dark man's distinctive, bright-colored robe shook as he kept rubbing the gold piece. Jarius stood behind the counter pointing out the superior craftsmanship in the design. Zeda stood to one side listening to the sales talk. Simeon remembered that the piece was difficult to sell so they had agreed to a low price of twenty-five shekels. Catching Zeda's eye, Simeon motioned for him to come outside.

"I am concerned—" Simeon drew himself up as fully as possible.

"Just tell me," Zeda cut him off.

"I cannot talk to Jarius. Lately no one can. But I am afraid of what may be ahead."

Zeda stroked at his beard and nodded.

"I don't know where you stand on this rabbi Yeshua." Simeon looked hard in Zeda's eyes. "You are always the peacemaker who doesn't tell anyone what you really think."

Zeda smiled but said nothing.

"Do you believe in these resurrection stories?"

"Go on."

"See! That is what I mean." Simeon threw up his hands.

"And?" Zeda shrugged his shoulders.

"Obviously, I don't believe in any of this rampant

madness, and I don't think Jarius does. But we can't talk." Simeon breathed deeply and exhaled, "I fear that Mariam believes. Of course, she feels she owes her life to him. She listened to his teaching and knows some of the leaders of the movement. Just the fact that she is alive makes her suspect. Matters could get out of hand, and I fear she might be hurt."

"Harmed? Come now."

"I did not believe that they would put the crazy man to death. Since they did, I must conclude that they could arrest a child. Or—her father. Nothing burns like fear and madness mixed together."

"Are such plans under way?"

"Not now, but I want you to talk to Mariam. Help her understand how dangerous it could be to associate with this sect. People who are willing to steal the body of their leader may be even more dangerous than the Zealots."

"So, you want me to take a message to her?"

"She will listen to you. You know how to do such things. Anything I do only seems to light fires that burn without sending out light."

"I understand," was all that Zeda said. "Let us see how our brother has fared."

When they reentered the shop, Jarius was congratulating the Ethiopian on driving a hard bargain and making a very good deal. The foreigner counted forty shekels into his hand!

———— • ————

"I am home," Jarius's familiar voice followed.

"Shalom, Abba." Mariam hugged his neck and squeezed his worn hands. No amount of scrubbing removed the discoloration of the silver and gold that had ground itself into his fingers and knuckles. The stain always lingered, leaving his long slender fingers a little rough.

"And peace to you, my child," he said, kissing her on the forehead. Mariam lit the candles, bowed her head, and waited for the blessing.

"Baruch atah Adonai," Jarius took a piece of bread, "who gives us this bread." He broke it and laid the pieces on the plate.

"Hamazaym Laham Makaha rash," Mariam answered.

Together they prayed the ancient prayer of the people, *"Ayn Kalohaynu. . . ."* Once the "amen" was said, the servant brought in two large bowls.

"Business was good today?"

Jarius only nodded his affirmation. The shadows covered his eyes.

"And you are feeling well?"

"Yes."

Mariam began eating and said nothing. Only the noise of the dishes broke the silence. Jarius offered no further comment, seeming to disappear in the dim room.

"The lentils do not please you?" Mariam hinted. "They were prepared with the spices you always like best."

"Oh, yes, of course. Fine. Thank you."

Silence fell between them once more. Nothing else was said until the servant woman offered to remove the flat clay dishes.

"Zeda came to see me today." Mariam tried to sound casual.

"Zeda?" Jarius blinked.

"Yes, he wanted to talk with me."

"Alone?" Jarius wrinkled his brow. "What in heaven's name did he want?"

"I think he is afraid."

"Afraid!" Jarius snorted. "Who in Yerushalayim isn't filled with fear these days?"

"Zeda thinks that more reprisals may be made against those who followed Yeshu. He numbers us in their company and is apprehensive." Mariam thought of Zeda's twisted ugly fingers and his flat bent hand, remembering the story of how her uncle had fallen in the street as a child. When soldiers paced past, a horse had stepped on his hand. The pain had lasted for years. "Yes," Mariam nodded, "Uncle Zeda understands well how disaster can suddenly arise from anywhere."

"The whole city has gone mad." Jarius reached to the center of the narrow table, pulling the oil lamp closer. "Every day the stories proliferate. Hysterical Sadducees frighten each other with their own ghost stories."

"Over a week has passed since his death." Mariam spoke slowly and deliberately. "Maybe the time has come to speak of the matter."

Jarius looked away as if distracted by some nonexistent object across the room, but virtually nothing had changed in their dining room since his wife's death so many years before. The dull stucco walls remained unadorned as if the household were still in mourning. At the far end of the room, the small corner fireplace sat empty with the hearth stained with soot. The blandness of the room offered no diversion to keep Jarius from answering his daughter.

"What do you think of the reports? The stories of his appearances?"

"He is dead, Mariam." Jarius's voice sounded distant and flat.

"What if he weren't?"

"Such cannot be." Jarius became even more faint.

"What if his teachings were meant to never die. He

knew how to conquer death. Can such confidence fade and disappear?"

"The aspirations and the man are two separate things, my child."

"But can they be cut apart?" Mariam insisted. "You saw him that day on the hill. He was not afraid to die. He was what he taught. The lion and his roar are one."

"I have not seen him," Jarius sighed. "He has not stopped me on my way to work and appeared in my shop."

"Father, I have talked to many of Yeshu's closest followers." Mariam pulled the lamp back closer to them again. "These people are sane and have no reason to deceive us. You know them. The followers of Yeshu don't chase ghosts, neither are they necromancers. Something new is happening. There is no precedent."

"Nothing new happens here," Jarius protested. "The only way we survive is by clutching to the old ways. Child, be prudent. We cannot afford to run after crazy notions that could hurt all of us."

"Was it crazy when you went to see him when I was dying? Didn't he say that he would come back if they put him to death? In three days he said he would rebuild the temple that was his body. He certainly rebuilt the one that I live in. Why not his own, Abba?"

"Mariam, loss and loneliness do strange things to people's minds. When the pain becomes great enough, all sorts of mirages and illusions dance in front of our eyes."

"Was that what happened to you the day he died? Did your ears deceive you?"

"I don't want to talk about it." Jarius turned away from the light.

"Don't run away, Abba." Mariam pulled him back toward her. "Everyone in Yerushalayim is running. The people hide from the officials. The Sanhedrin fear the people. The Zealots flee before the soldiers. The Essenes run into the desert. If he only appears in people's hearts and imagination, believers are still released from the bondage of their own anxiety."

"Mariam, I think Zeda is wise in his caution. We should not be seen with these people. If the word got back to Simeon—"

"You always worry about what Simeon thinks," Mariam interrupted. "Why is it you never talk to him unless you are arguing, and yet, his opinion is always very important to you?"

"You exaggerate." Jarius waved her away.

"No. You cannot say five words to each other without conflict!"

"You sound like your mother." Jarius was solemn. "I wouldn't allow anyone else in the world to probe and poke at me as you do."

"Zeda once told me," she persisted, "that Simeon was always the favored child. Is that so?"

"You are going too far now." Jarius leaned forward on the table. The candlelight slid across his face, leaving dark shadows under this eyes. "Matters need to be left in their proper place. Yes!" He pounded the table. "That's the problem! Everything once had its own order; now nothing fits."

"That's because this whole nation lives in raw terror," Mariam said respectfully, "afraid that death will strike at any minute. Even with his talk about tradition, Simeon is no different from the rest."

"And me?" Jarius's voice began rising. "Your father? What do I live by?"

Mariam closed her eyes for a few moments and then carefully continued without looking at him. "Justice, Abba. You live by justice."

"Yes!" Jarius pounded on the table again with both fists. "That is so!"

"But," Mariam continued very quietly, "justice is your final defense against fear. When wrong prevails, you are without hope."

Jarius stared at his daughter. Finally he lowered his head into his hands and silently peered into the rough planks of the table top.

"You do not know what to think, do you Abba? In your own way you are as troubled by his death as the rest of Yerushalayim is by his appearances."

"I do not know," his voice faded.

Mariam pulled his hand gently across the table and pressed it to her cheek.

"Several weeks ago you said to me," Jarius whispered, "'mercy will triumph over justice.' Where did you learn such an idea?"

"I don't know. So many thoughts fill my mind that I sometimes lose track of them."

"Perhaps," Jarius stood up, "it is best to let the past stay in the past. We have enough troubles with today. I am only concerned at these conflicts over the rabbi."

"No, Father," Mariam blew out the candles, "the matter is not ended. I think maybe it has just started."

SIX

Jarius had already been awake for some time when the slowly rising sun filled his narrow window with golden light. Trying to shake the dream, he turned uneasily to shield his eyes from the glare. Finally he sat up in bed, but the inescapable reccurring vision appeared again. Only a week had passed since he and Mariam had talked at supper, yet each night the same dream returned. Jarius closed his eyes, and the images danced into his memory once more.

A high tree began to appear out of the mist. As he watched, the trunk took the form of a man. Immediately little men appeared with axes and started hacking at the roots. The more they slashed, the larger the man-shaped tree grew. Two gnarled branches stretched out like long, extended arms, lifted up to heaven. They swayed in the wind, defying the destroyers. Finally the tree-shaped man said one word: "Mercy." Slowly the dream evaporated.

Jarius arose and washed his face, shaking his head. Night after night, he felt the weight of the strange reappearing images. He quickly dressed and headed for the door. The meaning had become increasingly clear to him, and he knew what must be done. After a quick explanation, he sent his servant scurrying into the city.

"Father, you are up early this morning."

Jarius kissed his daughter but said nothing.

"Your eyes are so swollen." Mariam pushed his hair back. "You look tired."

"The night has been very long," he said, patting her cheek. "I am afraid my mind is filled with too many thoughts."

"Don't worry. I will fix you something to eat."

"No," Jarius kissed her forehead, "nothing will be right until I know."

"Know?"

"Yes." He turned away.

"What is happening?"

"I must go." Jarius reached for his cloak. "I don't know when I will be back."

"Father, at least let me warm some milk—"

Jarius shut the door before Mariam could finish her sentence. He wrapped the cloak around his neck to protect himself from the cold morning air. As always, he touched the mazusseh on the door jam lightly. The hidden passage, "Behold how good and pleasant it is when brothers dwell in unity," came to mind immediately. He could not but reflect on the irony of the admonition. Walking briskly, Jarius was oblivious to his surroundings. Seeking out Roman soldiers could be dangerous. Should they turn on him, there would be no defense. He knew the chance he was taking.

Instead of choosing the street that led to his shop, Jarius turned in the other direction toward the Ephraim gate. A train of donkeys lumbered along, bringing firewood into the city. The huge bundles of sticks bounced on their sides when they brushed past him in the long, narrow passageway between the stone buildings. The street opened up again and bread vendors were standing around a little fire, warming their hands. Hard-crusted loaves were piled up on woven reed trays.

Jarius pressed a coin in one of the vendor's hands.

"Shalom," the man responded, tearing off a large hunk of bread. "Blessed be He who provides us with bread."

"Boker tov," Jarius peppered the bread with a sweet-smelling powder. "Did you see any soldiers standing guard in the plaza?"

"No, thank God." The vendor spit on the ground. "They have already left. You can pass without annoyance."

"Oh," Jarius said thoughtfully. "I suppose they have gone back to the Antonio Fortress."

Other men grunted their agreement. "Trouble is rumored today," one of the men whispered.

"Stay inside if you can," another mumbled.

"One never knows," the vendor added.

Jarius left the group and went back the way he had come. However, at the fork in the road, he turned toward the inner city. He had only gone a few hundred feet when he saw a group of women carrying empty water jugs.

"Shalom," he greeted them.

They smiled but looked away.

"Please," he stopped them, "may I have a word?"

Each woman looked embarrassed and ill-at-ease.

"I know this is most unusual," Jarius uncomfortably tugged at his cloak, "but I need information."

One of the women pulled her veil about her face and looked at the ground. No one spoke.

"Have you seen any Roman soldiers?"

They shook their heads.

"None?" Jarius sounded irritated.

"No," they only shook their heads.

"Romans are everywhere until you want them!" he snapped.

Picking up their vessels, the women scurried away.

Only then did Jarius realize that he might be putting himself in a vulnerable position with his own people by seeking out the enemy. Could his own motives be misunderstood? Discretion was important. For a long time Jarius leaned against the wall, rubbing his forehead.

Finally he started back down the street toward the shop. After several blocks, however, he left the boulevard and cut back across the city, going toward the market that he had passed on the day of the execution. The city was now more fully awake, and the food merchants had begun to do a brisk business. The smell of meat filled the air as goats and lambs were hung up on hooks in the open air. No one paid any attention when he walked briskly past the food stalls.

Once he recognized the Ephraim Gate, he knew the street that ran outside along the great wall was just ahead. Slipping past the sentinels at the huge doors, Jarius refused to look in the direction of the stone hill that had become one of the shapes that invaded his dreams. He walked along the narrow pathway and avoided looking at any sign that might indicate someone was being put to death on stone outcroppings. When he finally looked up, Jarius saw the line of rocks that provided the caves for the family tombs of some of the most prominent citizens of Yerushalayim. A familiar figure sat on one of the large rocks. The finely woven linen robe with the gold threaded girdle marked its owner as a man of wealth and prominence.

"Yosef," Jarius called to him. "Yosef of Ramatayim."

The white-haired man stood and waved him on.

"Forgive my sending you a message to come so early," Jarius hurried toward the man. "I hope I have not inconvenienced you greatly."

"Of course not." Yosef kissed him on both cheeks. "Your servant arrived early enough that I could easily change my plans to be here. I have not seen you since— since that terrible day."

"Yes." Jarius sat down on another rock beside his friend. "Indeed, that is why I have come."

"Oh?" Yosef sat next to him. "I don't understand."

"I'm not sure I can explain," Jarius began slowly, "but I have been deeply troubled ever since that morning. And then there have been all of the rumors." Jarius shook his head. "First they say he is here and then there. Supposedly the body has disappeared."

"I can tell you that the body is gone. He was buried here in my family tomb." Joseph pointed to the rock wall that was directly in front of them. The face of the limestone outcropping had been chiseled flat and worn smooth with a door cut in the center. A tall circular stone rested in a trough in front of the entryway. The exposed rocks were part of a formation that ran along the city wall and then trailed across the countryside. Here and there caves dotted the terrain. Spring grasses and flowers punctuated the rugged rocky ground.

"So the story is true!"

"Come and see." Yosef stood and pointed toward the slab door. "The stone is back in place now." He walked toward the rocky trough at the front of the slope. "All of my ancestors are buried here."

"I had heard you had given him a place." Jarius shielded his eyes from the sun as he looked intently at the tombs. "What happened?"

"I don't know." Yosef turned away. "I just don't know yet."

"But what did the soldiers tell you?"

"I never saw them. A servant came early in the morning to tell us that the door was rolled back, and the soldiers had left in the night."

"But his followers must have come and taken him away."

"Why would they do that?" Yosef looked at Jarius very intensely. "I have asked myself that question many times. They would risk death and bring dishonor on themselves to do such a thing. Why would they do that?"

"These are strange times." Jarius kicked at a rock on the ground. "Who knows why people do what they do?"

"If his disciples had come here, there would have been a fight with the soldiers. These common men would have fallen quickly. Romans are not easily overpowered."

"But the soldiers are saying that while they were asleep, the followers came."

"Come now, Jarius." Yosef chuckled. "Have you ever set the stone door without a loud grinding noise? Sepulchers are silent only from the inside."

"But the soldiers said—"

"Who knows what the soldiers said." Yosef shrugged his shoulders. "Rumors are rumors."

"And that is why I have come. I must find the Romans and talk with them."

"Such an idea could be very dangerous." Yosef shook his finger. "They'd suspect you of formulating trouble."

"I must take that risk. I hoped you might have gotten a name or some way to identify them."

"No, no." Yosef shook his head. "The three of them came Friday night and stayed all day Saturday, but we avoided any contact."

"Surely someone would know?"

Yosef turned back toward the tombs and looked for a

long time. "Possibly—" Yosef turned back to him. "There was a centurion in charge that day on the hill—a good man. I talked to him when we stood together at that awful place, and I was surprised that a Roman would be so compassionate."

"His name?" Jarius pressed, "Do you remember his name?"

"Yes," Yosef said slowly. "His name was Honorius. Surely he would know the other soldiers."

"Excellent." Jarius shook Yosef's hand. "I am sure he can be located at the Antonio Fortress. I will go there at once."

"Be careful, my friend," Yosef called after him as he quickly started back up the path. "Many a good Jew has disappeared inside that place and never been heard from again."

"I must go." Jarius waved goodbye.

The city had become so crowded that Jarius had to wind his way through the people. Hurrying down the streets, he could not avoid hearing the bargaining and bickering among the vendors. People seemed to be in an unusually surly mood. Conversations were sharp and acrimonious, making him feel uncomfortable.

Even though the press of the people slowed him down, he could soon see the towers of the fortress looming over the city. The Romans had built their lofty perch so that the soldiers could even look down into the closed areas of the Temple and observe any gatherings. The huge stone blocks of the stronghold formed a cold, unforgiving wall that forever separated the world of the Jews from that of the Romans. The high front gate was made of woven iron bars. Such a massive web of metal could withstand any attack. Any procurator could sleep well.

Jarius carefully approached the sentry at the gate,

being as respectful and obsequious as self-respect would allow. Guards stood on both sides of the gate. Jarius was met with the cold insolence he expected.

Surprisingly, his request to see Honorius was filled in a short period of time. A soldier led him down a long, cold stone corridor. Everywhere he looked, he saw men with spears standing at attention. Finally the guard led Jarius into an empty holding room. The man gruffly gestured for him to sit.

Jarius waited for what seemed an eternity, but nothing happened. He began to wring his hands and pace. The totally empty room looked more like a cell with bars on the windows, the stone block walls blended into granite slab floors. Even the dampness of the room couldn't prevent him from beginning to perspire. Jarius kept remembering Yosef's warning. Suddenly the door behind him swung open.

"I am Honorius." A tall, muscular soldier, wearing a leather breastplate that covered his shoulders, entered. A short sword was strapped over his toga. He was dignified and wore authority like the cape hanging from his shoulders.

"Thank you for seeing me." Jarius bowed from the waist, looking studiously at the man's familiar face.

"What do you wish?" Honorius's tone was unexpectedly straightforward, but not condescending or degrading.

"I am not here to cause anyone trouble or create difficulty of any sort," Jarius apologized. "I am glad to pay for the information I seek."

"Soldiers do not accept bribes." His voice immediately became hard and distant.

"No offense, no offense." Jarius gestured with both hands. "But I have come because of a rumor that some soldiers were reportedly paid to spread."

The centurion stared back at him.

"You see," Jariuś fumbled for words, "I was at the place of execution the day that a certain political prisoner was put to death. I was a—er—a—deeply affected by this execution. And you were there—several weeks ago."

"We do what we are ordered." Honorius seemed pained.

"I mean nothing," Jarius apologized again, "but his name was Yeshua Ben Yosef, and he was accused of making himself to be a king."

"Yes, I know who you mean," the soldier sat down. "I know his story, and I have heard the rumors."

"I thought that, perhaps, you knew the soldiers who were assigned to guard the tomb where he was placed—" As Jarius spoke, the centurion's face came into sharp focus. He had been the soldier standing at the foot of the cross, leaning on his spear.

"They are under my command."

"I am seeking to know what happened to the body, and I hoped you could possibly—"

"There is a certain jeopardy," Honorius looked intently at Jarius, "in asking questions about soldiers who have reportedly taken bribes." Honorius rolled his deep, soft blue eyes. Even though his face was leathery from long exposure to the wind and the dry Yerushalayim climate, he did not look hard.

"Did the followers of Yeshua steal his body?"

"No," the centurion said slowly, "they did not."

"Then?"

"Roman soldiers are trained to conquer anything they can see," Honorius said cautiously. "But none of us is able to battle with the imperceptible."

"I do not want to fight anything or anybody. I want to be able to live with what I heard on the day that this good man was dying."

"And so do I." The centurion's voice was low and

heavy. "Before I left Rome, I studied the philosophers. I know something about the gods, and I have studied your Torah, but I do not have any explanation for what is happening in this land today."

Jarius put his hand to his mouth and stroked his beard. His eyes narrowed. "Could it be—"

Without warning the door flew open and a helmeted guard burst into the room. "The Zealots struck in the lower marketplace—the one on the lower side. There's a riot. A unit has already been dispatched."

"Not again!" Honorius leaped to his feet. "Quick. My armor."

"In the corridor!" The soldier disappeared through the door. "Leave," Honorius gestured Jarius out. "Just leave."

Jarius hurried behind the centurion for fear of being left in the fortress without good explanation. He was barely able to get through the gate before another group of soldiers joined Honorius. Fortunately no one paid any attention as Jarius sunk back into the shadows outside the huge entryway. Eventually the noise of running soldiers was consumed by the sounds of city life. Satisfied that danger was past, Jarius hurried back to the shop.

———————————————

Jarius was panting when he entered their stall.

"You're still in business?" Simeon asked sarcastically from his workbench. He laid his small mallet down.

Without any acknowledgment, Jarius sat down at his workbench.

"Zeda left hours ago, and you never came." Simeon stepped in front of the table where he couldn't be ignored.

Jarius unfolded a piece of cloth in which a thin sheet

of gold was wrapped. He carefully flattened out the wrinkle in the metal on the table top.

"I deserve some explanation." Simeon leaned over the table.

"You wouldn't like it." Jarius picked up a small leather mallet.

"Well?"

"I was looking for soldiers."

"Soldiers?"

"The ones who said the body of Yeshua was stolen."

"Oh, no!" Simeon threw up his hands. "Now even you are chasing ghosts! I work while you pursue the crazy stories that mad people are spreading across the city."

"I learned today," Jarius smiled warily, "that it is very difficult to bribe a soldier."

"What do you mean?"

"Something has happened in Yerushalayim that is not as easily explained as your friends might think."

"You, a Nisi of the synagogue, are questioning the Great Sanhedrin?"

"I am questioning everything." Jarius pursed his lips. "I don't know what is going on and neither do you."

"We stand with the Law—the Traditions," Simeon snarled. "Thus we are saved from wasting time running after nonsense."

"Perhaps, you have been too close to your scrolls." Jarius leaned within inches of Simeon's face. "And you have lost the ability to know what you read."

"Listen to me." Simeon pushed Jarius back. "I will not be jeopardized by your stupidity."

"Really?" Jarius chuckled. "And what will you do?"

Simeon breathed deeply and clenched his fist. He stopped at the sound of a familiar voice calling from a distance.

"Father! Father!" the call came from outside the shop.

"Mariam? Here?" Jarius looked toward the door.

The flaps flew open as Mariam burst into the room. Before Jarius could move, she threw herself at him, clutching his robe. "I was so afraid that you might not be here." Her chest heaved in and out.

"Child, what has happened?"

"Our servant Jacob—" Mariam gasped for air, "was there and he ran to—" she panted, "—to the house at once."

"Speak slowly, speak slowly."

"In the marketplace," she heaved. "He was in the lower marketplace when—the Zealots attacked."

"Jacob was hurt?"

"Zeda," she panted, "Uncle Zeda was there. He was caught in the attack. Only Jacob got away."

"Zeda! Is he—"

"I don't know anything. I hoped he was here."

"I must find him." Jarius didn't even look at Simeon. "Stay with her until I return," he ordered.

"But I should—"

"Don't let her out of your sight." Jarius's voice was uncompromising. He shot through the door and was running by the time he was in the street. "Mind what I said," he yelled over his shoulder.

Jarius took a shortcut through the stalls. Jumping a stone fence, he dropped onto the street below. The market area was only several hundred feet ahead and around the corner.

Romans were everywhere. It looked like half the garrison had turned out to seal off the entire square. Jarius stopped running and approached cautiously, lest his intentions be mistaken.

Slaughtered people lay on the ground. Pieces of broken pots and jars were scattered there too. Food, vegetables, loaves of bread were here and there. Hunks of animal carcasses were mixed in with the debris. Shredded, torn canvas blew in the wind where stalls had been torn apart. Some of the merchants were struggling to get to their feet; others were badly hurt and had rolled over on their sides or backs. Although the soldiers were letting a few friends and relatives into the area to care for the wounded, each person was searched. As Jarius watched, soldiers walked along the roofs of the flat buildings, their swords and spears flashing in the sunlight.

Jarius came closer. He recognized some of the dead as Zealots; in contrast to the others, these men had been armed for combat. Their crumpled bodies were slashed open, and often their heads were bleeding. Bloody stains were all over the pavement. Some men still had spears sticking in them.

Shading his eyes, Jarius realized that Zeda was nowhere in sight. *He's escaped!* he thought to himself. *Taken a long route back to the shop to avoid any conflict.*

"Why are you here?" the question came from behind.

Turning to his left, Jarius found to his amazement that the Roman, Honorius, was watching him.

"What?" Jarius blinked.

"You came to the fortress before the attack, and you show up here afterward." The soldier's voice was hard. "You said you came as a friend?"

"Please," Jarius begged, "don't misunderstand. I am looking for my brother. He was last seen here."

"Humph," the centurion beckoned him to continue to look. "People are lying behind the stalls and tents. Some are on the other side of the square. Look over there."

Jarius moved quickly. "I am not a spy," he protested.

The soldier walked behind him as he looked to the right and left.

Jarius stopped and choked. Straight ahead one of the

booths had collapsed over several people. A hand was sticking out from under the canvas of the fallen stall. One could not miss the bent and twisted fingers. For years Jarius had tried not to look at that hand. And now it was all he could see.

Panic-stricken, Jarius grabbed the edge of the canvas and hurled it back. The enormous slash on Zeda's neck was still pouring blood into the pool beneath his face.

SEVEN

The dimness of evening felt especially comforting so Mariam only lit one candle, leaving most of her bedroom in darkness. Sitting down on her bed, she leaned against the wall. So much had happened so quickly during the last three days that Mariam barely had time to think on anything. Zeda had been buried immediately, as was Jewish custom. Taking care of the arrangements, as well as following the mourning customs, had been all-consuming and exhausting. And then there was her father. Jarius had been inconsolable.

"Oh, Daddy," Mariam felt a lump forming in her throat and could say nothing more.

Mariam removed her mother's necklace from around her neck and laid the lustrous beads back in the little chest. She had worn it for Zeda's funeral and had not taken it off since. For a long time she simply looked at the bright glass beads and the large pearl. Before closing the lid, she ran her fingers over each bead. Mariam placed the chest back in its hiding place.

"Oh, Mother," she sighed aloud, "if only you were here. . . . You would have been able to help Abba."

Jarius had tried to carry Zeda's body back to the shop, but had become so distraught that he had collapsed on the street. To the amazement of everyone, a Roman centurion had ordered two soldiers to help him return the body. He had stumbled into the shop, covered with blood and overcome with emotion. For most of the next two days he had either cried continually or was completely silent. Rachael, Zeda's wife, had even fared better.

Mariam became niece, daughter, wife, and mother. Now she could just be Mariam. And who was that?

Mariam thought of how in one year she had faced her own death and that of her beloved uncle and friend, who had been the guarantor of stability in her own family. Somewhere in that span, she had come to realize that her childhood was past. Although she was fourteen now, she felt much older. Reaching down, she ran her hands across her chest and down her hips. Both her body and her emotions had changed. Since that day of her own demise, Mariam's sensitivities had become razor sharp and were often equally disconcerting and painful.

Everything in Mariam's room was the same. Plain and simple, the bedroom had been her retreat for thousands of nights. One single window looked out on the courtyard. The world was sealed out; Mariam was secure, concealed, and protected in this space. Nothing had changed here. The first ribbon given for her hair had been decoratively placed on the wall. Now a swatch of ribbons hung from the wall. Although the assortment of colored strands had grown over the years, the cluster was still in the same place. On the ledge beneath the window was the candelabra that had been there forever. A simple wooden box held the tidbits and scraps of jewelry her father had brought home over the years. Only recently had Mariam grown to recognize seconds and rejects.

Everything was the same. Nothing was the same.

Even her spirit had changed. The little girl had been replaced by a strange sense of womanhood. But what was it to be a woman at all? There was no one to ask.

Of course, she couldn't ask her father about such matters, but neither could she ask Rachael, who had always been distant and inapproachable. Zeda had always taken a special interest in Mariam since he did not have children of his own. Mariam sensed that Rachael resented Zeda's closeness to his own family.

For the first time in three days, Mariam let herself remember how she felt about her kind uncle. Loneliness crept over her like coldness settling in on a winter's evening. The emptiness in her own family circle had increased once more.

"I will never see him again." Mariam covered her eyes. "He was such a good, gentle man to have died such a terrible death." The feelings that had been set aside surged up and Mariam began to shake. Finally she sobbed uncontrollably.

"Why," she intermittently gasped, "why has this happened to us?"

When the sound of Jarius's footsteps intruded, Mariam did not try to camouflage her feelings. She didn't even move when he came into her room. For a few minutes Jarius held her close before silently leaving again. She finally heard his shuffling footsteps disappear down the dark corridor.

Mariam doubled over on her bed. The cover around

her face was soon damp. She had no idea how long she lay there. When she looked up again, the candle had gone out.

"Adonai," she whispered, "please hear me." Silence settled around her. She remembered Yeshua had said to call Him Abba—Father. "Please help us. How much can we endure? Remember us as you did your people in Egypt and Babylon." She began crying once more as grief turned into despair. Hopelessness settled over her thoughts. Sitting upright, she held her hands upward. "I need your help or I don't think I can go on. Please be with me. Give me your peace."

Once more she dropped to the bed with her head down. The memory of her father pushed into her darkness. Jarius was younger, and there was no gray in his hair. He looked as he did when she was five years old. He reached down, picked her up, and sat her on his lap. "Will mother ever come back?" she asked him, and he answered, "I will never leave you alone." His strong arms and the warmth of his chest pressed through the heavy woven cloth. He began to hum as he gently rocked Mariam back and forth. "Do not be afraid," he kept saying.

The memory faded, but the comfort stayed. Only then did Mariam sense that someone else was in the room. Turning her head slightly to one side, she glanced completely around the room and saw nothing. Yet she knew she was not alone.

"Maranatha," she whispered, "come quickly, Lord."

Within her mind an almost lost but unforgettably tender voice resounded, *"Talitha cumi.* Do not be afraid to stand, my child."

Mariam hardly dared to breathe.

Once more he spoke, *"Talitha cumi."*

The Upper Room was packed with people. At least thirty to forty people could be squeezed into the main area beneath the huge wooden beams that crossed the ceiling. Side walls of adjacent smaller rooms had been removed to hold the overflowing crowds. With the walls out, at least a hundred people could assemble. At one time the upstairs had been a large dining area. At night people still slept on the floors, but the bed rolls had been cleared, leaving extra seating space on the rough wood. Mariam had come early because she knew the numbers were growing daily. The experience of the previous night made it imperative she be present.

At the far end of the room a heavy wooden table was always placed reverently in the center of the wall. No one but the apostles sat there. The mother of Yeshua and his brothers were near the front where they usually sat. Several apostles stood around the room. Overhead, an immense iron circular candle rack hung from the ceiling on a long chain. The links were secured to a large metal stob in the wall so that it could be lowered when candles needed to be replaced.

"We are struggling to understand," Yochanan was explaining to the group. Although he was unusually young to be a leader, Mariam knew Yochanan to be intelligent, warm, and very caring. "Each day we study together, searching the Torah, but none of us is ready to speak about the meaning of what we have seen."

Always gentle, Yochanan sounded unusually poignant. "I have seen with my own eyes, and yet I have no explanation for what I know is true." Although his smile was winsome and boyish, his words were authoritative. "We are being prepared for a new day. Surely God is opening a door to tomorrow."

"Is it true that he was lifted up and exalted?" a man spoke from the back. Small windows lined the top of the building. Dazzling light filled the room. "I heard that he disappeared into a cloud."

"Yes," Yochanan spoke slowly, "some of us saw this happen, but it is still difficult to understand." Yochanan's black beard covered much of his face, making his eyes seem more piercing and intense. "Yet he is no less with us now."

A murmur of affirmation went around the room.

"I come from the village of Ammaus*," an older man arose to speak, "and we have also experienced his presence among us. Our troubled minds are comforted and our spirits calmed when he comes. I am no longer afraid."

"Yes, yes," several added.

"He told us to wait here," Yochanan pointed to the other apostles, "and we would receive power to understand and speak. So, we are prepared to stay, fasting and praying, until his promise is fulfilled."

"Are these appearances real?" A little old man in the center of the group raised his hand. "I have never seen what others describe."

"Our experiences differ," Yochanan spoke slowly, "and yet they have special meaning for each of us."

"I don't belong among you," a tall distinguished man emerged from behind a wooden column in the back, "and yet you have been gracious to me. I know many of you must feel that I am the enemy and that you must keep separate from us." The man's toga was clearly Roman. His gray hair was combed down on his forehead in the way of the Romans. Mariam immediately recognized him as the centurion who had helped bring Zeda's body back to the shop.

"We welcome you as our friend," Yochanan saluted

*Emmaus

the Roman. "Your kindness has already helped us greatly."

"I have come," the Roman spoke apologetically, "because I was told that his family would be here. I must know who he was."

"Many of us thought he would be Ha Mashiach*," a larger and older man joined Yochanan, "and we asked him if it were so, but his answers were complicated."

"We couldn't comprehend what he meant," Yochanan added. "Often we seemed to be walking in the midst of a mystery."

"He told us," the older man put his arm around Yochanan's shoulder, "that when we are empowered, we will know. We welcome you to remain and wait with us."

"Thank you." The Roman bowed elegantly. "Please understand that death is no stranger to me," he paused, "and I saw him die. Surely there is no hope beyond the grave."

"Three years ago I would have agreed with you," the older man answered. "My name is Shimon Kefa.** You Romans call me Simon Peter. I was with him during these many months. I must tell you that I saw him defeat death many times before they put him on the cross."

"Yes," Yochanan added, "there are people here who are the living proof of what Shimon is saying." He looked around the room and saw Mariam. "Ah, who better to speak than one who was dead." Yochanan pointed to her. "Would you tell us?"

"If you wish," Mariam said quickly without looking up. "I am alive because he called me back. I know that death has not stilled his voice."

*the Messiah
**Simon Peter

"I know you," the Roman smiled. "It was your uncle—"

"Yes," Yochanan spoke for her, "you helped her family. How is your father, Mariam?"

"Please pray," she said very softly. "Nothing seems to comfort him. His pain is very great."

"When I awoke this morning," Shimon Kefa walked toward Mariam, "the words of the prophet were in my mind. 'Comfort, comfort my people, says your God. Speak tenderly to Yerushalayim, and cry to her that her warfare is ended.'" Shimon pointed toward her. "I think maybe this is a message for him, for you, for all who mourn. The battle is over."

"Since death has visited us again," Mariam looked up at him, "I pray for the fulfillment of that promise."

"Tell your father," Shimon Kefa added, "that he is remembered here. Let us all pray now with Mariam that each of us will be set free from fear and death's bondage."

As the men pulled their talliths over their heads, the women found similar covering. Some bowed their heads while others leaned forward on the floor, placing their faces in their hands. Shimon lifted his hands upward. As he spoke, the group followed, *"Shema Israel, Adonai elohaynu Adonai echod . . ."*

Closing the door to the Upper Room behind her, Mariam quickly descended the stairs that led down to the street. She adjusted the scarf on her head, swinging one end across her shoulders to partially cover her face.

"A moment please—"

Mariam turned at the bottom of the steps to find that the Roman had been waiting for her. "Yes?" she hesitated.

"My name is Honorius." He bowed slightly from the waist. "I spoke in your assembly earlier."

"Yes," Mariam was polite but distant, "and I was there when you helped return my uncle's body to our jewelry shop."

"Then you know that I mean you no harm."

"You have already proven yourself."

"I know it is not your custom to speak to men, much less to Romans." Honorius glanced up and down the street. "But I have a message for your father. I think it will be of help to him."

"A message?"

"But first I must ask you a question." The Roman smiled. "You see, I was there the day your rabbi was put to death." He paused and bit his lip. "I was on the hill, and I was deeply moved by what I saw and heard. I am not sure about some of the things he said while he was dying, but what I did understand overwhelmed me."

"You helped crucify him?" Mariam recoiled.

"Ah—no. No. Well—I—I was only a supervisor." Honorius gestured nervously. "I had orders to follow. Surely you understand."

"You have a question?"

"As he was dying, the ground shook and a storm broke. I have never seen such awesome sights. But you were brought back to life and never have I heard of such a thing happening to a mortal either. Please," he extended his hand, "tell me who you think the rabbi was?"

"No one spoke like him," Mariam furrowed her brow, "and no one understood as he did. Yes, he had awesome powers." Mariam shook her head. "But I have no complete explanation."

"I see." The centurion's eyes fell. "Thank you." And he started up the street.

"You are a good man," Mariam watched him pass, "and your pain will not go unredeemed."

"My pain?" He stopped.

"I think that you are not far from the Kingdom of God."

"What do you know of me?" Honorius turned back. "Someone has spoken to you of my private life?"

"No, I see the pain in your face. Your eyes have seen too much suffering."

"Please," the Roman looked shocked and dismayed. "Please—" his voice faded.

"You said you had a message for my father."

"Oh, yes. Yes," he muttered. "He came to see me the day of your uncle's tragedy. He had questions about the stories that were attributed to the guards who were posted at the rabbi's grave."

"Of course." Mariam nodded her head. "Father was very upset that morning. He was deeply disturbed by the stories circulating around the city."

"He wanted to know what really happened and why the guards left the tomb."

"You know?"

"I didn't then," Honorius ran his hand through his hair, "but I wondered. I had purposely overlooked the incident lest I uncover something I might later wish I hadn't discovered. So, the day after your father's visit, I decided I would question the men who had been stationed next to the rock door."

"And what did they tell you?"

"That is the message I have for your father." The centurion stepped closer to her. "The soldiers panicked and ran because the rock started to move."

"By itself?"

"At first they thought so, but that wasn't why they ran. An earth tremor could make such a large circular rock start to turn in its trough. Please tell your father the reason they left."

"Yes?" she beckoned. "Yes?"

"The men apparently watched for several moments before they realized that although the rock was moving, the ground wasn't shaking. The tomb was being opened from the inside."

———————◆———————

Mariam opened the weather-beaten rough door to the house. Leaves had again sprouted on the vines that covered the thick beam over the entryway. Mariam could hear angry voices. Obviously Simeon and her father were arguing. She shut the door very forcefully, sending a resounding bang through the house. Their voices lowered.

"Shalom." She tried to sound pleasant as she entered the living room.

"Shalom," Simeon acknowledged begrudgingly. He dropped some jewels into a leather pouch and pulled the drawstring.

Jarius said nothing, but continued to glare at his brother. "I must be going." Simeon ignored Mariam as he walked briskly toward the door. He closed it even harder than Mariam had.

"Trouble?" Mariam said as she hugged her father. She felt his strong arms.

"Zeda is sorely missed." Jarius held Mariam very close to him. "Without him, every decision has become difficult."

"You are both under a great deal of pressure."

"We agree on nothing." Jarius shook his head. "We will have great difficulty in purchasing our gold and gems. Perhaps, I want to pay too little, but Simeon is willing to pay too much."

"Don't worry, things will work out."

"No." Jarius sat down in his chair. "Nothing will ever be the same again. My hopes have been broken like a clay jar dropped on the paving. Death has called again."

"Father," Mariam spoke hesitantly, "maybe we are almost at the end of a dark night. Perhaps we will no longer have to wrestle with death—nor even the fear of death."

"I had thought—" Jarius stopped and slumped into a chair.

"But everything has become even darker for you?"

Jarius sighed deeply but didn't answer.

"When I was very frightened by mother's death," Mariam dropped to her knees beside him, "you told me you would never leave. Remember?"

Jarius looked blank for a moment, then nodded. His eyes softened as he remembered those special moments of closeness.

"Could anything have made you forget me?"

"Of course not!" he protested.

"So, even on stormy nights when I was alone in my room, you were really still with me."

"Mariam!" Jarius threw up his hands. "Everything is gone. We are in more than a dark night. We have been abandoned."

"Please listen to me." Mariam gently shook her finger at him. "I have more to tell you. The Roman centurion you went to see has sent you a message. He talked to the soldiers who were stationed at the tomb and discovered why they fled."

"Yes?" Jarius gestured for her to continue. "What did he learn?"

"The stone didn't move because men with poles pried it away." Mariam took hold of his fingers. "The rock was moved from the inside of the tomb. The guards ran because they were afraid of what they couldn't see."

"I don't understand." Jarius squeezed her hand.

"Yes, that's right, you don't. No one does *yet*. Perhaps tragedy never leaves us with any choice but to trust God. Maybe Yeshua was teaching us that truth through his death."

EIGHT

"**P**lease—Father." Mariam kept pacing back and forth in front of their house. "It will soon be past the first hour, and the city will be jammed with people."

"I'm coming, I'm coming," Jarius echoed from down the hall. "I can only move so fast in the morning."

"You know how the crowds are on Shavu'ot*." Mariam relentlessly continued, "Jews are here from every nation under the sun. For two days now they have even been camping all over the Mount of Olives."

"Yes, yes." Jarius waved her away as he walked through the door. "We are going."

"I fear there will be no room at the Temple. If you weren't the Nisi at the synagogue, we probably—"

"But," Jarius cut her off, "there will be a place for us." Jarius stepped ahead of Mariam. "And it won't be close to Simeon either."

"Hasn't anything improved?" Mariam walked faster to keep up with him.

*Pentecost

—100—

"No." Jarius looked straight ahead.

"Maybe I could—"

"On festival days we do not speak of business." Jarius walked faster. "Or pain."

"Please, I can't walk so fast."

"I thought we were in a hurry." Jarius glanced from the corner of his eye.

"You are being difficult."

Jarius said nothing, but smiled as he slowed a bit. He turned into the broad boulevard that went to the shop. Then he quickly turned away to the through street that crossed the Krystus Bridge leading to the Temple compound. Mariam had been right. By the time they passed the Palace of the Hasomdoeans, it was clear that the streets were already filling. Everywhere they looked were strangely different people of many, many lands. The Mesopotamians' long earth-colored robes blended into the dark brown weave of the cloaks of the men of Pontius. Here and there the bright greens and reds of the Phrygians and the Cappadocians dotted the crowd. The tall striped turbans of the Elamites bobbed up and down above the marching mass. Generally, they were all moving in the same direction—toward the Temple.

"Shavu'ot is a wonderful spring festival." Mariam put her arm in Jarius's. "I remember when you first told me the story of the Law being given to Moses on this day. Even though I was very small, I knew how important this day is."

"We will take the great stairway by the Western Wall." Jarius turned down a side street. "There may be more people, but the way is much quicker."

As the masses began pressing, Mariam hung on tightly, lest she trip on the cobblestones.

Even though only two hours had passed since dawn, the city was fully alive, preparing for the holy day. As the street became narrower, the sounds became even more intense.

"*Um gelion, sswaba,*" a man barked as she brushed him.

"*Marrtia benshama umtiona,*" a voice rang out ahead sounding like a protest.

"*Bya! Bya! Meona,*" a woman called back from another place.

"*Utguid?*"

"*Ya laymonia. Da a bia som mianiona.*"

"*Ego hupago.*"

"*Zwajwski Llguna oynewt.*"

The babble of countless, unintelligible languages filled the air, spreading the sounds of confusion over the crowd. Mariam clung more tightly to Jarius. Finally the bottleneck emptied into the area beneath the Western Wall where the crowd fanned out. The great Krystus bridge would carry them over the Tyropoeon Valley into the Temple compound. Jarius walked straight toward the stairs. Only then did he realize that a considerable crowd had already gathered at the base of the steps. The stairs led up to a landing that turned before going on up through the gateway into the Portico of the Temple. A group of men had filled the landing and were addressing the whole crowd.

"What's the problem?" Mariam tried to look between the people since she was too short to see. "Why aren't the people going up?"

"I don't know." Jarius pushed on through the milling crowd. "Someone seems to be making a speech."

"Surely, no one would provoke the Romans on a day like this." Mariam stood on her tiptoes.

The throng became quieter as the man speaking from the landing above the crowd spoke louder. Over the myriad of voices his voice became clear. Quickly, Jarius moved to within a few feet of the landing beneath the stairs.

"Look." Mariam pointed upward. "I know those people! That's Shimon Kefa, Yochanan—the other apostles! What are they doing?"

"I think they are drunk," a man next to them muttered. "Drunk or crazy—making fools of themselves."

"No!" a man answered from behind them. "Listen to what they are saying. He is explaining the strange stories that have run rampant throughout the city for weeks. Listen to him."

"If trouble starts," Jarius got a firm grip on Mariam's arm, "hang on and we'll go back the way we came."

"People of Israel: Yeshu of Natzeret was a mighty man, attested to you by God with mighty works, wonders, and signs which God did through him." Shimon Kefa stood on the edge of the landing and spoke so loudly his voice filled the square. His forcefulness and fearlessness commanded the crowd's attention.

Jarius was dumbfounded.

"This Yeshu you crucified and killed," Kefa sounded fearless, "but God raised him up, having loosened the pangs of death, because it was not possible for him to be held."

Jarius stared as if he were fixed to the spot.

"We are all witnesses that God has raised him up." Shimon Kefa pointed to the men gathered around him. "While David lies in his tomb to this day, we have found the place of Rabbi Yeshu empty."

"They are unafraid." Jarius slowly rubbed his mouth. "Look!" He pointed. "They seem to be indifferent to the consequences. What has happened to these men who have been hiding for days?"

"Let all the house of Israel know assuredly," Shimon Kefa shook his fist in the air, "that God has made him

both Lord and Ha Mashiach, this Yeshu whom you crucified!"

"Mashiach?" Jarius tugged at Mariam. "He is still
saying that Yeshu was the Messiah."

"Quiet!" a man spoke from the side of his mouth.

"Sh-hh," another hissed.

"Listen," came from the back.

"Silence," someone else said.

Across the plaza the unruly mass of people became
totally silent. Astonishingly, the entire crowd was looking up to the steps, straining to catch every word.

"Today God is fulfilling the words of Joel," Shimon
proclaimed. "Remember that he wrote, 'and in the last
days it shall be that I will pour out my Spirit upon all
flesh.'"

Jarius could only shake his head. For a moment he
felt as if something crazy were happening. The whole
scene seemed disorienting, strangely out of sync with
the reality that he knew.

Once more Shimon Kefa quoted the prophet, "I will
pour out my Spirit and they shall prophecy. And I will
show wonders in the heavens above—"

"Look," Jarius whispered to Mariam. "Look around.
How can everyone understand? How many nations
must be here? Shimon Kefa speaks Hebrew and they all
comprehend. Such is impossible!"

"The sun shall be turned into darkness," Shimon
pointed to the sky, "and the moon into blood. And whoever calls on the name of the Lord shall be redeemed.
Such is the mercy of God."

"What shall we do?" the man in back cried to the
apostle.

"Yes," an old man to the left of Jarius asked, "what
can we do?"

"Swaazahfa zafa obonpo emo?" cried a dark
skinned man in a high swirled African turban.

"Ad te, Domine, levavi." The sleeves of a youth's Roman toga slid back as he held his hands in the air.

"Baha! Baha!" The small woman next to Mariam bowed her head and prayed aloud.

To her left, a handsome Greek called out, *"Ti poiasomen, andrec adelpoi?"*

Other intelligible voices cried out what must have been the same question. While their understanding seemed to be identical, their ability to answer was not.

Jarius listened with no comprehension of what was occurring. He felt completely undone.

"Change your minds," Shimon called back to them. "Change your thinking! Call on the Holy Name, the name of Yeshu!"

"How?" a woman cried in Hebrew. "How do we receive the Spirit?"

"Call on the name of the Messiah for the forgiveness of your sins!" As Shimon Kefa answered, a wind started to sweep across the plaza. The powerful turbulence descended on the crowd and then swirled upward against the enormous wall, sweeping dust and debris toward the sky. Following the roar came the sound of weeping. As Shimon continued to explain, people began falling to their knees around the steps. Others held up their hands toward the men on the landing. The more Shimon spoke, the more people responded.

"Save yourself from this crooked generation!" Shimon had complete control of the audience. "The promise is to every one of you who will receive it."

"Empowerment has come!" Mariam turned to her father. "The new day of God's power is here. Do you see?"

Jarius stood with his hand over his mouth saying nothing. Consternation had turned into bewilderment. He felt as if his thoughts were scrambled.

"Many of the brethren here have seen the risen Lord."

Shimon pointed around himself. "They, too, bear witness to the truth. We have a God who suffers with us in our pain. He has done so through the cross of the Nazarene. Let my friends tell you what to do."

Immediately some of the apostles descended the steps and with them other men and women began calling to the packed square. "Listen to us! We shall tell you how to receive the promise!"

"Sit down," Shimon called to the expanding multitude. "Kneel down and talk with us!"

"Mariam! Mariam!" Yochanan waved to her. "Join us. You can tell of his victory over death."

"But I am only—" Mariam gestured futilely. And then she stopped. For a few moments she looked very puzzled. Finally she turned to the people around her and began talking. Many listeners were three and four times her age.

"Receive the truth," she told them fervently. "Although I am young, I have seen with more than my eyes. Redemption has come to the House of Israel."

Minutes passed before anyone realized that while there were no translators no one seemed to misunderstand. People nodded and responded, unable to answer in other than a strange tongue. No one argued or disagreed. Like thirsty sponges, the multitude absorbed the words of whoever spoke.

"Allow others to enter and hear the story," Shimon shouted down to the crowd. "Spread the word. Many are going now to the Pool of Siloe* to be baptized. Go with them and begin a new life. Follow us into the Kingdom of God!"

Immediately most of the crowd began following the leaders who led them along the side of the Great Wall

---

*Shiloam

toward the old part of Yerushalayim called the Jebusite city of David. Mariam could no longer see her father. People were walking past the place where he had been standing.

For a long time Jarius had stood staring at his daughter. Nothing in his past prepared him for the sight of his little girl speaking to a crowd of men and women as if she were a seasoned rabbi. While the very idea seemed inappropriate, nothing in her words and actions was unseemly. When Jarius looked around, he saw that the area was filled with small groups of people huddled around others who were telling their stories of Yeshua. He looked intently. No, these people were not crazy or diabolical.

Like a mighty wind, a holy enthusiasm had swept through the crowd. Everywhere he looked people were agreeing and affirming. The meaning of the ancient riddle was becoming clear to them.

At first it was as if his feet moved themselves. Jarius just walked with the crowd that was following Shimon Kefa. Intuitively, he knew Mariam would be all right. His own mind was the issue.

Jarius felt like a man who had spent years believing reality of one order only to discover that every perception was wrong. Words from a nearly forgotten conversation with Simeon floated strangely into his mind. "Redemption comes through suffering," he had said. Jarius realized he had always expected a Messiah who would force justice on the world at the point of a spear.

And yet was not the ability to bring grace and forgiveness an even higher way? The thought seemed almost out of reach—too profound to be grasped. As he walked oblivious to his surroundings, he kept reaching inward, trying to fasten the disjointed ideas together.

When the crowd descended down the Tyropoeon Val-

ley toward the Pool of Siloe, Jarius pushed his unre-
solved questions aside. Rather, he felt the disposition of
his heart. He hungered for the goodness that he had
seen in Yeshua the day that Mariam had been raised up.
Never before or since had Jarius observed such a blend
of strength and gentleness. If it were possible for the Rudach Ha Kodesh* to make such a thing happen in a person, Jarius wanted that gift.

Perhaps the world might be salvaged through love
rather than coercion. For the first time the idea that
Yeshua could be the Messiah seemed plausible. Yes, it
made sense. Suddenly, the ancient words of the
prophets locked together like pieces of a puzzle that
suddenly fit.

"I'm ready!" he exclaimed and rushed toward the
pool. "Yes." He waved at Shimon Kefa. "I want the gift."

The water was cold but Jarius leaped out into the
pool, dragging his robes with him. People on every side
were spilling into the pool. "Please," he said to Shimon
Kefa. "I believe. I am ready for the mikvah**."

When the last wave of people had passed, Mariam
again looked for her father, but could not find him. After
proclaiming his message twice, Shimon Kefa left with
the last group of people. The high holy services were
near completion in the Temple, and few people were still
entering the plaza. When she could no longer recognize
any of the believers, Mariam also left. She started down
toward the old city and the pool. Then Mariam saw one
of the disciples coming toward her.

"Have you seen my father?" she asked as she hurried
toward the man.

"Yes, he was with the first group to the spring, but he
has gone now."

*Holy Spirit
**ritual bath for purification

"Thank you." Mariam stopped and leaned against the wall. "Where would he have gone?" she said aloud. Slumped against the wall, Mariam folded her arms and rubbed her forehead for a few moments. "Of course! Of course!"

Quickly she turned in the opposite direction and began to walk as fast as she could toward the edge of the city. Leaving the city gate, she turned in the opposite direction from where Yeshua had been buried. Her family burial caves were part of the same rocky formation but at the opposite end of the terrain that boarded the high city wall.

When Mariam found the narrow lane that lined the small hillside next to the wall, she walked toward the iron gateway she knew so well. The garden was just coming to life, the spring flowers beginning to bloom. The path led toward the rocky base slope where a large circular stone leaned against a barren granite surface that had been chiseled and worn smooth. In the past Mariam had only known the family burial site as a place of pain.

"Father," she said gently.

As she expected, Jarius was sitting in front of the stone that sealed the door.

He turned slowly, as though not surprised by her voice.

"Abba, I was worried that something might have happened to you."

"It did."

"Are you all right?"

"Very much so. Sit down, my child."

Mariam took the shawl from around her shoulders and spread it on the ground. "You are still damp?" She touched his leg.

"No! Never have I experienced anything like today."

He looked straight ahead. "I knew I had to come here. I spent hours here after your mother died. But I did not think I could come again after we put Zeda in that tomb. The world had become a place of madness. The sun had turned into darkness."

"And now?"

"Now?" Jarius leaned back against the tree. "Now the night has passed."

"I don't understand."

"I know that death is not final and that the darkness has not triumphed. You were right, my child. Amazingly right."

"Right?" Mariam reached for his hand. "What do you mean?"

"Mercy has triumphed over justice." He turned to her. "I don't yet understand everything, but as Shimon spoke, my mind was opened. I came to see that what I had heard Yeshu say from his cross was truly God speaking to all of us. The Holy One deals with us according to His grace and not according to what we deserve. On that Friday morning the light of God was shining into our blackness. Justice doesn't bring hope, but forgiveness does."

"We did not understand him," Mariam answered, "because we wanted a Messiah who would rule with an iron rod and sit in a palace."

"But Yeshu reigns," Jarius stared at the jagged large circular rock in front of the tomb, "from the place of death, from his cross." He shook his head. "I cannot tell you how I came to understand, but these answers filled and renewed my mind like the cool summer winds sweeping in from the Mediterranean."

"A new day has come, Abba." Mariam squeezed his hand. "More than a festival of Shavu'ot, today is a new beginning for all of us. The Holy One of Israel has made a new covenant with us. Yochanan asked me to speak to the people around me. Of course, I was terrified. Then I remembered Yeshu's words. Once more he was saying, *'Talitha cumi.'* I knew I was called to stand and come forth."

For the first time in weeks Jarius smiled. "This garden has been transformed. The shadows have vanished. Winter has been overtaken by summer. Promise has returned to us."

PART TWO

"WHEN THE MOON TURNED TO BLOOD"

A.D. 33

NINE

Never before had so many excited people told their stories with such unbridled enthusiasm. Always rife with controversy, the populace of Yerushalayim was confounded by the emergence of the confident expectation that a new era had already begun. Rumors filled the streets and spread down the alleys. Like the overflow of a spring flood, the ancient city was inundated with the stories of a new faith springing from their religiously primeval soil. The marketplace hummed with the reports.

"You know what to expect from the Zealots," the vendor of spices stepped out of his stall to speak to the man selling wheat, "but what can one do with this new sect?" He ignored the two women buying grain. "They are not like the Essenes who hid in the desert. The People of the Way help the poor."

"I know, I know." The grain merchant threw up his hands as he counted change out into the hand of an older woman. "They are kind and gentle."

"Zealots hate." The first man shook his finger. "And

you keep your head down when they come around, but these people are different."

"Exactly." The merchant picked up a handful of his wheat. "These people nourish your dreams and feed your hopes. Perhaps, they are the most dangerous of all."

"Possibly," the spice man shrugged his shoulders, "fear and failure we understand. Goodness and generosity is not a commodity in our marketplace."

"Exactly," the wheat merchant repeated, shaking his head. "I just don't know." He turned back to his customers.

The swarm of shoppers were more distracted by their conversations than they were interested in the goods piled around them. Normally the lentils and bean merchants were shouting their bargain prices to the customers. Today the men sat on the grain sacks talking to each other.

"Over a week has passed since Shavu'ot," the older woman who had been eavesdropping said to the woman shopping with her, "and all I hear about is that this new group seems to be everywhere."

"Amazing, isn't it?" her neighbor agreed. "They say that the rabbi Yeshu's followers have the same magical power he did."

"Maybe they are all evil." The older woman widened her eyes in chagrin.

"But they are making the sick well," the other lady countered. "Can such results be so bad? I understand a lame beggar at the Temple was made to walk."

"Really!" The woman stepped backward, knocking a pile of gourds over. The oblong hollow shells bounced on the stone pavement, rolling in every direction. "Oh, my goodness!" She tried to push them back together with her foot, but the merchant didn't seem to notice.

"I wonder where they meet?" an Alexandrian Jew said from the corner of his mouth to his traveling companion. Both had been listening to the two women.

"Maybe these women know," the friend whispered.

"We dare not ask," the Alexandrian mumbled. "Dangerous to appear interested in subversive groups."

"Of course," the friend agreed.

"Ask for the Upper Room," a voice answered from behind them. Both men turned to discover a young boy sorting vegetables. He was separating the spoiled by throwing them over his shoulder.

"The Upper Room?" the traveling companion puzzled.

The boy looked very knowing, but only nodded.

"You know the place?" The Alexandrian bent over.

The boy smiled, but only raised his eyebrows in mock indifference.

"Perhaps a shekel might help." The companion dropped to one knee.

"Possibly." The boy stopped his sorting.

When the coin was placed in his palm, he was instantly on his feet, pointing and giving directions. The two men carefully listened to the details.

"There is a large old inn." The boy pointed in the direction of the ancient Dung Gate. "The place is near the top of Mount Zion."

When the boy finished describing alleys and back streets, the two men quickly turned back to the street only to bump into the two older women who had been standing behind them listening. Immediately behind the pair, other merchants and shoppers were also noting the directions. Everyone dispersed indifferently as if only the sheerest of circumstances and a quirk of fate had caused them to be intensely listening to each other during this mutual exchange of information.

———————— • ————————

The Upper Room was filled to capacity. Even the special head table was pushed against the wall. Candles once again had been placed in the candle rack hanging from the ceiling. Mariam recognized that there simply wasn't a place large enough to hold all of the people who had joined them since Shavu'ot. Men and women mingled together, talking and laughing in a way she had never seen before. Rich and poor stood side by side. The ancient customs of separation were clearly being strained and broken. Yet, no one seemed to notice. A large fat man with a strangely twisted nose stood next to a skinny little man.

Wherever Mariam looked there was an amazing amalgamation of people. A white-haired elderly man was standing next to a young boy. Women with children chatted with each other in the company of the men of the city. Elamites in their striped, sleeveless outer garments talked with the descendants of Moab, while the Jews of Yerushalayim mingled freely with the Egyptians. Greeks spoke with Romans. All the ancient distinctions blurred together into a new tapestry of diverse colors and contrasting shapes.

Mariam could feel the hopefulness that arose from the gathering. Anyone who entered the room was quickly buoyed up and filled with anticipation. Although the debilitating atmosphere of humiliation still hovered over the Yerushalayim streets, a new age was emerging in the Upper Room. Fear and despair had been swept aside.

Standing in the shadows observing, Mariam was thrilled by what she was seeing. Only one phrase captured what she saw and felt. *"Talitha cumi."*

"Excuse me," a young man spoke to Mariam, "I know

it is unusual for a young man to speak so directly but I have heard of your story."

"Yes." Mariam looked away.

"I saw you speaking to the people on Shavu'ot," he continued, "and I was amazed. Someone so young and so articulate—and a woman."

"Yes?"

"The Apostle Yochanan told me who you were and what happened." He smiled very confidentially. "I knew if you talked to an entire group, you would speak to just one person."

"Hm—mm—m." Mariam smiled. "Such is not our custom."

"I understand." He folded his hands in front of his waist and bowed. "But I am seeking the truth that only you can tell. My name is Stephanos, and I am from the Jewish colony in Athens."

"Well, Stephanos." Mariam looked out of the side of her eyes. "You are a persistent person."

"Such is the way of the Greeks," he grinned, "ah—when—ah—it comes to truth."

"And what is this truth you pursue?"

Stephanos's face changed, becoming very serious. "I want to know about death, about Sheol. They say you have been there."

"At your age?" Mariam studied his face carefully. She was immediately taken by his handsomeness. He was about twenty-two, twenty-three, not much older. While it was unusual for the local Jews, his hair was cut like the Romans, closely cropped to his head and combed down his forehead. He looked strikingly different from her friends, but his smile was warm and engaging. "Why would you want to know about death?"

"I'm not sure," he hesitated, "but I must know everything I can. Perhaps, it is because I have heard the

Greeks discuss the subject so often." Stephanos stopped and shook his head. "No, something more personal pushes for answers."

"Someone close to you has died?"

"My mother," his voice lowered, "died when I was young. I suppose I never really got over the loss. I have worried about her ever since. Often I think on death." His dark eyes looked moist and far away.

"You have been lonely."

Stephanos was startled. "What do you mean?"

"The pain has never gone away, has it? You struggle with your fears."

"You know?" Stephanos cocked his head slightly. "Such is not easily understood."

"My mother died when I was a child."

"Oh," Stephanos nodded, "you do know. Could we sit down?" He pointed toward a corner in one of the rooms where the walls had been knocked down. Two small benches were against the wall.

As Mariam sat across from him, she felt the distance between them dissolving. Mariam had never been this close to a young man, but she liked the feeling.

"So, our worlds are strangely alike." Mariam became serious again. "We know about the void."

"Did it ever get better for you?"

"No."

"Me neither."

"When I died, I hoped I would find my mother there."

"Did you?" Stephanos rested his chin on his hand. "Was she there?"

"I didn't find her." Mariam became pensive. "Then again, the experience seemed to happen rather quickly. Maybe if I had stayed longer, but then—"

"What?" Stephanos asked for more. "What are you thinking?"

"Time ceased to have any meaning." Mariam realized for the first time. "I could have been there a minute, a day, a year. All the past and future were gathered at that exact moment. There is no time in eternity."

"What does that mean?"

"I don't know." Mariam bit her lip. "I have no way to explain anything more than the awareness. Time was just swallowed up."

"There are moments like that," Stephanos mused, "fleeting moments, only a few. But I understand. Perhaps we are two of a kind."

"Possibly," Mariam hesitated. "You've had many friends?"

"No." Stephanos shook his head. "My father was a trader and I traveled with him even before my Bar Mitzvah. That's why we came to be here on Shavu'ot. He came for business."

"I've always lived here in Yerushalayim, but I didn't really have friends. I guess I have always lived in an adult world."

"Then we are alike! We can be friends."

"I don't know." Mariam looked away. "We have our customs, you know."

"No, I don't know." Stephanos was defiant. "I don't know what is happening, but many things are changing. Many believe we are at the end of the age. Why can't we be friends?"

"I must think on what you say." Mariam smiled. "But in the meantime, I can tell you about what happened to me."

"I'm ready!"

As Mariam described her lingering illness, she once more remembered the painful isolation and loss of her childhood. She talked about how the long hours of solitude had molded and shaped her life. A world filled with adult companions pushed her far beyond her years at the price of overpowering loneliness. Her memories cut into forgotten wounds and brought tears to her eyes.

Stephanos nodded with a knowing born of experience. Never before had anyone asked or listened to the dark side of her heart. His rapt attention beckoned her to speak of what she had seldom acknowledged. As she spoke of dying and the extraordinary light she had seen, Stephanos again understood as no one else had. He could see into her inner world with an awareness that both amazed and moved her. She finished her story by telling him how at the sound of *'Talitha cumi'* a new person had come forth.

For a long time Stephanos sat silently. Neither person spoke until he touched her hand. "Thank you," he said simply. "I will ponder carefully all you have said until we meet again."

And then Stephanos was gone. The crowd swallowed him and Mariam was by herself again. His touch had broken a barrier that never had been approached before. Yes, a young man had touched her. For the first time in a long while, she felt truly alone.

"Shalom alechim," Jarius greeted Simeon enthusiastically as he entered the jewelry shop.

"Shalom," Simeon puzzled.

"Many customers will still be here following Shavu'ot." Jarius arranged the jewelry pieces on the bright colored cloth. "I know we will do well today."

"I know it's well into the third hour," Simeon explained defensively. "I had to attend a meeting and was detained in the street." He avoided eye contact. "These things happen, you know."

"Of course, of course." Jarius smiled. "Such is life."

Simeon watched Jarius out of the corner of his eye as

Jarius went about the business of preparing their displays, whistling to himself as he arranged and rearranged the items.

When Jarius caught Simeon watching him, he smiled but said nothing.

"We have some important matters to discuss," Simeon began cautiously.

"Well," Jarius nodded, "nothing we can't solve."

"What is going on here?" Simeon threw up his hands. "Why this sudden cheerfulness?"

"We have much to rejoice about."

"When I last saw you," Simeon pointed his finger, "you were angry. Frankly, I can't remember when you weren't angry or sad."

"I hope to do better, my good brother."

"At your house you accused me of extravagance." Simeon folded his arms. "You saw no future for our business."

"Maybe the future has changed."

"Changed?" Simeon put both hands on the table and leaned forward. "If anything, matters are worse."

"How so?"

"I am late this morning because of more controversy that the Sanhedrin must consider, and you are right in the middle of the turmoil."

"Come now, brother. Matters can't be this serious."

"Don't try playing Zeda with me." Simeon's face began to darken. "I know what's going on."

"And what is that?"

"The demonstration you and your friends put on at the Western Wall disrupted the Temple service." Simeon's voice began to rise. "Oh, yes, you were observed. Don't deny it."

"Please," Jarius tried to calm Simeon, "why are you so upset?"

"Why?" Simeon pounded on the table. "I was

stopped by a loyal friend who said he saw you wading around in the Pool of Siloe with the multitude who tried to turn the place into a mikvah bath."

"You don't understand."

"No!" Simeon was almost shouting. "I don't comprehend why you are allowing yourself to associate with this band of fools who are becoming a new sect. Wasn't Zeda's death enough for you?"

Jarius caught his breath and then became silent.

"Well?"

"We must not ever speak of Zeda or his death in anger." Jarius gestured him away. "Please—"

"What have you turned into?" Simeon came around the counter. "Did the bath at the pool wash your brains away?"

Jarius studied his brother's hard, contoured face for a long time. "Simeon," he pleaded, "maybe we can find a new basis for how we deal with each other."

"I have heard of this 'turning the other cheek' business." Simeon stepped back. "But I never expected to find my own brother playing the fool. Forgive them? Is this the new game?"

"Simeon—"

"For decades all I heard was justice! Now you have turned into wet clay?"

"Would you prefer a fight?" Jarius turned away and walked toward his workbench.

"At least I would know what you were thinking." Simeon followed him. "You sound as if your arms have shriveled and your legs deteriorated."

"Why must we always be so angry?" Jarius tried to smile. "Life is hard enough as it is." He slowly sat down on the stool.

"The longer you talk, the more bizarre this conversation becomes!" Simeon slapped the top of Jarius' bench.

"We only have each other now," Jarius continued. "We must not always be adversaries."

"Then give up this messiah business!" Simeon pointed at him again. "Stop being seen in public with these fanatics."

"Would you deny me the right of my own conscience?" Jarius folded his arms across his chest.

"We are not speaking of ethics, but truth."

"And you are the only one who understands what it is?" Jarius's eyes narrowed as he challenged Simeon.

"How many arrests must be made before you stop? Is Mariam next?"

"Do not threaten her," Jarius's voice turned cold.

"She was seen actually preaching to the crowd! This mere child."

"You might learn a lot from her, Simeon." Jarius stood and pointed his finger in his brother's face.

"A—a—a—ah!" Simeon screamed. "Now you insult me by suggesting that a woman, a little girl, is going to instruct me—a rabbi!"

"Have you ever died and come back to life?" Jarius leaned into his brother's face.

Simeon grabbed a brass pot and threw it against the wall. "No! I haven't, but another exhibition like Shavu'ot and you may get the opportunity to try." Simeon pushed Jarius aside and stomped out of the building.

Mariam closed the door to her room as the last rays of sunlight fell across the walls. She lit the candles and oil lamps before settling down on her bed. Leaning forward, she placed her face in her hands and began to pray, *"Baruch atah adonai, me kalohaynu."*

Her prayer became silent as she allowed the unspoken urgings of her heart to arise like incense from the Temple altar. For a long time she rested in the spiritual presence that filled her room. Finally she said, "Amen," and sat up again.

She sat quietly for a while in the afterglow of the moment. Then her vision fell across the hiding place where she kept her most treasured possession. Mariam pulled the little chest from the wall and opened the lid. She looked in at the necklace and the magnificent pearl that immediately glistened in the light. She ran her fingertips over the roundness that looked so soft.

"Oh, Mother," she said aloud, "if we could only talk, and you could tell me."

She closed the lid and thought about Stephanos. His sparkling black eyes danced before her. Probing and penetrating, they were also incredibly knowing and perceptive. Surely he had read her soul. Strangely she did not feel embarrassed, but wonderfully alive when he had looked at her.

Disturbing and wonderful feelings churned around inside her mind and memory. Never before had Mariam known such a marvelous tension within herself. Since they were talking of holy things, there couldn't have been anything wrong with the conversation. Surely not. How could these unknown urgings be wrong? And yet . . .

Although she and her father had never spoken of a husband, she knew that at the right time he would find the right person for her. She would be betrothed, and whoever this unknown mysterious person should be, he would be right. Her abba would select only the best of all possible candidates. Occasionally she had wondered what he might look like, but the thoughts were only fleeting reflections. Now the matter was of new importance and urgency.

Stephanos's black hair, cut in the short Greek way,

made him look cosmopolitan and wondrously alluring. The finely chiseled features of his face were still ruggedly handsome. Never before had Mariam felt a presence that had been so commanding and confident. He had broken through their ancient customs of separation like a young warrior capturing a city without even using his sword.

And then he had touched her. No young man had ever touched her before. His hands were artistic, long and slender like her father's. Even his fingers seemed to speak their own language. They were soft, warm, and very strong. Perhaps, his touch had been the source of all of the magic. Of course, such an exchange was totally forbidden. No one had to tell her that fact of life. But why? No one had explained why either. Perhaps, the feel of a man carried its own forbidden power. Mariam wondered if all men felt the same way. Instantly she knew she didn't want to know. Stephanos's touch would always be enough.

"Oh my," she put her hands to her lips, "what is happening to me? Mother, if you could only tell me."

The familiar silence returned its emptiness and confusion. Mariam closed the lid on the little box and put it away. Leaning back against the wall, she rested her head on her knees. Immediately Stephanos's face drifted before her eyes again.

TEN

When Mariam looked up at the sun, she knew she was midway into the third hour of the day. As she wound her way along the edge of the marketplace, she found herself thinking of the charming Greek she had not seen for a week. The passing days had only peaked her interest. Noise at the other end of the market interrupted her thoughts. People were gathering. Mariam knew painfully well what could happen if a riot should break out in this place.

Mariam listened for any sounds of provocation. To her surprise, she heard a familiar voice in the distance. Quickly Mariam scurried toward the crowd where many of the merchants were listening. Commerce was coming to a halt.

"What God has prepared through the ages," Stephanos proclaimed to the crowd, "has now been revealed. As He led forth our people from Egypt when the Red Sea parted, so now Adonai has raised up Yeshu as the stone was rolled away."

Mariam was amazed. The throng listened with rapt

attention. Before her stood this dazzling young hero in serene confidence. His grasp of the message was profound with fervent sincerity. He looked almost radiant. Obviously Stephanos had a gift for speaking and argumentation.

"Love has triumphed." He gestured as if he were embracing the world. "We have been loosed from the chains of hate that once dragged us to our graves. Now we have the power to forgive even our enemies."

Covering all but her eyes with her scarf, Mariam moved further into the group. She stopped behind a large man who completely concealed her presence. Mariam realized it was not the message but the man that fascinated her the most. His powerful voice was wondrously enchanting. Mariam smiled as she recognized that Stephanos had the same compelling effect on the crowd as he had with her. This gentle strong man had also taken them captive for the moment.

Hidden by the crowd, Simeon Ben Aaron was standing on the opposite side of the throng. "Who is he?" Simeon spoke into the ear of the man next to him.

His friend whispered, "I don't know, but they say his name is Stephanos."

"A Greek?"

"No." The man shook his head. "He's a Jew from Athens."

"Sounds like a Greek to me," Simeon grumbled. "Probably one of their crazy wandering philosophers."

"Yes." The friend peered out of the corner of his eyes. "Street-corner preaching's not our style."

"Listen to me, men of Yerushalayim!" the black-haired young man thundered to his audience. "A new day is here. Don't miss the visitation of God."

The people pushed in more tightly around the young Greek. Business in the marketplace had almost completely stopped. A fat man with a flat nose stood next to a skinny little companion. Even the women crowded in on the fringes to catch every word.

"Many of you ignored the first hour of his coming." Stephanos pointed accusingly at the crowd. "Others of you did not know." Even though he was a young man, he had a commanding presence that demanded attention from his audience. "Some of you helped put him to death!"

"Damn him." Simeon clinched his fist. "If he's looking for trouble, he's going to find it today."

"Nevertheless," Stephanos defiantly proclaimed, "God has raised Rabbi Yeshua from the dead and established him as our messiah. A new covenant has been made. A renewed people called forth. The new era has begun!"

"New era?" Simeon shouted in a shrill voice. "I see no new day. We are still a captive people."

"Yes," someone yelled from the crowd. "Where has the throne of David been established?"

The crowd moaned and swayed uncomfortably as the spell of Stephanos's preaching was broken. Unexpectedly, from out of the shelter of the surrounding buildings, a small contingent of Roman soldiers emerged and walked quickly toward the crowd. At once the noise subsided.

"His throne has been erected in our hearts." Stephanos beat his chest. "Listen to me, you trembling, fearful men of Israel. No longer are we believers timid and intimidated. We have found the victory over fear itself."

As the soldiers proceeded, a tall gray-haired centurion stepped into the crowd, and immediately the people parted before him. Although everyone recognized the implications of his presence, Stephanos seemed indifferent.

"A new people have sprung up in your midst," the young Greek continued. "Where apprehension once bound us, now joy has filled our lives. The truth has taken the blinders from our eyes and unstopped our ears."

"Your messiah was a cheap criminal." Simeon's friend interrupted Stephanos. "He died like the rabble of the city."

"A fraud!" Simeon challenged Stephanos. "He was a magician who did cheap tricks."

Mariam gasped. Simeon's voice shocked her. For the first time she realized he was the heckler.

The gray-haired centurion turned and looked at the two men with a sternness that was foreboding and threatening. Immediately silence settled over the gathering. With regal bearing he turned again to listen to the Greek.

"You have misunderstood." Stephanos pointed at the detractors. "We wanted a messiah who would come with conquering armies to establish a new political order. We were wrong! His kingdom comes first in our souls, bringing a peace that dispenses with the need for armies. Shalom can exist among all peoples through him."

"Traitor!" Simeon Ben Aaron shouted as he and his friend bolted from the crowd and ran for a side street.

Mariam stared after her uncle as he disappeared. The taunting had not deterred Stephanos in the least. As the Greek continued to speak she found her attention being drawn to his message.

"Change your mind and believe," Stephanos concluded. "I will stay and talk with all who want to know more of the final truth that has come to us. Ask me any question. Come now together. Let us become brothers and sisters in the new family God is creating in these latter days."

While many of the people turned back to the market-place, about twenty men pressed forward. At once their questions came like arrows, but the young Greek seemed all the more energized by the exchange. Immediately he began answering as he beckoned others to come forward.

Mariam jumped when she felt a gentle tug on her sleeve. She turned to find the tall gray-haired centurion standing beside her. "Honorius!"

"He spoke well." Honorius bowed slightly as the Romans did when acknowledging ladies and nobility. "We shall hear more of him."

Mariam's scarf fell away as she nodded enthusiastically. "A new voice has arisen among us."

"He understands." The centurion waved good-bye as he joined his men who fanned out across the marketplace.

When Mariam turned back, she discovered that the crowd was dwindling; she was standing only about ten feet in front of Stephanos. When he looked in her direction, he stopped talking momentarily and smiled at her. His boyish grin was almost impish. The dynamic orator seemed to turn back into a young boy who had just successfully completed a contest before his favorite admirer.

Mariam blushed, but waved her encouragement. He waved back before turning again to his inquirers. At once Stephanos was plunged into the heat of passionate discussion. Mariam slipped away, watching him as long as she could. Only then did she recognize another man who had been watching in the shadows of the plaza. Shimon Kefa had been listening and observing.

"Your shopping was well done today." Jarius dipped

his fingers into a bowl of water. "The lamb was excellent."

"The supper is good?" Mariam asked.

"Of course, my child, you always feed me like a king."

"In this house you are, Abba."

"Where would I be without you to look after me," Jarius squeezed her hand. "Someday you will make a marvelous wife."

Mariam blushed and looked down.

"I met with the apostles today." Jarius handed Mariam the pita bread. "We had a most interesting discussion."

"What did they want?"

"Our numbers are growing at an amazing rate. But with such blessing, there are many problems to be considered. They are seeking direction."

"Who better to consult than the ruler of the local synagogue."

"I'm sure the authorities are increasingly concerned about us. They killed one man and in his place have sprung up a multitude. There must be great hostility in the Sanhedrin, so we need to find more men to help the apostles and share the leadership. Just as we have Tzedakah to care for the needy at the synagogue, we need overseers."

"I do know of one young man," Mariam kept her eyes on her plate, "who is certainly outstanding."

"What is his name?"

"Stephanos. He comes from the Jewish colony in Athens."

"Oh yes," Jarius shook his head. "Shimon heard him preaching in the plaza today. He was quite impressed with the power of his oratory."

"I was there!" Mariam's eyes widened, and a smile flashed across her face. "Stephanos was wonderful. And even many of the men came forward to talk with him. Just the other day I talked with him a long time—" her words slipped away. She started to mention Simeon, but her father cut her off.

"Talked with him? With a man?"

"At the Upper Room." She bit her lip. "All of the people were mingling together. You know how everyone greets each other."

"Yes," Jarius said slowly. "There is considerable freedom. You talked to him?"

"Well," she hesitated, "really, he talked to me. One of the apostles told him about my healing. You understand?"

"I see," Jarius said slowly, "a spiritual conversation."

"Of course, of course." Mariam kept nodding her head.

"Everything is changing so fast." Jarius leaned back and sighed. "Your mother would be horrified to think that you were talking to a young man. And yet, look at our meetings. There are no boundaries, but heaven knows, none of us has ever been happier." Jarius scratched his head and stroked his beard. "How can such exchanges be wrong if the apostles encourage it?"

"Then you won't mind if we talk together again?" Mariam instantly leaned across the table. "I—a—mean," she drew back slightly, "if he has more spiritual questions."

Jarius looked at her out of the corner of his eyes. For a moment he thought there seemed to be an unusual amount of color in her cheeks. "We must always be proper," he lectured.

"Oh, yes, Abba. Proper. Very proper. Of course. Proper."

Immediately Mariam jumped from the table and began clearing the dishes. Jarius stared in consternation.

Mariam smiled as she carried the dirty dishes from the room.

"We do have servants for this sort of thing," he mumbled.

Across the city Simeon was entertaining a guest in his living room. The last to leave home, he had inherited the Ben Aaron family residence. Located in the Lower City, the stone house was closer to the jewelry shop than were the other brothers' homes. From the front door Simeon could see the Great Hippodrome, where the Romans raced their chariots. His house looked ancient and worn, reflecting the lack of attention that Simeon gave to its upkeep. The large two-story edifice was now filled with empty unused rooms. He seldom went beyond his bedroom and the large meeting room near the front door.

Simeon settled back in his chair, carefully studying the small man who stood in front of him. Prematurely balding, the man's black, deep-set eyes added little to his Spartan appearance. He was short and slight, but his reputation was formidable.

"Where are you from?" Simeon pointed toward a chair for him to be seated.

"Tarsus," the man smiled. "Generally I am known as Shaul of Tarsus."

"They say you are a most accomplished student."

"I have had the honor of studying with Gamaliel." Shaul bowed his head in deep respect. He had the usual long shaggy black beard that was typical of Jerusalem. Nothing distinguished him from any man on the street, except that he had an exceptionally high forehead. "One's grasp of Torah naturally expands by just being in the presence of such a great teacher."

"But," Simeon drawled, assessing that there could not be a great difference in their ages, "they tell us that you are unusually skilled in disputations. Your logic and oratory are applauded by your teacher and fellow students."

"I work very hard." Shaul's voice betrayed a certain false modesty. "Diligence has its rewards."

Simeon often used the Greek style drinking cups. He picked up an amphora and set it before Shaul. "Nevertheless, we believe that you might be very effective in helping us combat the new pest that has infected our holy city." Simeon poured wine from a jug into the amphora. "Here. Take refreshment with me. We have important plans to make."

"You have a very nice home." Shaul looked around the large room. Colored strips were painted around the ceiling, bordering the room in a dull red. The terrazzo floors had a similar design. Chairs and tables were set around the room. "God has blessed you. You are married?"

"No." Simeon shook his head. "My time is consumed with business and Torah. Perhaps—someday—but now every hour is filled with the business of the Sanhedrin."

"I make tents." Shaul set the amphora cup down on the table and wiped his mouth. "I've been able to pay my way by plying my trade."

"You are known as a man who is able to find new twists to ideas and discover previously unseen truths in Halacha*." Simeon folded his arms across his stomach. "We need someone who can refute the strange interpretations that are being spread throughout the city."

"I hate those who pervert the Law." Shaul's face froze with a hardness that instantly stifled his pleasantness.

*The Law

"Yes, we must combat those who spread chaos."

"But there are boundaries—" Simeon pushed back with his hands.

"The Law cannot be violated." Shaul shrugged his shoulders. "But we have all the latitude that is necessary within its confines."

"I would hope so." Simeon leaned back against the chair. "I am not a man of violence. I am only interested in protecting the people from further abuse. I want you to publicly refute the teachings of these followers of the dead rabbi and expose their foolishness. Enlightened debate should prove to be enough."

"I understand." Shaul leaned forward on the table. "Tell me how a man who is in his thirties came to sit on the Sanhedrin."

"My family has always lived here—in Jerusalem. I literally grew up in the shade of the Temple. My two brothers and I knew all the leaders of our faith. Even though we were Pharisees, our family always associated with the cohanim*. My father was highly respected in their circles."

"One does not come to sit on the high council only because of political connections." Shaul saluted him. "At least, not at your age. You had to demonstrate unusual ability. Don't be modest. Tell me more."

"My ancestors have always been business people with a scholarly bent. My older brother, Jarius, was an excellent student and soon became recognized as a scholar. But as a child I excelled them all. While I was still at a very early age, my family discovered that I forgot nothing. At four I could read the Torah. I only had to look at the scroll once and I could see the whole sheet in my mind days later."

*Priests

"Quite remarkable," Shaul deferred. "They expected great things from you?"

"I suppose," Simeon sighed, "but with time their expectations became a burden. I tried to blend into the people, but my reputation followed me. Now I find that remembering does not always equate with wisdom. I have obligations of leadership that I do not always want."

"We all carry our encumbrances." Shaul looked away and grew silent. He took a final drink, emptying his amphora. "Yet, we do not choose our place in history. We must do what must be done. I will begin seeking out these fanatics."

"Contact me," Simeon concluded, "if you need anything. You may yet find your way to a seat on the Great Sanhedrin."

ELEVEN

Simeon stood with his back to the debate going on in the front of the assembly room of the Sanhedrin. He wondered how he had ever gotten himself in such a position. The Torah and Tradition were his loves. Comparing the teachings of the rabbis and reasoning from the Law was his passion. Simeon did not like being in the role of a power broker, but the younger Pharisees had pushed him to the fore. Even though his scholarly insights were admired and respected, he now thought that he should keep his mouth shut more often. In spite of himself, he always spoke out at the critical moments when the arguments were heated. Well, someone had to!

Ben Kaifa's voice irritated him. Simeon hated subtle manipulating politicians. Right was right! Truth should be enough. He tried to stare at the enormous wooden door that sealed the world out of the high religious tribunal's deliberations. Unfortunately the magnificent planks of mahogany were no obstacle to the impulses for power and control that governed the streets. There were no hiding places from evil. At best the hinged barrier only concealed the wranglings of the religious leaders from the people. The gyrations of the cohanim were best kept from the light of day as were most of the inner secrets of the Sanhedrin.

Each seat was empty. The vacant rows made the enormous room and the high ceilings feel very hollow. As the sun set, the light from the high windows faded. One of the servants scurried about lighting the candles. The shadows of the three men behind him stretched out in menacing form across the empty room.

Simeon suddenly turned and interrupted the discussion going on behind him. "But we must do the right thing!"

"Could the high priest do less?" The sniffling little man's voice became shrill. "In all the years that I, Josiah, have served the high office, I have never observed any other intent or motive."

"Really?" Simeon shot a glance at Yehosaf Ben Kaifa whose cold, unresponsive stare chilled Simeon.

Ben Kaifa leaned back in his chair, running his fingers down the length of the front of his purple silk robe. The high priest wore arrogance with complete casualness. The rich aroma of his expensive perfumes was the final touch that completely set him apart from everyone else.

"Unless we put a scare into the sect," the priest's assistant continued, "nothing will stop their continuing bold advances. They seem unafraid of anything or anyone."

"There is value in creating a healthy respect for the law," Simeon interrupted him, "but I continue to be opposed to violence. Each harmful act has only cost us."

The high priest looked at the young rabbi disdainfully, making no pretense of his dislike for Simeon.

"But violence has its place," the other Sadducee

picked up the argument. "We must remember that pain is a great teacher. The transgressors learn—"

"And the innocent die," Simeon broke in. "My own family is ample testimony."

Ben Kaifa looked away, as if to avoid acknowledging the loss of the Ben Aaron family. "Something bold must be done." The high priest's voice was condescending. "Matters can't continue as they now are."

"I have a plan and a recommendation." The administrative assistant tilted his head obediently to the high priest. "Each day these heretics teach on Solomon's Porch. They are well within the bounds and authority of the Temple police. We would not have to deal with the Romans. Our own people would have every right to arrest them for disturbing the peace."

"Your ideas are more to the point," Ben Kaifa gestured for his assistant to continue.

"Every day new rumors flood the marketplace. Crazy men say they have been healed. Some even claim the shadows of these so-called apostles affect cures. We must squelch these stories at once. Arresting their leadership would serve notice that we find nothing to respect in these frauds."

"I would suggest an alternative," Simeon spoke directly to Ben Kaifa. "We have identified excellent debaters to confront our opponents. We can defeat them with the truth. Is that not a more righteous way?"

"A—a—ah, righteousness is not the issue." The assistant Josiah protected Ben Kaifa from having to respond. "Expediency is more to the point."

"We have already seen what expediency accomplished for us." Simeon's answer was biting. "Why must we consistently use force?"

"Authority!" the other Sadducee thundered. "These upstarts must respect the office of the high priest."

"They are intelligent people." Simeon stood his

ground. "Jews will respond to reason more quickly than to pain. Persecution will only fuel the fervor of their convictions. On the other hand, exposing their error opens them to ridicule. Is that approach not more effective?"

"Perhaps," the high priest waved the arguments of his two allies aside, "both approaches are needed. Simeon can encourage his contacts to engage these disrupters in public debate, and we can also throw their leaders in jail to jolt their senses. Yes, I think that both approaches will be advantageous."

"I protest any use of force." Simeon's face hardened.

"Of course." Ben Kaifa smiled wickedly. "Our brother Simeon is most humane. No violence. Incarceration should be sufficient." He tilted his head, ending the discussion. Under his breath he murmured, "For the moment."

The three men quickly stepped from the bridge and entered the Temple compound. The noonday sun covered the paving stones with blazing heat. Business was brisk as worshipers bargained for pigeons and doves. The sounds of protesting animals being pulled to and fro filled the air. Stephanos was always distracted by the sights of the Holy Temple.

Yochanan led the way through the columns that supported the long overhang lining the edge of the Temple Mount. The entire area was already filled with worshipers. Philip followed behind.

Because it was common for rabbis to teach in the open area, students always assembled on the Portico. With talliths* already over their heads, pious Jews walked about saying their prayers out loud.

*Prayer shawls for covering the head

Stephanos shielded his eyes from the sun. "Must be about the third hour," he said to Yochanan. "The sun is nearly overhead. Tammuz* is truly here. I'm hot."

"Things will get warmer." Yochanan winked at him. "I think our adversaries will be out in force today. Our presence has not gone unnoticed. Don't be surprised if we have detractors."

"I'm ready." Philip's voice was strong and confident.

"My brothers," Yochanan called across the plaza of Solomon's Porch, "we have good news for you today. Come and we will share our glad tidings with you."

Philip waved for people to gather. Worshipers who were preparing to enter the inner precincts of the Temple turned toward him. Merchants who were bartering in pigeons and doves paused at the unusual invitation. The wind picked up the smell of the burnt offerings on the other side of the dividing wall, and for a moment the smoke hovered around them before it vanished.

"Look around you." Yochanan made a sweeping gesture toward the mountains that surrounded Jerusalem. "Behold the place where the Holy One has ordained to meet us." He stepped up on the ledge of the southern wall. The sheer drop nearly took his breath away. "I stand here on the pinnacle of the Temple, truly the highest point in all creation, to tell you of the mightiest thing our God has done for us."

Quickly several hundred people congregated before him. Philip blended into the front of the crowd.

"You're blocking the way!" a merchant shouted. But the men only packed in more tightly.

"You have heard of the extraordinary deeds of these last days and weeks," Yochanan continued, "but have you heard from eye witnesses? We are here to tell you

*corresponds to June—July

what we have seen and heard concerning Yeshua Ben Yosef, who was the unique son of the Most High. No longer do you have to depend on rumor. You can know the facts."

Immediately a murmur arose from the crowd. One of the merchants who had been complaining quickly put a bird back in the cage, grabbed the wooden crate, and ran for the stairway leading down to the great steps at the base of the Temple. Others waved to their friends to draw near.

"The prophet Zechariah predicted the world would come to Jerusalem to catch the coattail of the Jew, so that the Gentiles might be brought near to HaElyon. And it has come to pass. The final word has been spoken."

The pressing crowd pushed Stephanos up on the same ledge beside Yochanan. The throng's common Jewish heritage was wrapped in the robes of Egyptians, Parthians, Elamites, Greeks, and even Ethiopians.

"Louder, speak louder," a large fat man with a broken nose cried from the fringe of the crowd.

Yochanan's voice was clear but naturally soft. His shyness could not be concealed behind his initial boldness. He became even quieter as he talked.

Stephanos noticed that a group of men had come up the stairs with the bird merchant. The vendor pointed toward them. The elegant robes of the Sadducees lined with fringe were obvious. Their faces were hard and set. They watched a moment and then sent another man back down the stairs. In contrast to the eagerness of the crowd, they stood defiantly with their arms folded As the apostle continued to speak, they began edging their way forward.

"We can't hear you," a small, skinny man near the front intruded.

Yochanan turned and looked pleadingly at Stephanos. He gestured helplessly and then became silent. As he paused, his silence brought a hush to the noisy crowd.

The Sadducees immediately pushed forward, rudely shoving aside anyone who stood in front of them.

"I bear testimony to the truth of what you have heard," Stephanos boomed. His rich baritone voice was unusually resonant. He aimed his words at the opposition in the rear.

"All the prophets from Samuel forward proclaimed these days that have now been fulfilled in this Holy City. But you did not listen. Your leaders rejected this last prophet as they did the former prophets."

"How dare you speak profanely of the high priest!" one of the Sadducees interrupted.

"Did I say high priest?" Stephanos asked the men in the front row. "Did I utter those very words? Our friends seem unduly sensitive. Perhaps they know something that we don't."

The crowd laughed and parted before the hecklers.

"But then again, all of Jerusalem is now aware of the errors of those who sit on the Great Sanhedrin." Stephanos smiled warily.

Once again the crowd laughed.

"You are all children of the covenant made with Abraham," Stephanos spoke even more loudly. "But the time has come for the true sons of light to be separated from the false children of evil. The hour of separation has come. The Holy One of Israel has come among us in Yeshua Ben Yosef."

"Who are you to tell us the truth?" The short balding man in the middle of the group of antagonists pointed his finger accusingly. "Who are you and by what right do you accuse us?"

"I am Stephanos, a Jew from Greece. My authority is the Torah and the living word of the present. And who are you?"

"I am Shaul of Tarsus," the little man folded his arms across his chest, "a disciple of Gamaliel."

"Welcome the pupil of Gamaliel." Stephanos waved his arms above the crowd. "Who better to acknowledge the truth of what God is doing in these last days."

"How dare you accuse us," Shaul repeated.

"I don't accuse you." Stephanos smiled. "I simply point to the risen Messiah. Adonai has visited us in him. The fact of his victory over death condemns you."

"We are not crazy men. We've seen no ghosts." Shaul's words were bitter and sneering.

"Neither have we," Stephanos shot back. "Your ignorance and blindness not only crucified him, it keeps you uncomprehending to this very moment."

"A—a—ah," sounded throughout the congregation. Smiles flashed around the crowd whose sympathies were clearly with the young Greek.

"Come now." Shaul turned to the crowd around him. "Shall we allow the Hellenizers to have another run at us? Only a Greek would suggest that God could come in the flesh. Are you implying that this Yeshua is another Jupiter or Mars? Is there any more repugnant idea to a Jew than lowering HaElyon to being a man?"

"Yes—hear, hear!" Many of the men grumbled.

"We proclaim that the promised Messiah has come," Stephanos responded. "His mighty deeds proved who he is."

"His mighty deeds?" Shaul mocked. "You are speaking of the man that the Romans hung on a cross? Are you talking of the dead rabbi who even had to be placed in a donated tomb?"

"But God has raised him!" Stephanos countered.

"I haven't seen him!" Shaul taunted again. "If he's

alive, let him show up right now. Have him walk out from behind one of the columns where he must be hiding. Perhaps, he's too shy to show himself this morning. Or maybe he's afraid the Romans will kill him again."

The men surrounding Shaul laughed and applauded.

"Only your spiritual blindness keeps you from seeing what El Shaddai* has provided." Stephanos was undaunted. "The problem is not in your head—it's in your heart!"

"And the deficiency is in your empty mind," Shaul shouted. "The true Messiah will bring a new order of justice and righteousness. The wicked will be cast down, and our people will be raised up. I see no day of vindication. No new social order has come. All you offer is a dead rabbi easily disposed of by the Romans."

"The Kingdom of God has come!" Stephanos swung his arms open. "He reigns within us, writing the law on our hearts. Hate has been replaced by love."

"You preach madness!" Shaul hurled again.

"Madness," Stephanos pointed toward the Temple precincts, "to say that God is still fulfilling His promises? Madness to point out the same ingratitude and narrow-mindedness that greeted the prophets is still alive in the streets of Jerusalem? Tell me, my little friend from Tarsus, is it madness to love instead of hate?"

At the word "little," Shaul flinched and his eyes flashed. He clenched his fists, and the color rose in his neck. "Blasphemy. They defame the name of HaElyon. The Law is clear! Stone him," Shaul screamed.

"Stop it," a man in front of Shaul pushed him back. "We've had enough of your kind. You're nothing but a distraction."

Instantly Shaul returned the shove. Suddenly the

*God the Provider

crowd exploded. Pharisees screamed at Sadducees. Men swung at each other, tearing at each other's clothes. The large fat man and the skinny man began pushing people around them. Stephanos watched in consternation as his impromptu congregation turned into rioters.

"Arrest them! Arrest their leaders!" Shaul shouted.

Suddenly temple guards charged the unruly mob. Pushing men apart, they stormed their way toward Stephanos and Yochanan. Clubs knocked people to the ground as the guards made a determined thrust to reach the two men. Philip turned to block their advance.

"Quickly," Yochanan pulled at Stephanos's sleeve. "We must leave."

"Why?" the young Greek didn't move. "They started the trouble. We can—"

One of the guards leaped on top of the Greek, knocking him to the ground. He hit Stephanos twice before he could resist. Another man slammed the apostle against the wall, pinning him to a column. The sheer weight of the press of the crowd knocked Philip to the ground. Guards trampled on him as they pushed the men back.

"Do you want death in this sacred place?" The captain of the guard leaped on the wall swinging his sword above his head. "Stop now or someone will die." Men parted and the fighting stopped. Several fallen men struggled to their feet. Philip clutched his stomach, gasping for breath.

"Beat the blasphemers and take them to jail," Shaul shouted. Immediately he and his cohorts took charge. "Stop this desecration of holy ground. Those who will not receive reason must be instructed with pain."

One of the guards dragged Stephanos as he struggled to get to his feet. Another pushed Yochanan alongside of him. The crowd became silent as the men were hustled past them.

"Fear not," some anonymous voice called after them, "the truth is with you."

Philip slowly rose to one knee, still trying to catch his breath. When he looked up, his friends were gone.

———•———

Across the city in the Upper Room, the apostolic council was sitting down in a circle. The noonday heat permeated every inch of the room. There was no breeze to relieve the oppressive atmosphere. Every man felt the discomfort of summer.

"Where is Yochanan?" Shimon Kefa asked the group.

"He and the young Greek went to the Temple Mount to preach," Yaakov answered.

"I am very impressed with this Stephanos," Shimon Kefa spoke to the group. "The Holy One has given him a penetrating mind and a quick tongue. We will hear much from him."

"He would certainly make a tzedakah. Perhaps, we will have to say as the Greeks do—a deacon," Toma added. "We must recognize these younger leaders and organize their talents. I believe Philip, Timon, and Nicanor are also exceptional leaders."

"Indeed." Shimon Kefa nodded. "Today we must also embrace the new thing that the Rudach Ha Kodesh is doing with the women. Inspiration seems to come without respect to persons. Our old customs are being challenged."

"What do you mean?" Yakov Ben-Zavdai* asked.

"Mariam." Shimon beckoned for the group to come closer around him. "The daughter of Jarius is obviously

*James, Son of Zebedee

a person that the Lord has touched. She is remarkable."

"I agree," Taddai* nodded. "I listened to her speak to the crowd on the day of Shavu'ot. Regardless of their language, everyone understood her words. She was part of the miracle. The Rudach Ha Kodesh was with her."

"But women have never been permitted to instruct from the Torah," Toma objected.

"True." Shimon Kefa nodded his head gravely. "And we do not need to give unnecessary offense. Yet, we cannot dismiss what the Holy One is doing in her. She has visions and holy insight. Who among us is a greater witness to the power of Yeshua over death?"

"I understand," Mattiyahu** said thoughtfully, "that she reads and writes Hebrew well. Perhaps she could record many of these events for the inquirers who come from afar."

"Her modesty and demeanor speak for themselves," Shimon Kefa said, "but I fear for her safety. We are traveling down a dangerous road. Our adversaries are far from finished with us. We must expect more attacks."

"Do you know who Simeon Ben Aaron is?" Natanel*** reached for a piece of cloth to wipe the perspiration from his forehead. Most of the Twelve shook their heads and looked blank. The midday heat was casting its spell, spreading drowsiness.

Shimon held up his hand in caution. "We must not cast any dispersion on their family. None of us chooses our relatives."

"He sits on the Great Sanhedrin," Natanel continued.

"And?" Taddai raised his eyebrows.

*Thaddeus
**Matthew
***Nathaniel

"The man is Jarius's brother." Natanel gestured aim-lessly with his hand. "Could he not be a spy? Would he not betray his brothers?"

"Our Lord said, 'A brother shall be set against a brother.'" Shimon Kefa mopped his face. "I fear we have already found the fulfillment of His words. We may yet see that a sword will divide their house, but we can dis-miss any fears of collaboration."

"Surely." Taddai smiled. "Maybe the brother will prove to be an asset to us. In the meantime I believe we should encourage Mariam to speak and lead."

"Then let us pray for guidance." Shimon lowered his head into his hands. "Seek the mind of God that we might follow His complete will."

Talliths were pulled over their heads as the men bowed their heads. A soft murmur of prayer arose from the group. Someone reached out, and hands were joined. Finally, quiet settled while they continued in si-lence.

"Come quickly!" exploded across the room as the door banged against the wall.

Shimon's prayer shawl fell back on his shoulders. He leaped to his feet. "What's happened?"

"Yochanan!" Philip sputtered, trying to catch his breath.

"Stephanos!" he heaved. "They—have—been ar-rested."

"What?"

"Where?"

"In the precincts of the Temple," Philip blurted out. "Just moments ago."

"Who has them?" Taddai grabbed the young man's robe. "The Romans?"

"No, no, the Temple police."

"We must all go." Natanel bolted for the door.

"Stop!" Shimon shook his head vigorously. "We must be cautious lest we play into their hands."

"Yes," Yaakov*, the brother of Yeshu, agreed, "treachery demands caution. We could do nothing anyway."

"We can pray for their well-being," Shimon motioned for the group to sit down. "Natanel, go along with Philip and see what you can discover. We will wait here for your return."

"God be with you," another apostle called after Natanel and Philip as they disappeared through the door.

"He said," Taddai sighed, "that in this world we would have tribulation."

Once more the men joined hands and bowed their heads.

"Hodu l'adonai kee tov," Natanel prayed quietly.

"Kee l—oam chasdo," Taddai** cried fervently.

Kefa raised his head and looked upward, *"Baruch atah Adonai Elohaynu melech ha—olam . . ."*

———————————————

Mariam looked carefully about the kitchen. "We will need more vegetables," she said thoughtfully.

Immediately the servant picked up a woven reed basket.

"Perhaps, some fruit would be nice. See what is fresh."

The heat of midday intensified the smells of the kitchen. Spices, smoke, and the aroma of dried fruit gave the room a pungent but inviting scent.

"Of course," the little girl agreed. "The raisins and figs should be very good. Maybe the pomegranates from Jericho will have arrived."

"And find a piece of goat meat for supper. We have not

*James
**Thaddeus

had meat for some time. Father would like that, I think."

The servant peered into the wooden container on the ledge near the corner open fireplace where kettles were hanging over the fire. "The ground cornmeal is sufficient, but we need lentils."

"Possibly you should wait until the day cools," Mariam said thoughtfully. "The sun is particularly intense today."

"The merchants bargain best when they are sleepy," the girl laughed. "I will be fine."

"Whatever you think. I am going to my room and rest until midday passes. Just be cautious."

"Of course." The servant waved as she went through the door. Mariam walked down the hall and closed the door to her room. As was the custom of most, she prepared for a midday nap. "Blessed are you, O Lord," she whispered as she settled with her back against the wall. Her thoughts quickly drifted to the black-eyed young man who had come to fill her fantasies. What might he be doing right now? And did he think of her in his quiet moments?

Something unsettling began to stir within. As she thought about Stephanos, a great heaviness settled around her.

"What is wrong?" Mariam said aloud. "Why am I feeling this oppression? Surely nothing could be—" Her words ceased. Intuitively she could see her fiery young debater fearlessly bantering boldly before a crowd as if nothing in the world could touch him; naively, as if he could handle conniving murderers who spun webs of intrigue; foolishly, as if his youthful courage was enough to withstand the knives of hired assassins.

As if in a dream, she saw the images of men lunging at Stephanos. Her imagination was controlled by an independent force that revealed its own message. Stephanos jerked to and fro against restraints that pulled his arms down and pinned them to his side. An arm reached from behind him, pulling his neck back. A club smashed into his back, and a hand slapped his face. A foot kicked his stomach, dropping him to the ground. Somewhere behind him another man was pelted with a rod. Mariam froze before the scene. Her heart raced and beads of perspiration broke out on her forehead. She clutched at her throat.

"Pray," a voice from above her commanded. Mariam had become so familiar with the unseen Presence, which so often appeared in her room, that she didn't reflect on the charge. As the scene faded from her mind, she heard again, "Pray." Instantly the awesome Presence filled the room, and Mariam fell on her face on her bed.

"O Lord, protect Stephanos," she cried out. "Protect this man who is your servant. Whatever is happening right now, surround him with your strength. Be a shield and buckler for him. Do not allow evil to prevail. Keep him from pain and injury."

Silently she interceded while the internal urging surged through her breast. "Oh, let nothing happen to this man," she blurted out. "Save him from the fate that befell Uncle Zeda. Let nothing happen to this man— that I love."

TWELVE

Shimon peeked through a crack in the door to see who was pounding.

"We found them! We have them!"

"Where are they?" Shimon opened the Upper Room door wide. Two men stepped out of the blackness of the summer night.

Philip and Natanel darted into the dim chamber, quickly walking to the center of the room. Pulling back the hoods on their robes, they began explaining frantically.

"None of the officials would talk." Philip gestured wildly. "They dismissed us as if nothing had happened."

"Even the Temple guards wouldn't answer questions," the other added. "We feared that they were being held in seclusion."

"The silence of the cohanim made them all the more obvious," Philip continued, "but when no one would acknowledge anything, we feared the worst had happened."

"Then we went to the Sanhedrin to see if they would tell us anything. The Sadducees were even more arrogant."

"Until," Philip smiled as he spoke more rapidly, "we told them that we were going to get the Roman centurion Honorius and ask for soldiers to search the precincts of the Temple."

Shimon held a candle before their faces. "That idea must have sent them scurrying," he said caustically.

"We saw them send a runner back to the Temple Mount. Then they told us to go back and inquire again." Natanel shook his head. "And that's how we found them. Since there is no moon tonight, we found it difficult to move quickly or see. At first we only saw their shapes. They were slumped against the base of the great stairs leading to the Temple."

"They are hurt?" Toma wrung his hands.

"Beaten," Philip continued, "but in the darkness we couldn't tell how badly. Friends who joined us on the way are helping them. They should be here in a moment."

"Quickly." Shimon pointed to a water jug. "Pour water and prepare olive oil. Someone get cloths if it is necessary to make bandages. Prepare food since they have not eaten all day. Light all the lamps!"

Men immediately scurried in every direction. Lamps were quickly lit and set on the tables. The large central candle rack was lowered to provide more light near the tables. The large front door was uncharacteristically left open. Even the revered center table was brought forward to serve as a stretcher.

As Mattiyahu set the olive oil vase on the table, he heard footsteps. "Here they are now!"

Four men shuffled into the room. Yochanan and Stephanos leaned against the others for support, limping slowly toward the table.

"Sit down, sit down." Mattiyahu pointed to the benches.

"Are you hurt badly?" Toma helped Yochanan sit down.

"Nothing that won't mend quickly." The apostle smiled weakly. "But it has been a very long afternoon."

"I've had better days." Stephanos groaned as he eased onto the long wooden bench.

"What did they do?" Shimon sat across from his two comrades.

"The Temple police dragged us out of the Portico and turned us over to four men whom we didn't recognize. They took us through several alleys away from the Temple compound." Yochanan blinked several times and winced. He took quick, shallow breaths.

"They beat us with sticks until we fell to the ground," Stephanos continued their story. "There were too many of them for us to escape or resist. We had no choice but to take it."

"The sticks weren't too large," Yochanan spoke slowly. "It was more like being whipped, but the results were just as effective." He pulled open his cloak, revealing large red welts across his chest. As his sleeves fell back, the men could see the same angry streaks across his arms.

"Quickly." Kefa snapped his fingers. "Bring the olive oil. Your pain must be intense."

"Ah!" the apostle groaned. "It burns."

"They kept threatening us." Stephanos rubbed the back of his neck. "We were warned that death would follow if we did not desist."

Yochanan chuckled. "My young friend told them that we were not afraid of death and counted their attack an honor. In turn they kicked and stomped on us."

"I might have settled for a little less honor," Stephanos said warily.

"He just kept smiling." Yochanan shook his head. "Our little Greek brother smiled back no matter how hard they attacked." He looked Stephanos straight in the eye. "You are amazing!"

"Are we not to turn the other cheek? What else could I have done?"

"You might have covered your head and cowered on the floor like I did. No, my brothers, Stephanos showed extraordinary courage. He was fearless."

"I just kept praying." The young man shrugged his shoulders. "And I was astonished. An inner strength filled me. I simply knew I could endure anything they did to us."

"The more he smiled, the harder they kicked. I thought they would kill us." Once more Yochanan caught his breath and bent forward.

"They kept threatening us." Stephanos slowly peeled off his robe. "But I sensed they were more interested in frightening us than finishing us off." Abruptly he grabbed his side, pressing his ribs; a look of pain shot across his face.

"Look at his back!" Toma exclaimed. "By morning he will be a solid mass of bruises."

"You will be very sore," Mattiyahu groaned. "I've seen men flogged for not paying their taxes. Days passed before they walked easily."

"And so they flogged our Lord," Shimon added.

"To suffer as He did," Stephanos's voice sounded serene and steady, "is the greatest of honors." His casualness and levity were gone. "I will walk the streets tomorrow that none may know that I have passed through this hour. Let us never speak of it again."

The room became silent. The apostles stared at the young man. His strong muscular back was checkered with welts and abrasions. Down his arms ran streaks of red that merged into raised puffing mounds that would soon be black and blue. His eyes dropped, staring at the table as if he were momentarily embarrassed.

Nothing more was said as oil and salve were gently rubbed across the two men's backs. Wine and bread were set before them. Only after the medication was applied did either man reach for the refreshment, eating slowly. Several times the young Greek clinched his side and doubled over in pain.

"And then they released you?" Toma finally asked.

"No." Yochanan set his small clay cup down. "We were locked in the room for a long time. I thought we would be kept there all night."

"Not long before you found us, a man and his servant came," Stephanos added. "They unlocked the door and let us out. The man told us to leave quickly and warned us to stop our preaching around the Temple."

"I didn't know the man." Yochanan's eyes narrowed. "I thought maybe an angel had appeared."

Stephanos covered his eyes when the first rays of the morning sunlight fell across his face. He had started to turn over, but the pain warned him not to move quickly. Sleep once more overtook him, blotting out the constant throbbing that enveloped his total body. Strange images filled his sleep, keeping him near the edge of consciousness.

At first he thought the cool, soothing sensation in his feet was part of a dream. He peeked out of one eye and realized that a cloaked figure was kneeling at the end of his bed. A hood covered the face of the one who gently massaged his feet and ankles. The touch was so pleasant and soothing that he closed his eyes to fully drink in the relief.

The hands were small. Only a woman would have such a light touch. Stephanos wondered what a woman might be doing in this place reserved for the apostles. Yet, as the muscles were smoothed by the small fingers, warmth moved up his legs, pushing out the pain. Not unlike the unusual spiritual strength that emerged the day before as he was being abused, a healing power was beginning to surge through his whole body, sweeping away the residue of the beating. He felt warm and filled with a great sense of well-being. Closing his eyes, Stephanos thanked God for whatever was happening to him.

Presently the gentle fingers began anointing his head, working olive oil into his forehead and temples. A damp cloth touched his eyelids, carefully cleansing them. When he opened his eyes, a young woman was kneeling beside him.

"Mariam," he exclaimed.

"You are better?" she said softly.

"How did you get here?"

"Shimon called for me to pray for you."

"Pray for me?"

"I seem to be able to help hurting people."

"You have been here long?"

"A while."

"Most of yesterday and all last night," Shimon spoke from another corner. "I feared for your life."

"My life?" Stephanos looked slowly around as if he had not yet recognized the Upper Room. His fingers felt the edges of the table on which he had been placed.

"Men who received far less than they gave you have hemorrhaged to death." The apostle looked down on Stephanos. During the night you became feverish and grew worse. "We needed Mariam's prayers."

The young Greek carefully rolled onto his side. "Your

prayers work." Slowly he pushed himself up. "I think maybe I can stand."

"Careful," the apostle warned. "I'm sure you have several broken ribs." He offered his hand.

"I hurt," Stephanos said thoughtfully, "but I think I can get up." Slowly he swung his feet off the table. "I am surprised," he smiled. "I feel well."

"The power of love is amazing." Shimon offered his hand.

Mariam turned away, trying to conceal the color that she feared was filling her face.

"Your prayers do wonderful things." Stephanos carefully took a few wobbly steps. "Yes, I think I am none the worse for a little wear. In fact, I'm sort of hungry."

"Ah." Mariam beamed. "An excellent sign. I will prepare some fish."

"Perhaps you can keep out of trouble today." Shimon Kefa steadied the young Greek as he began hobbling around the room.

"I must walk the streets today," Stephanos insisted. "I will allow no one to think they have diminished me. We must minimize what has occurred."

"Slowly," Shimon Kefa cautioned. "We have important plans for you, and we don't want to spend you all in one week."

"I will be all right," the Greek insisted.

"Then let Mariam feed you," Shimon steered him toward the table. "But take it slowly. You received a terrible beating. No leaving this room for some time. Philip will bring food up from the kitchen. He is ready to eat," Kefa called toward the stairs.

As Mariam quickly set the table, the smell of fish soon filled the room. She placed bread and goat's milk before him. Saying little, Stephanos ate slowly.

"We will return to the Temple precincts today," Shimon Kefa addressed the rest of the group. "Yochanan and I must demonstrate that we will not be intimidated. The Sanhedrin is trying to frighten us and we can't let them think they have won."

"Is Yochanan able to speak?" Yaakov asked.

"I will speak for us," Kefa continued. "However, having my brother stand with me will be a message in itself."

"I will go," Toma stood up.

"No," the senior apostle shook his head. "They must not catch any more than two of us together at any time. The officials may yet be trying to arrest our entire leadership in one sweep."

"They fear us," Taddai said factually. "I believe the Sanhedrin is actually afraid of what we may do."

"They do well to tremble for touching the Lord's anointed." Mariam spoke quietly but firmly. "For His recompense is sure!" Sensing her possible impropriety, she immediately turned back to the hearth.

"You are respected here, child." Shimon smiled at her. "We always welcome your voice."

Mariam scurried about the fire trying to conceal her embarrassment.

"We will return by midday," Shimon concluded. "The Holy One will be with us."

"I should be with you." Stephanos laid the piece of fish down.

"No," Shimon shook his head, "you have been much more seriously hurt than Yochanan. And we have other tasks for you. Mariam will provide what you need. Stay here."

The apostles gathered around their two leaders and prayed for their safety. When the two departed, the rest of the group went their separate ways. Mariam busied herself about the kitchen as if she were the only one left

in the room. Stephanos smiled as he watched her scurrying about, obviously ignoring him. Stephanos patted
the top of the rough hewn bench beside him. "Come. Sit
down and talk to me."

"I'm not sure—"

"Come now, even Shimon has sanctioned your being
here. Sit down. The night has been long. You've earned
a rest."

Slowly Mariam crossed the room and eased onto the
bench across from Stephanos. Her eyes fastened onto
the table.

"Now, now," Stephanos laughed. "This isn't the first
time we have talked."

"But we've not been alone—like we are here."

"Oh, yes we have. You and I have always been alone.
We know the emptiness better than people twice our
age."

When Mariam looked up, she found his large black
eyes filled with both sorrow and kindness. The gentleness in his gaze left her vulnerable. She longed to touch
him, and at the same time she wanted to retreat.

"Yochanan and I lay in the dark on the cold, stone
floor for a long time," he continued. "The loneliness was
awful. Mariam, I am not a hero. My tears washed the
dust from my face. My pain was so great I thought I was
dying."

Mariam started to reach for him, but drew her hand
back.

"My mother died alone and I wondered if she felt as I
did there. And then you seemed to be in the room with
me. I could almost hear your voice talking to me."

Mariam blushed and looked away.

"I felt as if you were telling me I would survive.
Strength came back into my body. The emptiness was
filled—by you."

"No." Mariam shook her head. "Only my prayers were with you."

"I know of no one whose prayers are as yours. Your heart and soul travel in your intercessions."

"Tell me more about yourself."

"No, I want to talk of you. You are the most remarkable person I've ever known."

"Please—"

"Do not fear me, Mariam. I will only return the joy and life you bring to me."

"No, in Yerushalayim we do not speak of such things until we have been—betrothed." She tried to catch the word as if it could be retrieved.

"The customs of the Jews in Athens are not so different," Stephanos suddenly reached for her hand. "I understand what we are saying."

Mariam felt the warmth of his large, strong hands covering hers. She breathed deeply but did not move.

"Has not God brought us together? Are we not two boats seeking a common harbor?"

"Only parents should speak of such matters."

"The time is short, Mariam. Everyone says the Lord will return quickly. We cannot wait for the old ways."

"But that is all the more reason we must be prudent."

"Prudent? Yes." Stephanos's eyes became intense and penetrating. "But not passive. We still have this lonely space in which we must live."

"I—I—I don't—know."

"Don't retreat from me," Stephanos leaned closer. "We each have a God-given mission, but we don't have to fulfill it by ourselves."

"I must think. Pray."

"Of course. But don't be afraid."

Mariam looked apprehensively at the strikingly handsome face in front of her. He was strong like her father, yet there was no emotional distance. She did not know what to say to this man who spoke so directly to her heart.

"We must not offend the Lord." Her voice was apprehensive.

"Offend our God who made Adam and Eve for each other?" He turned her hand over and began tracing the lines in her palm with his other hand.

Mariam watched without resistance.

"You have taken the pain from my life," he pressed her palm between his. "Surely you are God's gift to me."

THIRTEEN

For a long time Simeon stared at the pieces laying unfinished on his workbench. The broken chain reminded him of prisoners set free. He thought of the two men he and his servant had released three days earlier. The believers had staggered out of their make-shift cell. Simeon was appalled that they had been beaten.

The high priest couldn't figure out how they had escaped and the crazy believers in Yeshua were saying that an angel had set them free. Simeon laughed aloud at his private joke. Who would guess that he was the liberator? If Kaifa ever found out, there would be a price to pay.

Pushing the chain aside, Simeon began to pace. Periodically he looked at the doorway, waiting for the canvas flaps to part. Simeon hated the contradiction he felt within himself. He wanted to be an unemotional dispenser of the truths of Torah. His continual prayer was that his every impulse would be disciplined and conformed to the Law. Yet an emotional underside within him would not allow an iron constitution to wall out the feelings that contaminated his resolve. Periodically a subterranean eruption of passion forced his better judgments aside.

The most difficult and confusing times for Simeon were when he had to deal with Jarius. He loved and admired his brother in a way that he could never express. When Simeon tried, his words became clumsy, and their mutual competitiveness spoiled the attempt. Jarius wouldn't let him come close. The fact that Simeon had always been the better student drove the wedge deeper. Jarius so often seemed afraid to stand on an equal plane with him.

Simeon thought of the message he had sent the night before, requesting that Jarius come to his house. Nothing had happened. No brother. No reply. Simeon was worried. Could Jarius have been attacked as were the two men—as was Zeda?

Simeon sat down again at his workbench, but his apprehension did not subside. Suddenly the canvas door opened and Jarius walked in. He stopped at the counter to adjust the display.

"Shalom." Jarius nodded to his brother, placing the bag in which he carried gold pieces home on the table.

"You did not come last night." Simeon turned his back and continued working on the chain he was finishing.

"I was in an important meeting." Jarius walked across their jewelry shop and sat down at his workbench.

"More important than family business?" Simeon sneered as he completed the latch on the chain. He realized that he sounded too caustic.

"More important than any business."

"The sound of fanaticism infects your every sentence." Simeon whirled around. "Even an intelligent conversation has become impossible." Again he regretted overstating his intention.

"Come now." Jarius sounded congenial. "The hour was late. When one is tired, speaking clearly is difficult."

"Tired?" Simeon put his hammer down. "Yes, I am very tired. I am tired of these endless conversations that go nowhere and change nothing. For nearly three years I have warned you of the disaster that this rabbi from the north would bring. Never in my worst nightmares would I have believed his madness would reach epidemic proportions. But now it is too late. Matters are completely out of control."

"Is it possible that only God is in control?" Jarius's eyes twinkled. "Even Gamaliel saw such a possibility."

"Don't twist the words of our greatest sage." Simeon glowered. "Everywhere I turn this craziness twists rationality into confusion."

"I do not feel confused." Jarius continued smiling.

"The insane often don't," Simeon shot back. *No, no,* he thought to himself. *Don't beg a fight.*

"You are a good man, Simeon. You rant and rave now and then, but you have a good heart. I do not think you want anyone injured."

"I have tried to tell you," Simeon measured his words carefully. "Many people are going to get hurt. You are sitting on a volcano. When it explodes, fire will fall on this city. I cannot be responsible any longer. I fear for you."

"Simeon, Simeon," Jarius pleaded, "our parents always put too much weight upon your shoulders. You were never a child, but a little man trying to lift the world." Jarius opened the bag and got a magnificent golden Yerushalayim dedaheba. "Mariam and I do not expect you to intercede for us with the Sanhedrin."

"But I must!" Simeon pounded his work table. "Don't

you understand that I can't idly stand by and watch these events happen. I am cursed if I do, cursed if I don't."

"We do not hold you responsible for what happened in the death of Yeshua." Jarius began rubbing the gold with a cloth. "We now know that he had to die for the power of God to be fully demonstrated."

"Don't talk like that!" Simeon's voice became even louder. "Such talk is blasphemy! Pure blasphemy!"

"I grant you your opinion—"

"But my opinions hurt no one. Your ideas split and divide people until they are willing to kill each other." Simeon inadvertently knocked the necklace to the floor.

"Yeshua predicted this division would come, setting brother against brother. Such is the nature of truth."

"Has not enough blood been shed?" Simeon held up his arms and shook his fists at the ceiling. "Daily I see the image of our brother lying here on this very floor dead. I cannot survive another similar sight."

Jarius rested his head against his hands and bit his lip. "I have found," he said slowly, "a mercy which is beyond all justice. We will be covered by that mantle of peace, regardless of what lies ahead."

"You talk madness! There is no mercy in this world." Simeon began to pace again. "You are surrounded by vicious people. They rule the Sanhedrin!"

"Yes. I know the cohenim wish us ill. I could not be more aware of the Zealots." Jarius put his dedaheba on the display counter. "And the Romans . . ."

"Stop it!" Simeon whirled around. "You don't get it." His eyes flashed. "We have spies in every one of your meetings. When speeches are made, the words are in our ears before they fall to the floor. Yochanan? You call him 'the beloved'. Stephanos? He has been seen talking to my niece a number of times."

"Stephanos?"

"This hellenized Jew even violates our customs and freely approaches your daughter. Oh, yes, my brother, we are well informed. I know you have become a leader among these people. In the days ahead your house will be marked."

"God will protect us."

"Like he did the rabbi from Natzeret?* Spare me the experience. I don't expect you to return from the grave!"

"You mean well." Jarius walked across the shop toward him. "I know you do not condone these excesses of violence." Jarius's outstretched arms held his brother's shoulders. "No, we would never blame you for what may be ahead. But the Lord has called us to walk this path."

Simeon's usual hard veneer fell away as his face twisted in pain. "You don't understand." He closed his eyes and shook his head. "I'm not being kind. I can take no more. I could not bear the sight of Mariam's being torn apart—or of you laying dead at my feet. I cannot tolerate thinking of what I know is ahead." He pulled away from Jarius's grip and walked to the corner near the small fireplace. Simeon stood in silence.

Jarius broke the pause. "I believe the stone moved. You do not. Yet we both serve the same God. We are sons of Avraham. We seek His will."

"Everyone seeks His will," Simeon interrupted him. "Each man who sits on the Sanhedrin thinks he knows the Torah, and that is why these matters have become so deadly. When people believe they speak for God, they feel justified in any course of action they take. The most vicious man of all is the one who believes his actions are sanctioned by God."

*Nazareth

"Perhaps," Jarius spoke more to himself, "this is why Yeshua forbid us to judge."

"You live in a world ruled by power, by evil—by Romans." Simeon's voice became hard. "The sword determines who finally prevails. If a sword pierces Mariam's heart, she will not return next time from Sheol."

"Yes, Simeon, you and I know that tragedy is always possible."

"You and Mariam are all I have left. Zeda's wife was never one of us. I cannot bear to place any more corpses beside the bones of our ancestors."

"What are you suggesting, Simeon?"

"I want to dissolve our partnership. You go your way and I will go mine. We will be spared further confrontation."

"No, no." Jarius lurched forward. "Surely this is not a solution. Closing our eyes will not stop our ears. Yerushalayim is a small world."

"We have both done well." Simeon again became the distant man of business. "Our reputations are well established. We will continue to bring customers from afar."

"But we complement each other—we profited because Zeda bought large amounts of gold and silver. Separate we will be diminished."

"Possibly." Simeon shrugged. "But I require little, and your new friends will become customers. I want this settled quickly."

"I cannot agree." Jarius threw his hands up. "We cannot replace this excellent location."

"Then I will move elsewhere." Simeon picked up the chain and dropped it in a little leather pouch. "I will begin making arrangements."

"No, please—" Jarius reached out to his brother. "A move will cost you greatly."

"Me?" Simeon turned on him. "Can you not understand the price you are about to pay? Wake up! The night is coming!" Simeon clutched the bag tightly and choked back the pain that stuck in his throat. He hurried out of the store, disappearing down the street.

———————◆•◆———————

Throughout the entire afternoon Jarius found it difficult to face customers and drive hard bargains. The conversation with Simeon kept running through his mind, leaving him feeling disjointed and confused. Finally he closed the shop and began to pour over their financial records and inventory. The afternoon slipped into the evening.

"Jarius. Jarius Ben Aaron."

For a moment, Jarius hesitated as if hoping the intruder would leave.

"Are you there?"

"Yes. But I am not open for business."

"It's Stephanos. I am here to talk."

Jarius untied the canvas flaps. "Come in. Come in."

"Perhaps I have come at a bad time."

"No, no, Stephanos. I am always glad to see you. Please sit down. Possibly a little refreshment?"

"Thank you." The young Greek bowed as the Romans often do. "I had hoped to talk with you if the time—the moment—is—uh—opportune."

"Certainly," Jarius spoke hesitantly but politely. "I am looking at some of our records. Let me set them aside. You are feeling well now?"

"Yes, much better."

"Please sit down." Jarius sat down.

"Mariam and I have been speaking to one another," Stephanos cleared his voice. "The apostles first suggested that she tell me of her encounter with death."

"Yes, I am aware of these matters."

"And her prayers for me have greatly enhanced my recovery."

"Mariam has great spiritual gifts. God has profoundly touched her life."

"We have both committed ourselves totally to His purposes."

Jarius nodded, saying nothing. The tone and directness of the conversation was not what he had expected. He stirred uncomfortably on the bench.

"Therefore, I feel it is appropriate for me to talk with you directly." Stephanos looked down, uncharacteristically at a loss for words.

Jarius felt uneasy.

"My mother died when I was young. During the past years I have traveled with my father. We came here to visit the Great Temple and worship. My father traveled on again, and I agreed to wait for him to return. Possibly in a year or so, he will be back. It all depends upon the caravans. So they are not here to speak for me. I must speak for myself."

"Yes." Jarius's eyes narrowed, and he wrinkled his forehead.

"From the moment I heard, I knew Yeshua was the Messiah. Like every good Jewish boy, I had memorized the Torah and the Psalms. I had studied the scrolls of Isaiah. All the teachings of the past blended in my mind. For the first time I understood."

Jarius picked up a wine skin that was hanging from the wall and poured red wine into two simple plain cups. Without speaking, he handed one clay cup to the young Greek.

"I heard Mariam speak to the crowd on Pentecost. Each word, like a new lamp, lit a dark corner of my mind. My insight multiplied, until my mind was filled with the light of grace. Never have I admired such a woman."

"Such a *young* woman," Jarius corrected and then looked away.

"In these last days I have found her to have the wisdom of a sage."

"What are you trying to say?" Jarius interrupted him.

"I want to become betrothed to Mariam," he blurted out.

"Betrothed?" Jarius's mouth dropped.

"Girls much younger have been betrothed for years," Stephanos answered quickly. "My request is not unusual."

"My daughter?" Jarius stammered.

"I am sorry my parents are not here to speak."

"This is most unexpected," Jarius stood up and began to pace. "I do not know what to say."

"My family is most worthy," Stephanos began to speak rapidly. "We trace our lineage through the exile to Moses himself. We have been orators and teachers as well as merchants. Mariam would want for nothing."

"For nothing? You have money?"

Stephanos's eyes darted back and forth, betraying that he had taken a wrong tack.

"You have resources that I cannot see?"

"Ah—a—no." Stephanos's eyes blinked. "However I am very clever and apt at trading. I even know something of the trade routes from which gold and silver come. I could be a buyer!" He blurted out as if inspiration had seized him.

"A purchasing agent?" Jarius's eyes widened for a moment. "Interesting."

"Of course," Stephanos picked up the opportunity, "I could easily open up new trade possibilities for you. I could purchase precious stones."

"And how much money do you have now?" Jarius asked warily.

"My resources are limited," he admitted grudgingly, "but I have ample time to open the doors that are before me."

"Perhaps the time has passed for marrying and giving in marriage. The Lord may come quickly." Jarius gestured with his finger pointed upward.

"Of course," the young Greek shifted uncomfortably, "all things await the Lord's will."

"You handle yourself well—very well," Jarius smiled, "and you are a young man without guile. Certainly you have impressed all of us. But once you have come seeking Mariam's hand, matters are changed. I must ponder carefully what you have said and we will talk again."

"Thank you. Yes—thank you."

"In the meantime, I wish to be present when you speak to one another. There are reasons for our customs. Do you understand?" Stephanos's eyes fell. Obviously he had not considered such a possibility. "Whatever you say," he answered mechanically.

"Good. We shall see what lies ahead."

Stephanos stood awkwardly for a moment before thanking Jarius again. He quickly left. Jarius did not have time to tie the flaps shut before another figure stepped into the shop.

"Honorius!"

"You are closed?"

"Yes, but you are always welcome. Come in."

"I've not been here since—" he stopped.

"Since we brought Zeda from the market. Much has happened since that fateful day. Let me light some lamps."

"Much indeed." The centurion unfastened his helmet and set it on the table.

"All that I have in my house is at your service. You

have proven to be a friend to the People of the Way." Jarius began lighting candles and oil lamps around the room.

"Possibly you have wondered how I can come to your gatherings so easily?"

"No." Jarius shrugged his shoulders. "I suppose we feel honored."

"My colleagues think I am spying. No one would think that I take you seriously. Consequently, there are no problems."

"Good, good." The oil lamps illuminated the faces of both men.

"But I have come to speak of spying," the centurion pushed his sword to one side as he sprawled out on the small bench. "The Sanhedrin has observers in your gatherings."

"Yes, I have just recently learned. But we have no fears. Maybe the spies will learn the truth."

"And I have spies that report to me about the Sanhedrin," the centurion smiled cynically. "Money can buy a great deal in Jerusalem these days."

"In the great gathering itself?" Jarius choked. "Is such truly possible?"

"Let us say that I know what they are about—all the time."

"I will tell no one." Jarius put his finger to his lips.

"Of course." Honorius acknowledged. "I want you to be very careful. The voices of restraint on the high court are diminishing as the priests become more frightened of losing control over the people. Like the Zealots, there are fanatics who will stop at nothing to achieve their purposes. Do not test these waters."

"What are you suggesting?"

"Shimon and Yochanan did well before the Sanhedrin the first time because they caught them off guard. Next time a confrontation will not fare as well."

"Why?"

"Each time you defeat them, they sharpen their knives."

"But we do not seek to conquer them."

"You are a naive man, my friend. Your goodness clouds your own eyes to the wickedness of power-hungry men. They have few alternatives left. When they lose the power of argument, only raw force remains."

"I see," Jarius said slowly. "I see."

"Do not give your source," the centurion placed his helmet back on his head, "but tell the Twelve to beware." He tied the string underneath his chin.

"Bless you, my brother."

"Thank you for calling me brother." Immediately Honorius left with the swift bold strides that always appeared so decisive.

Jarius quickly placed a barricade over the large doorway and secured it. He returned to his scrolls. For a few moments he looked at the columns of figures, then he put them away. He was too distracted to think of numbers.

How could he allow the family business to dissolve? Yet what could he do but grant the wishes of Simeon? Worse yet, how could he even think of his little Mariam leaving? Of betrothal? Even the thought left him lonely and pained.

And yet—and yet—

A son-in-law who was even at this moment so mightily used of God? A son-in-law who might know of the places that only Zeda had visited? Was Stephanos only a straw in the wind or was this the hand of God? Jarius slumped on the table, bewildered and unsettled. He fumbled as he put out the lights and closed the shop.

Spies? Apparently there were spies everywhere. Romans, Zealots, religious spies. And where did Simeon fit? No, in spite of his brother's competitiveness, their bond of love had always held. The worst of all alternatives was the realization that these very chords of love were now pulling them apart and Jarius knew there was nothing he could do. Simeon? A spy?

"O Lord," he cried out. "You said a sword would divide our homes, setting brother against brother. But the pain is too great to bear! Please help me know what to do."

Jarius trudged up the lonely, dark street toward his house with one thought in his mind. Could Simeon truly be a spy?

FOURTEEN

During the next three days Simeon did not come to the shop. He carefully avoided all contact with any member of Jarius's household. Most of the time he felt angry and confused, a man divided against himself. The obstinate mindlessness of his brother had created a terrible bind. Yet, their family ties were an unyielding bond.

Simeon was oblivious to his surroundings as he walked down the narrow street leading from his house to the jewelry shop. The many impossible demands of his situation crowded other thoughts from his mind. Whether he liked it or not, he would have to plot and scheme. "At least," he thought to himself, "I am going to stand on the side of truth regardless."

"I have news for you."

Simeon jumped when the voice broke his concentration. Without turning, he realized a man had fallen in alongside him. He also knew that Josiah, the servant of the high priest, had found him. "What?" he snapped. "What do you want?"

"You are to come with me, please."

"What is happening?"

"A special meeting has been called. I know the way and place."

"What sort of meeting?"

"Leaders of the Sanhedrin are meeting with your friend Shaul. They need you to come."

"Me?" Simeon barked. "Now?"

"Please come with me. The time is short."

Simeon considered Josiah to be nothing more than a sniveling lackey of the high priest. He tried to avoid conversation as they walked toward the opening in the south wall that would lead them to the Sanhedrin.

"Kaifa believes there are important decisions to be made."

"Humph."

"Your advice is considered to be most worthy."

Simeon picked up the pace as Josiah chattered away. He didn't respond further until the servant turned down a dark alley leading away from the Sanhedrin. "This is not the place where the Sanhedrin meets."

"A more secluded site seemed more appropriate." Josiah's smile was oily and conniving. "We are almost at the house."

At the end of the block, Josiah turned down a narrow passageway that led between the houses. When they came to the last door, he knocked softly. The door opened, revealing five men sitting around a table talking intensely. No one paused or acknowledged Simeon as he entered.

"Shalom," the high priest's voice was cold and distant. "Please sit down."

Josiah moved to stand behind his master.

The only light in the room filtered in through slits in

the closed shutters. Simeon blinked trying to see if anyone else was standing in the back. Only the outline of a
few items of furniture were visible.

Shaul was making a point by poking rapidly at the
man across from him. He stopped and saluted Simeon
respectfully.

The air was stale, and the room smelled musty. Simeon stood uncomfortably shifting his weight from one
foot to the other.

"But I will testify against them," Asa, a scribe from
the Synagogue of the Freedmen, continued. "I will
gladly say they blaspheme."

"Yes, yes," Yehosaf Ben Kaifa interrupted. "We have
many who will accuse. What we need is people who will
act. Men who will strike."

"Strike?" Simeon frowned. "What are you discussing?"

"The time has come." The high priest sounded condescending. "You should be aware that the time has
passed for talk. Those who oppose us will be swept
away," he said menacingly. "You are included today because you brought us our valuable brother Shaul."

"Then what do we need to do?" Josiah picked up his
cue.

"Their voices must be silenced!" The high priest continued as if Simeon were not even present. "We must
break up their sect. They must be scattered—and shat-
tered!"

"You know I oppose violence," Simeon bantered back.
"I am not intimidated by such talk."

"Simeon," the man at the end of the table spoke, "listen to me. Has old Zahor ever misled you? Was it not I
who influenced your selection to the Sanhedrin at such
a young age? Listen to what I say."

Simeon had studied under the old rabbi; Zahor had been a friend to the Ben Aaron family forever. He looked longingly at his old mentor, hoping for an ally.

"The hour has passed for negotiations, Simeon. These followers of the Way are growing too fast. We must do something immediately or lose our influence with the people. You must not oppose this action publicly."

"They have left us no alternative." Asa pounded the table.

"I will not be humiliated again." Shaul's eyes narrowed. "The next time I debate, I strike for the throat."

"So I have been invited to hear what you have already planned?" Simeon crossed his arms.

"No—o—o," Ben Kaifa spoke slowly but with the confidence of a man who sensed that he had already prevailed. "Your thoughts are always helpful. But we no longer waste time discussing our reservations. We must implement a plan of action."

"And I am ready." Shaul looked about the group as if he were counting heads. "With a few men I can move quickly through the city and put terror in their hearts. I am fully prepared."

"Excellent!" Ben Kaifa commended him. "You will be given full authority."

A smile broke across Shaul's face. Immediately he tried to conceal his satisfaction at the impression he had made with the high priest. He blinked, and the smile came again as a sneer. His eyes met the eyes of Kaifa and a tacit agreement passed between them.

As Simeon watched the exchange, his heart sank. The high priest had outmaneuvered him. He was isolated and alone. Nothing stood in the way of a violent response to Jarius and his friends. Shaul, his protege, was now the power broker. The final plans had been completed, he knew, before he arrived. His inclusion in the discussion had only been a final ploy to end his opposition.

"We must move quickly," Shaul continued. "Perhaps we can create a confrontation that will serve our purposes."

"Yes." Asa stroked his beard. "Then we must be prepared to move into their homes. I understand that they meet in a central large room on top of a building near Mount Zion."

"They have friends among the Romans," Zahor added. "Make sure we don't make a mistake and attack any group where a soldier might be present."

"Intelligence is necessary." Shaul looked around the group. When his eyes met Simeon's, he quickly looked away. "But—we must be prudent."

Simeon stared in disbelief.

"We seek only the will of God," Shaul became defensive. "Understand," he addressed Simeon, "we are only doing the work of the Holy One."

"You are so sure?" Simeon asked warily.

"Of course!" Shaul was emphatic.

"Then there is no hope." Simeon stood. "I want no part in your plans. We may all live to regret this meeting."

"Your family will be an exception, of course," Yehosaf Ben Kaifa played his final trump card. "Perhaps they will yet see their mistaken ideas." He smiled condescendingly. "You will want to make sure they stay in their house day after tomorrow so there is no problem of mistaken identity."

"In two days?" Simeon mumbled.

The five men looked at each other and nodded their agreement.

"In the afternoon to be exact," Shaul confirmed.

Slowly Simeon turned from the table and walked across the small room. He shut the door behind him as their intense conversation continued once more. He was completely alone.

———— • ————

Stephanos quickly spoke in Mariam's ear just as the assembly of the believers was beginning. He wasn't sure she understood that he wanted her to slip out and meet him in the alley behind the Upper Room. He paced for several minutes and worried that she might not come. The moon was bright and large. There were no clouds to obscure the hundreds of stars that dotted the black sky. Standing next to the wall, Stephanos was obvious, but only two steps into the shadows and he was invisible. He wrung his hands nervously. Five minutes passed before he heard the large wooden door open. A wisp of a figure hurried down the steps.

"Stephanos?" she called quietly.

"Here. In the darkness."

"Are you all right?" She bounded down the final steps.

"We must talk." He reached for her hand to pull Mariam into the dim. She didn't let go.

"Something has happened?"

"Yesterday I talked to your father. Did he tell you?"

"No."

"I told him that I wished to be betrothed to you."

"What?" Mariam gasped.

"I tried to make the arrangements myself since my father will not return for at least another year."

"Betrothed?" Her words trailed away into the night.

"I thought your father might have talked with you about his conditions."

"He has been gone." Mariam shook her head. "When

he was home, he was distant and preoccupied. Perhaps your talk is the reason, but he hasn't given me any idea of what is on his mind." She searched for Stephanos's face in the darkness. "Betrothed?"

"We must talk quickly," he squeezed her hand. "Your father told me that we are not to meet alone again. He must be present."

"Oh." Mariam smiled. "That is a good sign."

"But having someone with us will not be the same," Stephanos groaned.

"That is our way."

"But what if he says no—and the betrothal cannot be worked out. I couldn't see you again."

"Don't even think such a thought." Mariam touched his lips with her fingertip. "The Holy One of Israel will be with us."

"But I have so much in my heart that I want to tell you."

The moon's reflection bounced off his black eyes. Mariam could see the outline of his handsome features. Stephanos's nose was slender, and his lips fine like a Greek statue. He stood tall and erect like a sleek athlete. His hands were warm and strong. "We must honor his every wish," Mariam felt the back of his hand. "My abba will seek nothing but the best for us. I'm sure he will talk with me soon. Trust him, Stephanos. My father is a good man."

"I wanted you to know where my heart is."

"I must return." Mariam reluctantly pulled away. "Do not worry. What I can't say with my mouth, I will say with my eyes." Mariam quickly ascended the stone steps. Halfway she stopped. "I will pray for us every day," she called down.

Stephanos waited for what seemed an interminable time before slipping into the crowd. When he finally found the back of her head in the crowd, he watched intensely, hoping she might turn around. Even though one of the apostles was speaking, Stephanos's preoccupation muted his voice. He did not hear the group being cautioned that persecution might lie ahead and that they should not underestimate the intentions of their enemies. The young Greek's mind was clearly elsewhere.

FIFTEEN

Simeon stood fixed before the view of the ancient Holy City that stretched beneath his balcony. Everywhere he looked were remnants of the ancient past. To his left, the granite blocks of the city wall loomed above the Gate of the Potsherds. He could see the slope of the city dropping down to the Pool of Siloe and the other ancient pool that was a watering reservoir. On the other side, he knew their family shop was just below the line of the south wall. Because the weather had become considerably cooler, the noon sun no longer created the haze that almost concealed the farthest corners of the city.

As from time immemorial, merchants moved up and down the streets with their wares on the backs of mules and camels. Nothing distinguished this day from another. Nothing that could be seen. He knew his servant had returned and was waiting for permission to speak; yet he did not turn around.

Simeon watched the street in front of his house wind its way to the main boulevard and then disappear in the maze. The dull brown and the gray-white sameness of the houses and buildings swallowed the path he had followed for so many years to the jewelry shop. Herod's palace with the high towers caught his eye. The towers built to honor his family's victims remained a solemn landmark. Finally Simeon looked again at the south wall, tracing the rest of the way until he fixed on the spot where the little building would be. He tried to bring the details of their studio to mind. He would probably never go inside again. He knew this day would always be different from the rest.

The great Temple caught his eye. Its splendor set against the everlasting hills and mountains that surrounded Yerushalayim always gave pause to his reflections. Avraham had brought Yitzchak for sacrifice at this very place. David commanded the ark be carried to rest within the sacred walls. Down into the valley extended the ancient Jebusite city from which David had built Yerushalayim. Solomon had imported treasures from across the world to give the House of God glory, and when the enemies of Israel had burned it down, the faithful had built it again. So, it would go on until the Messiah himself came to enter the eternal gates.

"*Shema O Israel,*" Simeon said aloud. "The Lord our God is one God."

Simeon turned finally to his servant. "We must do what we must do. You spoke directly to Jarius?"

"Yes, master."

"You told him that I wanted my niece present when we talked?"

"As you directed."

"You were indecisive about the time?"

"I told them to expect an early hour, but warned that you could be delayed."

"Good." Simeon smiled at his employee. "That ploy

will keep them in the house. You emphasized the matter was of utmost urgency?"

"Yes."

"When I leave, you must stay in this house," Simeon extended his arms behind him for the servant to help him with his long outer coat. "If I do not return, stay at least until sunset. Today will not be a good time to be on the streets."

The servant bowed without asking any questions.

Simeon started for the door and then turned back. "Thank you, Nahum. You are a good friend. Perhaps the only one I have left."

"Master!" Nahum squinted. "What are you saying?"

"After today many things will be different. Maybe your loyalty is all that will remain."

"Of course, always." The servant bowed from the waist several times.

Simeon touched the mazusseh fixed on the door jam. He tightened the girdle about his waist, and started slowly down the lane that would take him finally to his brother's house. Never had he walked so slowly.

Stephanos and Philip bounded up the steps leading through the entry gate at the foot of the Temple Mount. Winding their way through the dark passageway that led up from the Jebusite city of David, they brushed past the many pilgrims who had come for the midday rituals. The press of people seemed unusually heavy. Yet, they moved through the group with single-minded determination.

"When we were attacked, the men from the Sanhedrin came out of this tunnel." Stephanos pointed to his left. "Who knows what lurks in the darkness around any corner?" he grinned.

"I think you enjoy danger," Philip chided him. "But being a gaba'im* doesn't exempt us from attack. Shimon warned of trouble."

"Greeks have always danced on the cutting edge of the sword." Stephanos laughed. "Who has more discoveries to proclaim than we do?"

"Surely your ribs must still hurt." Philip slowed down as the endless steps continued upward.

"Well—" Stephanos paused so they could catch their breath—"I wouldn't want to go through another beating today, but there is amazingly little pain left. I was touched by an angel."

"Angel?" Philip puzzled. "You jest."

"A real live angel," Stephanos laughed at Philip, pushing him onward to the entrance to the Temple Mount.

When they reached the top, the two young men stepped into the bright sunlight and covered their eyes. Silently they prayed for guidance and blessing. As usual the business of money changing and selling animals for sacrifices was moving at a brisk pace.

The young Greek led his friend through the Portico of Solomon until he found the exact place where he had previously stood with Yochanan. The flow of traffic had already slowed quick passage into the precincts of the Temple. "I believe I was interrupted." He winked at his friend. "I must finish what I was saying." Stephanos stood on the ledge, feeling the wind blowing at his back. Since the pinnacle of the Temple was one of the highest points in the city, he was balanced on the dangerous edge of the great wall.

"My friends, we have good news for you." The ledge put young Stephanos above the crowd. "Gather around and hear the exciting things that our God is doing. In

*Deacon

these days, signs and wonders confirm our story. HaElyon is fulfilling His covenant with Israel."

A crowd began to gather as Stephanos spoke in his rapid-fire manner. He recognized a fat man with a broken nose and his skinny companion from the Upper Room meetings. Stephanos winked, expressing his delight at their support. Each smiled back. Questions were hurled from the audience,and he pounced on them like a lion does his prey. "Don't be afraid to ask us concerning any matter." He motioned for the crowd to come closer. "We have nothing to hide."

Philip watched as his bold companion thrived and excelled in the exchange and banter. Stephanos never ceased to smile and wasn't offended when occasionally someone jeered. In a short time it looked as if several hundred men of all ages had crowded around them.

"May I introduce Philip." Stephanos gestured for him to stand on the ledge beside him. "What I say is confirmed by witnesses. My friend has seen and heard these matters of which I speak. Two other brothers are here." Stephanos pointed at the fat man and his little friend. "We do not tell idle tales but speak of the very things the prophets foretold. Hear the truth."

The crowd became intensely silent. Philip, too, was spellbound. Before his own eyes, the playful young man seemed to have grown in size as his voice expanded and deepened. Stephanos's jet black eyes were intense as if he were totally locked into the moment. Words, scriptures, and examples leaped from his mouth, hooking into the minds of his audience. His arms swept through the air with majestic gestures that made his message all the more compelling. Youthfulness was replaced by a formidableness that ended interruptions.

"Has not the Holy One, blessed be His name, always surprised us?" Stephanos pointed toward the sky. "Of course, we could not foresee how His Messiah would come. We humans are too limited. We must look at the wondrous healings and miracles of Yeshua to recognize Him. We are his witnesses." He pointed to himself and Philip.

The crowd pressed forward. Here and there an older man would cup his hand to his ear. Then any shuffling ceased, and Philip could sense that men were being persuaded and minds changed. The logic of Stephanos's arguments flowed from one idea to the next, like a spring stream that increased in power as it quickly became a river of thought sweeping away everything in its path. Sometimes Stephanos made his point in Hebrew and then switched to Greek. He punctuated his ideas with sprinklings of Latin. An accomplished scholar seemed to have mounted the acropolis hill of Yerushalayim and was speaking final truths. A gentle breeze swept across their shoulders, carrying the words to the very ends of the outer court. Finally Philip stepped down and into the crowd so that he, too, might observe and listen. Never had he heard such eloquence.

"Now is the hour to decide." Stephanos pounded his fist in his palm. "The hour is late, and the time is short. God has given you this final opportunity. You have all heard of these matters of which I speak. Are not your hearts touched?"

"What shall we do?" someone cried out.

"Yes," another voice demanded. "What is required of us?"

"Repent!" Stephanos hurled his challenge. "Change your minds! Think rightly and correctly, and you will find the path of righteousness. You must repent and be baptized to enter the Kingdom of God."

"Now!" exploded from the far corner of the portico. Philip had barely turned his head when a large group of

Temple guards charged the crowd. The men around him abruptly tumbled Philip, sending the young deacon crashing to the pavement. Several men fell on top of him, and for a second he couldn't catch his breath. Instantly, Philip remembered how the air had been kicked out of him the first time they were attacked. Others fell on the pile and Philip panicked. Barely breathing, he felt as though he were about to be crushed again from the sheer weight of their bodies.

"Get off! Stop it!" he yelled as best he could. Pavement stones tore into his knees and he felt the skin being scraped from his elbows. Someone stepped on his fingers. A sandal ground into his ankle and he cried out in agony. "Get off me!"

Slowly the men unpiled, but Philip found it impossible to move. Pain shot up and down his legs. From above him a hand reached down and helped him to his feet. When he looked up, a guard with a spear was standing where Stephanos had been. "It's happened again!" he agonized.

"Disperse! Now!" The guard brandished his spear in the air. "We will allow no further demonstrations."

The crowd became angry and surly. Someone jeered back at the man. Philip hobbled to the ledge to locate his friend. All he could see was a sea of men pushing and shoving. To his left he caught a glimpse of guards moving back in the direction they had come with someone in the center of the group. Suddenly the end of the guard's spear cracked across the back of his head, sending Philip crumbling on the stones in silence.

Simeon chose the back alleys, walking slowly from street to street. Several times he stopped to watch children playing. He realized how foreign their world was to him. He was four when the Ben Aaron family discovered his unusual abilities with language. Because Simeon had learned to read at such an early age, they had pushed him into studies with the older boys. Simeon remembered how he had devoured the scrolls, reading large sections at a sitting. Even the older boys squirmed on the benches and yearned for recess. Not Simeon! Words, phrases, even the form of language, had endlessly fascinated him. Because he progressed so rapidly, the world of his little peers slipped away before he had touched it.

In time the opportunities to find a wife also recessed. His all-consuming studies displaced any thoughts of having a family of his own. Torah had become his spouse. Disputations with his teachers became his whole way of life. Now the remembrance was painful.

Once Simeon walked through the Ephraim Gate, he turned away from the bend in the road that led past Golgotha. Simeon made sure that he didn't as much as glance in the direction of that place of defilement. Looking toward the Hill of Gareb, he took the northern path toward his place of dread. Because of the solitude his studies demanded, the family had been the only social world Simeon had known as a child. Consequently the death of each aunt, uncle, and worst of all, his parents was a source of staggering anguish. Even the thought of another loss was unbearable. Coming to the family tombs was a difficult obligation. Today seemed to be the worst time of all.

Locking the gate behind him, Simeon found the familiar seat before the stone-sealed cave where the rest of his family slept eternally. Gardeners had done a good job removing the spring weeds. Here and there the lilies of the field dotted the terrain with their bright red splashes of color. Looking at the crypt, Simeon waited for the quietness and solitude to invite the past to come forth again. Quickly memories brought tears to his eyes.

"I have tried to be a good son," he spoke to the foreboding rock that blocked the door to the past. "I have worn my responsibilities like a weight around my neck. Please release me, for I shall break if you do not."

Only the wind answered him.

"We are being destroyed by Romans and fanatics, fear consumes us, and we no longer hope in righteousness. No one listens to me." He sighed deeply.

Silence seemed to mock him.

For a long time he thought of what he must say. In the end, he came back to the same speech he had made to himself many times during the past few days. A way of life was disappearing and there was nothing he could do to stop it. The empty gnawing loneliness was more than he could bear. Finally, he got to his feet and continued on his way to the house of Jarius.

***

Kaifa sat in the chair in his private chambers behind the assembly hall of the Sanhedrin. The high priest shifted nervously and growled at his servant. "Where is Gamaliel?"

Josiah fidgeted with his robe. "We have made sure that a group of his students have engaged him in lively debate. They have been instructed to take the whole afternoon."

"And the other witnesses?"

"They are waiting in the council chambers."

"Good." Kaifa turned to Shaul. "You are ready?"

"Of course." The little man from Tarsus sounded almost cavalier. "I am prepared for any argument they bring. All we must do is elicit blasphemy."

"And if they don't," Josiah added, "I have witnesses who have heard them speak before. They cannot escape our accusations."

A pounding on the door interrupted them. When the servant opened the door, a man rushed in.

"We have him." The man was breathless from running.

"Him?" The high priest frowned. "I thought there were two of them. They always go in pairs."

"Only one was captured." The runner gulped for air.

"Bungling fools!" The priest struck the table. "What happened to the other one?"

Josiah shrugged, and Shaul threw up his hands.

"Can I depend on no one?" The high priest stormed around the room.

"Do not worry," Shaul tried to calm him, "we are prepared to strike throughout the city. All we need is one to bring charges. We will move swiftly."

"We have the young Greek." The runner tried to apologize.

"Ah." Shaul shook his fists in the air. "That is the one I want. We have met before."

"Not one of their twelve?" Kaifa slammed his fist into the table again. "I wanted the fisherman, the ring leader!"

"There was only this young man speaking this morning." The runner squirmed.

"Damn!" the high priest screamed. "Fools!"

"No, no," Shaul insisted. "The Greek is brash and will quickly say the wrong thing. He is an easy prey."

"He made you look like the fool." Kaifa turned on Shaul. "If he does so again, you will pay."

"He had the crowd with him." Shaul backed away. "This time he will not have an unfair advantage."

Kaifa turned to the runner. "When will they be here?"

"Shortly, quickly." The messenger kept shaking his head.

"Then let us go to the council chambers now." Kaifa stomped to the door as the men quickly followed him.

"And Simeon Ben Aaron." The priest stopped in the doorway. "Where is he?"

"He knows nothing of the meeting," Josiah mumbled, "and besides, you warned him."

"He had best not show." Kaifa turned to Shaul. "But if he is so foolish as to oppose us, you are to strike the house of Jarius first. If not, go to their special meeting place. Understand?"

Shaul nodded his head.

"Now, let us go and be about God's business." The high priest walked quickly down the hall.

SIXTEEN

Mariam wrung her hands and shuddered. "Something oppressive hangs over us—worse than the summer heat."

"I feel nothing." Jarius looked around the open patio in the center of their house. "The noonday heat is always unbearable during this time of the year."

She uncharacteristically pushed her father. "For days there has been a cloud over you. Your face has been drawn. There is heaviness in your every word."

"I suppose so." Jarius took her hand as he walked toward a bench under the eaves.

"When I tried to pray this morning, something ominous moved in my soul. Be forthright, father. Tell me what is happening. Why is Simeon coming to see us?"

"The world is changing too fast." Jarius threw up his hands. "First it was Simeon, and then it was Stephanos."

"Stephanos?" Mariam tried to look innocent as she sat down. "What did he say?" She pulled her father down beside her.

"Say?" Jarius cocked his head and looked at her from the corner of his eye.

"You sound as if he said something unusual to you."

"He came seeking to be betrothed." Jarius settled back and measured this daughter whom he loved more than life itself. She had even become the son he would never have. Surely her happiness was more important to him than anything else in the world.

"You have had unusual contact with the young man," Jarius drawled slowly. "Maybe that has been good, maybe not."

"We have only sought to understand the great things that God has done in these last days."

"And the young Greek is most impressive," Jarius continued as if he were talking to himself. "But who knows what lies ahead? These are explosive times. Nothing is settled. Nothing is stable."

"But Eve was made for Adam," Mariam answered instantly.

"You've thought on this matter," Jarius probed.

"Every girl thinks on these matters." Mariam danced away.

"You are so young," the father muttered.

"Come now," Mariam scolded him. "Girls much younger than I have been betrothed for years."

"But they were promised to men who were older—who had money."

"Money?" Mariam frowned again. "In light of what Yeshua has taught us about the Kingdom of God, how can we speak of money in such a matter as this? The issue is God's will."

A smile broke over Jarius's face. "You are taken with our new gaba'im. Something has already stirred in your heart," he chided her.

Mariam's face flushed and filled with color. She

turned away as if suddenly preoccupied with a distraction behind her, but there was no basket of fruit, no piece of sewing to offer her an excuse.

"My child," Jarius beckoned to her. "Come here. Do you think your father cannot see? Yes, I was taken by surprise when Stephanos came, but I have paid attention since. There is much between you."

Mariam extended her hand and looked gently in her father's eyes. "Stephanos is the only boy—the only man—I have ever talked to. But I have looked into his soul and found only goodness there. Sometimes he is like a mischievous little boy, and then when he speaks, he becomes a mighty warrior with words. He truly loves the Holy One with all of his heart, mind, and soul. What more could I want in a husband?"

Jarius tried to fight back the knot that was forming in his throat. He blinked hard. "I suppose this day was inevitable, but it has come so quickly. What am I to say? How could I deny your heart's desire? If this is your wish, then the matter is settled."

"Oh, Abba." Mariam hugged his neck. "Stephanos will be a wonderful, wonderful husband."

"Now, now," Jarius cautioned, "there is much to be discussed. He must be able to support you. There are business matters to be resolved, and there are proprieties that must be observed."

"You are the best father who ever lived!" Mariam kissed his cheek.

The council room was packed when Yehosaf Ben Kaifa finally entered and took his seat on the platform. The noon day heat was oppressive, making the members even more irritable. The prisoner stood between two guards. Ben Kaifa's eyes darted around the room, assessing the composite of the assembly. The rows of benches and desks were full. Annias had already taken his seat against the wall. He listened momentarily to the scribe continuing to read the list of charges. Then the high priest turned his attention to the Greek.

The appearance of the young man did not please him. Ben Kaifa would have preferred one of the Gallileans who had been a personal follower of the Nazarene rabbi for several years. This foreign youth was too easy a prey. The burly Temple guards who surrounded him made the Greek look even smaller.

"And how do you answer?" Asa, the scribe, lowered his scroll.

"I am innocent and falsely charged." The young man smiled at the Sanhedrin.

He isn't even astute enough to be afraid, the high priest thought to himself. *Shaul was right. He will fall quickly.*

"Indeed!" Asa, from the Synagogue of the Freedmen, stood. "I am a scribe who makes special note of such matters. I have listened as he and the others stirred up trouble in the Temple precincts."

"And what was said?" the interrogator asked.

"Blasphemy!" Asa pointed his finger at Stephanos. "He preaches against Moshe and defames our God. He preaches that Rabbi Yeshua was a divine messiah. He leads the people astray. He has broken the Commandments!"

"Come now," Stephanos began when the scribe stopped to catch his breath. "Never have any of us detracted from the Law. Yeshua himself said that not one dot or comma was to be removed until all was fulfilled. Before you I swear allegiance to all that our father Moshe spoke to us."

"Silence!" The council scribe stomped his foot. "You are not to interrupt."

"Am I not allowed to speak?" Stephanos pulled away

from the guard holding him. "Is this the way you treat your brothers?" He held his bound hands in the air. "Even in the pagan city of Athens where we have many debates over the writings of vile men, we respect difference of opinion. Would you treat one who debates over the Law as a criminal?" He walked before the Council, extending his arms in the air.

"Stop him," the interrogator ordered the guard.

"No, untie him," a white-bearded member of the Council broke in. "We are not a Roman tribunal. Such behavior on our part is unseemly."

Yehosaf Ben Kaifa stirred uncomfortably. He had misjudged the young man who was quickly playing on their sympathy. It was more than brashness. The young Greek truly was not afraid.

"Cut the ropes," he commanded his servant. "Give him space."

"Do not be deceived," a Sadducee rose to speak. "These men are constantly disrupting Temple worship, and they spread confusion. They claim new visions and novel ways we haven't known before. The guards have only been prudent. Who knows? Maybe these followers of the Way are insane."

"Mad?" Stephanos laughed. "Look at me. Are my eyes glazed? Do I babble? I came to your city seeking truth and the things of God. Is that the act of a crazy person? What I have found has given me supreme joy. Come now. Where there is pain and brokenness, the People of the Way have left happiness. Have not the lame been made to walk?"

"Exactly!" Shaul charged from his chair. "Moshe himself warned us of deceivers who perform magic and miracles. Remember the Law's warning, 'If a prophet arises and gives you a sign or wonder, and if he says, let us go after other gods, he shall be put to death.' Like

Dathan and Korah, these men lead our people astray."

Shouts erupted from the chamber and angry men shook their fists. Pandemonium broke out across the room.

"Silence! Silence!" The scribal interrogator kept motioning for the group to be quiet. "Order, order!" he clapped his hands together.

"Hear me!" Stephanos suddenly shouted above the confusion. "*Shema Israel, adoni eloheuni adoni echod.* I believe our God is one."

His sudden affirmation of the Shema shocked the Council and they subsided. Then once more the shouting began.

He is taking control. Ben Kaifa's eyes narrowed to slits as he thought. *He is much more dangerous than I thought.*

Yehosaf Ben Kaifa's cunning instincts had obtained a wife for him from the family of Annias and propelled him into the highest office in Israel. His intuition warned him that possibly no one in the Council was a match for the young orator from Greece. Fear tugged at his mind. *We must not be defeated again,* he thought.

He rose to his feet and stood until the entire room was quiet. "You will follow the rules of order," he commanded. "Young man, you will have ample opportunity to answer after the charges are stated, but you will be silent until then. If you interrupt, I will have you held on trial." Slowly Ben Kaifa sat down, satisfied he was now back in charge. "Continue, brother Shaul, with your statement."

"Moshe is clear. The Law is precise. When false prophets lead the people astray, they shall be put to death. This 'Yeshua' was not content only to declare himself to be the Messiah. He made himself on a level with HaElyon. These fanatics who stole his body now teach that Yeshua is still alive. Have any of you seen him?" Shaul suddenly shouted.

"No! No!" the chamber echoed back.

"Indeed!" Shaul pointed at Stephanos. "This man makes a dead rabbi into a God! These followers of Yeshua destroy our customs. I call for the death of this man and all who are like him."

An eerie quietness settled over the Council. The intent of the gathering had become obvious. Months before they had gathered at night to hear similar charges against the Rabbi Yeshua and what followed had torn the city apart. They had already chosen a road that was becoming increasingly familiar. Men settled back in their chairs, staring at the walls.

"This stranger's particular beliefs are not as important," Shaul shook his fist at Stephanos, "as is the fact that he leads people astray. His group undercuts your authority. We caught him preaching in the Temple compound. In the end they will destroy the Sanhedrin itself." As he looked around the room, Shaul knew he had finally found an argument that couldn't be resisted. "We only seek God's will," he concluded.

Perhaps, I have misjudged Shaul, Ben Kaifa thought to himself. *How could any of the Council reject his arguments? Virtually every man has expressed fear of losing control of the people. Shaul has given them a legitimate legal reason for a severe judgment. The stage is set.*

When Shaul sat down, the witnesses began. One after another they accused.

"As did Yeshua, these men violate the Sabbath! I heard it with my ears!" a small skinny man declared.

"Yeshua had no respect for the Temple. The prisoner is no different. This man created a riot in the holy place today. I saw him incite and inflame pious worshipers," Asa, the scribe, spoke from his place in the assembly.

"I, myself," Josiah strutted back and forth before the council, "heard this Greek preach blasphemy. Our brother Shaul certainly does not overstate the seriousness of these matters. We must act." Council members nodded as if agreement was a foregone conclusion.

"Now," the high priest turned to the young Greek, "your time has come. Are these charges true?"

For several moments Stephanos didn't speak. Then slowly he turned to the high priest and smiled. His demeanor was unnerving and haunting. No animosity, anger, bitterness. He simply smiled.

"I count it all honor to speak of the Messiah." Stephanos turned to Shaul and looked compassionately at him before he continued. The man from Tarsus looked away.

"Brethren and fathers, hear me. The God of Glory appeared to our father Abraham," Stephanos paced slowly before the Council, recounting the history of Israel. Carefully he retold the ancient story of their past. "And so Abraham became the father of Isaac and circumcised him on the eighth day." His words came quickly, crisply, and melodiously.

In spite of themselves, the Council was forced to listen. His eloquence increased as he continued. Strangely, Stephanos not only maintained his composure but kept smiling. The Sanhedrin members did not seem to be able to look him in the eye.

"Moshe received living oracles to give to us," Stephanos beamed, "but our fathers refused to obey him, and thrust him aside." Stephanos stopped before Asa, but the scribe looked down.

Where is he going with all this? Kaifa crossed his arms. *Who could disagree with what he has said? Unless he gives us better excuse to attack, this debate could go on all day. Surely he is not going to try and put us on trial. He doesn't even seem angry.*

"The issue is not the sanctity of our God nor of His Law," Stephanos concluded. "The question is one of His Messiah and the perpetual blindness of our leaders, of *your* blindness." He continued smiling.

Their eyes returned to his as each man remained totally attentive. Kaifa stroked his chin and pulled at his beard. The silence was deafening.

"You stiff-necked people, uncircumcised in heart and ears, you always resist the Holy Spirit." He pointed at the Council and then at Shaul. "As your fathers did, so do you. Which of the prophets did not your fathers persecute?" Finally he pointed at the high priest. "And they killed those who announced beforehand the coming of the Righteous One, whom you have now betrayed and murdered."

Yehosaf Ben Kaifa leaped from his chair and tore at his elaborately embroidered robe. "Enough! We have heard more than enough."

"He blasphemes!" the scribe from the Synagogue of Freedmen screamed.

"The death penalty!" Shaul demanded. "He, himself, calls for the death penalty!"

Stephanos threw his head back and looked toward the ceiling. "Behold, I see the heaven opened, and the Son of Man standing at the right hand of God."

Ben Kaifa had been waiting for such words. Immediately he leaped to his feet and tore off his outer robe. Other Council members had been waiting for his signal. They, too, flung their robes aside. Hand-picked lackeys leaped to their feet and pushed their chairs aside. The chamber was being stampeded into violence.

"No more!" the high priest demanded. "I will hear no more. What is your verdict?"

"Kill him!" they screamed.

"Away with him!" Council members rushed toward

the young Greek. "Take him away!" The crowd surged forward, sweeping Stephanos toward the door.

"Stone him!" someone screamed. "Stone him!"

Simeon followed the servant down the long hall into Jarius's family gathering room. The dimness of the hall offered a cool tunnel out of the sweltering summer furnace. Thick adobe halls made an excellent insulation against the dry heat. The servant pulled back the thick curtain allowing Simeon to enter first. Mariam stood in front of the empty little fireplace in the corner of the room, while Jarius stood stiffly rubbing his hands together.

"Sit down, my brother." Jarius offered the best chair in the large living room. "It is good to see you." His casualness sounded forced. "I am sorry it is so hot today. The noonday heat is always a problem."

"Uncle!" Mariam hugged his neck. "I have missed you."

Simeon stiffened, and his response was wooden. He shuffled to the chair and sat rigidly. "Perhaps we should get to the point," he blurted.

"A little libation will cool us." Jarius offered a finely painted amphora. "I have found a fine Greek wine that I save for special occasions. Possibly—"

"No," Simeon shook his head. "Since we have much to say, I want to begin immediately. Have you told Mariam that we are dividing the business?"

"Breaking up the family business?" Mariam put her hand to her mouth. "Oh, no!"

"I had hoped that—" Jarius gestured aimlessly. "Well, there is still hope—"

"No." Simeon steeled himself. "My mind is made up. The brothers Ben Aaron are finished."

"Why?" Mariam pleaded. "Surely there is another way."

"The House of Israel is being divided by the way you have chosen," Simeon lectured her. "I can no longer stand by and watch what is surely going to happen to you."

"What is he saying, Father?"

"Yes, Simeon. Tell us clearly what you mean."

"Zeda's death was not warning enough?" Simeon rolled his eyes. "What more can be said?"

"Zeda was killed by Zealots." Jarius shook his head. "He was caught up in tragic circumstances. You are as vulnerable as we are to such outbreaks."

"Listen to me." Simeon's demeanor broke. "Fanaticism grips our land. The Zealots are only a symptom. Terror is the cause. Fear has replaced rationality."

"Even as we speak, terror is breaking loose in the streets. You are safe this afternoon only because I have struck a bargain, which is the last one I can make." Simeon smashed his fist into his palm. "I am isolated. Used up. No more!"

"What is going on?" Jarius pulled his chair forward. "You are not telling us all you know."

"I have already said too much." Simeon ran his hand through his hair. "You must go your way and I mine."

"Uncle," Mariam bit her lip, "please tell us what is going on."

"Do not leave this house," he said emphatically. "By tonight the moon will have turned to blood. There will be no place to hide from the men who believe they have a divine call to cleanse the House of Israel by force."

"The Romans will never stand for an uprising." Jarius tossed his brother's comments aside. "They will restore order."

"Order? What good was order to Zeda?" Simeon's

voice again became hard and controlled. "Yes, things are orderly in our family tomb. Order after the fact is of little value."

"This morning—" Mariam looked toward the window. "I was almost swallowed by a terrible ominous feeling that welled up in my soul. The pain left when—" she smiled feebly. "Father, might we tell Simeon our good news?"

"I don't think so," Jarius sighed. "Now is not the time." He stood up. "You have always known more than you told us and today you surround us with a mystery again. If our friends are hurt while we escape, do you not think that fact will be a burden for us to bear. No, my brother, we want no advantages."

"Then be ungrateful!" Simeon bolted from his chair. "Keep what is in the shop. As of this afternoon our connections are broken." He marched toward the door. "I have fulfilled my responsibilities. I dust off my sandals." Simeon did not look back or close the door behind him.

"He had to be angry." Jarius rubbed his forehead. "Simeon could not complete this deed until he found a reason that inflamed his passions. The break is final." Jarius slumped into his chair. "Call one of the young servants who can run much faster than we can. Dispatch him to the Upper Room immediately. Tell them to leave. Simeon has given us a signal. We don't have much time left."

"Perhaps I should warn—"

"No, Mariam, do not leave the house. Simeon may have paid a high price to warn us. We must heed his advice. He knows much more than he is telling us."

———————————————

The wind suddenly swirled down the dirt highway spraying the crowd of men with grit. Travel on the well-used road had stopped when the attack began. A few people now pushed on, keeping a considerable distance from the assault. Heavy outcroppings of limestone and gypsum provided a sordid selection of stones. The rocky terrain allowed only the scrubbiest of bushes to survive. On the far side, the Roman's stark hill for execution with its skull-like countenance leered down at the executioners. Far off in the distance a few soldiers stood on the high walls of the city, casually looking down. They could not have missed seeing what had transpired.

Shaul slowly handed their outer coats back. The afternoon heat had subsided somewhat. Each man took his flowing robe without saying a word. Their frenzied enthusiasm had turned to cold soberness. Here and there men stole back into the city.

"He did not cry out." Asa puzzled and looked away. "I don't understand."

"Fanaticism changes people." Shaul sounded defensive. "We must be strong and not be swayed by our emotions."

"He seemed almost serene." The scribe's face twisted. "I did not expect such behavior. I had thought he would resist—fight—"

A blast of cool evening wind caught the dirt along the side of the road and hurled the grit in their faces. Each man covered his face and shielded his eyes.

"I feel dirty." An older man brushed the dust from his turban. "Very—dirty."

"Do we just leave him?" One of the young men looked bewildered and confused. "Shouldn't someone—do something?"

"We must leave," Shaul spoke too loudly. He began to move quickly and nervously. "The Romans may happen onto us and want explanations." He pulled his own outer garment on and wrapped it close to his body. "Throughout the city our people have begun cleansing the city of this pest. We must join them immediately."

"Moshe commanded death—" the older man kept reminding each person who remained. "The Law called for death. Didn't it? Well, didn't it?"

When Shaul looked about him again, the crowd had almost completely dispersed. The remaining council members hurried toward the city gate. He felt a sudden impulse to run as well. But he stopped to look back.

The necessity to be the backbone of the conspiracy was gone. Whatever point he had to make that day blurred in his mind. All he could see was the crumbled figure that lay sprawled in the ditch. The shower of stones that had avalanched on him still dotted the length of his body. As if drawn by a magnet, Shaul inched forward.

Not once had he looked. Holding their garments had been a carefully planned strategy to avoid having to throw even one stone. No one realized that Shaul had turned away when the mob had begun their pelting. He already knew that he would never forget the black piercing eyes, the countenance that wouldn't break, the smile. Shaul tiptoed, trying to peer into the ditch without getting any closer. Only then did he realize that the face was turned upward toward the sky. The sight jolted Shaul to the core of his soul.

Nothing had broken the young Greek's composure.

SEVENTEEN

No one noticed the fifteen men as they hurried down the main boulevard that led toward Mount Zion. All talking ceased when the group turned into the narrow side street. The small band slipped along the alley walls, silently following the two dirty beggars who pointed out the direction. To their surprise, they found the neighborhood was also unusually quiet. The children had disappeared from the streets. Falling into single file, the men edged their way along the buildings. The lengthening shadows offered little assistance to their efforts to stay concealed.

"That's the place," the large fat man with the flat nose whispered. He pointed up the stairs to the Upper Room. "Their leaders will be holed up inside."

"Should we light some torches?" the little man beside him asked someone behind them. "Night's going to fall fairly soon."

"No, no." A temple guard pushed both men aside. "You're bungling everything. Fire will signal that we're coming. Don't spoil the surprise."

"But they may hide in a closet or escape through a dark passageway," the obese man protested.

"Five of you go to the other side of the building." The guard ignored the fat man and instead motioned to his compatriots. "Make sure there aren't other stairs down. Do it quickly. We will charge the door immediately."

"Can we break the door down?" the skinny little man peered up the plain stucco wall to the landing in front of the door.

"Of course," the guard brushed him off. "You said the door is secured only by a single piece of wood." The guard pushed the fat man up the stairs. "Hit the door first and we'll be right behind you."

"Now wait," the large man balked. "There might be—"

"Get on with it." The guard shoved him. "You had your choice of the stoning or the assault. Now move!"

"What if they pile furniture against the door?" The smaller man hung back.

"Stop stalling." The guard waved the three men standing behind him forward. "Both of you have been paid enough. Faster!"

Stairs creaked as the band charged forward. Although the fat man hit the door hard, he only bounced back into the men who piled up behind him, nearly knocking the last man back down the stairs.

"Fools!" a lone man at the bottom of the stairs chided them. "A single wooden bar?" The fat man grabbed his shoulder. "Someone must have changed the barrier. I think I broke a bone."

"Hurry up," the guard hissed. "They'll arm themselves. Break the door down!"

When the group threw their weight once more into the heavy planks, a crackling, splitting noise rewarded their efforts. Their final heave against the door sent it crashing into the wall. The temple guardsman drew his sword and rushed into the huge room. Quickly the little man picked up a piece of the splintered door brace and began swinging in all directions. The others had to duck as they scattered across the room.

"Where are they?" A guard jabbed his blade at the shadows in the corner. The hanging candle rack swung back and forth in the large empty room. Even the central table had been removed.

"Someone's coming up the stairs over there!" One of the men pointed to the inner staircase in the center of the room.

"No one's down there." The first man in the second group of soldiers bounded up the stairs. The rest of their group followed him. "The whole house is empty."

"It can't be!" The guard stomped his foot. "We were told that they gather here every evening. Are you sure?"

"Didn't you notice?" The last man came up the inside stairs. "Even the streets were empty. They were expecting us. The whole neighborhood cleared out."

"Damn!" The guard charged through the outside door and down the steps. "No one is here," he called to a man who had stayed next to the wall.

Josiah, the servant of the high priest, stepped forward. "Someone warned them. They have to be hiding somewhere in the area." He began pacing. "Go back to the compound and get all the guards you can. I'll go on with these men. Turn the city upside down! Strike down everyone who gets in your way." Josiah beckoned the guard to come down. "And get rid of those two fools who led us up this blind alley."

"Strange, very strange," the fat man emerged in the doorway muttering. The rest of the group pushed past him, clomping down the stairs. "They can't be far away—" his voice trailed away.

"Listen carefully," Josiah spoke rapidly. "Move on to the other places where they may be hiding. Give us more names," he demanded of the fat man and his friend. "Shaul and the others will sweep through the south edge of the city. Who else is in the area?"

"A brother of the rabbi Yeshua named Yaakov lives up there," the frail little man pointed up the street. "I can lead you. And there are several homes we can sack along the way."

"And do you know of other possibilities?" The priest's servant growled at the large man.

"Some of the apostles might have gone to the Ben Aaron house," he mumbled. "Perhaps—"

"No!" Josiah cut him off. "Leave them alone."

"But," the man rubbed his flat, twisted nose, "I think—"

"No one asked you to think," the priest's servant poked him in the chest. "If anyone touches that family, I will hold you personally accountable. Understand?"

"Sure, sure."

"On to the house of this Yaakov!" Josiah shook his fist. "Strike those who resist. Arrest the rest."

Immediately the band fell in behind the little man. Josiah walked behind the group, keeping in the ever-deepening shadows. Behind them the broken door to the Upper Room swung awkwardly in the increasing wind. Sounds of patting sandals pounding on stones faded away, leaving the neighborhood in uncharacteristic silence.

Across town a Roman soldier walked briskly down a long stone corridor inside the Antonio Fortress. Flickering light from torches danced along the walls of the forbidding passageway. At each turn soldiers with spears stood at attention. Other than the scavenging of usual stray dogs, there was little activity. Night had settled over the occupiers.

When the young soldier rapped hard on the chamber door, the response came quickly. A commanding voice bid him enter. Shutting the door behind him, the soldier stood stiffly at attention, his eyes fixed straight ahead. Nevertheless, he could see that the centurion was studying a Greek manuscript lying on the desk in front of him.

"What is it, soldier?"

"Problems in the city, sir."

"What?" The graying distinguished centurion looked up for the first time. "What do you mean?"

"Bands of men are reported running through the streets breaking into homes."

"Zealots?" Honorius stood up.

"I don't think so," the soldier stared straight ahead. "At least the situation seems to be different."

"How?" The centurion shifted his weight uneasily from foot to foot.

"Temple guards have been observed leading attacks. Prominent Jewish leaders are taking part."

"At ease." Honorius crossed his arms. "Who are they attacking?"

"Strange," the soldier began talking directly to his leader. "Houses seem to be selected at random. Most of the people are just ordinary folk. There doesn't seem to be a pattern other than the fact that the Temple guards are taking some prisoners."

"Prisoners? They have no right to act outside of the precincts of the Temple!"

"Certainly," the young man shrugged, "but the reports tell us that they are striking all over the city."

"Anything else?"

"Apparently they put a young man to death outside the Ephraim Gate. Stoned him!"

"I think I understand," Honorius said slowly. "Any reports from our informants inside the Great Sanhedrin recently?"

"We have not heard from the spies in some time. At least there's been no recent alarms."

"What about the fat man?" Honorius began slowly, walking about the room with his hands behind his back. "You know—the one with the broken nose. He always has some tidbit that a few shekels can pry from his mouth."

"He seems to have disappeared."

"Yes." Honorius rubbed his chin, "I suspect the caldron has finally boiled over." Honorius reached for his leather breastplate. "And we may well be too late. Possibly the Jews have started their own religious war." Honorius clapped his hands and pointed to the door. "Send men into the streets to restore order. Find out if the Sanhedrin is behind this and get a report to the Procounsel immediately. Have a dozen soldiers ready to go with me into the city at once. Quickly."

Before the soldier could leave the room, Honorius was strapping on his sword. He quickly shut the door behind him, jogging to the room where the armor and helmets were kept. He emerged with a bronze battle chest shield in place and a cloak fastened to his shoulder. A contingent of men were waiting for him in the courtyard. He briefed them on what might be ahead as he led the soldiers into the city.

Honorius said little as they marched double-time, though he periodically spoke to the man next to him. "Double-crossed," he mumbled. "We have been double-crossed at the crucial moment. There's just no other explanation for the lack of warning. Hope my friends are—" He said no more, but picked up the pace. "Up this street." He waved to his men. "We will stop at this house first. Mind your manners. These are prominent citizens."

A soldier knocked on the door of the house of Jarius Ben Aaron several times but got no response. Honorius stepped forward and pounded harder. Finally several of the soldiers called out. Nothing happened.

Honorius put his mouth to a crack in one of the door timbers, cupped his mouth, and yelled loudly. "Do not be afraid. It is Honorius. The soldiers are here to protect you."

"Honorius?" a familiar voice answered. "Is it really you?"

"Time is of the essence," the centurion replied. "Let us in!"

The safety bar clanked to the floor with a heavy thud. The door slowly opened. A figure was silhouetted against the blackness. He bid them enter.

"Stay here." Honorius stationed the men by the door. "I will return."

"Follow me," Jarius said, leading him down the hallway.

"We have received reports of attacks throughout the city," the centurion continued. "Your friends are in trouble."

"You are truly a brother," Jarius said over his shoulder, "and a wise man. Yes, an attack is under way."

"I am concerned that the Twelve will be in great danger. The Sanhedrin knows all about the Upper Room."

"The Holy One has blessed us," Jarius assured him. Jarius opened the curtain at the end of the hall, "Let me show you something."

Seated around the room were over twenty people.

"Peace," Shimon Kefa greeted him.

"You're safe!" the centurion exclaimed. "You're all here!"

"No weapon formed against us shall prosper." The apostle looked around the room. "We have no fear."

"Amazing!" Honorius relaxed. "But others may not have fared as well. We will move quickly to put an end to their campaign of terror, but we know that one man has been killed."

"Who?" Jarius implored.

"I don't know, but we understand he was left beyond the Ephraim Gate."

"We will send men to find the body." Shimon looked carefully around the room at several young men.

"You must be careful."

"Don't worry. We will be cautious, but we cannot but observe all the customs of the Law. Whoever our brother is, he must be honored. The body must be prepared."

"Be very alert. I will send one soldier with you to grant passage through the gate at night. Unfortunately, I may need all the rest of my men before sunrise. I would suggest that your leaders stay hidden until the storm passes." Turning toward the entry, Honorius paused. "Trust no one."

———————————— • ————————————

Simeon, too, tried to hide in the blackness of the cold night as he watched the entryway to the prison. Although the temple guards came and went at a fast pace, time dragged by. He pulled the hood of his cloak over his head when the winds picked up. Stench from the depths of the prison floated up and made him feel slightly nauseous. Everything about the dungeon made Simeon feel disgusted and wore on him as the night lengthened.

Simeon was also repulsed by the realization that he

was spying. If any group in Israel was to be trusted, it should be the religious leaders. Now he knew the depth of their deceptiveness. The benevolence of Simeon's own intentions had been betrayed again and again by those who sat on the priestly throne.

Simeon mused that the religious enemies who had converted his own family were the only predictable and trustworthy group in the country. The more Simeon felt aversion to what he was doing, the more isolated he felt.

At first the sound was so slight, Simeon almost didn't hear it. Then the muffled sound of many feet trudging up the pavement became unavoidable. Flickering torches preceded the small army that dragged up the boulevard toward the prison. As they came closer, Simeon could see that children were clinging to their parents. Women were weeping, but no talking was allowed. The first wave of men who passed Simeon were chained together. A quick estimate suggested at least fifty people were being herded into the prison. Simeon studied every face that passed him.

Crouching behind a column, Simeon hid as the temple guards funneled the remainder of the people through the large iron gates. Most of the captives were inside before he saw a man he recognized. "Josiah!" Simeon stepped forward. "I want to talk to you."

The servant of the high priest spun around. "Who dares call me?" His voice was strained.

"Over here," Simeon demanded.

Josiah grabbed a torch from one of the guards and thrust it toward the shadows. "Who are you?"

"Simeon," he said flatly.

"What are you doing here?" Josiah sneered.

"Observing."

Before Josiah could reply, another crowd of prisoners emerged from a different street. They were much louder, hurling their protests at the guards. In turn, the guards threatened and warned.

"Fools!" Josiah stomped toward the group. "Shut them up," he commanded the lead guard. "We want silence. Get them inside."

"You were to act as quietly as possible," Josiah confronted one of the leaders near the front. "This is not a circus."

When the man stepped out of the march, Simeon recognized Shaul. At once Simeon joined both men while he continued watching each face that passed him.

"We have done well," Shaul began. "I have captured many of their leaders. The night has been well spent."

"People have been hurt?" Simeon's eyes narrowed.

"We are most humane," Josiah scowled. "Better than they deserve."

"Only those that resisted," Shaul shrugged.

"Many struggled?" Simeon probed.

"Surprisingly not." Shaul watched the last of the group disappear inside the prison. "This new religion seems to make people remarkably docile. Rather gentle."

"And the Ben Aaron family?" Simeon's voice was low and intense. "Have they been troubled this night?"

"Of course not," the high priest's servant snapped. "Those were my orders."

"I trust so." Simeon turned away. "Others are coming. More prisoners?"

"Certainly," Shaul beamed. "I am very thorough."

Simeon turned back to where he had been standing.

"Where are you going?" Josiah called after him.

"I will be watching," he answered without looking back. "I will be observing." Simeon merged back into the black corner behind the column.

Josiah and Shaul exchanged a troubled glance and

then hurried inside the prison, trying to ignore the silent sentinel who scrutinized their efforts.

"I knew this hour would come." Jarius looked around his living room. Many of the group were asleep huddled under blankets. "So many came to us—it was inevitable."

"I suppose." Toma leaned back against the wall. "For weeks we have seen the signs. I fear for our families with children. I hope the young men have found the brother lying outside the gate."

Jarius stared at Mariam cuddled up along the opposite wall, sound asleep. Rather than staying in her room, she had chosen to sleep with the believers.

"God will grant the fallen one a special place in our memory," Mattiyahu answered from the corner. "I only pray his death was not prolonged."

"I am sure many of our people will flee the city." Shimon Kefa stared into the embers in the fireplace. "Some will seek refuge in Galilee, but in time the persecution will pass."

"For the time being, we have the protection of our friend, Honorius." Jarius walked back and forth. "I am sure order will be restored quickly, and possibly the Sanhedrin will be prevented from carrying out such raids in the future."

"I am not sure what to make of these attacks." Mattiyahu shook his head. "I had expected the throne of David to be restored quickly. Pieces of the puzzle still don't fit together."

"Perhaps," Toma said slowly, "he is going to return suddenly in the midst of this confusion and vindicate us. Maybe he will bring the fallen one with him."

"No," a small voice spoke from the corner of the room. "I don't think so. His victory will be the triumph of love."

"Mariam!" Jarius turned to his daughter. "I thought you were asleep."

"I had the strangest dream." She sat up, rubbing her eyes. "I saw a great sword sweeping through the air, cutting people down on all sides. And then a bleeding hand reached out in front of the blade. The sword slashed again and again, opening deep wounds, but every time it struck the hand, a piece of the blade broke off. The wounds were more powerful than the steel. Finally I heard a voice say, 'The victory is in my hands.' Then I woke up."

"H—um—m." Shimon Kefa inched his way toward the young woman. "What do you mean, 'the triumph of love'?"

"I don't know." Mariam shook her head. "The words just came to mind."

"Surely the Radach Ha Kodesh has made you a prophetess," Shimon spoke softly to keep from waking anyone. "Can you tell us more about the dream?"

Mariam shrugged her shoulders.

Shimon Kefa spoke to Mariam. "Could you not have seen the wounds of the Messiah?" Shimon narrowed his eyes. "Remember?" He began to quote, "'He was wounded for our transgressions and with his stripes we are healed.' Was not Isaiah writing that the Messiah would redeem through his pain? Yes, yes and it shall continue to be so."

"Amazing." Mattiyahu rubbed his beard. "A prophesy of victory fulfilled through defeat. We must ponder such an irony."

"Yes, yes." Toma sat up excitedly on his knees. "Did

not our rabbi teach us this principle? The least would become the most. The Kingdom comes to those who mourn—through their pain, the world is redeemed."

"Is this city not controlled by the Sanhedrin?" Jarius's eyes widened. "Are we not the most powerless of all? And yet tonight we are pursued because they fear us."

"In some way that I can't fully explain—in His death, we died," Shimon Kefa said to the little group. "No longer are we tied to the bondage of fear."

"Could it be," Jarius mused, "we are the only free men in the city?"

Sounds of a door hinge creaking interrupted the conversation. The entryway curtain flew open.

"Men are at the door," a servant interrupted them. "The young men you sent out have come back. They have returned with—" He stopped and looked at Mariam. "With—with the body of the one who was killed."

EIGHTEEN

Mariam took the little jewelry box from its hiding place and set it on her bed. She opened the lid and looked at the necklace for a long time before picking it up. Her fingers gently traced the contour of the large pearl in the center.

"I don't wear you anymore," Mariam said aloud, "except in mourning. My connection to life—you have become my attachment to death." She slowly lifted the pendant to her neck, tying the string in back. Tears ran down her cheeks.

Mariam adjusted her long black dress, trying to smooth out the wrinkles, only to sink back on the bed with her face buried in her hands. For a long time the morning sunlight poured in on her huddled, motionless figure. Silence was broken by an occasional sob or moan. Twice the muffled sounds of sandals padding down the hall slipped through the door, but nothing broke the pain and ominous silence that had seeped into the very texture of the walls. Emptiness filled the room.

The tomblike quietness felt like the abyss from which none escape and into which all perish. As if to defend herself, Mariam drew herself into a smaller and smaller ball, gently rocking back and forth.

"Daughter?" Jarius's kind voice called. "Are you there?" Twice more he called.

"Yes," she finally said hesitantly.

"Shimon Kefa is here. There are final details to be discussed."

"I am coming," she said slowly, struggling to get up from the bed. "Just a moment."

Mariam blinked her eyes. The previous night was a strangely distorted dream, both real and an extension of madness. Her lack of sleep could not blur the memory of the men coming through the door with a body wrapped in a sheet. Each recollection sent her reeling backward into the oblivion that kept swallowing her thoughts. In front, Philip and Timon stood holding one corner of the sheet. Parmenas and Nicholas were in back with the shrouded limp form hanging between them. Nowhere in the circle of faces was the one countenance she most sought. Instantly Mariam knew what she had refused to consider. Vaguely she remembered everything in the room fading, going white. When she awoke in her bedroom, a servant was placing a cold towel on her head.

Now Mariam had to fight each pulsating thought in order to make herself take one slow step after another toward the door.

"Coming." She reached for the latch.

"I'm sorry to disturb you." Jarius's face looked old and drawn. "Unfortunately there has been a change of plans that we must discuss."

Mariam nodded mechanically and followed her father down the hall.

Shimon Kefa turned when they entered the living room. He put his arms around her shoulders. "Your father told us about the plans for betrothal and how close you had become." He hugged Mariam. "My heart is very, very heavy."

"Thank you," Mariam mumbled.

"Since none of Stephanos's family is here, the Twelve felt you should sit in their place." Shimon led her to a chair. "I will announce that you were betrothed if you would like."

"Oh—please do," Mariam squeezed his hand. "Please do."

"We had planned to gather in the Upper Room," Shimon spoke softly, "but we fear that this Shaul and his followers might try to disrupt us. We felt we must change the place of the funeral. Yaakov, the brother of Yeshu, has offered his house for our gathering. They are not as likely to attack him again. The body has been prepared and is in state there."

"I offered our family tomb," Jarius continued, "but my brother's objections were so violent that I felt we should not proceed."

"Yosef of Ramatayim in turn offered his crypt," Kefa smiled. "Such a holy place seemed most appropriate."

"His tomb!" Mariam's eyes widened. "The same—"

Shimon nodded. "Where better than the site of the first resurrection?"

"Stephanos is honored." Mariam wept.

"If all is agreeable—" Jarius once more took her hand. "We must go quickly. We sent word to meet at the second hour."

"Stephanos is honored," Mariam kept repeating as they left the house and walked down the street.

"*Adom Olam,*" arose from across the congregation, "*Ashalom malan.*" The familiar words floated up from the mourners. "Before any being was created at the time when all was made by his will," they sang as the Ben Aaron family filed into the special place reserved for them. "And at the end, when all shall cease to be, God alone will awesomely reign." The voices sang the ancient hymn to the last line. "He is without beginning, without end; might and mastery belong to Him."

The house of Yaakov, the brother of Yeshua, was not as spacious as Jarius's. Yet the single large family room opened out into a large courtyard multiplying the seating capacity. Even before Jarius and Mariam arrived, the crowd had spilled over, filling the area outside. The room was simple with unadorned walls. Two large windows opened out onto the thoroughfare that ran through the heart of the city.

Mariam kept her veil over her face, barely revealing her eyes. She sat close to her father with her head down.

One of the Twelve began. "*Shema O Israel, Adoni Eloheunu adoni echad.*"

Believers fell into the cadence, "The Lord is one. And you shall love the Lord your God with all your heart—"

Jarius kept his arm around Mariam until it was time for him to speak. Shimon Kefa finished his prayer and nodded to Jarius. "My friends, while most of you do not know, Stephanos was betrothed to my daughter." Jarius stood tall and erect. "We loved him dearly, and I honor him for the son that he was to me in the faith. Before my beloved wife and our newborn son died—" Jarius choked and for a moment stood in awkward silence. "When they passed away," he began again, "I knew I would never have a son. What a wonderful replacement this young man would have made. I will always remember him for the place he would have filled." Jarius sat down slowly.

When Jarius sat down he stared into the hard clay floor. Time, traffic, heat, and wear had beaten the simple dirt covering into a rocklike surface. Sacred history had flowed over this surface. Yeshua had walked in this room with the Twelve. Miryam had stayed here often with her son, Yaakov. Jarius looked up at the long low ceiling of beams that supported the clay tiles. He hoped that in some way Stephanos was hearing what was said.

Philip walked to the center of the room. "He was my best friend. We were both from Greece." Tears ran down his handsome face. Like Stephanos, Philip wore the close hair cut of his people. He seemed much older than his eighteen years, but his boyish face gave him away. Philip had the muscular athletic build that was so admired in the hellenized world. Although he wore the long flowing robes of the people of Yerushalayim, he was clearly a Jew of the diaspora.

"I admired Stephanos because he was the finest and bravest person I ever knew. He wanted to take the message of Yeshua to our country. He believed the story was for the whole world. I would gladly have died in his place that he might have done so." Philip stopped abruptly and put his hand to his eyes. Finally he said, "Praise God for my brother, Stephanos." Philip quickly stepped back into the crowd.

People stirred. The low ceiling made the room feel stifling. Yaakov stood in the middle of his crowded house. "The People of the Way will always hold dear the memory of this one who is our first martyr. He was fearless in facing all opposition. Did he not speak with the authority of a sage and prophet? Did God not do mighty works through him? Now a brother has come forward to tell us the story of Stephanos's final defense of our faith. Nakdimon* comes to us now at great risk to himself. He often sat with the Messiah at night to learn from him."

"No more!" The tall dignified man stepped from the crowd. "I came at night because I was afraid to be identified with the rabbi."

A sudden murmur of recognition arose from the group.

"Yes, I sit on the Great Sanhedrin. Do not fear." His eyes were filled with pain. "As I listened to this young Greek argue before the court, I saw in him a boldness that I lacked. I felt ashamed and convicted by his courage. My cowardice kept me at a safe distance from Rabbi Yeshua. Listen to what Stephanos told us."

Nakdimon slowly expounded the brilliant defense Stephanos had made before the rulers. He became increasingly animated as he elaborated the message. "And so I have come to believe in Yeshua Ha Mashiach. I watched this Greek fearlessly turn his face toward the heavens," his voice cracked, "and he did not flinch as the rocks fell on him. In that moment I knew I could never return to the Sanhedrin. I had to become one of you publicly. The valor of this martyr has given me confidence and faith." Nakdimon's voice faded.

People embraced Nakdimon as he stepped back into the crowd. From somewhere a hymn began spontaneously as the deacons stepped forward to lift the bier on their shoulders for the procession through the streets. Only then did Mariam move. Quickly she knelt beside the linen-wrapped figure. An aroma of the spices and ointments filled her nose as she ran her hands across the linen covering draped around the face. Then she

*Nicodemus

lifted the cloth. The sight took her breath away, and she bit her lip. Yet she continued loosening the binding around the neck.

Very carefully Mariam reached behind her neck and untied her necklace. Her greatest treasure tangled in her fingers. The hymn faded away as the group stared. Mariam reached down and tied the strands around the neck of her betrothed. When she replaced the napkin, Mariam made sure the treasured pearl clearly showed on top of the linen bindings. Here and there she tucked the cloth in place as one gives a final touch to a child being sent off on a long journey. Finally she adjusted the pearl so that it was perfectly in the center.

"With certainty in the resurrection," Shimon paused to reach down for Mariam's hand, "we go forth from this place, not defeated but as the victors." He helped Mariam to her feet. "By the power of his cross that overcame death, so shall we overcome. It has been given to us to follow in his footsteps. By his wounds are we healed now and forever."

Mariam stepped aside, and the young men hoisted the bier on their shoulders, turning to the door. Believers fell in behind them as Shimon Kefa and Yaakov led the way. Silently the procession wound its way toward the edge of the city. As was the custom, people ceased speaking as they passed.

Yet at each thoroughfare, others fell in with them until a mighty throng filled the streets, stretching out for blocks. At each intersection, their gait became more certain and determined. What began as the usual lethargic funeral pace increased in tempo until they became a marching army. As they marched through the gates of the city, the certainty and forcefulness of the procession's advances sent an awed hush through the last marketplace.

Two days later Honorius appeared at the home of Jarius Ben Aaron. His small company of soldiers stood respectfully before the door, waiting for the servant to announce them.

"Ah," Jarius came to the door, "welcome, you have—" He stopped immediately when he saw the two men who stood bound in the center of the soldiers.

"We must speak privately." Honorius nodded toward the hallway.

"Of course, of course." Jarius bid them enter.

The centurion motioned for two of his soldiers to bring the prisoners in. "Please call your daughter." His voice was unusually brisk and factual.

Jarius dispatched his servant to find Mariam. Turning down the long hallway, he led the men toward the familiar gathering room. Jarius held the heavy woven curtain back to allow the soldiers to enter before him. They spread out across the large plain room pressing their prisoners against the center wall. Honorius stood in front of the empty fireplace in the far corner of the room. Mariam came through the dining room from her room in the back of the house.

Mariam's face was pale and her eyes listless. The black limp robes of mourning looked strangely inappropriate on one so young. She smiled but said nothing.

"Do you know these men?" Honorius said bluntly.

Jarius searched the soldier's face for some clue as to whether he could dare to be forthright before the other men.

"Have no fear," the centurion reassured him. "You can be candid."

Jarius looked hard into the face of the fat man with the strange broken nose and then at the skinny little man who stood cowering next to him. Both stared at the floor, avoiding any possible eye contact.

"Yes," Jarius said slowly, "they are our brethren. They have often been in our meetings." He turned to Mariam. "Is this not so?"

She only nodded.

"I'm sorry," Jarius spoke directly to the odd pair. "I do not know your names. Perhaps I have forgotten."

"I doubt if they ever let you know," Honorius sneered. "May I acquaint you with the most significant spies the Sanhedrin placed in your midst."

"What?" Mariam's eyes blinked.

"I don't understand," Jarius fumbled.

"They are a worthless lot." Honorius poked the fat man in the chest. "They were actually turned in to us by one of the Temple guards to avoid paying them for informing. Little did the guards know that these two had been paid by us as well."

"Informers?" Mariam strained forward. "Yes, I've seen these men in many of our meetings. They often sat near the front."

"They listened carefully to all of your secrets." Honorius shook his head. "Tell them what you told us."

The fat man turned away.

Honorius abruptly grabbed his cloak, yanking him nearly out of his sandals. "We can't hear you," he yelled in his ear.

"A—a—ah—" he stammered. "I—ah—knew something of where this Shaul came from." He leaned back. "Is—is that what you mean?"

"Speak of it." Honorius jerked him forward again.

"Your brother," the fat man blurted out, "your brother solicited him."

"Simeon?" Mariam's eyes widened. "Shaul? The man who helped kill Stephanos?"

"I thought you should know." Honorius's countenance changed. "I do not wish to bring more pain to your house, but neither do I want you exposed to danger." He tugged at the fat man again. "Give them the whole story."

"I don't know all of it," he stammered, "but your brother did introduce this man from Tarsus to the Sanhedrin. All of them put the raid and the killing together."

"Is that so?" The centurion scowled at the little man.

"Yes." He shook his head obediently.

"I am sorry." Honorius looked from father to daughter. "I wish I had other news."

"Did Simeon participate in the stoning?" Mariam asked haltingly.

"I don't think so, but I don't know." Honorius turned back to the fat prisoner. "The truth! Speak it!"

"Shaul," his twisted nose was becoming increasingly red as he spoke, "I only know about Shaul for sure. He did it."

"Brother shall be set against brother." Jarius turned away.

"So Simeon separated himself from us," Mariam spoke only to her father, "in order to have a free hand in these evil deeds."

"Protect yourselves." Honorius pushed the prisoners back toward the entryway. "We will take care of the likes of these."

"Thank you," Jarius followed them toward the door. "You have always been more than a friend."

Jarius paused only for a moment at the door before returning to the gathering room. When he found it empty, he called for his daughter. For several minutes he walked through the house trying to find her. Only then did he realize Mariam was gone.

During the month that followed Honorius's visit, Mariam became increasingly silent. Finally, Jarius knew they must talk. He put his tools aside and secured the door. He knew where Mariam was likely to be. Immediately he started across the city for the place of the Tomb.

The once obscure path to the family sepulchers of Yosef of Ramatayim was now well beaten as increasing numbers of visitors came to the place of the Great Resurrection. Undaunted by the possibility of being seen by Temple guards or spies, pilgrimages had continued even during the worst winter months. When Jarius came close, he could see that at least a dozen people were scattered around the stone outcroppings, silently meditating. Still wearing the black robes of mourning, Mariam was seated on the usual large rock in front of the portion of the tombs where Stephanos lay. She looked unkempt and disheveled. Jarius slid in beside her without speaking. Mariam reached for his hand.

"You are well today, daughter?" He broke the silence.

"I suppose." She didn't turn her head. Dark circles ringed her eyes.

"But not your soul?" Jarius squeezed her hand.

"Perhaps not so good with my soul." Mariam's expression did not change. The wind pushed the scarf on her head back. Her uncombed hair hung in uncharacteristic tangles.

"You still grieve?" Jarius's voice was factual.

Mariam looked down at her hand in her father's. "My pain comes from another place."

"Try to tell me," Jarius spoke softly. "I have so often wished that your mother were here. I make a poor substitute."

Mariam reached up and kissed him on the cheek.

"My dear Abba," she smiled for the first time, "no one could be more compassionate, but the struggle is very deep within me. Yes, I miss Stephanos, and I feel as if I will never love another. But I fear to speak of what I find inside. The anguish is more like rage. You do not want to hear my thoughts. I must confess that I have no sense of the Presence; emptiness has replaced fullness."

Jarius bit his lip and looked down.

"I just don't understand." Mariam's entire body sagged. "I just don't understand."

"What, my little one? What?"

"Our people are so powerless in the face of the onslaught that has befallen them. How could the Holy One raise us up so high only to let us fall so far? Lies prevail while truth lays battered in the gutter."

Jarius stroked his beard as his eyes darted back and forth across the garden. "I see." He groped for some word to say.

"There is no equity!" she suddenly blurted out so loudly that several people turned to look. "Why have all these innocent people been slaughtered? Why do we fill the jails? Why could such a thoroughly good man as my Stephanos be cruelly stoned to death by heartless fanatics? Tell me, Father. Why has God made us to be His sacrifices!"

"Now I see." Jarius flinched. "Bitterness," Jarius answered very slowly. "The pain within has turned to bitterness."

Mariam refused to look at him. Silence fell between them once more.

"I drank from the waters of Marah after your mother died, and I pitched my tent by the same place of brackish water when Zeda was killed. Unless the springs that feed our souls are sweetened, everything in us will become rancid."

Mariam said nothing for a long time. When she turned around, her flashing eyes had become hard and dark. Her jaw was uncharacteristically tense and set. Enmity had settled into Mariam, devouring the gentleness which had been her very essence. "Do—not—speak—to—me—of—our—family again," she snapped. "What have we ever given each other but pain?"

"Mariam," Jarius gasped. "I don't understand."

"Hours. It has taken me hours," Mariam's voice accused him, "to understand why I hurt so deeply, but now I understand. Perhaps our family has always thrived more on death than life. I did not want to face the truth, but in this graveyard, it has become obvious. Even my own mother left me behind to take the final journey."

"Oh, no," Jarius begged. "Don't even utter such a thought."

"And what happened to my good uncle? Perhaps he left the shop that day because he could no longer stand the confrontation between you and Simeon. Maybe that's why he was in the marketplace at that ill-fated moment. How do I know?"

"No, no, such was not true."

"Simeon was always a plague in our midst." Mariam began to clinch her fist. "Was he not like a dog that carries disease from one house to the next?"

"Mariam, this is not you speaking."

"But it is!" She shook both fists in his face. Her knuckles were white against the taut skin. "The one opportunity that I had for true life was destroyed by Simeon. Whatever was his part, he orchestrated the plot that destroyed Stephanos." Her eyes widened, and her lips trembled. "I never want to hear his name again."

"Something terrible has happened to you. We must talk." Jarius reached for her hand.

"I can't," Mariam abruptly slapped his wrist. "I won't," she added bitterly. "If I were to pray, I would ask that Simeon be struck with a death as agonizing as the one he visited on Stephanos. Now you know what is truly in my soul." Her neck had become crimson; her cheeks flushed. "Leave me be. There is nothing to be said."

"Please." Jarius struggled for words, but could find none. "Please—"

Mariam groaned, "I went to the place of death. But now death has come back for me. I walk in it, and its mantle of blackness has settled over everything I touch. You have no idea how difficult it is even to talk. I never want to speak of any of this again. But should my uncle cross my path, I tell you that I will strike him with the first object upon which I lay my hand. Now leave me be, Father." Mariam abruptly stood. "Death has become my portion. There is no hope left within me."

Before Jarius could answer, Mariam turned toward the path. She took only a few steps before she broke into a run. Jarius could not move. Her words thundered in his head like an avalanche of boulders from high cliffs. The delicate creature that had blossomed into an awe-inspiring prophetess of the Most High had been uprooted and wilted before his eyes. Jarius clutched his throat as he breathed heavily. When he looked around, the others in the garden had also left. Jarius felt completely alone, as if the rock in front of his family's tomb had once more opened to receive another victim.

PART THREE

"... SIGNS ON THE EARTH BELOW"

A.D. 35

NINETEEN

Spring warmth that always came with Iyar* brought more people than usual to the market. The citizens of Gitta filled the market square, crowding the local merchants away from their self-claimed territories. Halfway between Sebaste, the capitol of Samaria, and the coastal city of Caesarea, the thriving village of Gitta was always a crossroads of commerce and ideas. Possibly their openness saved Philip, a Jew, from the initial rebuff that was expected in the Samaritan villages of the north.

The two months since Stephanos's death had been spent preparing his message. However, the enthusiastic response of the people to his impromptu speech was beyond Philip's wildest expectations.

Philip had forced his way to the center of the square. Closing his eyes for what seemed an eternity, he stepped up on the rock ledge that surrounded the city water well and began his speech. As he had seen

*corresponds to April-May

Stephanos and Shimon do, Philip boldly proclaimed that the God of Avraham, Yitzchak, and Yaakov had now acted in his servant Yeshua. From somewhere deep within his soul, the words had started flowing like water from the well. The rest became a blur.

The usual company of cripples and beggars that plagued every public square were the first to listen. Philip had never grown accustomed to the stench from the filth, disease, and rotting flesh of this human refuse. He had tried to preach without directly looking at their sorry lot. Starting with them, a wave of affirmation swept through the crowd.

Philip was unusually tall, and his unusually light, long brown hair flipped back and forth as he tried to speak in all directions at once. Nineteen years had left no marks of wear on his handsome boyish face. The straggly stubble of a sparse beard around his chin only added to his naturally youthful appearance. Yet Philip's eyes and voice had an authority of far greater consequence than his physical weight. His black, dark-set eyes burned with intensity as he scanned the scene that was exploding around him.

Naively Philip had no plan for what should follow his preaching. The friends of a paralyzed woman pushed her forward, challenging his proclamation that the power of God was now unleashed. No one was more surprised than Philip when she suddenly stood when he prayed for her. She took one step and the crowd exploded with excitement. Pandemonium followed. Like a rushing wind bearing down from the mountains, restorative power had settled over the broken and maimed. Awestruck, Philip had gone from person to person, just as he had seen the apostles and Stephanos do. The dazzling results had been constant. Samaritans were having their own Shavu'ot.

Philip carefully backed away from the surging crowd, trying to edge his way toward asylum in the Samaritan synagogue behind him. The plain large stone and staccato building appeared to be the only available sanctuary from the mob. The pressing horde made it difficult to escape gracefully from the sea of hands that reached out on all sides to touch him.

"The Taheb* has come." One woman waved to another.

"We are being healed," another cried out. "Look and see!"

"Touch me." A beggar pulled at Philip's robe. "Do as you did for the lame man."

Philip tried not to panic, but their grabbing hands alarmed him. His cloak was nearly pulled off. "The Kingdom has come," he kept waving with his hands raised above their heads. "Believe and receive." Hanging onto his outer robe he took two more steps away from the crowd.

"What you have seen is a confirmation of the authority of our Messiah." He pointed upward as he inched back toward the door that was only five feet and an eternity away.

Finding the resolve to speak in the marketplace had been one of the most courageous acts of Philip's young life. As he had walked the long miles from Sebaste to Gitta, he had thought again and again on the boldness of Stephanos. Children of the hellenized world, both men's visions were far broader than their brethren who had never been beyond the narrow limits of the villages of the Gennesaret or the towns around Yerushalayim, Stephanos had insisted that the message must go beyond the house of Israel even though no less a person

*Samaritan Messiah

than Shimon Kefa himself had disagreed. Philip had to keep faith with the dream of his beloved friend.

"Change your minds!" Philip kept backing away from the adoration being offered him. "Receive the message of the Messiah!" He sensed that the door to the synagogue was just behind him. "The day of the Lord is at hand." He grabbed the handle and ducked inside, shutting the crowd out.

For a moment Philip blinked trying to adjust to the darkness. He knew of no Jew who had ever ventured into the forbidden precincts of the holy place of the Samaritans. *Perhaps,* he thought, *now they will turn on me. I should have gone elsewhere.*

Every Jew knew that the hatred between Jews and Samaritans was as ancient as the walls of Yerushalayim themselves. Jewish contempt for these assimilated mongol remnants of the Northern Kingdom had simmered for nearly five hundred years. Because the northerners had failed to keep separation from the Goyim, their unfaithfulness was held in total contempt. Ancient cousins, they were the butt of jokes and objects of scorn. Undaunted, Samaritans returned Jewish snobbery with their own special brand of hate. They had even attempted to hinder the rebuilding of the Yerushalayim walls when Nehemiah began the project. Philip could quickly switch from hero to victim.

"Who are you?" a voice called out of the darkness.

"Philip," he answered apprehensively, "a—a Jew, a follower of the Way."

"Why have you come here?" a different voice probed.

"Our people have been scattered by persecution." His voice sounded high and inappropriately boyish. He tried to lower it. "I felt called to come to your village. I believe in telling everyone the news of what God has done for us."

As Philip's eyes adjusted to the dark he saw three elderly men standing directly in front of him. Behind them was a large open sanctuary of worship. The high stone walls were unadorned. Tall columns ran up to the ceiling. The synagogue didn't look particularly different from a Jewish synagogue.

"We observed your deeds from the upper windows." The oldest man with a long white beard stepped forward. "We heard the potency of your words. No one does such things unless God is with him. I am Nebat, the Nisi of the synagogue. I welcome you."

"Like you Jews, Samaritans have always expected a Taheb. Two years ago we sent envoys to hear your Yeshua. We pondered the reports of his teaching but could not decide if he was the one."

"Today," the second man continued, "you made us understand for the first time. I believe we have found our Taheb."

Philip stared. The acceptance of his message by obviously important men was as stupefying as the whirlwind of signs and wonders in the town square. "I am only a messenger," he fumbled. "I share what I have seen. I proclaim his name."

"We hear you gladly." The last man bowed from the waist. "Teach us. Continue to speak." His words were muted by thundering fists on the door. The pounding could no longer be ignored.

Philip shrugged his shoulders and gestured feebly with his hands. "I'm—ah—not sure—what to do next."

"Come here." The elder motioned toward the thick wooden door. "We will place a bench so you can stand in the entryway and explain to the multitude. Teach us more."

Before Philip could protest one of the men opened the large door while another motioned for the crowd to back up. The third man pushed a bench forward and pulled Philip toward the entrance. Standing with him, the elder entreated the crowd to be silent. "Hear this man." He turned to the trembling evangelist. "We believe our God has sent him to us."

"Oh, Stephanos, why aren't you here," Philip moaned under his breath. He looked out over the sea of faces that had only multiplied in the short time he had been inside. His mind raced back to what he had heard the young Greek say to the crowds. Desperately Philip sought for the correct phrases, the words, the ideas, the story.

"Brethren and Father," Philip began as Stephanos always did. The crowd immediately quieted. "The God of glory appeared to our father Avraham." Philip sensed that the right chord had been struck when he said *our*. Knowing that the Samaritans only recognized Torah, Philip remembered to avoid the later prophets and the Psalms shunned by the Northerners. The early demise of the Northern Kingdom had frozen their Scriptures before these books appeared. He must not offend ancient sensitivities. Apprehension turned to boldness as Philip discovered personal authority he had never known before.

"What happened today?" Simon Magnus stepped back from his balcony, which overlooked Gitta's town square. "Never have I seen such a thing!" Consternation was an unusual and uncomfortable posture for the magician who made deceiving people his career. The nimble fingers that could make flowers appear in mid-air tapped against Simon's thin, narrow lips. Long ago he had learned how to roll his eyes after one of his sleight of hand tricks, increasing the illusion of mystical power.

Now he could only blink in amazement. "Never have I seen such capacity!"

"I don't know," his woman stammered. "I heard the commotion and watched from the street. Everywhere people are saying the young Jew made the blind see and cripples walk."

"Yes, yes." Simon turned back to the balcony. His long flowing silk sleeves swirled with the flair that wrapped him in mystery. "There was no deception or chicanery in what I saw. Neither was his hold over the people cleverness."

Simon leaned over the railing, staring down on the nearly empty marketplace. He kept stroking his beard, which narrowly bordered the side of his face, coming up in a thin line above his upper lip. This carefully manicured beard made him appear strangely knowing and menacing at the same time. Simon continued to search the square for any clues that he might have missed. His massive exotic ring with a golden Cobra's head turned heavily on the side of his finger.

"In all of the incantations I have ever known," he turned back to his woman, "none even suggested that such potential was possible. I must find this man."

"Perhaps," the woman spoke slowly, "we should fear him." Her naturally seductive eyes were heavily lined in blue, making them appear longer and more enchanting. The bold colors painted around her eyelids were strangely alien to the modest people of Gitta. Hesitation was equally foreign to her. "You almost had the city in the palm of your hand. Could our position be jeopardized?"

"Come now." A wicked smile broke across his face. "Do you doubt me, my love?" Simon stepped back into the room and reached for her. "When one finds a greater skill, one pursues a new opportunity." Simon ran his hands up her slender neck, tracing the line of her ears until he plunged his fingers into her cold black hair. "There is nothing that money can't buy." He looked at her with knowing intent. "Right? Money buys everything?" Abruptly he closed his fingers around her hair, jerking with just enough pressure to cause a hint of pain.

The woman flinched and closed her eyes tightly.

"Pain and pleasure and power," Simon relaxed his clutch, "what more is there?" His fingers began a return journey down her neck, continuing toward her ample cleavage. "A new mystery religion is invented everyday," he chuckled. "When there are new secrets to be learned, Simon the Great will master them. Never doubt me!" His eyes narrowed. "Now go find where they have taken our new friend."

For a long time Philip looked around the room that the rulers of the Samaritan Synagogue had offered him. Plain, spartan, a bed was in one corner and a table in the other. Expecting to sleep beneath a tree, the gift of accommodations only added to the wonder of the day. The small fireplace in the wall offered warmth that would be a reprieve from a cold night. He adjusted the olive oil lamp so that light fell on the parchment they had also provided. Always very expensive, writing materials were saved only for the most important communiques. The Samaritans had quickly provided ink and a sheet of parchment when Philip asked.

He dipped the reed pen into the little dish with the pool of ink. "Greetings in the name of our Messiah, the Lord Yeshua," he slowly made the Hebrew letters. Because of his hellenized upbringing, Greek would have been easier. But, not wanting to give any offense, he continued in Hebrew. "I know that many will question going beyond the House of Israel. And yet God has done great works here among our estranged relatives. Hear what has transpired before my eyes." The words came faster and faster as Philip described the details of the wondrous results that had occurred during the afternoon. "I need your help," he concluded. "I implore Shimon Kefa and others to come. Surely God will bless such a journey. A new door has opened."

Rolling the parchment into a scroll, Philip tied a thin piece of cloth around the little bundle. Perhaps, two or three days, or a week, might pass before the epistle reached Yerushalayim. If his urgency registered with the leaders, someone might return in a week or two at the very most. Philip extinguished his light but didn't leave the table. Late into the night he pondered what he might tell these former adversaries during the long days that were ahead.

"Stephanos," he sighed, "if only you were with me. You would know."

During the week that followed, Simon Magnus carefully observed everything that Philip did. His woman had exchanged her exotic and revealing gowns for the clothes of the peasants. He watched from the balcony while she stood near the front. The crowds did not decrease nor the ministry diminish.

Yet the more Philip spoke, the more he felt his limitation. Unexpected questions exhausted his insights even though the results continued to be dramatic. Philip had no grasp of how the signs and wonders occurred, but the results clearly and decisively authenticated his talks.

And yet something was missing. Philip sensed a

problem he could not define. In the next days and weeks he struggled to find the important dimension of their newfound faith that seemed to be lacking. Only then did Philip dare to consider emulating what the apostles had done. Possibly, the mikvah baptism was the answer.

On Shavu'ot the people who entered the Pool of Siloe had come forth with new life. An invitation to the mikvah had been an essential part of Shimon Kefa's message. Philip reasoned that it should be added to his. Once Philip made the announcement, the response was immediate.

Philip called the leaders of the synagogue together. Standing in Philip's room, they listened carefully to his instruction. Once or twice the old men interrupted, but only for clarification. Nebat, the Nisi, kept nodding his approval.

"If you please," suave intonations interrupted Philip's discussion with the elder. "I desire a private word." A man stepped into the room.

"Simon Magnus!" the elders exclaimed.

"We have not met." The tall magician walked between the young Jew and the old Samaritan. "I, too, am much taken with your message," he extended his hand. "I wish to discuss the ritual that is about to be performed."

"Simon is well known in our city," Nebat, an elder, narrowed his eyes and set his jaw, "and known to be a man who dabbles in spiritual power."

"Therefore," Simon fixed his eyes on Philip, "my participating in the ritual of washing would speak to many skeptics." He stared at Philip as if casting a spell or seeking to enter the deepest recesses of his mind.

"You believe?" Another elder pulled at his beard.

"I must!" Simon threw up his hands. "The results speak for themselves."

"I speak of a messiah," Philip crossed his arms, "a man whose name was Yeshua."

"A man of unspeakable power," Simon's eyes widened. "Yes, I want to follow him. If the ritual is the way, then I will be the first to enter the water."

"Others will proceed you," Nebat spoke through his teeth. "You must stand among the people."

"Will I be able to do the things you do?" Simon spoke as if the elder were not present. "Will I be able to pray for sick people and obtain the same marvelous results?"

"I—ah—I don't know." Philip scratched his head. "But you will receive a new life and be released from the bondage of evil."

"A new life." Simon's eyes moved away from their fixation on Philip for the first time. "Amazing! Yes, of course, I believe. I am ready."

"The people will gather by the river bank," Philip continued factually. "Those who believe will walk out to me and be placed under the water, even as Yeshua was baptized by Yochanan. As we go down, we enter into his death, so that we may receive new life from the Holy One."

"Ah," Simon Magnus drawled, "going down to death, as if you have found a door to the underworld. Yes, I know of similar procedures. You will not be sorry to have me numbered among your people. I will be there." With a great flourish, Simon disappeared through the curtain.

"He is an evil man," Nebat warned. "Seducing women and confusing the young. Neither Jew nor Samaritan, he preys on the fears of our people. Stay wide of his path."

"Perhaps he seeks a new heart," Philip reassured the elders. "I am among those who believe that the message of Yeshua is also for those who are not the sons of Avraham. Maybe this strange man can be among the first."

"Caution!" One of the old men shook his head. "Caution. I do not trust him."

"Of course," Philip smiled. "Your wisdom has prevailed often in these last days. Now that we have the details in place, who will be the first person to be baptized?"

"I shall." Nebat humbly lowered his head "*I* will be a sign to our people."

When Shimon Kefa and Yochanan arrived in Gitta five days later, the city was still teeming with excitement over the multitude that had gone down to the river for Philip's mikvah bath. The sight of Simon Magnus wading out in his extravagant silk robes had dumbfounded the most obstinate of doubters. Across the marketplace people were talking of the new fortunes that must surely lie ahead for the people of Samaria. The age of fulfillment was at hand. Dreams would come true. The two apostles could not overlook the mood of triumph and conquest that permeated the marketplace.

"Our Taheb has come," one enthusiastic seller of figs instructed them as he counted out their change in denari. "Now those snobs in Yerushalayim will be forced to accept the righteousness of our father. True?" he asked and then continued talking before they could answer.

"We shall be vindicated." The vegetable vendor shook his finger in Shimon Kefa's face. Only then did the Samaritan recognize their Jewishness. Abruptly, he bore down, "You shall see who is superior!"

The awe that Philip had inspired couldn't be missed. The aura that surrounded his message left both men disconcerted. In sharp contrast to the vicious opposition of the Sanhedrin, Gitta was intoxicated by their new faith. By late afternoon the two men had found their way to the inn where Philip was staying.

Although that inn looked no different from one in Yerushalayim, there were subtle variances. The centuries of distance between Samaritan and Jew had left many marks. The swirling multicolored floral design on the pottery was unique; the zig-zag weave with dark green bands on the covering on the bed was singular. Although the Samaritans spoke Aramaic and Hebrew, little quirks in pronunciation filled Jewish ears. Such diversity was common to the hellenized world of Philip, but Shimon Kefa, the fisherman of Gennesaret, balked at the nuances that felt vulgar and common to him.

"Brothers!" Philip rushed out to greet the apostles. "Come back to my room. I have much to tell you. Samaritan elders will be here shortly. Everyone anticipates your arrival."

"We have come," Shimon spoke hesitantly, "with considerable reluctance. I am not sure that we should be here." He sat down on the crude wooden stool against the wall.

"And yet the Holy One of Israel seems to be at work," Yochanan smiled, "and we must recognize what He is doing."

"Something is missing." Philip ran his hands through his hair. "I have been amazed at the miraculous things I have seen and yet—" He began to walk slowly around the room, "—yet something isn't right."

"Indeed," Kefa snapped, "I have heard the sound of it in the street. Just as I feared, these Gentiles have misunderstood."

"I don't understand." Philip froze in place, "I tried to be faithful," he apologized.

"My son," Yochanan kept smiling, "do not fear. The

error is not yours. We, too, had these problems and mis-
conceptions."

"Even in the House of Israel, people stumbled." Shimon lectured. "How much more will the pagan world
trip over its own greed?"

"Now, now." Yochanan shook his finger at Shimon.
"Let us not lose sight of the great work that Philip has
done. We will have ample time to clarify the problems."

"I have only . . ." Philip gestured futilely.

"You have only," Shimon interrupted him, "been an
excellent witness to our faith. We are pleased with you."

"Well," Philip heaved, "so much has just happened. I
wasn't sure what to do. I did all I knew." He stopped and
smiled. "How are things in Yerushalayim?"

"All goes well," Shimon answered. "Our enemies continue to persecute us, but they are only spreading our
story. No, we are not discouraged."

"And Mariam?" Philip asked. "She yet grieves?" He
realized how often thoughts of Mariam filled his mind.
Even asking about her well-being made him feel awkward as if there was something inappropriate in his feelings.

"Her wound is deep." Yochanan looked out the window. "We do not see her often. I fear for Mariam."

"I see." Philip rubbed his forehead. "Perhaps when I
return, I . . ." his voice trailed away.

"No," Shimon Kefa shook his head, "only the Holy
One can help Mariam. Now tell us when we are to meet
these new converts."

"Tonight." Philip stared blankly. "Tonight . . . yes, tonight we have a meeting."

"Excellent," Kefa stood decisively. "We will quickly
speak to these problems."

"Don't worry." Yochanan squeezed Philip's shoulder.
"All things are in God's timing."

Philip smiled but his mind was elsewhere. Mariam. She had been in his mind for days. At first Philip thought that he was being spiritually prompted to pray. And yet the tug was in his heart. Slowly he was beginning to recognize that Mariam had touched him at a place where no one had been before. He longed to see her.

"I said," Yochanan repeated, "in God's timing."

"Ah yes . . . yes," Philip blinked remembering where he was.

———————————•———————————

The three men passed the afternoon with intense and animated discussions. Shimon intensely probed the meaning of the baptisms while Yochanan urged wider understanding of the response of the Samaritans. Philip held his ground, insisting that the faith must go beyond the House of Israel.

Philip hungrily pounced on each new insight from the apostles. Slowly he began to sense what the two seasoned veterans had quickly recognized in the streets of Gitta. Yes, the Samaritans had embraced a messiah. Unfortunately they shaped him in their own image.

Finally, the two leaders knelt on the floor and put their faces in their hands for the evening meeting. Before he joined them, Philip looked at the sight before him. Shimon Kefa was big with massive arms, and Yochanan was small and slight. Yet they both looked no different than any ordinary Jew that might have stumbled into a Samaritan village by mistake.

Philip wanted this scene etched in his memory. Centuries of animosity and bitterness were about to end. Shimon Kefa might not like the feel of the Gentile world, but in spite of himself he had stepped across an ancient boundary. Whether he knew it or not, his small step was an extraordinary leap into the world Philip knew best. Philip watched the two leaders lost in their deep prayer, sensing that he would be telling unborn generations of this time and place.

TWENTY

Every space in the Samaritan synagogue was filled. The stone ledges around the walls were packed with men sitting shoulder to shoulder. Around the room, torches were set in iron holders high upon the walls. Outside, crowds of men and women milled around, hoping to find a place inside. Fire from the large torches around the entryway flickered against the night sky. Candles and lamps dotted windows throughout the village.

Philip and the apostles entered through the rear door, following Nebat, the leader of the synagogue. Simon Magnus stood unnoticed, wrapped in a plain brown robe with a hood over his head. Taking the unusual posture of anonymity, Simon blended into one of the far corners of the building.

Men reached out to touch Philip as he walked past. Nods of deference and respect followed him. When he began speaking, silence immediately fell over the room.

"Brothers," Philip welcomed the group. The men clapped. "Tonight we have two of our most significant leaders to teach us. We must listen well. Shimon Kefa is a fisherman of the Gennesaret. He will explain."

A hush of respect fell over the room that indicated that no interruptions would be permitted.

Shimon Kefa towered over his audience. His broad massive shoulders gave him a commanding presence, which was increased by his deep resonant voice. He began slowly, carefully choosing his words. By speaking of their common ancestors Moshe and David as well as the patriarchs, he was on acceptable ground. As he talked of David, even greater agreement could be seen in their faces. After a half hour, the esteem given to Philip now encompassed him. Only then did Shimon Kefa turn to the heart of the matter.

"Yeshua from Natzeret demonstrated that he was from God by the powerful works, miracles, and signs he performed. We are eye witnesses. Even after evil men put him to death, HaElyon raised him up and freed him from all suffering." Shimon paused as if measuring his audience. He was receiving rapt attention. Not even in Yerushalayim had there been such intense interest.

"Even our father David died and was buried," Shimon continued. "Therefore God has clearly brought us one of greater power."

"Our Taheb!" someone spontaneously cried out.

"Yes," the crowd erupted in mass. "Yes, yes!" The night air was charged with explosive energy.

Shimon Kefa stood quietly until an uneasy silence settled over the congregation. Quietly but defiantly he answered. "No, my friends. No." His pause was deafening.

He shook his head, "I also misunderstood the nature of Yeshua's mission. What Jew did not want a Messiah who would slay the Romans? Power is seductively corrupting. For centuries we have tried to put words in

God's mouth so that the Holy One would satisfy our hunger for security and our lust for prominence. We want the Almighty to baptize our evil intentions."

A murmur of consternation rose over the synagogue. Man turned to man, questioning what they had heard. Shimon Kefa watched carefully but his face showed no apprehension. Finally he began again. "You want a Taheb who will restore your nation and give you preeminence. We Jews want a Messiah who will elevate us over both the Romans and you. But both nations have been wrong! The Rudach Ha Kodesh cannot fall on us until we renounce the governments of the world and enter the Kingdom of God."

"Where is this kingdom?" a frustrated leader of the Samaritans cried out.

"In your heart!" Shimon shot back.

Once more the crowd was dumbfounded.

"Stop being seduced by the offer of political power, and the rule of God will give you divine security. Let go of your old desires for a Taheb who will fight for you. Let the risen Lord give you a new mind!"

A sudden gust of wind brought an invigorating breath of cool night air into the room. The torches flickered and bent low. The evening breezes pushed the canvas coverings on the small square window openings aside.

Across the room men whispered in each other's ears. Some gestured with exaggerated motions of their hands. Everyone appeared to be perplexed and confused. Shimon Kefa silently watched their consternation.

Finally, the leader of the synagogue stood. "We do not understand," he spoke slowly and respectfully. "Our fathers taught us to hope for one who would restore the kingdom of Israel. We have seen the sick made well.

Surely such power would make an army invincible. But you are saying that God does not intend to defeat our enemies?"

"Who are your adversaries?" Shimon bore down. "Rome or evil itself? Soldiers or fear? Poverty or greed?" His voice became fiercely intense. "Oh yes, I know of the desire for prominence and rank. Yes, I have been lured by self-aggrandizement. When I walked with the Messiah, my heart burned with the desire to be first and vested with all authority. Yet at the most important and decisive moment when he needed me, I found that I had the heart of a coward. I know of no hope for any of us unless the evil, the compromise, the duplicity is taken out of us. Only then can we begin to understand the meaning of the kingdom Yeshua brought us."

When Shimon stopped, Yochanan began. "My friends, we are still struggling to understand everything Yeshua taught us about the Kingdom of God, but this we have learned. It is not a political state, a restored throne of David. No, it is much more. . . . Our God intends to restore the Garden of Eden itself to us. We are meant to live in peace with the Holy One, with everyone, and with ourselves."

"You are of the House of Avraham," Shimon began again. "The promise is surely for you, but you must not make a Messiah of your own fashioning. You must allow him to be who he is. From the beginning of time, men have tried to use the power of God for themselves." Kefa became even more intense. "War, cruelty, injustice, abuse have followed. Even religion itself has been a tool of prejudice and malice. But now a new light has come among us."

Yochanan raised both of his arms high in the air like Moses commanding the sea to part. "Hear us!" he boomed. "The Evil One has fallen. Even the demons shutter before the name of Yeshua. The principalities and powers of the air have been defeated. Flee from your sin. Through the name of Yeshua you can be set free. We bring the way of love." Yochanan slowly lowered his hands. "Nothing, not even death, can defeat the love of the Holy One of Israel. When you want to be filled with the power of love, then the Rudach Ha Kodesh can descend upon you."

"I have hated Jews all of my life." Nebat, the leader of the synagogue, rose to his feet. "Oh yes, I know that of which you speak. How many times have avarice and fear controlled me? But my soul hungers for goodness. If my heart can be purified, then I want what is offered. What more must we do?"

"You have followed the outward ritual," Kefa instructed. "Now the time has come for the inner work to be done. Ask the Rudach Ha Kodesh to come in and fill your heart. Ask Him to give you the love of Yeshua."

The old man dropped to his knees on the stone floor. Shimon Kefa placed both of his hands on the elder's head. Closing his eyes, Kefa began to pray under his breath. Immediately other men rose and walked to their leader. They, too, knelt at the apostle's feet. Philip joined Yochanan as they moved from person to person, laying hands on them and praying.

Suddenly a wave of weeping arose from the large group. Men were groaning in agony for their sin. Those kneeling at the front began to pray in different languages. People inched forward for the apostles to touch them. Weeping continued unabated until the sound of many diverse languages filled the room. Shimon, Yochanan, and Philip moved from person to person, laying on hands and praying.

Eventually singing began. Men stood and locked

arms, swaying back and forth to the rhythm of old Samaritan hymns. Finally their voices faded into the lateness of the night. Men hugged each other, shook hands, and talked of the amazing experience the apostles had imparted to them. Too much had occurred even to be explored out loud. The evening would have to settle before it could be sorted out.

"We can return to the inn," Philip suggested to Shimon Kefa. "I suppose I have as many questions as they do."

"What you have seen tonight, my son, is the distance between ideas and the Holy One Himself." Yochanan looked across the empty synagogue. "When they let go of the god they had created in their image, they found the true God. And so the Spirit comes."

"Will you continue to preach to the Samaritans?" Philip turned to Shimon Kefa.

"What else can we do?" The big man shrugged his shoulders.

"Good." Philip smiled. "Let's go home." The three men pulled their cloaks over their shoulders and turned to the back door.

"Wait," a man called from the back, "I wish a word." A brown hood concealed his face. "I want to inquire further about this great power you have."

"Yes?" Shimon peered at the faceless form.

"I have spoken with your associate." Simon Magnus cast the cloak aside. "And have even been baptized by him." His well-groomed appearance made a striking contrast to the coarse heavy woven robe he had used to conceal himself. "Your power is even greater than his." Simon offered his hand.

"Simon is a magician," Philip said bluntly.

"But I seek the true way." Simon's thinly trimmed beard made his smile appear sinister. "I, too, want to place my hands on people and see this Rudach Ha Kodesh come. I am prepared to pay your price."

"Pay?" Shimon's mouth dropped.

"Buy the Spirit of God?" Philip flinched.

"I have considerable resources . . ."

"Your money can burn in hell!" Shimon Kefa cut him off. "You think the gifts of the Holy One can be purchased?"

Yochanan stepped forward, looking intensely into the magician's eyes. "Your soul is filled with bitterness and malice. The Evil One has placed his claim upon you. You will perish, swallowed by your own greed."

"No." The magician's eyes widened. He shook his head vigorously. "I meant no offense. I simply wanted the ability . . ."

"Your offense," Shimon interrupted him again, "is that you were offered God and instead you choose power. These good people of Gitta had the same choice, and they gladly received him who is life. *Your portion will be death.*"

"No, no," Simon Magnus begged them. "No! Please do not consign me to perdition. Please pray that what you have said will not be so!"

"Repent!" Yochanan demanded. "Change your evil ways of thinking. Go home and put your house in order."

"We will be leaving tomorrow," Shimon Kefa warned. "If you have done these things, we will pray for you in the morning. If not, the curse remains on your head."

"But, but . . ." Simon reached out to the three men who quickly walked through the back door, disappearing into the night.

"But . . ." he reached out once more, but no one answered. Simon Magnus stood alone in the empty building.

Bright morning sunlight filled the room. Guests ate together around rough plank tables scattered around the large common dining hall. The local people silently watched the three Jewish celebrities. Servants moved from table to table. The apostles hungrily ate the figs and fruit that had been prepared for them. Shimon Kefa tore off a hunk of bread before passing the round flat loaf on to Philip.

"We will instruct the elders this morning," Yochanan explained. "We can help them understand more about the new way of the resurrection life, and then we will press on throughout the region as we return to Yerushalayim."

"What do you wish me to do?" Philip reached for another fig.

"Unless the Lord directs otherwise," Shimon answered, "return directly to the brethren at the House of Yaakov in Yerushalayim and tell them what has happened. We all have much to consider."

"But be cautious," Yochanan warned. "The persecutions continue. One cannot be too careful."

"One thing more," Philip said slowly. "Perhaps you have a message to send to the house of Jarius Ben Aaron?"

"Jarius?" Shimon Kefa shook head. "I don't know what it would be."

"Why?" Yochanan looked puzzled.

"Earlier," Philip casually shrugged his shoulders, "you spoke of Mariam's trouble. Perhaps, I might take a word of encouragement to her."

"You?" Shimon frowned.

"Mariam has become infected by bitterness," Yochanan leaned back. "She walks through a dark night and is not easily approached. I appreciate your concern, but I think you might do well to walk wide of the house of Jarius."

"You know more than you are saying," Philip probed.

"To talk of the troubles of others," Shimon Kefa cut him off, "blesses no one. Matters that aren't our personal business are best prayed about—not discussed."

"Yes." Philip looked down.

"You must return to Gitta in three or four months," Yochanan instructed Philip. "We will tell the elders that you are the personal representative of the apostles and will have oversight here."

"Well, Philip," Shimon Kefa answered patting the young man on the back. "You have served the memory of Stephanos well. The Holy One has used you to make us see that our vision was too small. But the Gentiles are another matter."

"Who knows?" Yochanan laughed at Shimon. "How many times have you been wrong before, my good brother?"

Shimon Kefa shook his head without answering.

"Philip." Yochanan's countenance changed, and his voice became serious. "You have forced us to go through a new door that we did not even want to see. Your youthful eyes have served us well. Bless you. A new day has begun for all of us."

TWENTY ONE

"The lilies of the valley are so profuse." Jarius pointed toward a large clump of flowers along the city street.

"I love spring." Mariam took her father's arm as they walked down the familiar lane toward their house. "The warm breezes are so invigorating."

"I'm glad you came today." Jarius tried to sound casual.

"Many of the believers have asked about you. I know people were glad to see you again."

"Good. If it makes you happy."

"Your happiness is my happiness," Jarius patted her hand.

Mariam said nothing, returning to her all-too-familiar silence.

"Perhaps we might sit down." Jarius pointed to a low wall. "We don't have to return home quickly. The Sabbath is a good day for just seeing what is around us."

"The hills are becoming green again." Mariam looked toward the skyline that surrounded Yerushalayim.

"The rains were good this year. The grasses will be full. Yes, let's sit here."

Jarius looked at his daughter. Her little-girl hands had turned into facsimiles of her mother's. Long and tapered, Mariam's fingers had taken on the elegance of cultured women. Her vibrant olive skin softly covered the veins that rose across the back of her hand like little rivers meandering into a maze of tributaries. The slender, graceful lines from her palms to her wrists artistically blended into the hands of a woman.

"Business has been good, but I miss . . ." Jarius picked up several smooth stones that he rolled around in the palm of his hand. "We should do well during the festivals."

"You are the best craftsman in the city." Mariam turned and smiled at her father. "No one makes the Yerushalayim dedaheba as you do."

Jarius reached out to touch his daughter. The childhood chubbiness had vanished and her cheek bones had became more prominent. Mariam's neck was more slender now. The delicate fine profile was the same, but her mouth and lips had become more defined. Mariam had become a young woman no man would miss.

For a long time they sat together silently looking out over the city. Jarius ground the little rocks together in his hands, searching for something to say. Too many areas had become sensitive, and Jarius could not adjust to Mariam's new sharpness. He simply waited, hoping for some significant point of contact.

"Perhaps, we should go on," Mariam stood.

"Of course." Jarius followed her lead down the narrow street that was virtually empty. Vendors, merchants, and artisans alike avoided even the slightest hint that any work was being performed on the Sabbath. Here and there children scurried between the houses, laughing and chasing each other. Yet nothing broke the all-encompassing peace of the Holy Day. Divine reprieve sheltered everyone from the confrontations and abrasions of daily life.

As always Jarius touched the long, thin mazusseh on the door post of his home and blessed the name of God.

"You have a guest," the servant said as he met Jarius in the entryway. "Come quickly to the living room. Simeon has been waiting for some time."

"Who?" Jarius quickly followed the servant, who nervously swept the curtain aside.

"Simeon!" Jarius opened his arms wide offering an embrace.

His brother stood, courteously bowing his head. "I thought that we might talk." Simeon lowered his eyes.

"Well—yes, yes, of course."

"Uncle!" Mariam broke into the room.

"It has been some time," he said apologetically.

"Much, much too long." Jarius hugged his brother, kissing him on both cheeks. "Wine! Some honey cakes." He pushed the servant out of the room. "Brother. Please sit down." Jarius pushed a chair to the center of the large open room.

"I trust business goes well." Simeon sat stiffly in his chair. He looked around at the plain walls and the corner fireplace. Nothing had been added since his last visit.

"Oh, yes," Jarius beamed. "Here—Mariam—sit down. We haven't seen your uncle in months."

Mariam continued standing near the door. "And your business?"

"I have had a good winter," Simeon's expression did not change, "but it has not been easy to find gem stones at a good price. Zeda was the master of the art."

"Oh most certainly." Jarius smiled nervously.

"I should have come earlier." Simeon rubbed his

hands together, turning the back of his hand over in his palm. "I know we have all struggled with the difficulties of these past days."

"No question." Jarius vigorously nodded his head. "Lots of uncertainty everywhere."

"I tried to do the right thing," Simeon continued defensively.

"Of course, of course." Jarius encouraged him.

"I have been very disillusioned." Simeon ran his hand through his hair. "Disgusted with the actions of many of my colleagues. I thought," he sighed deeply. "I thought . . ." Simeon shook his head. "The arrests have been a disaster. The high priest and his cohorts panicked." Simeon pulled at his beard. "The whole matter has gotten completely out of hand."

"People have died." Mariam's voice was cold and distant. Slowly she walked toward the fireplace standing with her back to her uncle.

"I know." Simeon hung his head and gestured feebly. "I feel very badly about these matters."

"These matters?" Staring into the hearth filled with cold ashes, Mariam tightly crossed her arms. "How about these people?"

"I never wanted anyone to be hurt!"

"Possibly you have heard of a young rabbi called Shaul?" Mariam asked cynically.

"Mariam." Jarius shook his head, implying she should lower her voice. "We are talking to your uncle."

"You have heard of this Shaul?" Mariam turned slowly toward Simeon.

"Yes," Simeon answered slowly, looking perplexed.

"He seems to be somewhat of an executioner," she sneered.

"An executioner? No, no." Simeon shook his head in surprise. "But I know of Shaul."

"Of course, you do!" Mariam snapped. "You are the

one who introduced him to the Sanhedrin!" Mariam
thrust her finger in Simeon's face. "You are the one who
unleashed this mad dog on us."

"No!" Simeon's mouth dropped. "You are distorting
everything." He stood slowly. "I insisted that your family be protected."

"Then you admit it." Mariam poked Simeon in the
chest. "You even have spared us at the expense of our
friends. Perhaps, you only wanted to avoid the embarrassment of having your own family dragged to the
prison."

"Mariam!" Jarius pulled at her sleeves. "Your uncle is
a rabbi."

"You are twisting the facts." Simeon's voice became
shrill.

"Twisting?" Mariam's eyes widened. "I will tell you
about twisting. The night they brought the body of the
man I loved into this very room and laid him on this
floor, I saw the meaning of twisted. The rocks and
stones that this Shaul caused to be thrown at him left
his body twisted and broken."

"Mariam," Jarius pleaded again. "We are still a family."

"You killed him!" Mariam shouted in her uncle's face.

"I was promised that there would be no violence,"
Simeon pleaded. "I thought Shaul would only debate
with the young Greek. Nothing more . . ."

"Young Greek?" Mariam clenched both fists. "Young
Greek!" she shouted. "So there is not even a question
that you knew about Stephanos."

"They were only supposed to debate. We had a responsibility to the truth."

"The truth?" Mariam mocked him. "You would not
even listen to the experiences of your own family. You
treated our testimony as lies. What would you know of
the truth?"

"Please." Jarius tried to step between his daughter and brother.

Mariam pushed him aside. "You are fortunate," her voice was cold and measured. "If there was not some remnant of my faith left in me—" She shook both fists in Simeon's face. "I would try to do to you what they did to him. Now get out of this house or I may lose even that final restraint."

"But," Simeon tried to protest. "We must not be—"

"You declared us dead to you." Mariam bit her lip. "Now hear me. You are dead to me. Don't ever let me see you again."

"Jarius—" Simeon pleaded with his brother.

When Jarius reached for Mariam, she turned back to the fireplace, locking her arms across her chest again.

Jarius looked down shaking his head and wringing his hands.

"You are dead to *us*." Mariam stared at the black and gray ashes in front of her.

Slowly Simeon walked toward the hallway. He paused and looked back. Mariam did not move. Jarius continued staring at the floor. Simeon reached out and then dropped his arm. His steps echoed down the empty hall. After he opened the door, Simeon stopped one last time. He ran his hand across the rough wood of the door jam touching the mazusseh lightly. His hand froze in place. Instantly, he remembered the moment years ago when he and Jarius had placed a fragment of Psalm 133 in the little box. "Behold how good and pleasant it is when brothers dwell in unity." Slowly Simeon's hand slid down the wall. He pulled the door shut behind him and began the long walk away from his brother's house.

———————————— • ————————————

The whole assembly of elders and leaders sat spellbound as Philip described what he had seen in Gitta

three weeks earlier. He spoke of the new insights that he
had gleaned as well as the strange story of Simon Magnus. The older men shook their heads in amazement,
while the younger people were enthusiastic and excited.

"Only eternity knows fully what these walls have
heard," Philip pointed toward the huge timbers overhead and to the hanging candle rack of the Upper
Room. "In this very place the old ways have crumbled
before the onslaught of the new. But I tell you another
surprise. God is surely calling us to carry the message
of the Messiah far beyond the House of Israel. Did
Yeshua not say, 'to the ends of the earth'? Well?" He
slowly looked around the room.

When Philip paused the crowd erupted in response.
Older men wrung their hands as the younger men enthusiastically held their fists in the air like warriors
poised for the battle. A few of the elders grumbled. Jarius smiled at the growing excitement.

"Many of us come from the Gentile world. Was not
our first martyr, Stephanos, a hellenized Jew?" Philip
strategically invoked the name of his friend. "Have not
we had this call from the very beginning? The time is
coming when we will no longer be able to avoid a decision. The darkness of the Gentile world awaits the light
that we bring."

Some of the younger men applauded, but many of the
group were clearly perplexed.

"Peace to you, Philip," Toma took the floor. "We will
await the reports of Shimon Kefa and Yochanan with eagerness. They will soon return from the north. You have
given us much to consider." Toma moved quickly to
avoid any further discussion. He held his hands in the
air. "May his grace continue with you always. Go in
peace."

The brisk night air rolled in as the doors were opened for the people to go out into the night. Many continued talking as others moved to the door. Philip walked through the crowd, seeking Jarius.

"Might I have a word with you?" Philip asked respectfully.

"Ah," Jarius turned around, "I would be pleased to speak to you, Philip. You are the hero of the hour."

"Or a troublemaker."

"Yes," Jarius agreed, "you have raised questions that are hard for us to face. Many do not welcome an open door to the north."

"Mariam is here?" Philip asked cautiously.

"No, I'm sorry that she is not."

"I understand that she is troubled."

"She struggles." Jarius smiled weakly.

"I have thought of her very often." Philip's face flushed. "I would like your permission to speak with her."

"Really?" Jarius stroked his beard. "Mariam has been very distressed. Recent events have changed her a great deal."

"Stephanos was like a brother to me." Philip shifted his weight from one foot to the other. "Maybe I could help her find new hope—a new perspective."

"Hmmm." Jarius patted the young man on the back. "Maybe you could be of help in getting Mariam's mind on other things. Please come as often as you wish."

"Thank you." Philip shook his hand. "Thank you. I will come by in the near future."

"Yes." Jarius continued shaking his hand. "You are a fine young man. I trust you will waste no time in coming to my house."

The sun rose earlier and stayed later as spring's promise continued to unfold. Spirits lifted as the days lengthened. The uneasy lull in the Sanhedrin's battle against the People of the Covenant continued. The wave of fear that had gripped the church during the winter was disappearing. Old rumors of impending doom were silenced by new reports of success and victory. During the three weeks since Philip's return, consternation had shifted to the debate over the inclusion of the Gentiles.

When Jarius first heard the latest extraordinary news, he waited for further confirmation before bringing the report home. Two days later another caravan from the East confirmed the early reports. Yaakov told him that some of the apostles had heard the same story. However, Jarius and Yaakov agreed that the message could be only a ploy to cause believers to lower their defenses.

Three days after Jarius talked with Yaakov, a communique came from Barnabba also confirming the earlier stories. Jarius knew that it was time to tell Mariam the remarkable news. He waited for supper, hoping that she had not yet heard.

Once they had eaten, Jarius silently stared into the adjoining family gathering room. The lone candle in the far corner filled the room with shadows that evoked painful memories. After a few moments, Jarius turned his head away, focusing his attention in their dining room. "As always, you have proven to be the woman of the house. The supper is excellent." The fire in the corner fireplace cast dancing shadows along the wall. A tall clay pot filled with tall flowers had been set in the opposite corner. The fresh spring flowers filled the room with fragrance.

"Thank you, Abba." Mariam offered him a bowl filled with lentils. "Perhaps, some more?"

"No, thank you. I want to offer you something."

"You have a surprise?"

"Yes." Jarius beamed. "I believe I have something astonishing to tell you."

"It is about Philip?" Mariam smiled coyly.

"Philip?"

"Yes." Mariam acted nonchalant. "He was here today and said he came with your blessing . . . Philip means well." Mariam was distant and indifferent. "I know he wanted to encourage me. I sent him away."

"Pain has shallowed you daughter," Jarius was uncharacteristically blunt, "and bitterness has blinded you. Once you read the hearts of others, now you do not even perceive how you hurt them. Even I felt the sting that you left on Simeon's face."

"Father!" Mariam's eyes widened.

"No, Mariam." Jarius shook his head. "We have waited too long to speak of these matters. Before my very eyes I am watching you turn into someone I do not even know. I was the one who always demanded justice until you helped me find a better way. I fear my old preoccupation has become yours. You have lost the ability to forgive."

"You should not say such things to . . ." She stopped and her voice faded. Mariam stared at the table but made no response.

"Simeon was wrong when he abandoned us," Jarius's voice was even and steady. "But we were wrong when we turned him out."

Mariam folded her hands in her lap and she dropped her head even further.

"Hear me child. God's mercy also triumphs over injustice. As you sat hour after hour in the garden, you lost sight of what Yeshua's death meant. Surely the death of our rabbi was the greatest injustice of all. But I heard him say from the cross the words that make both justice and injustice irrelevant. Mercy endures and will not be thwarted."

Mariam looked away, rubbing her forehead, trying to regain her composure.

"We have no choice but to receive and extend the same mercy that God gives to his enemies—that he has chosen to bestow on Rabbi Shaul."

"Shaul?" Mariam looked at her father for the first time. "What are you saying?"

"The story has now been confirmed." Jarius was factual but intense. "The Holy One of Israel has chosen to be very kind to this man who has been the persecutor of His people. God has touched our brother Shaul."

"Our brother?" Mariam scowled.

Jarius chuckled. "While Shaul was pursuing our people, an extraordinary experience happened to him on the Damascus Road. Shaul was struck blind until our brother, Chananyah*, prayed for him to receive his sight."

"Chananyah? The disciple?"

"Yes. After Chananyah prayed, Shaul's eyes were opened. This self-proclaimed avenger of God's justice began to proclaim that he had seen Yeshua alive and risen."

"I can't believe it." Mariam's hand automatically covered her mouth. She stared at her father.

"The last report we received from Damascus was that Shaul was thrown out of the Damascus synagogue for arguing that our rabbi is the Messiah."

"Shaul?" Mariam slowly shook her head. "The man who helped kill Stephanos? Shaul?"

"Rather unjust thing God has done. Unjust but so very merciful."

*Ananias

"But Stephanos . . ." her voice trailed off.

"Mariam, let go of your disillusionment, your bitterness, your pain. Our God has offered us a better way. We have no war with Simeon, with Shaul, with anyone. Mercy, Mariam. Don't be afraid of mercy."

TWENTY TWO

Yehosaf Ben Kaifa slouched uncharacteristically in his chair, glowering at the Great Sanhedrin assembled before him. His jeweled breastplate hung slightly off center. He tugged at his beard, periodically staring at Simeon. His lacky, Josiah, walked nervously among the zekenim* seated on the front row, whispering instructions in their ears. A speaker continued making his report as if he were completely unaware of the distraction being caused by the servant of the high priest.

The speaker lowered the scroll. "Finally, the report from the synagogue in Damascus states that Rabbi Shaul was ejected for his teaching. He is now living somewhere in the city with the followers of the Way. He has defected and now preaches for them." His words echoed back from the high ceiling, bouncing off the wooden paneled walls in ominous tones.

Angry discussion broke out across the room. Ben Kaifa shifted in his chair but did not cease to stare at

*Spiritual leaders

Simeon who sat isolated in his silence as the men around him talked to each other. A ray of sunlight from one of the high windows fell on the table in front of Simeon as if the Divine had even chosen to mark him.

"And where did this Shaul come from in the first place?" One of the men on the front row stood up. "How did he ever come into our midst?" He hammered the long mahogany desk top with his fist.

"Perhaps," the high priest pointed toward the huge wooden door at the back. "Simeon Ben Aaron can explain."

"He was a student of Gamaliel." Simeon rose slowly. "He was recommended to us as an excellent debater."

"To us? I believe you are the one who brought him," Ben Kaifa charged.

"He was sought as an alternative to the violence which has been so counterproductive," Simeon answered bitterly.

"He tries to hide the fact," Josiah interrupted, "that this Shaul avoided attacking Simeon's own family who are apostates and idolaters. Perhaps, there is more that he also has not told us."

Simeon stared at the servant who stood smirking in the front. He said nothing.

"Yes," an older zekenim at the front stood and addressed the Sanhedrin, "it is convenient that the rabbi from Tarsus converts immediately after we have given him papers representing us. Are *you* next, Simeon Ben Aaron?"

"I have tried to be a voice of moderation," Simeon protested. "I wanted no more deaths."

"Except the whole nation of Israel," the high priest mocked. "You have opposed my plans from the beginning, Simeon Ben Aaron," he bore down. "But nothing equals the confusion that this turncoat has caused.

How can we possibly trust you or your advice again?" The high priest made a sweeping gesture with his dark blue robe, inviting the response of his supporters. Instantly the zekenim at the front stood and applauded. The whole room broke into an uproar. Ben Kaifa slithered back into his chair. A sly sinister smile broke across his face.

Simeon watched his former associates shake their fists at him. His closer comrades looked down. No one spoke for him. The sheer weight of the cold isolation pushed him back onto his bench.

"Now let us give our undivided attention to our God-given leadership," Josiah spoke over the noise. "Let us no longer be distracted nor divided by duplicitous voices in our midst. Hear our high priest."

Simeon watched Yehosaf Ben Kaifa stand again, adjust the breast plate, and clear his voice. He strutted back and forth as if pondering a great and weighty statement. Simeon had seen the performance many times before but never at such expense to himself.

"Of course, it is difficult to assess what sort of plot may be afoot," the high priest said slowly and deliberately. "Perhaps only time will clarify the full truth. However, one thing is clear." Yehosaf looked carefully around the room. "We can no longer tolerate any division in our ranks. I expect unqualified support."

Immediately the room broke into vigorous applause. The high priest placed both hands on his hips. With his feet set far apart, he looked like a potentate surveying his domain. Simeon sunk deeper into his chair. Even his best friends did not look his way.

The gentle spring breezes made sitting outside a popular preoccupation with the Yerushalayimites. Almond trees exploded in their array of white flowers as the grapevines sprang to life again. Children chased each other through the streets. Even the Roman soldiers seemed less caustic and abrasive.

The conversion of Shaul was the preoccupation of both the followers of the Way and their opponents. Many praised God while others saw only an elaborate plot to fool the brethren. The traditional Jewish population was defensive and spoke of infectious madness. Some of the believers thought that the remarkable story was yet another sign of the imminent return of Yeshua and the end of history. While everyone had an opinion, the man from Tarsus was essentially an enigma to all. The rumors of Yerushalayim had no rest.

Philip thought about the mystery of Shaul's change of mind as he waited for a servant to answer the door. Standing in the doorway of the Ben Aaron household made the totally unanticipated turn of events seem all the more improbable. What does one say about the redemption of the man who has brought the death of one whom you love? One should rejoice—and yet.

"Mariam is expecting you," the servant said as he opened the door and bid Philip follow him.

Nothing more was said as Philip followed the man through the house and out into the open courtyard in the center of the house. Once again the grapevines had sprung to life. Flowers had come again in the bed around the stone patio. A small almond tree was still exploding with blossoms. Mariam was sitting in the warm sun with a scroll in her lap. Her fingers moved lightly from word to word.

"You read Hebrew?" Philip smiled.

"And Greek," Mariam rolled up the scroll, "and I write each as well." She handed the scroll to the servant.

"Thank you for asking me to come back." Philip sat down beside her.

"Thank you for coming." Mariam smiled. "I owe you an apology. I'm afraid that I was rather abrupt when you were last here."

"No, no." Philip beamed.

"I would like to ask you a few questions." Mariam's face became serious. "Is it true that this Shaul has become a believer in the Way?"

"Every report confirms what we first heard. Yes, God seems to be breaking down all doors of opposition, and Shaul has come in."

Mariam's eyes narrowed. She rubbed her chin and settled back on her little stool, saying nothing.

"I have seen the Samaritans embrace our faith," Philip continued. "Anything is possible. Is not the resurrection itself the guarantee of the power of our message?"

"Then why do we seem so weak and helpless?" Mariam did not snap as she had when Philip was last there. Her eyes looked uncertain and pained.

"You are thinking of Stephanos's death?"

"I can't seem to get beyond what I saw that night when you helped carry his body into this house. The horror of his bruised broken skin still rises in my dreams. If our Rabbi Yeshua had such power, how could we be so vulnerable?"

"I—I—I don't know." Philip's forehead and brow were deeply furrowed. "No one has asked me such a question."

"I know that I should rejoice over the conversion of this Shaul." Mariam wrung her hands. "But I lost my way in all the terrible things I have seen in these last few years. Can you help me?"

Philip looked into her probing eyes. In the last few

weeks he thought of this wondrously beautiful face so many times. Her soft olive skin and the delicate line of her profile were more alluring than ever. And yet the turmoil that was in her soul had become like a hood over her face, covering the light that usually shown there. Philip realized that he had envisioned himself as the hero from Gitta, sweeping in once more, bringing a breakthrough. Now his tongue was frozen in his mouth.

"Can you explain this contradiction?" Mariam reached for his hand. She clutched it with such intensity that any thought of romance was squeezed from Philip's mind.

"I admit that I have avoided our gatherings." Mariam suddenly let go of his hand. "I have so few to talk with. When Zeda died, my aunt returned to her people in the north. I have exhausted my father's ideas. Of course, I cannot talk with other men, but I need help if I am to get beyond this place. Would you pray for me?"

"Yes, of course. Right now?"

"Perhaps . . . now."

Philip stood, placing his hands on her head as he had in Gitta. He poured out his compassion for her, asking the Rudach Ha Kodesh to come and wash away her pain. He could feel Mariam's head shake as she began to weep. He prayed even more intently. A great sense of peace finally settled over Philip. He left after that moment, feeling awkward in her presence. He wanted to take her in his arms, and yet he had just prayed for her. The contradictions confused him. Philip knew he couldn't be the answer for the house of Jarius Ben Aaron. As he walked down the street he realized that Mariam had an almost fathomless sensitivity that was totally foreign to him. There was a depth in her eyes that arose from a soul shaped of different clay than his own.

Philip kept remembering her words. "I have so few to talk with . . . My aunt returned to her people . . . I have exhausted my father . . . I cannot talk with the men . . ." Philip pondered the conversation and the uncrossable chasm between them.

"I know!" he suddenly said aloud. "She has been talking to the wrong people." He changed directions and took the Street of the Chain, which led finally to the Upper Room.

———————————◆———————————

The Upper Room was unusually quiet when Mariam entered. The late afternoon sunlight streamed through the windows, casting shadows around the room. Mattiyahu pointed to the opposite end of the room where Yochanan and Toma sat reading from the Torah.

"Shalom unto Mariam, daughter of Jarius." Yochanan laid the scroll down. "Thank you for coming. Please sit with us."

Mariam took a seat at the table. She lowered her head respectfully and waited for one of the men seated at the table to speak.

"Philip came to speak with us two days ago," Yochanan began. "We have carefully pondered what he said to us."

"We have been keenly aware of your distress." Mattiyahu sounded matter of fact. His years as a tax collector had left a sharpness in his voice that often concealed his tender heart. "We have worried about what was best for you."

"We have prayed often," Yochanan's voice was warm and compassionate as always, "but there has been no clear direction . . . until Philip came."

"We wish to discuss two matters with you today." Mattiyahu was precise. "We believe that we can help resolve the confusion that has overcome you."

Mariam sat quietly, saying nothing.

"My child," Yochanan spoke softly, "you have a way of touching the center of people. On the other hand, we are men who have survived the brutality and cruelty of a world that devours the gentle. We have little understanding of a soul like yours. We erred in not recognizing that fact earlier. Philip's concern for you has opened our eyes. I think we know what to do now."

"Yes?" Mariam looked back and forth between the three men. "What are you suggesting?"

"First," Mattiyahu said factually, "we feel you need a constructive task that will engage your quick mind. You have spent too much time alone."

"I don't understand." Mariam shook her head.

"Philip has opened the doors to the north." Mattiyahu pointed toward the window. "The story of Yeshua must be written down as the message spreads quickly. You know many details of the ministry. Between the two of us, we can compile an account of the Messiah that will teach them the truth."

"Write an account?" Mariam puzzled.

"We need your help." Yochanan smiled. "You can read and write Greek and Hebrew. Because you have servants, you have the time to write. We believe that the Holy One of Israel would have an accurate account made of these matters."

"I . . . I don't know . . ." Mariam blinked her eyes. "I am surprised. When you sent for me, I was afraid someone else had been killed. I just don't know what to say."

"I have already begun the work," Mattiyahu spoke in rapid staccato tones. "Right now I am compiling all of the basic teachings of the Messiah. You can help me select some of the incidents that people should remember."

"I am not worthy." Mariam turned away. "I have lost my way in my own struggles. What have I to say?"

"All of us have gone through times of confusion and doubt." Yochanan reached for the Torah scroll on the table and moved it back in front of him. "We have had to search the sacred writings to find our way, but we have grown through the struggle. The same will be true of you."

"But there are matters," Mariam bit her lip, "that still leave me defeated and beaten. I . . . I just don't know . . ."

"That is the second matter." Yochanan took her hand. "There is one who understands your pain better than anyone else."

"One of the apostles?" Mariam asked.

"No," Yochanan stroked his beard, "Philip suggested that you need to talk with a woman. More than anyone she knows what it is to have a sword pierce the heart."

"A woman?" Mariam shook her head.

"She spends most of her time in seclusion, praying for us and our work, but she was glad to offer herself to you."

"Who?"

"I speak of another Miryam*," Yochanan answered. "We want you to talk with Miryam, the mother of Yeshua. Who could help better than the woman who stood at the foot of the cross when her own innocent son was put to death?"

"Miryam awaits your visit." Mattiyahu smiled for the first time.

At first Simeon had resented his Arab friend Ishmael's makeshift canvas tent, where he now practiced his trade. The Ben Aaron family building had offered durability, warmth, and, of course, reputation. Nevertheless,

*Mary

the landing near the Pool of Siloe had proven to be profitable.

Simeon laid the array of golden chains across the wide piece of silk cloth. He ran his hand across each one, like a father caressing a child who is the source of great pride.

"This is your best price?" The burly man in front of him crossed his arms. "You understand that buying the whole lot is a considerable sum?"

"There is no better workmanship in this city," Simeon did not budge. "Each chain will sell quickly."

"I don't understand." The gruff-looking man shook his head. His beard quivered. "You have an excellent business. Why would you sell out your entire stock?"

"My offer to you is more than fair."

"Yes, yes." The customer picked up one of the chains and held it to the sunlight. "We both know the price is right. Why are you doing this? I have known you for years, Simeon Ben Aaron. I just want to know what is going on."

"I am leaving," Simeon said flatly.

"Leaving?" The man's eyes widened.

"Yes." Simeon fixed his eyes on the chains, "I am leaving and have no idea if I will ever return."

"You hold a prestigious position! Many of us are only merchants, but you sit with the powers that be."

"I need to explore the trade routes." Simeon tried to sound indifferent. "I want to go to the places where jewels are sold."

"But you have an established reputation . . ."

"Reputation?" Simeon snapped. "Yes, I suppose I have come to have a reputation here. One cannot control such things. Now, do we have a deal or not?" His rough inflection ended any further inquiry.

"Well," the man shrugged, "I suppose we do." He

pulled a leather pouch from beneath his robe and began emptying gold coins on the table. "When will you leave?"

"Soon," Simeon scooped up the coins, "very soon."

TWENTY THREE

Mariam carefully chose her path down the sloping street, trying to keep up with Yochanan. The old Jebusite city of David was honeycombed with narrow, meandering streets, winding toward the Valley of Hinnon. Because Mariam had seldom been in this ancient section of Yerushalayim, she watched Yochanan carefully to see which of the streets he turned down. She knew the tomb of King David was ahead, and the Tower of Siloe was near. Turning abruptly to the left, he pointed ahead. Mariam looked up at the muddy brown house that loomed at the end of the passageway. Her own home was obviously more expansive than this plain, one-story stucco building. The house was well-hidden in the maze of back streets. A wall and gate guarded the front door.

"Miryam has lived with me ever since the day of the crucifixion." Yochanan slowed his rapid pace. "She has become as my own mother."

"She does not stay with Yaakov?" Mariam stepped lightly over a large hole in the cobblestone street.

"At times she visits, but Yeshua gave me charge of her well-being."

"You have many visitors?"

"In the beginning," Yochanan opened the gate, "many people came. In fact, we had an endless procession of inquirers." He closed the gate and secured it. "Finally, Miryam was exhausted by the pressing crowd. And then we became concerned that she might be caught in the persecution. So I found a secluded place for us."

"She must be very lonely." Mariam paused at the doorway.

"No, I think not," Yochanan said slowly. "Each day Miryam prays constantly for the People of the Way. Her world is filled with unseen companionship."

"Oh?" Mariam pursed her lips. "She must be very unusual. Miryam knows that I am coming?"

"Of course." Yochanan pulled the leather tong that opened the wooden latch. "Occasionally she speaks with young women and people that we feel have a special need to come here." Yochanan touched the mazusseh on the door lightly and swung the door open.

There was no hallway or fine entry area. Instead, they stepped directly into a sparsely furnished room. The plain walls blended into the hardened clay floor. A large wooden table with two benches was in the center of the room. In the center of the opposite wall was a door. The low ceiling with protruding wooden beams made the whole room feel very close.

A fire crackled in the small gray fireplace in the corner. Over the hearth hung a cooking pot hung on blackened chain. The aroma of the vegetables stewing and the ancient smokey scent of the house blended together into an inviting warmth that reminded Mariam of her kitchen. A little woman whose head and face were covered with a hood was sitting near the fireplace on a wooden stool.

"Shalom," Yochanan called. "We are here."

Miryam stood and pulled the hood back. Her graying hair made her look about the same age as Jarius. Her face was small and delicate. Miryam's unadorned homespun dress was like the common women; yet she carried herself with an unusual bearing of gentle but regal authority. Miryam still wore the widow's black robes of mourning.

"I have eagerly awaited your coming." She offered her hand. "I am Miryam."

"I am honored," Mariam fumbled.

"Come, sit down, my child." Miryam led her toward the table. "The walk from the steps of the Temple entrance is long and steep. You must be tired."

"Let me just look at you for a moment." Miryam slipped onto the bench across from Mariam. "Yes, you do remind me of my own daughter. Your visit will be like my child coming to see me." Her kind smile was obviously meant to put Mariam at ease.

"Thank you." Mariam kept looking down.

"You have known much suffering," Miryam observed gently.

"I have been so terribly lonely." Mariam continued to look at the floor.

"I understand." When Yochanan placed several small pieces of wood on the fire, Miryam turned to him. "My daughter and I are going to have a wonderful time together. Please leave us until the ninth hour. We have much to discuss."

Yochanan nodded and piled several more large pieces of wood on the hearth. After setting an earthen jug of wine and cups on the table, he left.

"My son spoke of you," Miryam rested her head

against her hands, leaning forward. She looked across the table lovingly.

"He did?"

"Yes, he told me of your recovery, and he said that one day we would meet. I have been expecting you for a long time."

Mariam stared in amazement.

"Not having a mother has been hard."

"How . . . how, do you know?"

"The Holy One, bless His name, has given me a special task. Now I am the mother of the motherless. Such matters are clear to me."

"Her absence has been very hard. I have longed to talk with someone who can tell what only a woman can know."

"And Adonai will use *you* to tell what only a woman can understand." Miryam's voice became intense. "No one can comprehend the pain and loss that death brings as does a woman. My child, the Rudach Ha Kodesh will use the agony of these days for the glory of God."

"But," Mariam protested, "I have lost my way. My perspective has been twisted. I am not worthy to . . ."

Miryam put her finger to Mariam's lips. "Do not let the noise of the battle confuse you. The wounds of the warfare strain the integrity of every soul. Except for the strong arm of the Lord, none of us would be able to stand."

"I haven't endured. I have been so confused." Mariam wrung her hands. "Everywhere I see the innocent caught in the web of evil. The inequity, the injustice is monstrous. I do not think that I can stand it any longer."

"My son left a message for you. During such bad times when death is on the prowl, you are to answer with *his* words—not yours."

"His words?"

"He said you should recall what he said that day. 'Talitha cumi'."

"He did remember!"

"Talitha cumi," Miryam repeated softly.

"Talitha cumi," Mariam murmured.

For a long time, the two women were silent. Mariam sat looking down, while Miryam rested her forehead on her hands, prayerfully waiting.

Finally Mariam sighed deeply and looked up. "I know. He has spoken those words to me twice. I must go on through what I do not understand. I just don't know how."

"These outrages often make it difficult to trust our heavenly Father," Miryam observed. "When life turns upside down, it is hard to believe that Adonai is in control."

"I am sorry," Mariam acknowledged, "but my faith has bent under the load. I am so confused."

"Now I want to tell you a story." Miryam walked to the fireplace and began stirring the vegetables in the pot over the fire. "None are left to remember those dark days. They are all dead and gone now." The pungent aroma drifted across the room once more.

"I know well how hard it is to trust our Abba when we are caught up in circumstances that are unexplainable, unknown, improbable. But God uses such times to prepare us for the greater things that He intends to do through us. We learn how to trust Him through our failures and doubts, regardless of what we cannot see nor understand."

Miryam put the lid back on the pot and sat down again.

"I was just about your age when it all began. One afternoon I was walking through the meadows when I suddenly discovered a man watching me from the trees on the edge. Immediately I was afraid of him and started inching my way toward the little road that would take me back to Natzeret, my village. Suddenly he called me by name and told me to stop. Panic gripped me. I had never seen him before."

"And?" Mariam leaned forward.

"He called out, 'Shalom Miryam, favored lady! Adonai is with you!' I was disturbed, troubled by such a greeting. But he walked quickly across the field until he stood directly in front of me. Being so young, I had not spoken to many men outside of my family. I was bewildered. Then he said, 'Don't be afraid, Miryam, for you have favor with God. Look! You will become pregnant, you will give birth to a son, and you are to name him Yeshua. He will be great, he will be called Son of HaElyon, God will give him the throne of his forefather David; and he will live in the House of Yaakov forever. There will be no end to his kingdom.' The messenger's words still burn in my ear."

Miryam threw her hands in the air. "I asked the man, 'How can I have a baby?'"

Mariam shook her head in dismay.

"The man answered, 'The power of HaElyon will overshadow you. The child that is to be born will be holy.' All I could think of was that the elders would stone me as an adulteress! I was terrified."

Miryam slowly stood and walked to the window. She looked out into the late afternoon. Silhouetted by the fading sunlight, Miryam glowed with a softness usually reserved for the young.

"That night I had a wondrous dream that I was walking into a great sunburst. The sun seemed to spin out of orbit and was coming to greet me. The radiance was warm, good, engulfing me like a spring day beside the

Gennesaret. Although my eyes were closed, I thought that if I looked I might be blinded by the brilliance. I felt as if I had been chosen to make the high priest's yearly entry into the Holy of Holies. I fell asleep bathed in warmth and wrapped in the arms of God."

"I know about the life-giving light." Mariam's voice was filled with awe.

Miryam turned away from the window. "In the weeks that followed my body confirmed the words that I had heard in the field. Then I knew that the man was a messenger of the Most High. Even though I was betrothed to Yosef, I knew that there was no way in the world that I could convince him of what had happened. I was quite alone. Do you understand? I was quite alone. With fear in my heart I dared to wonder what sort of God would lead an innocent girl into a place of total embarrassment, ostracization, condemnation—the source of injustice, but the Almighty himself."

"And your parents," Mariam ventured gingerly.

"Consternation consumed them. They were humiliated. I knew that they were sure I was not telling them the truth. Finally they sent me away to stay with my cousin, Elisheva*. Some day I will tell you that story. But I want you to know that many times each day I would ask myself, 'What has God done to me? Why?'"

"You must have been terrified! No one could have believed such a story."

"The night of my visitation I knelt down by my bed and put my face on the floor. I cried out to Adonai, declaring that I was his servant. I prayed, 'Let it be done according to your word'. At that moment I found a peace to which I could return again and again. As the months passed, I started to realize that the Holy One

*Elizabeth

often allows the unthinkable in order to achieve the unattainable.

"And that is what you must remember, my child. Our Messiah rose out of poverty, confusion, and the semblance of injustice. He is part of the mystery of a universe whose order is constantly being disrupted by chaos. Yet his birth, life, and crucifixion are an assurance that these unjust and unexplainable intrusions finally will be made to serve the purposes of our God."

Mariam rubbed her forehead. "I hear," she said slowly. "I hear your words," her voice trailed away. "But I have lost one that I loved so . . ." Mariam stopped abruptly, gesturing awkwardly as if she might catch her words and snatch them back.

"The loss of one who is innocent," Miryam's eyes clouded, "violates everything in our souls. My destiny has been to carry these hideous assaults in my heart— even from the beginning, it was so. When Yeshua was born, soldiers came to destroy all the babies in our village. I knew well the mothers whose cries filled the night. Their only crime was to have their babies in the season of reckoning. And my innocent baby was the reason for the assault on them. As we escaped in the night, I carried their cries in my heart, I still hear Rachael crying out for her lost children. Oh yes, my son grew up in the shadow of persecution and transgression.

"But I tell you the most unspeakable day of all was when I saw him stagger down the street with a cross on his back. I had watched Yeshua grow up before my eyes like the purest lamb in the flock. He had worn goodness like others wear a mantle. When I saw the unspeakable evil, I could not even find a voice to cry out. My soul was torn as if the wild dogs of Gey-Hinnon* had turned on me."

*Jerusalem garbage dump, origin of Hell

Miryam clinched both fists so tightly that her knuckles became white. For a few moments her hands shook. Then she relaxed and breathed deeply. "When he was a boy, our family studied the Psalms together. Yosef would read, and Yeshua would memorize. He drank up the words like a thirsty sponge. Almost from the instant he heard, the words were etched in his mind. He listened and then repeated them back to us. When we went to the Temple for Yeshua's Bar Mitzvah he sang the Psalms like one of the choir."

Miryam paused and silently reflected for a long time. "On that bleak Friday afternoon," she began again, "he looked down at me. His words were barely audible but those who were closest heard him speaking Aramaic, 'Eli! Eli! L'mah sh'vaktani?' Those who didn't understand thought that he had cried, 'My God, my God, why have you forsaken me?'" Miryam spoke confidentially. "The observant ones knew he was quoting Psalm 22. But I know why he chose those words."

"My father was there that day," Mariam exclaimed. "The injustice, the terribleness of the cruelty overwhelmed him."

Miryam shook her head. "Virtually no one understood. But I knew why he quoted that psalm. Remember, my child? Remember the rest of the words? Many times I heard Yeshua recite the heart of that Psalm. 'My praise shall be of you in the great congregation. The afflicted shall eat and be satisfied. Those who seek him shall praise the Lord! All the ends of the world shall remember and turn unto the Lord. For the Kingdom is the Lord's!' Do you see it?"

Mariam shook her head in bewilderment.

"At the black moment my son knew that he was in the center of God's will. He was proclaiming that every injustice and tyranny would fall before the reign of God. The seeming contradictions of evil will finally be forced

The Dawning

to serve Adonai. He was not abandoned by God. The sunburst had only been momentarily obscured by the clouds. He knew the light would prevail."

"Oh—my," Mariam muttered.

"My son was saying, 'Let it be according to your word'! He was proclaiming in the darkest hour of the battle that the Evil One could not win. The mystery of redemption could not be thwarted even by the death of the innocent. Only when I stood before an empty tomb did I fully grasp his words. My child, our small minds stumble over what we cannot fathom. Only one posture is possible for us. We must trust and worship in the face of what we cannot grasp."

"My head swims," Mariam rubbed her temples. "Your words are like honey but how can I ever digest them? The diet is too rich."

"Remember his words to you," Miryam urged. "You're a walking symbol of the answer. Remember what happened. In the face of death, you stood. We must stand up again and again until nothing can take us down. We may face momentary defeat, but the victory cannot be denied us. Now is the time for you to stand again."

"I did it once . . ."

"Child, death comes in many shapes. The death of dreams, hopes, and even loves. Death comes when all joy is lost and the promise seems gone forever. We have to stand up at those moments. We cannot let what others do not understand keep us from standing nor can we allow the tyranny of lies and the monstrous abuse of power bend us to the ground. We know that the door into the tomb swings both ways. You *can* arise once more."

Suddenly Mariam hurled herself at the little woman. Mariam's body shook and heaved with her sobs. Miryam held the young women's head against her breast. When Mariam's crying subsided, the old woman began to rock her gently back and forth.

Miryam softly recited a psalm as she cradled her broken child. "Unto You O Lord, do I lift up my soul. O my God, I trust in You: let me not be ashamed, let not mine enemies triumph over me." Then Miryam began to sing the lines as they were sung in the great Temple services. "Yea, let none that wait on you be ashamed: let them be ashamed which transgress without cause."

At first Mariam's voice was barely audible, but then she sang along softly with Miryam, "Show me your ways, O Lord; teach me your path. Lead me in your truth . . ." Her voice died out as she clung to her new-found mother.

"Now my child," Miryam hugged her one more time, "there are important things to be done, and you have an important place to fill in the movement."

"I will try." Mariam dried her eyes.

"When I was overpowered by the Rudach Ha Kodesh I discovered an amazing thing. The love of God turned into life within me, and the birth that followed brought forth life. The world is filled with so much death that we must constantly allow the same transformation to happen again and again. We are to receive the Abba's love and give life to everyone that we meet."

"When I went to the tombs every day . . ." Mariam stopped.

"You fastened onto death," Miryam interrupted. "Eventually, you were overcome with its depleting effect."

"That's right! That is exactly what I did."

"Now reach out for life. You can stand in precisely the same place and be granted a blessing. Immerse yourself in the love of the Father, and you will once again be filled with life."

"Yes," Mariam said slowly. "Yes." Conviction returned to her voice. "Yes." She clinched her fist tightly. "The time has come for me to leave the shadows of the tombs. The night is past. The day is at hand."

"Hear me child." Miryam stood before her placing one hand on Mariam's shoulder. "I have seen the future, and it shall come to us in these terms. Proud rulers shall fall from their thrones as the humble are raised up. The rich will be sent away empty while the hungry are filled. The House of Israel shall be split asunder but out of the ashes will yet arise the fulfillment with the promises to our father Avraham. In this hour we are small and few in number. Yet we have already become an army on the march. The People of the Way shall arise until the empire sits in their shadow. You will live to see the day when Rome itself will be in awe of us and our Messiah. The day will come when you stand in the streets of Rome and proclaim the glory of HaElyon. Your words shall go across this world and be heard by people yet unborn. Praised be Adonai, the God of Israel, because he has visited and made a ransom to liberate his people by raising up for us a mighty Deliverer."

"I am overwhelmed." Mariam's voice broke. "I must ponder these matters."

"Sit by yourself a while," Miryam walked to the door. "I will leave you now. Be quiet until Yochanan returns. Shalom."

For a long time Mariam did not move. Finally, she got up and walked to the hearth. Taking a twig she poked at the ashes and stirred the embers. The radiant heat leaped out, stinging her hand. She rubbed her hand as if there was something reassuring about the twinge. "Ah, I am truly alive," Mariam said to herself. "Oh, El

Shaddai, grant me wisdom," she prayed softly. And then spreading her arms, she exclaimed, "According to your word! Let it be!"

TWENTY FOUR

As the time for Pesach approached once again, workmen began repairing the road and bridges leading into Yerushalayim. Shopkeepers were already stocking their shelves for the yearly flocking of pilgrims that would soon fill the streets. Workmen were whitewashing the tombs so that the visitors could see the graves of relatives and past heroes without being contaminated should they inadvertently touch the sepulchers.

Shepherds eyed their flocks for the animals that would be used for the Temple sacrifices. The carefully chosen lambs without blemish would be between eight days and a year. Even during the sacrifice, great care would be taken as no bones could be broken. Once within the precincts of the Temple, their throats would be slit as the owners drained the blood of the innocents into gold and silver bowls. The bowls would be dashed at the foot of the great altar where the blood would flow into a hole in the enormous rock where Avraham had nearly offered up Yitzchak centuries before. The underground drain emptied into the Kidron Valley where the usually dry stream bed turned into a spring river of blood. So began the rituals of spring.

Jarius had worked hard during the winter months making Simeon's share of the jewelry. His profits would be less as he had to buy the chains that his brother's more nimble finger made best. On the other hand, there would be no division of profits. Jarius was hopeful.

Mariam had made few journeys to the garden tombs. Rumors of increased warfare by the Zealots made everyone apprehensive about walking beyond the walls. Moreover, her interests had changed. Spring was also returning to the house of Jarius Ben Aaron.

When the smell of warm freshness filled Mariam's bedroom, she looked out the window at the radiant white blossoms of the almond trees, which could be seen everywhere. The invitation was too much to be denied. The walk through the city would be good for her. Mariam reasoned that a stroll beyond the wall would be good for her. Yes, she would sit again before the tomb. She had been there only a short time when she heard someone calling.

"Mariam! Mariam!" Jarius was running toward the tombs as fast as he could. "Where are you?" Mariam saw him leap over a large rock and cut across the grassy mound.

"Over here, Father. I'm here." Mariam stood and waved.

"Come quickly. We don't have much time."

"What's happened?" Mariam began walking toward him.

"Yochanan is calling for you." His chest heaved up and down. "You—must—pray."

"I don't understand."

"There's been a—a terrible attack. Our friend—" Jarius bent over to catch his breath. "Honorius—has been seriously injured."

"Speak slowly." Mariam gripped his shoulder. "Start at the first."

"Attack—ambush—an attachment of soldiers near the Essene Gate! The Romans were outnumbered—but they killed most of the Zealots. Honorius was stabbed in the back. He has lost a great deal of blood."

"Where is he?" Mariam threw her cloak over her shoulder.

"The Romans took him back to the Antonio Fortress. He has called for us to come. The soldiers allowed Yochanan and Yaakov to stay with him. And Yochanan sent for you."

"I don't understand. What can I do?"

"Yochanan believes it is particularly important for you to pray with our friend. But we must hurry, his condition is very grave. We must run as fast as we can."

Jarius reached out for Mariam's hand, pulling her back down the path. Mariam jogged as fast as she could beside her father. They quickly rounded the corners of the great wall of the city and hurried toward the Ephraim Gate. Once inside they wound their way through the treacherous maze of vendors that filled the large marketplace. Having cleared the plaza, Jarius darted for a back alley that provided a short cut across the city. Father and daughter hurried down the narrow passageways that took them through the labyrinthine streets and unmarked sections of the city. The entangled winding streets followed nothing but their own bewildering logic. Only a child of the city such as Jarius could find his way.

"There's the fortress!" Jarius pointed toward the towering bastion of stone that loomed above the low-roofed buildings in front of them. "Once we pass these houses, we must walk slowly or the guards will be suspicious. Hurry now, we're almost there."

Jarius and Mariam walked with determined pace toward the entrance. On each side of the central gate, helmeted soldiers with long spears and battle shields stepped in front of him.

"What business do you have with Rome?" the youthful soldier asked insolently.

"Honorius, the centurion, sent for us." Jarius was polite but firm.

"Oh, yes," the guard deferred. "You have been expected. This is the woman that was requested?"

"Yes," Jarius answered simply.

"Follow me." The guard beckoned them inside. No one became accustomed to the fortress's atmosphere of impending doom. Jarius pulled Mariam close to him as they hurried behind the young man. The huge thick walls were damp as always, and the corridors were musty. Even during the day, torches lit most of the longer passages.

The soldiers were menacing and overpowering. When Jarius and Mariam passed, the Roman guards' steely-eyed stares never changed. Disdain and contempt were obvious.

Turning a corner, Jarius and Mariam saw five soldiers gathered outside a door that was just ahead. The young soldier motioned for them to stop before he walked ahead to speak to the man in charge. Each of the soldiers looked around at the two Jews as though refuse collectors had interrupted their high-level meeting. Finally, the man in charge snapped his fingers at Jarius and Mariam.

"I have no idea why Honorius called for you," his voice was clipped. "He seems to have picked up a fascination with local magic. But I tell you that if anything happens to him neither of you will ever walk out of this fortress again—understood?"

Jarius looked straight ahead without responding.

"Send them in." He pointed toward the door with his thumb.

In the center of the bleak, empty room, Honorius was stretched out on a long, low table. Light from a small window illuminated the heavy, dark, splotched blanket that covered him. Blood had completely soaked through the covering along the contour of his body. His face and arms were uncharacteristically white. Honorius moaned as he slowly moved his head from side to side. Yochanan and Shimon Kefa stood beside him. A Roman in a toga leaned against the wall, watching.

"We're here with you, good friend." Jarius gripped Honorius's hand."

"*Voca mea ad Dominum.*" He spoke in halting Latin. Honorius moved his fingers slightly.

"Thank you for coming quickly," Yochanan spoke directly to Mariam. "The situation is very grave. The doctors cannot stop the bleeding."

"His wounds are serious," the man in the toga interjected, "but not fatal. If the bleeding were to stop—" he hesitated and walked forward. "They say you have healing powers. As a doctor, I respect such things. Do as you wish."

"It has been some time." Mariam nervously ran her hands through her hair, "I don't know."

"We felt particularly drawn to call for you." Shimon put his large hand over hers. "I believe the time has come to start again."

"Then I must stand up." Mariam reached out to touch Honorius. "No," she turned toward the doctor, "I do not have healing powers, but I serve the One who does. We shall call on Him."

Mariam dropped to her knees on the stone floor. Reaching up, she held Honorius's hand in her own. His large hand was very coarse. Mariam could feel the large scar that ran across the top of his hand. His skin was cold and clammy. The apostles and Jarius moved around Honorius, placing their hands on his head and chest.

The room was quiet until Mariam's small gentle voice broke the silence. The beautiful lyrical sound was soothing and fresh like the bird's first song in the morning. She hummed and then the words of a Temple hymn became clear. The Roman doctor obviously couldn't grasp the Hebrew but he walked to the foot of the make-shift bed. Yaakov opened his eyes when he caught the phrase, "My God, my God, why have you forsaken me?" Yochanan looked up in surprise.

Mariam kept singing the psalm, and all three men joined her. Together they chanted, "I am poured out like water—my strength is dried up like a potsherd."

Mariam became louder, "O my strength, hasten to me, deliver my soul from the sword—" The men's voices diminished as her hauntingly penetrating voice floated through the room. "All the ends of the world shall remember and turn unto the Lord and all the kindreds of the nations shall worship before you." Mariam continued humming, singing, praying as she slowly swayed back and forth.

None were aware when the doctor left the room, nor were they conscious that the door had been left ajar so that the other soldiers could watch. The Romans stood reverently and respectfully watching the strange scene of their captives sincerely pleading for the restoration of the life of one who was a ruler of their people.

The four intercessors seemed untouched by the slow passage of time. Eventually, the soldiers slipped away until only the guard at the door remained. The sunlight had long since disappeared through the small barred window when the doctor returned with a torch. He walked around the table several times touching the blanket at different places before he lifted the covering over Honorius's chest. Finally, he reached down and patted Mariam's shoulder.

"He has stopped bleeding," the Roman observed thoughtfully. "Now he has a good chance to recover."

"Three days have passed since we prayed for Honorius." Jarius looked around the Upper Room at the apostles who sat on the rough hewn benches listening. "I am pleased to report that he fairs well. During my last visits I have found a new respect from the soldiers. In fact, several officers have gone out of their way to talk with me."

"News spreads," Toma added. "We are receiving more and more inquiries about our faith. Gentiles are pressing in upon us. We cannot avoid the outsiders much longer."

"Our gaba'im Philip baptized an Ethiopian when he returned from Samaria," Yochanan spoke to the group around him. "Although a Jew, he shared the word with his countrymen, and now we are being urged to go to their cities. The world is listening."

"I think the time has come for me to begin writing an account of what Yeshua said and did." Mattiyahu stood.

"But," Yaakov objected, "the Messiah may return at any moment. The age will end. Books and scrolls will be unnecessary."

"We have argued this point before," Mattiyahu countered. "We must use the time we have left well. A written story could be studied carefully. In the absence of eye witnesses, the believers would have an accurate account. Gentiles have no objective version of these matters."

"I have come to believe Mattiyahu is right," Shimon Kefa acquiesced. "If the report were written in Hebrew, it would preserve our Jewish heritage as we debate the matter of the propriety of our preaching to the Gentiles. Have you not already spoken with Mariam about helping in this matter?"

"Indeed." Mattiyahu turned to Jarius. "Is Mariam ready to begin?"

"Mariam has been returned to us." Jarius smiled. "The dark night is over."

"Life has come back to her hands," Yochanan agreed thoughtfully. "Her prayers for Honorius stayed death itself. I believe Mariam is ready to return to her unique place among us. She will have much to add to the story that Mattiyahu writes."

"Once the scrolls are prepared," Shimon Kefa instructed the group, "they can be circulated among our people."

Some of the men reluctantly nodded their heads and commented quietly to each other. Jarius, Yochanan, and Mattiyahu exchanged knowing glances. An agreement had been struck and the dye was cast.

"I will keep you informed on the progress of our friend Honorius." Jarius bowed formally to the group.

"*Shalom*," they roared back.

"*Shalom aleichem*," Jarius answered as he shut the door behind him. When he looked down at the bottom of the steps, he saw a familiar figure leaning against the wall. "Philip! *Boker tou.*"

"Do you have a moment?" The young deacon bowed awkwardly.

"Of course." Jarius extended his hand.

"I was not sure this was the best time to talk." Philip

gestured nervously. "I knew you would be busy if I came to your shop. And I didn't want to come to your house." He rubbed the toe of his sandal in the dust. "Possibly we might talk as we walk."

"Splendid!" Jarius gently slapped him on the back. "I have wanted to tell you what a brilliant idea it was to take my daughter Mariam to Miryam. You understood what none of us realized. Perfect insight!"

"As a matter of fact," Philip continued as he fell in alongside Jarius, "I wanted to talk with you about Mariam."

"Good." Jarius smiled. "I believe she is ready to return to the tasks God has given her to do. Perhaps, you can be of help."

"Yes," Philip said slowly, "this was something of what I had in mind."

"Excellent! What would you suggest?"

"I have come to speak to you about being betrothed. I want to ask for Mariam's hand."

Jarius stopped in mid-step. "What?" He slowly leaned forward.

"I care deeply for Mariam." Philip began speaking rapidly. "Together we could be of great benefit to the People of the Way. I would fill her life with joy and would withhold no good thing from her. HaElyon would bless us with long life and many children."

Jarius swallowed. He looked at the handsome young man as if he wasn't sure he understood what he had heard. "I had no idea," he muttered.

"I have thought and prayed on this matter for months."

"Does Mariam know?"

"No." Philip looked down. "She has no idea—"

"I see." Jarius nodded his head back and forth. "Then your request is certainly proper and in order." Jarius's brow furrowed. "You know that she loved Stephanos deeply?"

"We all did." Philip shrugged.

"Yes," Jarius said haltingly. "We all did. But of course those days are behind us. We must go on now."

"Exactly!" Philip nodded enthusiastically.

Jarius looked carefully at Philip's pleading eyes. His face was apprehensive and taut. The hero of Gitta looked more like a schoolboy recoiling before the possibility of a reprimand. Such a man without guile could not conceal the depth of his emotion.

"You're a very good man." Jarius smiled kindly. "I always feared that some wealthy family would come seeking Mariam. We would haggle about the dowry and argue over how much money they would provide. When the deal was struck, it would be as if I had purchased diamonds and emeralds from afar. The idea of bartering over the future of my most priceless treasure always left me sick at my stomach."

"I have very little." Philip opened his empty hands. "But—"

"But," Jarius stopped him, "you come offering a pure heart and genuine love. These are gifts beyond price.

"My son." Jarius put his hand on the young ga-ba'im's shoulder. "Surely our Messiah has freed us from measuring the future in terms of wealth. Perhaps, in a year or two or five, he will return. Maybe not. But Mariam's future will not be settled by a pile of shekels."

"I'm not sure I understand," Philip muttered.

"I will pray about your request. And I will talk with Mariam. We will seek the mind of the Lord."

"You will?" Philip's eyes widened.

"Yes," Jarius said slowly. "And in the meantime, I want you to talk with Mariam. I no longer find many of the old ways to be useful. I will not consign Mariam to a future to which she has not agreed. We will let these matters work. If all goes well, we will talk of betrothal on another day."

"Oh, thank you." Philip kissed his hand. Then realizing that he looked foolish, he shook Jarius's hand vigorously. "Yes." he bowed twice from the waist. "Yes, I will come to see Mariam." Philip took several steps backward, bowing and bobbing up and down. "Indeed, I will come soon. Thank you. Yes, in the immediate future I will visit."

He kept moving up and down as he walked backward. "Thank you for being so understanding." Philip waved as he turned to run up the street. "Soon!" he waved over his head. "I'll be there soon."

Jarius watched in astonishment as Philip ran up the street waving his arms over his head. At first he chuckled, then Jarius laughed aloud as he continued walking back to his house.

As he crossed the plaza, a vendor offered him a golden necklace. Jarius quickly recognized the poor workmanship and brushed the man aside. For the first time in weeks, he thought of Simeon.

———————————— • ————————————

At that moment Simeon was walking down the central street of Damascus. He has just passed the palace and was seeking the main marketplace. The rabbi was pondering his strange journey into a foreign world.

Simeon had had no trouble in finding a caravan traveling to the north. Many merchants traveled in the spring before the heat of summer became unbearable. He could choose his fellow travelers. A few drinks, laughs, exchange of lies, and he knew that the squatty Syrian trader and his five would be congenial and safe. Well before dawn, he had fallen in with the long line of donkeys and camels that wound their way through the deeply eroded canyons leading down from Yerushalayim to the plain. Once they found the King's Highway, their safety was virtually assured. Neither nation nor bandit would dare disrupt the main artery of commerce to the entire world.

Before the dawn of time, pharaohs and kings had traveled the same broad thoroughfare from Egypt to Mesopotamia. As centuries passed, the ancient kingdoms of Summer and Akkad had given way to names like Assyria and Babylonia. The Elamites disappeared, and the people of Cush were swallowed by their captors, but the trade on the King's Highway continued unabated.

Father Avraham was the first Hebrew to travel down the dusty passageway. Later the children of Israel wound their way back up from Egypt, following the well-beaten trail. Half a millennium before Simeon Ben Aaron's birth, the Seleucids had marched down over the cobblestone way to become the new law of the realm. When the Maccabees broke the yoke of the Seleucid dynasty and Israel became independent for the last time, Judas Maccabees and his sons had quickly restored trade on this very highway. In a short time, the Romans found the route to be equally useful for their purposes of conquest. Now an obscure Jewish merchant again used the ancient way seeking his fortune.

Simeon might have traveled in the opposite direction toward the port of Elilat. Amalekite, or Elilat Stone, was plentiful there. The mines of Solomon were just beyond the city in the mountains that bordered the Gulf of Acaba. The blue-green amalekite was the gem of choice for his jewelry. Nevertheless, Damascus offered more options for trade than did the remote regions of the south.

Damascus would also be a better place to explore than Elilat. The oldest continually inhabited city in the world had been founded by Uz, the grandson of Shem. The ideal location made the city of antiquity a major trade center. Named for the patterned cloth called damask, Simeon knew that the city would be a good place to start again.

Simeon walked slowly down the street called Straight. Never having been in Damascus before, each sight fascinated him. Because the boulevard ran in an unbending line completely through the city, the main street provided a quick preview of what one would find. At various markets, Simeon stopped and asked for directions toward the Jewish sector and the major marketplace just south of the Amana River. Everywhere Simeon saw the signs of brisk trade.

"Jewelry!" a voice called across the market. "The finest in gold and gems! Visit the best of Damascus!"

Simeon looked across the crowded square. Against the backdrop of a great stone wall, vendors had laid their wares out on long-flowing strips of cloth. Probably there would be many gem merchants in the vicinity.

Simeon ambled among and through the peasants with vegetables spread out on the stone street. The smell of dried hot peppers nearly made him sneeze. Catching his breath, the sickeningly sweet smell of figs knotted his stomach. Picking up the pace, Simeon slid between two camels that were tied to a pole near the wall.

"You have amalekite?" He tried to sound casual.

"Ah—much better." The vendor frowned. "We specialize in lapis. Come and see the finest treasure that Syria has to offer."

"I was seeking amalekite." Simeon kept walking.

"No, no." The vendor tugged at his sleeve. "Once you

have seen our lapis you will completely forget the inferior green stones."

Simeon looked carefully at the man. He was dressed well enough. His long flowing robe was silk, and the girdle at his waist appeared to have strands of gold woven through it. Even his leather sandals looked new. Not many people could afford to dress as well.

"I have a special connection." The vendor kept pulling Simeon toward his stall. "Few merchants can quote you such prices as can we. Lapis is what catches the eyes of the women."

"I seek amalekite from the caves of Solomon." Simeon walked alongside the vendor. "Such stones only come from around the Port of Elilat."

"Yes, yes." The man waved his hand. "In Yerushalayim they specialize in such trivia. But now you have come to the world of sophistication. Lapis is the mark of culture."

Simeon felt uncomfortable as he stepped into the man's little shop. The gold was acceptable but not exceptional. Some of the rings looked good, but others were rough and poorly finished. Jarius would never put such work on their counter.

Jarius, he thought to himself, *I wonder what he is doing this afternoon. Perhaps, a visitor from some foreign country has come as I have to look. There would be no problems in finding amalekite in our—* His mind snapped back to the moment at hand.

"I can make you a very good price on this lapis necklace," the vendor's smile was too patronizing, too wide to be trusted. "You obviously have an eye for fine workmanship."

Simeon ran his fingers gently across the gold clasp at the end of the strand. Only then did he fully realize that his knowledge of lapis was too limited to recognize a good bargain. Amalekite was familiar, but lapis had seldom been used by the Ben Aaron family. Zeda had always handled such matters. Now Simeon must learn.

"Thank you." Simeon abruptly put the necklace down. "I must hurry on." In three long strides he was out of the store, leaving the startled vendor with his mouth open.

Simeon quickly walked down the first alley he saw. He had no idea where he was going but wanted to appear decisive, in charge. The realization of how little he knew about his own trade was unnerving. Zeda and Jarius had provided more insight than Simeon realized.

The side streets of Damascus were not particularly different from Yerushalayim. The gray stone and dull stucco buildings and houses looked the same everywhere, with little to distinguish one from the other. Dirty streets tied the houses together in an unplanned meandering flow of cobblestone. After several blocks Simeon stopped, realizing that it was pointless to go further. Leaning against a wall, he looked around a neighborhood that looked familiar but was completely foreign. In this entire city there was not one person who knew him or cared for his well-being. Simeon, the young man who sat in the Sanhedrin, was an anonymous merchant passing through town like a grain of sand blowing in from the desert. Like the legions of the forgotten, none recalled his passing.

Simeon crossed his arms and drew tightly within himself. For the first time he allowed himself to glimpse at a fragment of the idea that was lurking in the shadows of his mind. Could he be the one who was wrong? What if Jarius and Mariam were right? He clutched his fists tightly as every muscle in his body became taut.

"No!" he said aloud and straightened up from the

wall. Simeon knew he could not let himself ponder what was swirling around in his mind. It would be far better to wander forever than allow himself to be captured by such thoughts. "I have become," he said aloud, "a wandering Jew."

How strange, he thought to himself as he walked aimlessly. *No one can remember when the Ben Aarons were not jewelry makers working under the shadow of the Great Wall.*

Suddenly everything is gone! Zeda is dead. I cannot even face Jarius. A sword has pierced our house and cut the ridge pole asunder. I told them to walk wide of that rabbi! They would not listen.

A noise interrupted his meditation. At first the sound was no different than the usual racket of the street. Someone was talking loudly; men were arguing. When Simeon looked closer, he could see a group of men bantering back and forth.

To his surprise, Simeon realized that he had stumbled into the Jewish section of Damascus. The Morgen David* was on many of the houses. Mazussehs were posted on doors. A group of men were standing in front of the synagogue debating in typical Jewish fashion. Reassured, Simeon walked quickly toward the group. Undoubtedly some point of Torah was at stake.

Simeon smiled. "Two Jews, three opinions!"

Fifteen men were crowded around the front door of the little synagogue, apparently arguing with a man in the center of the group. Simeon slipped into the crowd with his hand to his ear, trying to catch the gist of the discussion. When the man at the center answered one of his questioners, Simeon froze in place.

"You must search the prophets," the familiar voice

*Star of David

crackled, "or you will make the same mistake as have our brethren in Yerushalayim. It was necessary that He die and be buried in order to fulfill the plan of Adonai."

Simeon stared in disbelief as he listened to Shaul, the disciple of Gamaliel.

"We stumble over the crucifixion." Shaul pointed forcefully toward his questioner. "We wanted a political king who would rule with the weapons of war, but God has given us the ultimate victory. Death itself was defeated when Yeshua of Natzeret stepped from the tomb of Yosef of Ramatayim."

Simeon ducked behind a large man shaking his head in disbelief.

"I see no restored paradise," the old man angrily responded. "Peace and justice have not come to us. The world is no better today than it ever has been. How can you even suggest that the Messiah has come?"

"We always expected the wrong thing." Shaul threw his hands in the air, "Have we not always been a stiff-necked people? Our blind hearts have shut our eyes to the truth."

"How dare you call us blind?" a younger man nearly shouted at Shaul.

"Because I was the blindest of all," Shaul immediately acknowledged. "No one was more zealous for the truth than I. I organized attacks on the People of the Way. I was willing to condone killing in the name of truth. Believers and their children were jailed. But I was wrong."

"How can you be so sure?" someone sneered.

"The Messiah came to bring peace to our hearts. The new order must begin within us and then move into the world. He has begun to restore the creation by making all things right within each of us. HaElyon has made a new covenant through the Messiah. Even the goyim are included. I have seen the coming of the risen Lord!" Shaul held both of his hands toward heaven and looked upward. "The light of the world had to blind me in order that I could learn to see. Yes, my brothers, I have seen the Lord."

No one answered. Men shook their heads and looked perplexed.

"I was blinded by His light as I came to your city," Shaul bore down. "As I sat sightless, I realized that the darkness in my soul was far deeper than any night. I knew that I had been wrong. When I cried out to HaElyon, I envisioned a man coming to pray for me. Even as I pleaded before the Holy One of Israel, I felt hands being laid on me. Suddenly my eyes opened again and before me was the face I had seen in my mind. Chananyah, whom many of you know, had prayed and my eyes were opened."

Simeon ground his teeth and clinched his fist. He shook his head vigorously mumbling under his breath.

"You have rejected our brother Chananyah, but I am living evidence that his message is truth. Far more than vision was restored to me. I know now that Yeshua is the fulfillment of all that Adonai has been doing through our people for centuries."

Simeon put his hands over his ears. "No!" he suddenly shouted. "The man blasphemes!"

Men turned and for the first time Shaul saw Simeon.

"He has betrayed his people!" Simeon pointed an accusing finger. "He has betrayed those who trusted him! This man is the worst traitor of all."

Shaul batted his eyes as if seeing another vision. "Simeon? Simeon Ben Aaron?"

"His treachery knows no ends. He tricked all of us on the Great Sanhedrin," Simeon exploded. "He must have been a plant from the followers of Yeshua. We were all deceived. I tell you that this man is from the Evil One!"

"What are you doing here, Simeon Ben Aaron?" Shaul asked in astonishment. "Has the Holy One driven you out of Yerushalayim as well?"

"No! No!" Simeon shook both of his fists at Shaul. Simeon began backing away. "I will have none of this. None of this madness."

"We cannot run from him." Shaul stepped toward Simeon. "I was wrong. God's truth can't be denied. Don't run from the truth."

"No!" Simeon covered his ears. "No," he started to run back up the street. "Deliver me from the insane." Simeon ran toward the market.

Only after Simeon had run blindly down several different alleys did he realize that he had no idea where he was. North, south, east and west were scrambled. Damascus, Yerushalayim, Caesarea, Jericho—maybe Sheol itself— had all blended together. Flat nondescript houses and streets smeared into a sameness that meant nothing. Nothing made sense. Simeon mashed one fist into the other. "No!" he screamed at the top of his lungs.

A young woman with a water jug on her head was walking only twenty feet away. She stopped at his defiant outburst. Pulling her child closer, the lady quickly detoured. Simeon slumped against the wall, slowly sliding down to the pavement. He sat alone, periodically shaking his head as the afternoon sun traveled on toward the evening.

TWENTY FIVE

Jarius took full measure of the woman sitting across the dining table from him. Only yesterday, a month ago—or two years ago, or maybe longer—Mariam was a little girl, a fragile flower of the field about to be cut down before the spring had even begun. He found it difficult not to think of her as a delicate child to be guarded at all cost. In such a short time so much had changed. His conversation with Philip the day before kept returning. His little girl could quickly become a bride.

Jarius stared at Mariam's face, remembering the way she had looked. He recalled the hallow sunken eyes circled in gray and the thin drawn cheeks. He could still see the pale thin lips and the blue tinted fingernails. When he blinked his eyes, the subtle but dramatic shifts in the contour of her face metamorphosed into the beautiful young woman of radiance and health who was smiling at him.

"Something wrong?"

"No—no daughter." Jarius smiled. "I was just thinking that you have become a woman that men would fight to possess."

"Abba!" Mariam recoiled in mock consternation. "Really!"

"It's quite true." Jarius's eyes widened. "You are a rare beauty."

"True beauty is of the heart," Mariam chided her father.

"And yours is pure," Jarius countered. "You are my greatest treasure."

"Thank you, Father," Mariam answered coquettishly.

Jarius reasoned that finding a correct match for such a prize would be difficult. Few men could fully respect her spirit and not be intimidated by her strength. Only a man of considerable spiritual depth could provide the happiness Jarius knew that he must give his daughter.

"Are you ever lonely?" he asked.

"I am alone a lot," Mariam said thoughtfully. "And sometimes I am lonely. Yes, sometimes."

"Perhaps, the time has come to seek a suitor."

"Come now, Abba." Mariam picked up the goblet in front of her, "I am hardly in need of that much diversion. I have more than enough to keep me occupied with my work among the People of the Way."

"Nevertheless—" Jarius stroked his beard and drew himself to his full height. "A father must think of such matters."

Mariam cocked her head coyly. "The time for marrying and giving in marriage may have passed. Our Messiah could return at any moment."

"Yeshua said that the Temple would be torn apart stone by stone. Daughter, when I looked yesterday it was still standing."

"Come now, Father." Mariam reached for the large jug in the center of the table. "You have something on your mind. Just tell me." She filled her father's cup.

"I have had an inquiry," Jarius spoke very slowly as

he continued to stroke his beard. "A fine young man has come to speak of betrothal." He toasted her with the cup.

"Betrothal!" Mariam's mouth dropped.

"Young women all over this city would have worried about not being engaged for the last two years. But even now, you are more affronted than pleased."

"Heavens!" Mariam shrugged. "I have much to do." Mariam got up from her chair and poked at the small fire in the corner fireplace.

"And you would just as well not face the pain of your recent loss."

"Father," Mariam pleaded. "I don't think that I want such complications now." She moved the simmering pot of soup to the side of the hearth.

"No, my child." Jarius shook his head. "Few of us were created to be alone. When your mother died, I could not have endured if you had not filled the emptiness. There is a fullness that comes only through love. I must do everything in my power to find such a gift for you."

"I don't know." Mariam stared into the ashes.

"I believe Philip is a very fine young man."

"Philip!" She whirled around.

"I was somewhat surprised myself. Yes, Philip has come seeking your hand."

"Why, he was Stephanos's best—" Mariam stopped abruptly. She walked slowly back to her chair and set the soup in the center of the table.

"Stephanos will not come again," Jarius's voice was tender.

"Yes," Mariam said haltingly. "I know."

"Philip has come alone, as Stephanos did, but I am impressed. He is obviously a good man. However, I would never make any agreement that was not acceptable to you my child. Unless you are completely happy, I could not agree to betrothal."

"Thank you, Abba. No one could be a better father than you." Mariam turned uncomfortably in her chair.

"Perhaps, you might think on the matter. Philip is far from a stranger to us. I believe you should talk together, even though many would be offended. Time will soon tell."

"My heart has always spoken clearly. I trust it more than time itself."

"You are to be the judge, Mariam. If you encourage the young gaba'im, fine. If not, then the matter will not be spoken of again."

"I will pray. We shall see what follows." Mariam ladled the soup into both of their bowls.

As Mariam ate, Jarius again wandered into his own solitude. Finally she broke the lull.

"Abba, do you ever wonder where Simeon is? Do you ever worry about him?"

"They say he has left the city." Jarius stared into space. "I heard that he left with a caravan going north."

"You heard?"

"So, I inquired." Jarius shrugged.

"I was wrong." Mariam looked down at her bowl. "I knew better. Yeshua taught that we must forgive and I didn't."

"Your pain was too deep." Jarius continued staring.

"If I had accepted his apology—"

"The issues were too great." Jarius slowly turned toward Mariam. "The rift is too deep, too fundamental. A line was drawn, and neither of us knew how to cross the mark. The line became a chasm."

"Perhaps we should go to him."

"But we cannot compromise the truth that we have seen with our own eyes. Therein is the permanent gulf.

We cannot compromise, and Simeon cannot entertain the possibility that he might be wrong. We can reach but we cannot touch."

"When he returns—" Mariam stopped. "Surely he will return. Won't he?"

"I don't know." Jarius shook his head. "I also hear that the family of Ben Kaifa is fighting to maintain control of the Sanhedrin. Simeon is seen as one of their enemies. The cohenim are systematically spreading rumors that Simeon is a traitor, a spy. If they succeed, Simeon would have a hard time even being accepted by old friends."

"He had so much."

"Simeon still has one of the brightest minds anywhere. If he must start again, he will find a way."

"Then we must wait for him to come to us?"

"Daughter, we have no alternative. Once any man starts down the King's Highway, no one can predict where his steps will lead."

"Yerushalayim remains the center of the universe. He must come back again. Next time I will be more forgiving."

"And in the meantime, we have the matter of Philip to ponder. You will see him tonight at the Love feast."

"Yes." Mariam smiled. "I have Philip to consider."

———————————— • ————————————

The candles in the hanging rack were all lit. Torches had been placed along the walls of the Upper Room. Believers laughed, talked, inquired about their mutual well-being. Many women huddled together on one side while the men mingled on the other. Yet the sheer numbers pushed them together. The traditional separating wall remained permanently cracked.

Even though many of the believers met regularly in

the house of Yaakov, the Upper Room was always packed with people. Those who fled when persecution began were replaced by new faces.

In the center of the room six tables were filled with kosher food. A small mountain of little green cucumbers were piled on a platter next to a tray filled with tomatoes and large radishes. Steamy corn porridge was waiting to be ladled out. Though it was not usual for the season, boiled meat had been set out for this special gathering. Small bowls of raisins and figs were set close by to provide a final balance of sweetness. Next to the crushed grain cakes was a large vat of honey. At the end of the far table were the usual array of grapes, mulberries, and pomegranates for dessert.

At the far end of the room was the special head table. The treasured goblet that had been used during the final Seder night was in the center. Unleavened bread was set next to a wine jug. After everyone had eaten, one of the apostles would recite the story of that sacred night and all would drink from the holy cup.

"Shalom," Toma called loudly from the front.

"Shalom alechem," echoed back as the crowd quieted.

"The time has come to celebrate the gift of life that Adonai has given to us. Once more we remember the resurrection that has set us free from the fear of death. Let us thank the Holy One of Israel."

Men pulled their talliths over their heads and lifted their hands in prayer, and Toma began, "*Shema O Israel, Adonai eloheunu adonai echad.*"

The group responded in unison. "The Lord our God is One God." Someone prayed, "*Barauch ata adonai Elohenu Melech holam hamotzi lechem min haretz.*"

And so the prayers began. Spontaneously men and women uttered simple short prayers of joy and affirmation with responses of praise and devotion. Someone began a simple little song. Immediately the chorus filled the room. No longer afraid of interruption by persecutors, the group sang joyfully for a few minutes. Slowly the singing faded into brief silence.

"Amen. Let us begin." Toma pointed to the tables.

Immediately people gathered around the tables allowing the widows and the elderly to go first. Mariam stood by the wall, waiting for others to fill their clay bowls.

"Shalom."

Mariam turned to see who had spoken to her. "Philip," she blushed, "I—I didn't see you when we entered."

"I saw you." His voice was low and quiet.

"Peace be unto you." Mariam sounded distantly polite.

"And to you." Philip bowed slightly. "My, aren't we formal this evening."

Mariam blushed and then rolled her eyes. "It's not like we don't know each other."

"Indeed." Philip laughed. "Perhaps we might talk a moment before you leave tonight?"

"Yes," Mariam said lowly. "I would like that."

"Good!" Philip beamed. "Excellent."

"Philip?" A young man tugged at Philip's sleeve. "Please come."

"What?" Philip frowned. "Is something so urgent?"

"Shimon Kefa calls for you."

"I suppose I must go. I will be back."

Mariam deferred without speaking. She turned back to the table, smiling. Once Mariam had filled her bowl, she found her way to a place among the women. Talk turned on the details of families, children, and everyday life. Occasionally Mariam made a comment, but most of the time she only observed. Periodically she glanced around the room. Finally, she found Philip standing with a group of young men.

Philip talked with great animation. His gestures were like wide swipes of a sickle harvesting the listener's attention. Obviously he was the leader among his peers. The men laughed and joked as Philip continued his tale of some adventure to which women were not privy.

For the first time Mariam realized that Philip was a fascinating man. Tall and muscular, he looked like the young men who ran in the races at the great Roman hippodrome below the Temple Mount. The Greek cut of his hair was different from the long-hanging style of the men of Israel. The more she watched, the more Mariam realized how much she had not observed about Philip.

Unique? Yes, he was unique. The style of the Hellenized world was a charming layer over his Jewishness. Oh yes, Stephanos had the identical fascination for her. As a matter of fact, Philip had the same rugged handsomeness.

"You're not eating?" a woman next to Mariam asked softly.

"Oh! No—just thinking."

"My but they are a handsome group of young men," the older woman patted Mariam's hand.

Mariam blushed.

"We will gather shortly," Toma announced from the front table. "Tonight, Shimon Kefa will share a word with us before we receive the cup of the Lord. Let us prepare."

Immediately the men moved the food tables out of the center of the room and back to the walls. The remaining food was quickly prepared for distribution among the poor. Several apostles were seated there as well. In the shuffle Mariam lost sight of Philip.

"Before we begin," Toma held up his arms to silence the group. "I want to ask our dear brother Honorius to speak. Perhaps, many of you do not know that he stood at the foot of the cross on that fateful Friday. He has been an observer of all that has transpired in these last days. Honorius is a true friend of the People of the Way. We welcome him as a righteous Gentile and one of us."

Honorius stood slowly. A heavy cloth bandage still ran across his shoulders and down his back. Honorius shifted his weight carefully from one foot to the other. "I have been reassigned to Rome," he announced slowly. "In the beginning I feared that I might never return there. Now my heart is filled with sadness. I feel as one about to be separated from his family forever."

"When?" Shimon Kefa broke in. "When will you leave?"

"There is a boat setting sail in a week. I will be on it."

"Are you well enough to travel?" a man near the front asked.

"I have no choice but I will endure." Honorius looked carefully around the room. "My friends, I want to re-member each of you just as you are tonight. I lived through the most incredible adventure any man could know. We began as enemies and have ended as com-rades. Together we have witnessed what the ages have longed to see. My whole life was changed by what I thought was just another routine execution. I can still see Jarius Ben Aaron running down the Golgotha hill. I could never have dreamed that eventually he and his daughter would save my life. Time and eternity have blended together in this place." Honorius choked with emotion.

"Will we see you again, my friend?" Jarius asked.

"Perhaps," Honorius pursed his lips, "we will all be surprised. Jarius, I sense that in a most unexpected way we will be together again. Who can say? Has not the God of Israel proven that His surprises exceed any of our expectations?"

"Then tonight will be your last time to worship with us?" Yochanan rose to his feet.

"I am afraid so. Tomorrow I must travel down to the port and make the final arrangements. I will not be back."

"We will pray for you tonight and as you journey." Yochanan raised his hands in a blessing.

"I will tell this story wherever I go." Honorius straightened up to his full height. "I am to return to the Pretorinum guards that protect Caesar. I know that you still are not sure of how the people of my world fit into the plans of your God. But I believe I have found what Rome needs most. The matter will not stop here in this small land. Believe me, a ripple goes forth that will not cease until it has become a tidal wave sweeping over all the shores of the world. You cannot wait long because the Gentiles will come to find you. More is afoot here than any of you yet realize. Get prepared my friends, for the walls are tumbling."

"Let us gather around our friend," Yochanan motioned for some of the group to circle, "and let us bless him and pray for his journey."

Across the room, people edged forward. Standing around Honorius, they placed their hands carefully on his shoulders, back, and head. One by one their intercessions began.

Jarius and Mariam stood beyond the circle watching. For a reason that neither could define, they sensed that it was not appropriate to be severing ties with their friend. Even though Honorius was leaving, they knew the bond was not being cut.

"You have the pouch I gave you to carry?" Jarius whispered to Mariam.

"Yes."

"Two days ago Honorius told me that he was leaving. I made a special chain and I want you to give it to him now."

"You've known about his departure?" Mariam blinked. Jarius said nothing.

When the prayers were ended, the People of the Way hugged their friend and wished him well. The battle-hardened soldier kept wiping the tears from his cheeks and shaking hands.

As the people separated, Jarius and Mariam stepped forward. "Until then." Jarius extended his hand. "We are not finished with each other."

"I pray not." The soldier bit his lip.

"My father has made something I want to give you." Mariam opened a little leather pouch and pulled out a long gold chain. On the end was a long slender cross made from hammered gold.

"I know this is a strange gift." Jarius picked up the cross. "Perhaps, your fellow soldiers will think it strange to wear a symbol of an execution. But I want you to always remember the day that you and I stood together at the foot of his cross. We share a unique bond. When you wear this chain, remember us. Let this be a mitzpah* between us."

Honorius wept as he hugged Jarius. "God bless you always."

"And the Lord watch between us together and apart." Mariam reached up and placed the gold chain around the Roman's neck. Carefully she adjusted the cross so that it hung in the center of his neck.

*A covenant of blessing and peace

Honorius hugged Mariam and across the room the believers applauded their approval. Several men helped the soldier ease back on the little bench where he had been sitting.

"We shall see our friend again," Mariam said to her father as they returned to their place. "In my spirit, I know that God is not finished with our relationship."

"I believe so." Jarius shook his head thoughtfully. "I believe so."

The flickering flames of the candles sitting around the room made the chamber glow. The blandness of the barren walls was transformed into golden refractors of light. Singing began. Slowly and spontaneously the People of the Way offered their praise in simple songs, each blending into the next as if led by an unseen conductor. Although the songs were quiet, the emotion was profound.

Prayers followed. Some prayed for friends and relatives that had traveled to other places. Fervent and straightforward, the petitions rose ever-upward with the smoke from the candles. The air was alive with light and love.

As the intercessions faded, Shimon Kefa spoke. "I must share a dream with you," he carefully chose his words. "It is not easy to change one's most basic convictions and beliefs. Yet we have been forced to rethink everything as we wait for the day of the Lord to come."

Quietness settled over the congregation.

"As you know, we have been traveling in the north among the Samaritans. While I was traveling to Yafo, a Roman officer in Caesarea was visited by an angel of Adonai. As these strange events were unfolding, I went out on the roof of the house where I was staying to pray. It was there I had the most extraordinary vision.

"A large sheet was let down from heaven, filled with

all sorts of unclean animals and crawling creatures. A voice called to me, 'Get up, Kefa, slaughter and eat!'" The clay lamps cast shadows under Kefa's eyes making him look much older. Like Moshe before the burning bush, Shimon Kefa appeared to be a man about to be called forth on a new journey.

"I protested but the voice said to me, 'Stop treating as unclean what God has made clean'."

Mariam leaned against her father as she listened. Intuitively, she knew the ending of the story. Stephanos had been the first sign and Philip's journey to Gitta the second. Perhaps, Honorius himself was the true omen. Mariam looked around the room at the faces of the people. Old men were perplexed; the young were excited and eager.

Shimon Kefa described further how the Rudach Ha Kodesh had fallen on the Roman's household and many gasped. The idea of goyim being included among the People of the Covenant was obviously painful.

Mariam smiled at their consternation as Kefa finally admitted that he allowed the Roman family to be baptized. Honorius applauded but not many joined in. A few of the apostles at the head table silently stroked their beards and looked down.

Mariam could see the turmoil working like leaven among the People of the Way. Something new was rising up and nothing would be quite the same again. Yet Mariam also knew she was watching other pieces of an ancient wall fall. She turned slightly to see how the people behind her were receiving the message. To her delight, she found Philip. He was positioned in the back like a carefully stationed observer. He, too, seemed amused by the perplexed congregation.

Peering between two women, Mariam watched Philip closely. His eyes darted back and forth quickly scanning the room. The sparkle in Philip's knowing, intelligent eyes had a hint of mischief. Yes, Mariam thought to herself, there are many things that I have not noticed about this man. In the days ahead, I must come to know him well.

THE BEGINNING

GLOSSARY OF HEBREW

abba—Daddy
Adonai—Lord, Name of Jehovah God
Ammaus—Town of Emmaus
Avraham—Abraham

Barnabba—Barnabus
Ben Aaron Family:
    Jarius—Ruler of a Jerusalem synagogue
    Mariam—Jarius's daughter
    Rachael—Wife of Zeda
    Simeon—The youngest brother and member of the
        Sanhedrin
    Zeda—The eldest brother
boker tov—Good morning

Caiaphas—High Priest and leader of the Sanhedrin
Chananyah—Ananias
cohanim—Priest

Elisheva—Elizabeth, the mother of John the Baptist
El Shaddai—Name for Jehovah God, indicating Him to be
    the provider

Gaba'im—Deacons, men who conducted acts of mercy and
    charity, sometimes called Tzedakah
Gennesaret—Sea of Galilee
Gey-Hinnon—The Jerusalem city garbage dump, the origin
    of the ideal of hell
Goy, Goyim—Gentiles, non-Jews

HaElyon—The highest God
Halacha—The Law
Ha Mashiach—The Messiah

Kaifa, Yehosaf Ben Kaifa—Caiaphas, high priest and leader
    of the Great Sanhedrin

Marah—The bitter swamp Moses sweetened when Israel
    faced death by thirst
Mattiyahu—Matthew

mazusseh—Ornament on doorways with a scroll inside, touched as a sacred remembrance
menorah—Jewish ceremonial candelabra
mikvah—Ritual bath of immersion for purification
Miryam—Mary, mother of Jesus
mitzpah—A pact, a covenant between people invoking God's blessing and oversight
Morgen David—Star of David
Moshe—Moses

Nakdimon—Nicodemus, who came by night
Natanel—Nathaniel, one of the Twelve
Natzeret—Nazareth
Nisi—President of a Synagogue

Ramatayim—Arimathea
Rudach Ha Kodesh—The Holy Spirit

Sanhedrin—The highest ruling body in Jerusalem
Shalom—Greeting of hello and goodbye, wishing peace and well-being
Shaul—Saul or Paul
Shavu'ot—Festival marking the Giving of the Law to Moses, a harvest festival
Sheol—The place of death
Shimon Kefa—Simon Peter, leader of the twelve apostles
Siloe—The Pool of Shiloam

Taddai—Thaddaeus
Taheb—Samaritan Messiah
Talitha Cumi—Hebrew phrase, "Little girl, arise"
Talliths—Prayer shawls worn around the neck or over the head
Toma—The apostle Thomas
treif—not kosher
Tzedakah—Agents of charity of the synagogue, Hebrew for deacon

Yaakov—James, brother of Jesus, also Jacob
Yakov Ben Zavdai—James, son of Zebedee, an apostle
Yavo—Modern-day town of Joppa
Yerushalayim—Jerusalem

Yerushalayim dedaheba—Elegant woman's golden
 headdress made in Jerusalem
Yeshu, Yeshua—Hebrew for "He shall save his people from
 their sin"—the name of Jesus. Yeshu is the affectionate,
 familiar form of Yeshua
Yhudah of Kriot—Judas Iscariot
Yitzchak—Issac
Yochanon—The apostle John
Yosef—Joseph

Zealots—Fierce extreme patriots
Zekenim—Spiritual leaders in the synagogue; elders in
 church

The Jewish Calendar:
  Tishri—September to October
  Heshvan—October to November
  Chislev—November to December
  Tebeth—December to January
  Shebat—January to February
  Adar—February to March
  Nisan—March to April
  Iyar—April to May
  Sivan—May to June
  Tammuz—June to July
  Ab—July to August
  Elul—August to September

The Jewish Day:
  First Hour—Sunrise to 9:00 A.M.
  Third Hour—9:00 A.M. to Noon
  Sixth Hour—Noon to 3:00 P.M.
  Ninth Hour—3:00 P.M. to Sunset

ABOUT THE AUTHOR

Author of nine books, including *When the Night Is Too Long* and *When There Is No Miracle*, Robert L. Wise, Ph.D., is a long-time student of the Hebrew language and of Jewish culture. He has traveled extensively in the Holy Land, as well as across the world.

Robert lives in Oklahoma City with his wife, Margueritte.